CW00687249

Highwayman:
The Complete Campaigns

Ironside
Winter Swarm
War's End

Michael Arnold

© Michael Arnold

Michael Arnold has asserted his rights under the Copyright, Design and Patents Act, 1988, to be identified as the author of this work.

HIGHWAYMAN: IRONSIDE © Michael Arnold 2013
First published 2013 by Endeavour Press Ltd

HIGHWAYMAN: WINTER SWARM © Michael Arnold 2015

First published 2015 by Endeavour Press Ltd

HIGHWAYMAN: WAR'S END © Michael Arnold 2020
First published 2020 by Sharpe Books

This omnibus edition published 2020 by Sharpe Books.

Table of Contents

HIGHWAYMAN: IRONSIDE

PART ONE: THE CHASE

Beside Pruetts Lane, North of Petersfield, Hampshire, November 1655

The storm was long spent, but its legacy lingered, the mud now deep and slick.

The horse's iron-tipped limbs slipped and scrabbled for purchase as it fought to maintain its gallop, scoring deep furrows through the lane's sunken, waterlogged belly. But still it forged on, snorting its efforts to the threatening clouds that scudded across the evening sky. It stumbled, whinnied wildly, squealing a plaintive cry that fell on deaf ears before gathering chaotic limbs in thunderous rhythm, guttural grunts pulsing steam that rose in roiling jets to briefly swallow its rider.

The rider pushed himself into the steed's billowing silver mane, the stench of horse flesh and sweat filling his nostrils. He touched his spurs to the dappled grey flanks. The horse snorted again, jerked its granite-hard neck in annoyance, eyes blazing white in the slate dusk. But it quickened all the same. The rider grinned.

A branch flashed into view like a low-flying gull, whipping out of the oppressive haze in a blur, sending the rider into a desperate crouch, hugging his mount's moist neck. They raced below its swiping range, relief pulsing atop each rasped out-breath, and the rider crowed his exhilaration into the dripping canopy, invigorated by the thrill of the chase. And there it was, suddenly and brilliantly, emerging from the hazy half-light like a wheeled ghost. His quarry.

The coach grew in size and definition, blooming a hundred yards off like the pall of smoke from a spark-touched bag of gunpowder. The rider held his breath, gritted his teeth till they ached, heart beating like a Naseby drum, scalp prickling, muscles tense. He revelled in the speed, in the danger, in the spray of mud and the eye-stinging air.

And then he was beside the clattering vehicle, veering to the left of the rear wheels. He took the reins in a single gloved palm and let his free hand drop, groping for the smooth handle of his pistol. There it was, jutting up from his saddle holster, the metal-bound butt hard and reassuring. He jerked it free, luxuriating in its brutish weight, and kicked again, the horse mustering a final burst of speed so that they drew up alongside the driver. The rider looked straight ahead, alert to the hazards of the road, but his arm swept out like a sailboat's boom to bring the pistol level with the coachman's head.

"Slow 'em up, cully, lest I clean your ear with lead!" From the corner of his eye he could see the coachman glance across at him. The thundering pair of bays harnessed out front did not falter. "Rein them in, friend!" he called again. "Do not make me kill you!"

The beasts whinnied as their harnesses pulled taut and, as though the mud had deepened in that instant to suck at the crashing fetlocks, the bays fell to a canter, to a trot, and finally walked to a steam-shrouded halt.

The rider wheeled his mount back to face the coach. It was a splendid thing indeed, like the jewellery box of a giant, half gold, half cornflower blue, the doors draped with patterned curtains of silver and black. He kept the pistol up, steady and level. "Jump down, there's a good fellow."

The driver dropped his reins. A musket lay on the timber platform at his feet, and he cast it a surreptitious glance.

"Do not be a dullard," the rider warned.

The coachman swallowed hard, nodded, and scrambled down to earth. He was a short, plump man, probably in his early forties, with warts on his chin and a syphilitic nose. He snatched off his felt hat to reveal a pate of thinning brownish hair and nodded emphatically. "Don't kill me, sir, I beg you. I've four chil'ens and..."

"Away with you," the rider snapped. The terrified driver needed no further encouragement and bolted into the tree line, vanishing noisily amongst the safety of the undergrowth like a startled fawn. "You inside!" the rider called as he dismounted and strode up to the inert coach. "Out you come, and be sharp about it!"

Nothing moved. The bays whickered nervously as though they discussed their plight with the rider's big grey, but from the coach there came nothing but silence. The rider took a step nearer. "Do not be foolish," he called in a steady tone, "for you will not live to regret the mistake."

The coach swayed like a milkmaid's hips as someone moved inside, huge springs creaking noisily beneath, and he braced himself, one foot in front of the other like a man striding into a gale.

"I am stepping out!" a voice called from within the gilt shell. It rocked more vigorously.

The rider noted the depth of tone. The stentorian edge that made him think of his time with the cavalry. It made his neck prickle. "No weapons! Raise your hands where I may see them, and move slowly!"

"To whom am I speaking?" the voice barked back.

"Lyle!" the rider replied strongly, knowing the revelation could only serve to move matters along more swiftly.

The sticky earth trembled. More hoof beats. Lyle peered past the coach to see the approach of a black gelding and a roan mare. The black was ridden by a man wearing a buff coat that sagged across the shoulders to betray a painfully thin frame beneath. His face was creased deeply with age, fringed by a neat beard of wintry whiteness, and made severe by a long, hooked nose that was bright red at the tip. His neck convulsed in a violent twitch as he waved cheerily. "Shall I take the reins?"

"You'd better," Lyle snapped, irritation bubbling in his veins. "For you've done nought else of use this day."

The old man twitched again and grinned. "The branch wasn't long enough, Major, 'pon my life it was not." He slid down from the saddle and spread his palms. "A miscalculation is all."

"We'll discuss it later," Lyle said. "And cover your ugly face."

The old man flashed an amused sneer and drew a silken scarf up from his collar to envelope his head. A pair of holes had been cut in the material through which his blue eyes gleamed.

"He's right, Samson," the second newcomer said. The face was already masked, and the body clothed in the garments of a man, but her feminine voice seemed to jar against the deeper tones of the others.

Lyle looked up at the diminutive figure who deftly brought her powerful steed to a halt. She was twelve, they reckoned, but she might have been twenty, such was her confident bearing, and he suppressed a smile. "I said later. Now to your business."

She nodded, cocking a long pistol in one smooth, practised motion. "Let's see what's what, then."

"I have placed my pistols inside!" the voice from within the coach announced.

"Let us see you then, sir," Lyle replied.

After a brief pause the curtain at the small door was swept aside and a head poked out into the chill evening air. The man had seen perhaps fifty winters. He had a broad, ruddy face and straight grey hair sprouting from beneath the rim of a wide, feathered hat. His eyes were dark and bright with intelligence, and his lips thin - pressed into a hard line. He ducked back for an instant, a clunk announced the door's catch had been freed, and it swung outward. The man edged out like a rat easing from its hole, a rotund torso and short legs emerging in turn. He wore the attire of a soldier - a suit of oiled buff hide and metal - but one of high rank, for the shapes cut out of his rapier's guard were ostentatiously intricate, and his coat was lined with golden thread.

Lyle sighed. "Stone me for a base rogue if there isn't a guard for even the smallest carriage these dull days!"

The elderly man who had gone to take the reins of the mud-spattered bays gave a wet-sounding cackle. "As if the roads ain't safe, Major."

Lyle glanced quickly back at him. "Quite so, Mister Grumm, quite so!" He returned his gaze to the well-upholstered fellow who now stood with his back pressed against one of the coach's big wheels. "But what exactly is he guarding?"

The armoured fellow squared his shoulders and widened his stance, standing like a sentinel before the coach. "I protect a man whose boots you are not fit so much as to lick, sir."

Lyle trained the firearm at his face. "I will decide that, sir. And if I must blast a hole 'twixt your eyeballs to do it then I am ready and willing." He saw the man eye the pistol with interest and twitched the twin muzzles a touch. "She's Dutch. You like her?"

"What manner of weapon is it?"

"A flintlock as you'd know it, sir," Lyle said, "though she has a pair of barrels mounted 'pon an axle pin. So I may choose to shoot each of your stones out in turn, should you give me cause."

"What do you want?" the voice of another man broke the tension. It was slightly muffled, coming from within the vehicle, but not so much that Lyle could mistake the rounded notes of an East Anglian accent. "I say, Walmsley! What does the blackguard want?"

The guard, Walmsley, kept his gaze fixed upon the poised firearm. "He wants you to fear him, sir. This is the infamous Samson Lyle." He spat. "The *Ironside Highwayman*."

Lyle touched a finger to the brim of his hat. "At your service. Though the name is not something I encourage. A creation of the news sheets, I'm afraid."

The curtain crumpled suddenly and was thrust aside. Out of the coach stepped a man in simple black breeches and doublet, with a tall buckled hat and tidy falling band collar. To Lyle's eyes he was dressed like a puritan preacher, except that the clothes were stretched so tightly over his corpulent midriff that such an austere vocation seemed unlikely. Besides, Lyle knew from the accent that he had found his man and he inwardly thanked God for it.

"Ah ah ah," Lyle warned as he noticed Walmsley's hand snake to the small of his back. He twitched the pistol in his grip. "What have you hidden there?" The guard's jaw quivered. "Ground arms, my man, or you'll find yourself staring at the clouds."

Slowly Walmsley eased a small pistol from his belt and let it drop to the ground. "I have no more, save my blade."

Lyle nodded. "Try any more tricks, and things will go badly for you." He winked. "There's a good fellow."

"You are a bastardly gullion, Lyle," Walmsley growled.

Lyle gave a weary sigh. "Bark when you have teeth, sir. For now, mine is the only bite that matters." He looked beyond the soldier to the plainly attired passenger. "Let me see you, sir."

The fat fellow stepped tentatively to the side, though he remained firmly behind his bodyguard. "You know this man, Walmsley?"

"Every military man knows him, sir," Walmsley replied. "A soldier, as was. A good one. A good man, no less. But now?" He shook his head pityingly. "A scoundrel of the very worst kind." His little eyes examined Lyle, from the tall boots pulled high over his thighs to the crusty buff coat and long cloak that was the dark green of woodland moss. He scrutinised Lyle's face with its broad, clean-shaven chin and thin lips below a long, slightly canted nose. "I had hoped to run into you, Lyle, truth told. There are so many stories."

"All good, one hopes."

Walmsley spluttered derisively. "All ridiculous, judging by the measure I now have of you." He glanced quickly over his shoulder at his soberly presented companion. "The Major. Terror of the highways, scourge of the new regime." He hawked up a gobbet of phlegm, depositing it amongst the churned mud between Lyle's boots. "And yet here you are. A simple brigand."

Lyle cocked the pistol. "And yet I have you, sir." He let his gaze drift beyond the belligerent soldier. "And I have Sir Frederick Mason, do I not?"

The portly man in black seemed to colour at the mention of his name. "How...?"

"Lawyer by trade," Lyle went on. "I have been tracking you, sir. Waiting for you. You are my prey this night."

"Why?" Mason said, finally finding his voice.

"Because you are courtier to the new power in the land. Goffe's adviser and Cromwell's lapdog. A beneficiary of England's misery."

"He is the man," Walmsley cut in defiantly, "who'll drink a toast when he sees you dance from Tyburn Tree."

It startled everyone to hear the coach creak again and Lyle forgot the blustering soldier in an instant. He adjusted the pistol so that its muzzle was in line with the door, while he sensed the girl, still mounted to his right, bring her own pistol to bear.

"More of you?" he said to Walmsley, though he could hear the tension in his own voice. He imagined the coach might be more Trojan horse than gilt treasure.

Before Walmsley could respond, the head of a woman emerged from behind the curtain. Lyle simply stared. She was quite plainly clothed, in a dress of soft yellow, her auburn hair restrained about her scalp by a white coif. And yet Lyle found her utterly striking. It was the eyes, he knew. Dark and glittering, like nuggets of jet, the shape of almonds and the depth of oceans. They seemed to burn, boring right through him, reading his mind.

He swallowed thickly. "Your servant, mistress."

The woman stepped lightly out of the carriage. She was tall and slender, her lips full, scrunched together in a pout that he supposed was born of anger, though he found the gesture captivating. Sir Frederick, he realised, was speaking, and he shook his head, reluctantly tearing his gaze from this new vision. "By your leave, Freddy. I was too busy admiring your rather sumptuous friend."

The lawyer's cheeks filled with crimson. "Why, you devil-eyed villain. Insult a man's niece, would you?"

"Insult, sir? Far from it." He looked back at the woman. "I would but worship."

"How dare..." Sir Frederick began, but he was interrupted by the very woman he defended.

"It seems you know your captives, Major Lyle," she said. Her voice was surprisingly calm. "And we know you."

"Seems that way," Lyle agreed.

"Then why do your confederates cover their faces? Are they so hideous that they must not be beheld?"

That was a shrewd comment, thought Lyle, and he could not stifle a smile. "Adds to the mystique, mistress."

Her implacable expression did not falter. "Perhaps it masks their shame."

Lyle heard his companions chuckle at that and he could only laugh. "It is for their protection, mistress. For my part, I would have a jewel such as you gaze freely upon me."

"Haggard, is he not?" Grumm chirped from his place at the nervous horses, a bridle in each hand.

The woman appraised him. "You do not appear to take your vocation seriously, sir."

He knew she would be seeing a face more deeply lined than was befitting his twenty-six years, and eyes that, though a sparkling shade of green, had been described by former lovers as too cold to be truly attractive. Like the eyes of a hunting tomcat, one had said. He snatched off his wide-brimmed hat to reveal a mop of sweat-matted hair that was the colour of straw, and offered a short bow. "I have grieved too long to waste another moment on matters maudlin."

Her thin brows twitched a touch. "You chased our coach, sir. What kind of highwayman chases his quarry?" Her voice was hard, scornful, though he sensed a note of amusement too. "Would not a competent brigand have lain in wait? Blocked the road and so forth?"

Lyle cast a caustic glare at Grumm. "The element of surprise, mistress." He jerked the pistol, indicating that his prisoners should move to the side of the coach. "Now, if you would be so kind...."

They did as they were ordered, forming a line before Lyle. The girl dismounted too. "I'm Arabella," she announced in a friendly voice, though, as she ran a hand down the bristling Walmsley's flanks, her other still firmly gripped the pistol.

Lyle moved close to the woman. She seemed to stiffen under his gaze and he offered an impish grin. "I'll not check you for weapons, mistress, have no fear. I am a highwayman, not a lecher."

She made a display of sniffing the air. "I'd think you a gong farmer, sir, to tell by your aroma."

Lyle brayed at that. "You are a fine thing, and no mistake." He winked at her. "Might I have a name to put to the esteem?"

She seemed to be fighting back a smile, for the corners of her mouth twitched. "Felicity Mumford."

Lyle took up her hand and kissed it. "Angel."

"Unhand me, sir," Felicity protested, though she did not pull back.

"Push me away and I will be gone, by my honour."

Sir Frederick Mason was, Lyle knew, a political animal. One of the new men, risen by guile and wit in the aftermath of war. A grey-bearded snake. He was a wielder of quill and ink, rather than steel and shot, and, until now, his demeanour had reflected this fully. But the exchange with his niece seemed to invigorate the lawyer to action, for he stepped forward, jabbing a finger into Lyle's face. "Honour? Honour? You know nothing of the word!"

Lyle let Felicity's palm drop and stepped away. "This nation knows it not, Sir Freddy. No longer."

"Ah, here's the nub of it!" Mason squawked. "*Ironside* Highwayman. He dares use the name. This is no ironside. A *king's* dog, Felicity! Long gelded, but still he yaps!"

Lyle glanced across at Grumm. "Eustace, are the horses calmed?" He waited for a quick nod. "Then see to the loot."

"A pox on your thievery," Mason hissed. "God-rotten Cavalier."

"Innocent of that charge," Lyle replied, "I'm pleased to say."

"This man," Walmsley interceded, relishing his moment, "was once a hero of the rebellion. Would you countenance such a thing? A friend to Cromwell himself."

"Surely you jest, sir," the lawyer muttered, visibly thrown by the revelation. "Friend to the Protector?"

Lyle felt himself tense at the name. "Now his sworn enemy." He flashed a grin at Walmsley. "And always proud to school crusty old Roundheads in the ways of honour."

The soldier bridled, his blood up now, but it was his employer who spoke. "Cromwell is the best, godliest man in these islands. What depths do you plumb, sir, if you would make him your foe?"

"If those depths," Lyle replied levelly, "are to harangue, harry and plunder the men of Cromwell's new order, then they are waters in which it is a pleasure to swim." He let his eyes fall to the bulging flanks of Sir Frederick's heavy coat. "Now shall we peer into those deep pockets, sir?"

Walmsley stepped between them. "Stay where you are, Sir Frederick."

Lyle narrowed his eyes. "Steady, old man, lest you wish for some tutelage."

"Old man? I am Kit Walmsley. Formerly of Sir Hardress Waller's Regiment of Foot."

"Another of Oliver's toadies."

"Speak of the Lord Protector in such a manner..." Walmsley said through gritted teeth.

"Protector nothing, sir!" Lyle shot back scornfully. "That blackguard protects himself and nothing more. He ought to take the crown and abandon the obfuscation."

"Pup!" Walmsley blustered, his throat seeming to puff up like that of some red-faced bullfrog. "I'll cleave out your malignant tongue!" With that his hand was on his sword hilt, a third of the blade already exposed.

Lyle rolled his eyes. "Precious Blood! Must we?"

"Shoot 'im, Major," Eustace Grumm called impatiently. "Let's be on our way."

"You disgust me, Lyle," Walmsley went on, the rest of the sword sliding free. "You're a traitor and a coward and a quartering would be too lenient for you." His face warped into an expression of pure malice. "Perhaps we'll dig up your good wife and make her dead eyes watch."

Samson Lyle knew he was being goaded. He knew, most likely, that the sly Walmsley was playing for time. And yet the bastard had mentioned Alice.

He discarded his hat and tossed the pistol to Bella, who caught it with one hand, and released his own blade, its length slithering through the throat of his long scabbard. Taking half a dozen measured paces backwards, he held it out in front, dancing before Walmsley, the last light of the autumn eve dancing at its tip like molten silver. He felt good, powerful. He was tall, just touching six feet, with a body that was lean and spare, with muscles like braided match cord. A figure that betrayed a life of hardship, fight and flight. He cast a final glance at Grumm. "Take Star, Eustace. Turn him about."

Kit Walmsley stepped out, turning his shoulders to present the smallest possible target, right foot well advanced. "Turn him about? The horse cannot watch?"

"He cannot," Lyle said.

"Cannot witness his master take a beating?" the soldier asked incredulously. "Is the beast your mother, sir?"

"My companion through many horrors."

Sir Frederick called a subdued word of encouragement. Walmsley muttered something low and inaudible, his fleshy face suddenly taut with determination.

Lyle eyed him warily. A noise grumbled somewhere to his left, and he could not help but catch Grumm's sideways glance. He pretended to ignore the warning it contained, but acknowledged it inwardly all the same. For all Walmsley's advancing age, he retained the easy agility of a man much younger. Moreover, the way he drew his sword told of quick reflexes and a man not lacking in confidence. Indeed, the more Lyle saw of Walmsley, the more he thought the older man looked formidable: a leather-faced, compact, bullock of a man, exuding power and vigour.

Walmsley rumbled a challenge, waved him on. The highwayman stepped in. He was taller by a couple of inches, but a deal lighter. As the blade tips touched, tinkling musically, he felt the weight of his opponent push back, forcing him to brace himself as though standing before a great wave. He thought how it must have seemed to the onlookers like a fight between mastiff and whippet.

With a slash, Walmsley swept Lyle's blade aside, lunging straight in with an aggression that might have sent his steel all the way through the younger man's breast had not the whippet been wise to it. The highwayman jumped to his side, forcing himself to laugh contemptuously, though the hisses of his companions spoke of the closeness of the strike.

Walmsley thundered past like a wasp-stung boar, managed to keep his footing and wrenched his thick torso round to meet a counter from his enemy. None came, and he coughed up a wad of phlegm, deposited it at the roadside, and sneered. "What halts you, whelp? Your arrogance finally fades now that you face a real swordsman?"

The highwayman's blade was poised out in front, and he flicked his wrist so that the fine tip jerked. "Come."

They clashed, a flurry of clanging blows echoing from tree to tree like the song of mechanical birds.

"Were you at Worcester?" Walmsley asked as they parted again. "Or did you hide like the louse you have become?"

"I was," Lyle said. "And Naseby. And every other damnable place I was sent. My horse was with me, and it took its toll on him too, which is why he must face away for this. He dislikes fighting."

Walmsley shook his head in bewilderment, while Lyle could have sworn he heard Felicity Mumford laugh.

"I was at all the blood-soaked brabbles," Lyle went on, "fighting for the Parliament. And what was it all for? King Oliver the First!"

Walmsley's thick neck bulged as he grimaced, affronted by the insult, and he dipped his chin like an enraged stag, bolting forwards once more. The highwayman was again surprised by the bulky fighter's speed, and this time he had to offer a riposte before he could twist away. The weapons met high, crossed, blade sliding against blade in a teeth-aching hiss until hilts clanged.

Walmsley shoved forth, hoping to throw his opponent off balance, but Lyle gave ground willingly, letting the heavier man stumble in like a collapsing wall. They parted again, and this time Walmsley paused, heaving great, face-reddening gasps into labouring lungs. His eyes narrowed, the light of understanding glinting across their surface. He evidently sensed the younger man's game. Remain passive, cool and calm, venture no great attack, and offer no openings. Allow the bigger, older man to expend his energy, all the while defending, deflecting, moving clear.

"Blast you, sir, but you are a slippery knave," he rasped.

Lyle nodded. "And you a brave old curmudgeon. For that you have my utmost respect, sir, but I cannot allow you to carry this duel."

"Allow?"

Lyle looked across at Felicity Mumford and winked. "Observe."

Now he attacked, jabbing and cutting at Walmsley with speed. He saw each gap in the soldier's admittedly robust defences and took his chance, darting the razor tip of his sword through like a striking adder, forcing the rapidly tiring opponent to donate every ounce of strength in protecting his skin, all the while turning circles that would numb his legs as surely as if he ran all the way to London. Eventually, when he could see that Walmsley's face had taken on a purple hue at its edges, Lyle disengaged. "See that I battle with my elbow nicely bent?"

"What of it?" Walmsley blurted, bent double in an effort to coax air into his lungs.

"I use only my forearm to keep you at bay, while your hot forays drain you like a pistol-shot wine skin."

Walmsley grimaced. "Damn your impudence!"

"And my leading foot, you will observe, remains fixedly in front, ensuring my movements are made in a single line. Efficiency is key."

Walmsley attacked again, humiliation perhaps as invigorating as rage, but Lyle parried four ragged diagonal strikes, thrust his own blade along the lower line, as Besnard had taught him, and sent the soldier skittering rearward lest he lose a kneecap.

"You see, Kit," Lyle said, keeping his tone light, as though sharing some jolly anecdote with an old acquaintance. "May I call you Kit? One must fight to one's strengths. Paramount of which, for my part, are height, speed and stamina. The latter, particularly, will be nicely preserved whilst you hack and snarl your way to exhaustion." Lyle also reckoned upon his calmly delivered assessment, though entirely accurate, would serve to light a flame beneath the cauldron of Walmsley's rage, compelling him to lose all reason and bow only to furious temper.

The onslaught came as Lyle had expected. Walmsley drew himself to his full height, grasped the beautifully decorated hilt in both hands, and bolted forwards. A thunderous, snarling barrage of blows followed, each one propelled by white-hot fury and each carried on the crest of a wave given force by Walmsley's full weight. Lyle, for all his training, found himself compelled to retreat, for the jarring blows juddered up his fingers and wrist and arm, bludgeoning his shoulder like a cudgel. One of the old soldier's crushing downward thrusts bounced clear of Lyle's blade, only to sail perilously close to his right ear. It startled him into action, and he swayed out of range of the next backhanded swing and stepped smartly inside Walmsley's reach, thumping his hilt into the bullock-like opponent's face. The nose cracked noisily, Walmsley brayed, and blood jetted freely in a fine spray. Lyle came on, unwilling to afford his enemy time to recuperate, and Walmsley blocked his strike desperately, grunting with each move and staring through his new bloody mask with narrow, baleful eyes. A man, Lyle knew, with murder firmly on his mind.

Walmsley fell back suddenly in an effort to throw Lyle off balance, but the highwayman had anticipated the move and went with him, pricking the air before Walmsley's face in a series of staccato thrusts that had his eyes screwed tight as though a swarm of hornets buzzed about them. Walmsley, breathing hard now, gave more ground, slashing his blade in horizontal arcs as though swatting at the head of a leaping dog, all form vanished from his bearing. Lyle bore down swiftly upon him, so he twisted away, turning like a scarlet-cheeked acrobat, and lurched forth in a desperate lunge.

Lyle parried easily, twirled clear himself, and brought the blade down hard in a blow that would have split Walmsley's skull like a hammer against a boiled egg. The soldier blocked but had no riposte to offer, and Lyle let his sword slither along Walmsley's expensive steel, the rasp reverberating up his arm and through his ribcage. The guards met, Walmsley's ornate sword pressing hard against the functional bars of Lyle's weapon. There they stayed for a second or two, steel entwined like silver snakes, before Lyle darted back to break the zinging embrace. He allowed Walmsley to recover his feet. "Have you had enough, sir?"

"Never!" Walmsley snarled. He charged forth, slashing the sword wildly at the highwayman. Lyle parried the first mad blow, ducked below the second, stepped past Walmsley's thrashing body, and lashed the flat of his own blade against the soldier's rump. Walmsley howled, stumbled, and Lyle kicked him square in the back.

The fight had taken them near twenty yards away from the coach, and Samson Lyle paused to check that his captives were still where he had left them. Content, he advanced on his stricken foe. "Do you yield, sir?"

The fight had gone out of Kit Walmsley. He sat on his haunches, peering up at his conqueror, all defiance ebbed away. His round face was still bright with exhaustion, but no longer with rage, and his heavy jowls seemed to sag more than they had before. He tossed his sword away, ignominious defeat complete. "Where did you learn, sir?"

"To fight?" Lyle shrugged. "With the New Modelled Army."

Walmsley shook his head, beads of sweat showering his shoulders. "To fence."

Lyle thought back to the hours he had spent in the school of Charles Besnard, learning the great master's forms. The more he had absorbed, the less the memory of Alice had haunted him, and so he had worked day and night. "France. Rennes, to be exact. I did not enjoy exile, I admit, but it had its benefits."

He flicked Walmsley's sword into the air with his boot and caught it by the hilt, then turned away, leaving the broken man to trudge back to the coach nursing his shattered nose. "Eustace!"

Grumm, waiting patiently with Star and the two bays, looked up. "Major?"

"Is my most esteemed comrade well?"

Grumm patted the huge grey stallion on its dappled flank. "He's as irritable as ever, Major, aye."

"Good. Now, if you'd be so kind, please see what weighs so heavy in Lord Bed-Presser's pockets."

"Aye, Major." Grumm left the animals and moved quickly to where Sir Frederick Mason stood, his face a picture of indignation.

"Major?" Sir Frederick hissed, as Grumm took two purses from about the lawyer's person, both chinking with metal. "You're no officer, for you are no gentleman."

Grumm chortled. "I never yet seen a gen'lman made by his commission."

Lyle smiled. "Nor I."

He watched as Grumm moved swiftly to the rear of the coach and lifted a stout chest free. It was small, but clearly heavy, for Grumm groaned with the weight of it as he set it down. He turned when he sensed Walmsley at his back. "What is it?"

Walmsley glanced at the ornate blade still in Lyle's grip. "You'd leave a soldier without a sword, sir?"

"No, you're quite right, sir," Lyle agreed, slashing once through the air with the exquisite weapon, revelling in its astonishing balance. He drew his own sword and tossed it to Walmsley. "Enjoy," he said as he saw the rage come over the soldier again. "That piece of tin has bested many a great swordsman." He winked. "Including you." He looked abruptly away, not willing to enter into a discussion with the deflated soldier, and was pleased to discover the new blade fit snuggly into his scabbard.

Retrieving his pistol from Bella, he aimed it at the chest and fired. The crack of the gun echoed about the forest's darkening canopy, rooks and sparrows bursting up into the sky in fright, and the strongbox jumped back, its lid flung violently open in a spray of splinters. He turned to the prisoners even before the smoke had cleared, twisting the pistol's barrel and cocking it once more. "Two shots, remember." If Walmsley had intended to act, he evidently thought better of it, his gaze searching only his boots, and Lyle grinned broadly at Mason. "Now back in the carriage, Sir Freddy, and keep that blubbery jaw clamped or you shall see me upset."

Sir Frederick Mason hesitated, for he was incandescent with fury, yet he had seen the easy defeat of his experienced bodyguard and evidently preferred his skin to remain intact.

With an almighty sigh, the lawyer waddled back to the vehicle and clambered awkwardly inside.

"Empty the box," Lyle ordered Bella, who immediately went to the damaged chest, a sack appearing in her hand. He looked at the auburn haired woman who so captivated him. "Miss Mumford?"

Her eyes blazed with indignation. "You'll want my jewels, I suppose, you ruffian."

Lyle dropped his jaw as though scandalised. "Why, Felicity, we've only just met." She shot him a withering look, blowing a gust of air through her sharp nose, and he took her hand, guiding her to the coach door and helping her up the single step. He offered a quick bow. "It was a pleasure to make your acquaintance."

She turned back briefly, dark eyes searching his face. He thought he saw her lips lift in the merest hint of a smile. "I wish I could say the same."

*

Samson Lyle drew Star to a halt outside the barn. It was becoming dim now, and the old structure looked like a black rock amongst the trees, but he found its looming fastness reassuring, for they often used the abandoned place to regroup after a raid.

He slid nimbly off the side of the saddle, hitting the ground softly enough, though he felt his knee crack above the squelch of his boots. "Jesu, but I'm getting too old for this."

"Whereas," Grumm said as he reined in just behind, "I am still in fine fettle."

Lyle shot him a withering look. "Then next time, Eustace, you may wield powder and steel, while I shall hold the horses." There was a gnarled crab-apple tree nearby, its branches bare, clawing at the air like a crone's talons, and he tied Star to its trunk. He lingered for a short while to stroke the large patch of mottled pink skin that blighted the horse's handsome grey flank. The beast snorted irritably. "There there, boy," Lyle whispered, keeping his tone soft, soothing. "You did me proud as ever."

Grumm jumped down with an agility that belied his advancing years and brought his big black horse to the tree. "Rest up, Tyrannous."

Lyle sighed. "Must you call him that?"

"It means tyrant in the Greek," protested Grumm.

"I know what it means, Eustace," Lyle said as he checked the weapons held about Star's saddle. He had two pistols - the double-barrelled Dutch piece and a standard flintlock manufactured in London - along with the horseman's hammer he had carried through the civil wars. He tugged on each, ensuring they were firmly in place and always ready for deployment, and glanced up at the old man. "But it sounds ludicrous."

"What is ludicrous, Major," Grumm replied hotly, his neck sinews bulging, "is a highwayman with a cowardly and ever-vexed bloody horse!" He planted his hands on his hips. "You need a new mount."

"I need a new accomplice."

"I'm serious. His temper worsens by the month."

Lyle touched his fingertips to the grey's long face, tracing the white diamond that seemed to glow between its eyes in the darkness. Star pressed its muzzle into his palm and he glanced down at the damaged flank. "So would yours if you carried such a wound."

Grumm nodded. "If a cannon had exploded beside me, I'd be dead and gone, and I knows it. He's a strong bugger, no one's sayin' different. But you can't trust him." He tugged the strands of his straggly beard in exasperation. "It ain't right to have to avert the gaze of a destrier whenever there's a scrap."

"I trust him more than I trust you, old man," Lyle replied, thinking back to the ambush. "What happened back there?"

"As I already told you, Major, the branch we set was not long enough. It did not cover the road, and they went around."

"Leaving me to give chase. Christ, Eustace, it ain't good enough."

Grumm screwed up his face. "I'm a bloody smuggler, Major. I know weights and measures and the true value of goods. I know how to get things off the coast, where to keep 'em hid, and who to sell 'em to. We're all learning this new profession. All three of us together. Give us time."

Lyle snorted ruefully as they strode towards the large timber building. "Time? If they catch us we'll swing. No second chances, Eustace."

"Pah!" Grumm waved him away. "Quit your whining. Next time the branch'll be just perfect." He scratched at a globule of food that had dried fast amongst the tangles of his chin. "What did we get?"

Bella's mare, Newt, named for the jagged nature of her tail, was already tethered to an iron ring near the entrance to the barn, and the girl came striding out to greet them. She had long since discarded her scarf to reveal a face free of the blemishes of time. Her fresh, white skin only punctuated by a smattering of orange freckles across her nose and cheeks, and partially concealed by the shadow cast by a wide hat that she wore at a slant. "Some coin, a nice string of pearls, three gold rings, and that Walmsley's hanger."

Lyle nodded, drawing the sword he had taken from his bested opponent. "It is a Pappenheim."

Bella wrinkled her stubby nose, freckles briefly vanishing in the creases. "A pappy-who?"

"Pappenheim-hilt rapier. The style taken from Count Pappenheim, one of the imperial generals in the European wars." He held up the weapon, turning it slowly as though it were a rare gem. "Double edged and long enough to use from horseback. A gentleman's blade, but a murderer nevertheless." He ran a finger tenderly across the patterned hilt. "The guard is made of two distinct pieces. Not the full cup that one often sees, but a matching pair, like twin oyster shells, one set either side of the blade." Even the grey dusk failed to conceal the weapon's harsh beauty, and he could not help but marvel at the killing tool. Its pommel was ornately designed, heavy to offset the weight of the blade, but forged with some skill into the shape of a mushroom. The grip was tightly bound in good quality wire, and the sweeping knuckle bar twisted on its way from hilt to pommel, a subtle nod to the smith's craft.

"It is magnificent," Lyle said quietly. "But look here. The *pièce de résistance*." He fingered the holes that had been pierced into the two halves of the shell guard. "Stars and hearts. Perfectly formed," he turned the hilt over to examine the opposite half, "and perfectly symmetrical."

"Pretty," Bella said, lifting an eyebrow sardonically. She plucked off her hat, batting it with her other hand to send plumes of dust into the cool air.

"What was in that box?" Grumm asked impatiently.

"Hold your reins, Eustace," Lyle chided, smiling as he caught the glint of greed in the old smuggler's face.

Bella spat. "Paper."

"Paper?" Grumm echoed disbelievingly, his head wrenching hard round at the mercy of his tick.

Lyle raised a hand for quiet. "But what was written on it?"

She shrugged. "Piss-all, Samson."

He sighed. The girl had become his ward not long after Worcester, when Lyle still basked in the glory of revolution. The days when he had loved life, before things had turned sour between him and those for whom he had shed so much blood. She had been Dorothy Forks then. A snot-nosed urchin of six or seven, grubby-faced and barefooted. Lyle had been sent by his friend and master, General Cromwell, down to Portsmouth to issue special orders to the garrison. Now, four years on, he could not remember the content of those orders, only the road along which he had travelled and the brief rest stop he had made. It was near a little hamlet in a winding part of the road that was thick with forest and birdsong. Star had dipped his muzzle into a tiny, moss-fringed stream, and Lyle had sat back on his rump and let the canopy-split sunlight dapple his face.

"Give us a groat, squire," the girl had said.

Lyle remembered his eyes snapping open to gaze up at the feral face with its twinkling hazel eyes. "Give?" he had asked, amused by her precociousness. "You do not work for your keep?"

"Oh, I work, squire. Work 'ard." She had been wearing a baggy shirt that was almost the colour of the soil at their feet, and she wriggled her bony shoulders once, twice, and the garment was bunched at her waist. "Work on you, if it please ya."

Lyle had been astonished and repelled at once. "On me? Christ, girl, but you're a child."

She had winked in a perverse attempt at appearing coquettish. "One what can polish your privy member till it gleams."

Lyle had found himself on his feet, as though the very notion had put him on edge. "You do this often?"

"Aye, sir, as oft as I must."

"Must? Who puts you to such a task? What manner of man?"

The man in question had appeared then, stalking round the bend in the road with a face ravaged by pox and sharpened by greed. He had grinned obsequiously upon eyeing the exchange, bowed low over his gnarled cane, and explained in more detail the services his girl could offer a fine gentleman with coin and discretion. Lyle had snapped the cane across its owner's skull, leaving him senseless in the long grass, and gathered little Dorothy up into his saddle. They had not parted since. He had insisted she learn her letters, and she had insisted he never address her by her old name again.

Bella had travelled Europe with him in the intervening years, learning skills with weapons as well as books, yet she still wielded the brazen tongue that had so intrigued him at that first meeting. He watched as she went to fetch the sack into which the chest's contents had been thrust. "Piss-all to your eyes, maybe, but what exactly do they say?"

She grimaced as she took out a handful of sheets. "It's just a bunch o' letters, Samson."

Lyle held out a hand. "Let me see."

"Shouldn't bother," Eustace Grumm muttered as he went to urinate against the barn. "It's too damned dark. You'll bugger your eyes."

"Aye, I suppose," Lyle relented. "Back at the Lion then. We'll study them by candlelight."

"Don't know why we didn't just ride there direct," Grumm said as he hoisted up his breeches. "Ale's what a man needs after a take. Gives him a thirst."

"Gives a woman a thirst too," Bella agreed, nodding enthusiastically. "And we've some pigeon pie left over."

Grumm grimaced, his tick rampant. "Mightn't be the case, young Bella."

"You greedy old beggar," the girl said, an accusatory finger stabbed in Grumm's direction.

"As I've told you before," Lyle cut in quickly, "we do not make for home immediately after a take. If we're tracked, then let them track us here."

He felt a tremor then. It took a few moments for the sensation to filter up through his boots, but the feeling was so familiar that he knew instantly what it was. The others were staring at him. They had both come a long way since joining him in this new perilous adventure, but neither had stood on a battlefield and let the earth's vibrations whisper to them. Neither had that perception of danger that only experience could give. "To your mounts," he heard himself say.

"Major?" Grumm asked, his bearded face suddenly tense.

Bella stepped forward a pace. "Samson, what is it?"

"To your mounts, damn you!" Lyle snapped suddenly, spinning on his heels to make for the crab-apple tree where Star grazed. "We are hunted!"

Bella and Grumm rode clear of the barn as soon as the horsemen were in sight. It was an oft practised ploy, for Lyle's pursuers seemed to grow in number and tenacity with every robbery he committed, and the only way the three of them could hope to even the odds was by splitting the hunting party. Thus the girl and the smuggler would ride in opposite directions, while Lyle would take a third route, and they would trust their skins to the speed of their mounts and the encroaching darkness, hoping to meet much later at the rendezvous point.

Lyle cursed his nonchalance as he clambered into the saddle. Felicity Mumford had mocked him for playing at criminal as though it were a game, and, he inwardly admitted, it was a sharper thrust than she knew. He had become good at his new profession, and that had made him blasé, while his fury at the world had made him reckless. He had always insisted that Bella and Grumm conceal their faces during an ambush, telling himself that it would keep them safe, but deep down he knew that his own behaviour would eventually negate any such safeguard. Why had they spent so long at the barn? Why had he chosen to inspect his loot before they were safely back home? No reason, he chided himself as Star gathered pace to a brisk canter, beyond pure arrogance. He prayed they would make good their escape.

Star burst through a stand of withered brown bracken and out onto the moonlit road. Lyle stood in his stirrups to squint at the approaching posse. There were six of them, and he knew their presence was unlikely to be mere coincidence, for they each wore scarfs the colour of saffron about their torsos and waists, the device carried by many of the men who served William Goffe, the new Major-General of Berkshire, Sussex and Hampshire. Such men were no longer simply the army - they were the law - and to see them riding in strength about a night-fallen backwater spoke of a purpose beyond routine. Orders were bellowed from the lead rider and the main group seemed suddenly to dwindle, the rearmost of their number peeling skilfully away. Good, Lyle thought. Divide and conquer. He raked his spurs viciously along Star's flanks and the big stallion roared its anger, reared briefly, and sped away. He twisted in the saddle to see how many of the pack remained. To his surprise, there was only one, and, though the distance was too great to make out the man's features, he could see enough of the rider to identify him. He was clad in the ubiquitous hide and metal of a cavalry trooper, his head encased in a helmet with a single sliding nasal bar and a tail of riveted steel sheets to protect his neck. In all this, the horseman might have been any nameless trooper thundering along this rain-softened bridleway, but for his scarf. Swathing his torso diagonally, fastened in a large knot at his side like a vast flower in bloom, the garment was made unique by a black smudge at the point where the voluminous material crossed its wearer's shoulder. Lyle could not see the detail, but he knew the device well enough, and the revelation gave him pause. He hauled on Star's reins, stooped forth to whisper into the skittish stallion's pricked ear. "I won't run from him."

Lyle instructed the snorting beast to turn with deft movements of his wrists and thighs, and Star did as he was bidden, hooves sliding alarmingly in the mud. But he was steady enough, and soon they faced their pursuer, moving into a lively trot.

The man in the orange scarf was at a gallop now, and his big black horse devoured the ground in a matter of moments. Lyle saw him draw a pistol and he produced the short English flintlock holstered to his left. He was reticent to fire, for Star hated the sound, and the report would doubtless tempt the rest of the posse back to his position, but the armoured man discharged his weapon immediately, its sharp cough making Lyle shrink low behind his steed's thick neck. Star bellowed like a bullock at Smithfield and it was all Lyle could do to keep control, but eventually he was able to straighten and take aim. He shot when the rider was still thirty paces away, knew he had missed, and dropped the reins so that he might draw his second firearm. His attacker had another pistol too, and it was fired quickly, the report agonisingly loud now that they were so close. Lyle ducked, even as his hand groped madly for the butt of his double-barrelled gun, but the lead flew over his right shoulder to smack into a tree some distance behind. Now he had the advantage, levelled his pistol, but the trooper raced past before he could cock the hammer, slashing at Lyle with a hefty looking broadsword, and the highwayman only just managed to avoid its murderous arc, the pistol skipping from his grip to tumble into a muddy rut.

The foes wheeled about to face one another again. Lyle felt Star's huge bulk judder beneath him, and he knew the battle-scarred animal was beginning to panic. He had to forgo his blade so that he might cling on with both hands, desperate to keep himself in the saddle, even as the saffron-scarfed pursuer bore down again. He knew he would be skewered this time and, just as the horses were about to meet, he wrenched savagely on Star's reins, tearing the bit to compel the steaming grey away from the line of collision. Star slewed violently to the right, Lyle felt himself sway in the saddle, his rump sliding precariously out of position, and his thighs screamed in pain as he clamped them tight. Somehow he stayed on, the trooper's blade cleaving nothing but crisp air, and then he was into the trees, pounding along a narrow track that was fringed with tangled branches and perilously dark. He could not hear a thing above Star's thrashing breaths, but he twisted back to see that the armoured man had given chase, despite the risk to his own mount. Lyle leaned in to whisper encouragement in the horse's ears, and was immediately gratified to sense a calming in the frightened animal's demeanour.

"There you are, Star, old thing," he said, slapping the stallion's hard neck. "Keep your nerve and we'll see what can be done."

The trees thinned and the track widened until Lyle found himself in a small grove. It was skirted by ancient looking boughs, the kind Grumm often talked of when telling tales of the first people of his native Cornwall, and strangely illuminated by the moon. He let Star run across it but wheeled him around as soon as they reached the far side.

The man on the black mount burst out from the woods to meet them and drew his horse to a halt. "I have you now, Lyle!"

Lyle felt exhausted from the chase, but he forced himself to doff his hat in mock salute. "Well bless me, if it isn't the Mad Ox of Hampshire!"

The trooper's face was bisected by the nasal bar and obscured in the horse's billowing breaths, but Lyle caught the flash of white teeth below a bushy black moustache as he sneered. "Have a care, sir, for the life of a brigand seldom ends well."

"Soldier, Francis!" Lyle called back. "Not brigand."

"You are outside the law!"

Lyle laughed. "Because the law in this county is but one man; William Goffe. And you, Francis, are Goffe's creature."

The trooper bristled, kicked forwards a touch, sword still naked and glinting. The black motif embroidered at his shoulder now resolving into the gaping maw of a roaring lion. "It is Colonel Maddocks to you, Lyle."

Lyle drew his own sword now that he was confident that Star had found some semblance of calm. "And it is Major Lyle to you."

Maddocks urged his mount to the right so that it walked the perimeter of the clearing. "You relieved Sir Frederick Mason of some valuables this night. I want them back."

"Not possible," Lyle countered. A thought occurred to him. "You clung to my tail with impressive haste, Colonel. Too soon for Sir Freddy to have reported our encounter. Were you supposed to have been his escort?"

"I'm warning you, Lyle," Maddocks snarled. "Return the items forthwith."

Lyle laughed. "I'm right! You should have been protecting him. Stone me, sir, but such a thing will not go well for your prospects, eh? But why would they appoint you personally? The Major-General's private mastiff sent on an errand such as this. A tad beneath you, is it not?"

"How long do you think you can last?" Maddocks called suddenly. "Out here on the road."

"Long enough," Lyle called back, moving Star to mirror his opponent so that they circled one another like a pair of ban-dogs in a Southwark pit.

"Goffe has made me your nemesis, Lyle. I am his chief huntsman now. The snare closes around you, never doubt it."

"And yet I will ever wriggle free."

"To what end?"

He had often wondered upon that question. The war was over. The old king dead and gone, his son hiding away in France. The bastions of the Royalist cause; Prince Rupert, Lucas, Montrose, were scattered to the wind, or rotting in mocked graves. The Scots cowered to the north and Ireland was subjugated. It was what Lyle had prayed and worked towards his whole life. Complete victory. And yet, the sweet taste of a true republic had quickly soured. "There is no end as long as tyrants stalk the land. We fought and died to throw off the yoke of one, and were straight-way given another. Goffe is no better than Laud or Strafford."

Maddocks spat. "Major-General Goffe is invested with the Lord Protector's authority. He is a righteous man. Anointed by..."

"By God?" Lyle shouted across the grove. "Do you not hear yourself, Maddocks? The Divine Right of Major-Generals!" He shook his head in disbelief. "What did we fight for all those years? You and I, side by side, taking back these isles inch by bloody inch, and for what? A king in all but crown. A nation carved up and served in slices for Cromwell's friends to feast upon. A land ruled on the private whims of generals."

Maddocks seemed to be grinning behind the iron bar. He levelled the sword, pointing it like a steel finger at the outlaw. "You were Cromwell's man once, Lyle. Do not play false with me. You were content enough with your lot until it no longer sat pretty with your feeble sensibilities."

The image of the colonel across the grove seemed to dim then, as though his darkening silhouette became part of the elm-thrown shadows, and other shapes slithered over Lyle's mind. Other men, womenfolk and children, running, screaming, weeping. They were shrouded in a mist that was red as an April dusk, a shade ever branded upon his memory; blood and fire.

Ireland. That was where it had all started. He had been there for some months, serving Ireton, mopping up the last remnants of resistance at Carlow, Waterford and Duncannon as the New Modelled Army rolled over the land like an inexorable storm cloud. The battles had been hard fought and well won, and he had thanked God daily for His providence. And then came the massacres. There had been plenty of blood spilt already, for the Confederate War had raged since before even the English struggles, but Lyle had not borne witness to it, and he had learnt quickly that tall tales were the currency of soldiers and civilians alike. Yet at Limerick his eyes had been prized open like clams in a cauldron. He had seen things - done things - that even now he could not begin to reflect upon, lest bile bubble to his throat. So many innocents had died, all for a greater good that he increasingly found impossible to espouse. What still astonished him was his own arrogance. The conceited nature of a young, brash, infamous soldier that told him to confront his commander as if his voice could possibly be heeded. He had considered himself friend to Henry Ireton, a brother-in-arms, and that had convinced him to speak his mind. How foolish he had been.

Maddocks attacked. He spurred forth with a sudden kick that had his horse bellowing and his opponent reeling. It was all Lyle could do to urge Star into a run, and he managed to raise his blade in the nick of time as the pair met in the open ground, suddenly close enough to see the whites in each other's eyes. The weapons met high with a clang, pressed in, flashing in the moonlight as they filled the deep forest with the song of swords. Lyle looked into Maddocks' face to see his old comrade's rictus grin, lips peeled back in a grimace made all the more horrifying by the black eyes that were screwed narrow with determination. Lyle twisted the blade to free the deadly embrace, felt the tip of the colonel's sword bounce off one of the shell guards protecting his hand, and was immediately thankful to have obtained such a weapon, even as he was forced to parry two more strikes from the formidable opponent. He managed to sway back to avoid the third short thrust and steered Star out of range.

"You are a mad cur, Lyle," Maddocks rasped as the horses wheeled about. "Foolish, blinkered and vain."

"Better a free fool than chained."

"Chained? That horse bolted a long time ago." Maddocks swiped the air with his heavy sword. "It'll be the noose or nothing for you."

Lyle laughed. "Then I choose nothing."

"The choice is not yours to make."

The colonel came again, bolting impressively forwards from a standing start, but this time Lyle was ready for him. He squeezed his thighs lightly, flicked the reins, and Star slewed away, leaving Maddocks' mount to charge into the cool air in his wake. He turned, even as Maddocks rallied for another assault, slicing his own arc above Star's tall ears in an ostentatious blur. "You may chase me, Mad Ox, but you will not take me alive! I'll fight Goffe's creatures as long as I draw breath!"

"The war is over, Lyle," Maddocks countered.

Lyle shook his head as he rolled his shoulders for the next engagement. "Not for me."

"It was Ireton killed her, Samson," said Maddocks, his tone softening a touch. "His orders. Not Goffe, not Cromwell."

"But Ireton is dead."

"Then the debt dies with him."

Lyle dipped his head as he kicked. "No."

They raced inward, closing the ground in a heartbeat, but this time Lyle released the reins, gripping with legs only, and unhooked the iron war hammer that hung beside his shin. It was two-thirds of a yard in length, the four-sided hammer counterbalanced by a lethally sharp pick, and he hurled it at Maddocks' horse. The big beast cried out as the heavy club slammed into its shoulder, and it lost its step enough to put Maddocks off his swing. The colonel's broadsword found nothing but clean air, and Lyle brought his own blade round to clatter the side of the soldier's head. Maddocks' helmet saved his life, but the force of the blow knocked him sideways so that he slid halfway off the saddle. The disquieted horse, still whinnying in pain, reared up, throwing him clear so that he finished in a heap of leather and metal in the centre of the grove.

Lyle was upon him in moments, snatching up the war hammer as he moved to stand over his stricken enemy. He held it up as Maddocks stared forlornly back, wincing with each breath. "An outdated old thing, really. Made for smashing plate armour. Has its uses, though, I'm sure you'll agree."

Maddocks spat a globule of blood that looked like tar in the night. "Get it over with."

"When they killed her," Lyle said, "were you there?"

Maddocks seemed surprised at the question, but he managed to shake his head. "I was not."

"I never saw her body. Never had the chance to kiss her cold lips or put her in the ground myself."

"Alice had a good burial, Samson," Maddocks said. "But you were on the run. A deserter."

Lyle nodded. "It was my fault, I know. And the knowledge that I was not at home when the soldiers came has eaten me alive these four years. I was not there to protect her, as was my duty." He forced a smile that seemed so at odds with his feelings. "But that knowledge has driven me too. Given me purpose that had all but leaked away in Ireland."

"Just kill me now, damn you!" Maddocks snarled suddenly, the wait for his demise crushing his spirit as he gazed up at the stars.

"I will not," Lyle said. He went to gather up Star's reins and clambered nimbly into the saddle, putting the weapons away and offering a sharp bow. "You are bested, Francis, and I will best you again, and again, for as long as you hunt me. The war is not yet done. It is a war of vengeance, against those who wronged me, chased me away from my home and murdered my wife. A war against the Protector's creatures. It will never be done."

*

The Red Lion was a modest establishment just off the Portsmouth to London Road at a village called Rake. It had stabling for half a dozen horses, lodgings enough for the same number of travellers, and a decent sized taproom stocked with good local ale and a passable claret. It was also the perfect place from which a highwayman might launch his campaign.

"What happened?" Eustace Grumm's voice came from the darkness as Lyle dismounted in the small courtyard outside the inn.

Lyle peered into the gloom. He could see the reed-thin profile of his friend leaning casually against the red brick wall, soft candlelight streaming through the windows to highlight him a touch. "It was Maddocks."

Grumm had a clay pipe clamped between his crooked teeth and he pulled it free, blowing a large pall of smoke as he spoke. "In the flesh?"

"Aye."

"Knew it were Goffe's men by the scarves, but I hadn't expected the Mad Ox to ride with them. You're sure?"

"I knew from a long way off," Lyle nodded, whistling softly for the stable hand to collect Star. "Saw his crest."

"The black lion?"

Lyle tapped his shoulder. "Embroidered into his scarf, here."

Grumm snorted. "Very nice. Must be doin' well for himself these days."

Lyle nodded. "He is tasked with hunting me down, it seems. Major-General Goffe's right-hand."

Grumm stepped out of the shadows, his eyes like white orbs in the night. "You spoke?"

"We fought."

Grumm's jaw dropped, but footsteps scraped on the yard's compacted chalk and both men turned to see a young girl appear from the stables. "Take yer 'orse, m'lord?" Bella asked with a mischievous grin.

Lyle smiled as he handed her the reins. Her role in charge of the stables was a source of great pride, but many of her customers were also victims out on the road, and the irony was not lost on her. "I am glad you made it."

She grinned. "Never in doubt. Those old buggers in armour never outrun me an' Newt." Her freckled nose wrinkled as she inspected Lyle's saddle, and she reached up to draw the double-barrelled pistol. "You didn't have the same luck though, I'm guessin'."

Lyle took the weapon from her and turned it in his hand. The piece was caked in half-dry mud, from muzzle to butt, and would need a thorough clean before it would function. "Dropped on the road. I was lucky to retrieve it."

"Dropped?" Bella echoed incredulously.

"Christ above!" Grumm blurted as he squinted at the filthy weapon. "I knows why you bloody dropped it." He thrust a spindly finger in Star's direction. "That nag'll be the death of you, Major."

Lyle followed the former smuggler's gaze. "Will you sing that same tired tune all your life, Eustace?"

"I'll sing it every time he near kills you, aye!"

"There was a moment," Lyle confessed, "after Maddocks and I exchanged fire, that I almost lost control. He panicked, looked to bolt. I could feel it."

Grumm fiddled with his straggly beard. "Damn me, Major. If you're not fighting the toughest bugger in Goffe's retinue, you're wrestling with your own mount."

Bella patted the horse. "Ah, don't mind him, Star." She glared at Grumm. "He's a sour old thing."

The old man jammed his pipe stem back between his teeth. "Not so sour as that bloody animal."

Lyle went to the horse, scratching the white diamond between its big eyes and receiving a soft nudge of its snout for his trouble. "He may be shy on occasion, but did you ever see a swifter beast? He's saved my skin more than times than I could count. I'll not turn my back on him now. Besides," he added, speaking into the animal's twitching ear, "we won, didn't we, boy?"

"Good work, Samson," Bella declared happily. "The Mad Ox is a proper fighter."

"When we rode together with the ironsides," Lyle said, tucking the pistol into his waistband, "he was one of the very best. Better than me, that's for certain."

"What's changed?" Eustace Grumm asked.

"All that fencin', I bet," said Bella. "Them hours an' hours with that glum-guts Besnard."

Lyle could not help but laugh at that. "Actually, I threw my hammer at his horse. Now come along. I need ale."

The three of them sat at the taproom's rearmost table, lit by fat beeswax candles and wreathed in smoke from Grumm's pipe. There was one other patron, slumped in a far corner cradling a pot of strong beer, but they recognised him from the village and knew he posed no threat. Grumm had fetched victuals while Bella had seen to the horses. There were some hard-edged offerings from the cheese cratch, thin strips of bacon, and good bread, cooked in the ovens on the premises, and the trio were soon enjoying a well-earned meal. If the bell jangled at the door, they would shift into well practised action. Lyle would be gone, vanished into the shadows and out through the small rear door that would take him to the woods beyond, while the others would inhabit their roles of tapster and stable-hand like a pair of players in the long-defunct theatres that had hugged the southern bank of the Thames. Eustace Grumm ran the tavern, going by the name of John Brown, while Bella was his great-niece, Lucy. It had worked for a year, ever since Lyle had returned from France with his two rather incongruous companions and a tidy fortune made at the sharp end of a duellist's blade. The charade had given them a business, a place of relative safety from the wolves of the road, and it had become the home none of them had thought ever to find. A secure bolthole away from their life of crime, and yet all the while funded by it.

Lyle took out his prized pistol and placed it on the table. He began to pick at the flaky mud with his fingernails, scraping away the road's grime to reveal the magnificent weapon beneath. When the larger lumps were scoured clear, he took up a cloth and worked at the more intricate parts of the lock.

"You threw your war-hammer at him," Grumm muttered in amusement, bits of half-chewed bread flecking his beard as he spoke. "What would Master Besnard think?"

"He would congratulate me on staying alive. And he'd tell you not to stare down that beak of yours so sanctimoniously."

Grumm crammed a chunk of cheese into the side of his mouth. "He'd advise you to pick your fights more carefully."

Lyle looked up from the pistol. "I won, didn't I?"

"Barely."

As she worked her way through a plate of bacon that was scorched crisp, Bella leafed through the pile of papers she had taken from Sir Frederick Mason's strongbox. She glanced at Lyle, her expression sour. "Like I said, Samson. Piss-all in this lot."

Lyle gnawed a grubby fingernail. "Keep looking. Sir Frederick must have been carrying something of significance for Maddocks to be shadowing him."

"Fat lot o' good he did," Grumm said happily.

"Yet the fact remains," Lyle said. "He had Walmsley in the carriage for close protection, but Maddocks was already out on the road. He tracked us so quickly, he can't have been far behind Mason."

"Lucky we jumped him when we did," Bella said.

Grumm cackled. "They was to rendezvous before they hit the Combe, I'd wager."

"You may be right," said Lyle, for it seemed reasonable. Between the villages of Hill Brow and Rake, the London Road climbed above a deep, wooded vale known as Harting Combe. In the summer months, when the going was firm, travellers could gaze down upon the Combe as they thundered along, enjoying the clean air and the stunning view. But the road south of Rake was very steep as it plunged off the high ground, becoming almost impassable during autumn and winter when the terrain was water-logged and filthy. Those on foot might still risk the shorter route, or even skilled riders if they possessed a good mount, but no heavy vehicle could begin to negotiate so sharp a gradient in such precarious conditions. They would be forced, then, to risk the low, forest-choked bridleway that curved along the foot of Harting Combe, meeting the main highway again at a point beyond London Road's steep drop. It avoided that difficult section of road, which was a blessing, but it forced pilgrims to take their chances in the dense woodland of the isolated vale, compelling those travellers of a wealthier nature to ensure they were well protected. Mason, Lyle had guessed, would be one such person, and he had decided to strike the lawyer at the Combe's southern edge, for many a coach had met with an armed escort before taking the road down into the forest's infamous embrace. Evidently it had been a good gamble to make, for Colonel Maddocks and his troopers were almost certainly due to link up with Mason at Hill Brow. They had intercepted their quarry in the nick of time. He gnawed his lip as he considered the implication. "Why Maddocks?"

"That Mason's one o' Goffe's big wheels," Bella answered. "You said so yourself."

"But so is Maddocks." He shook his head. "Why set his best man to protecting a lawyer? No, it was not Mason himself that was significant. Rather what he was carrying. We must reflect upon our takings."

Bella shrugged. "Not much. Just a few trinkets."

"Which means," Lyle persisted, "it was the strongbox."

The girl sighed theatrically as she delved into the scraps of paper again. "How many bushels o' corn they got in store. A letter from the Major-General askin' Mason to settle a dispute 'tween farmers down at Rowlands Castle." She waved one crumpled sheet. "Message informing Sir Blubber-Belly that a prisoner's to be moved from Newbury to Portsmouth."

"What prisoner?" Lyle asked.

She shrugged. "Don't say." She looked through the papers again, pausing at one. "Now this'n is an invitation from Sir John Hippisley for Mason to attend a masquerade, whatever that is."

"A masquerade ball," Lyle explained. "A grand dance. Very popular in France. The people will wear disguises."

"Surprised Goffe would allow such a decadent thing," Grumm grunted. "Smacks of Cavalier to me."

"He probably doesn't know," replied Lyle. "Hippisley's out at Hinton Ampner, is he not? On the Winchester Road."

Bella scanned the paper and nodded. "The manor house, aye."

Grumm looked up with a mocking sneer, a trail of fat wending its way down his beard from the corner of his thin mouth. "Surprised you don't attend, Major, given your apparent lust for death." He shook his head in exasperation. "Congratulate you for staying alive, would he? Besnard would have you whipped through the streets for such recklessness."

That was true, thought Lyle. When he had enlisted with Besnard after a couple of months of listless wandering, he had been an angry, desperate, grief-stricken youth. He had sold his armour to buy food, leaving only the grimy clothes on his back, a big, wounded horse, and his much dented sword. Charles Besnard had seen him fight an ill-judged duel over an unpaid debt - one he had been lucky to survive - and had seen some spark of promise in the way Lyle had handled his blade. He had taken the Englishman on, given him and Bella lodgings, and taught him the ways of the great fencing masters. Besnard had saved Lyle, without a doubt, but he could still be a strict disciplinarian who would not have entertained or condoned the rekindling of Lyle's thirst for danger. "Come now, Eustace," he said calmly, "you know more than most about staying alive. For a righteous man, you've done your fair share of unrighteous acts in the name of saving your skin."

Grumm sat back and took a drag on his pipe. "We are not discussing me, Major."

"How many ships did your false light guide onto Clovelly rocks so that you might eat?"

That hit a nerve, for the old man lurched forwards to jab the clay stem at Lyle's face. "I was never a wrecker, damn your forked tongue!"

Lyle smiled, holding up placating palms. "A smuggler then."

"Aye, a smuggler," Grumm conceded, aware that Lyle was goading him and at pains to cool his ire, "and proud to say it. But a wrecker never. If you were any other man, Major Lyle, I'd stick my boot in your behind for such slander."

"Easy, Eustace, easy. My point is that we play the hand life deals us, and do what we must to survive."

Grumm eased back again, half disappearing in the billowing smoke. "Amen to that."

"And next time I shall open Maddocks from chest to ballock."

Grumm chuckled. "No you won't. You enjoy the chase as much as he."

Lyle offered a shrug, for he could not argue with so observant a man. He held up the pistol instead. "Look at her. Such beauty." It had been made by a gunsmith in Rotterdam, though Lyle had picked it up after a tavern brawl on the outskirts of Rennes not long after his flight from England. It had been there that he had bade his time after his world had collapsed, and there that he had learnt a modicum of French and a great deal of swordsmanship. He lifted the pistol with both hands, for, though barely heavier than a typical English flintlock, it was longer by the length of his hand, from wrist to fingertips. He blew gently over the lock to make sure no loose powder or debris from the ride had lingered amongst the mechanism. Satisfied, he checked the strikers. There were two, which was what made this weapon so special - and so lethal. Double-barrelled handguns were rare enough, but one with only one lock was almost unheard of. This pistol had two barrels, one set above the other. When Lyle fired the piece, he need only depress the barrel release, twist the twin muzzles round, and fire again. The same lock, cock and flint would be employed, making the process swift and simple.

Grumm stared at it. "Just don't drop the damned thing next time, Major. She's your talisman. That extra shot will save your life one day."

The sound of Bella chuckling excitedly made both men look down at her. She had a heavily creased square of vellum in her pale hand, which she thrust under Lyle's nose. "Finally the cull cackles!"

"What is it?" Lyle asked.

"That prisoner, Samson. Goes by the name of James Wren."

"Sir James Wren was a lieutenant-colonel of harquebusiers. Rivalled Prince Robber in the saddle. I fought him once."

It was late. The last patron had staggered out into the crisp night air, and the Red Lion's heavy studded door had been locked and barred. The candles guttered, throwing eerie shapes on the whitewashed walls, while the last remnants of flame danced in the hearth. Bella had cleared away the detritus of the meal, replacing their ale with steaming pots of spiced wine, and now the three outlaws sat together at the age-scarred elm table, a strangely concocted family who knew that each night together could be their last.

"Fought *with* him?" Eustace Grumm asked, staring at Lyle over the rim of his wooden pot.

"Fought him," Lyle repeated. "A skirmish in the days before Worcester." He took a swig of wine as he remembered those frantic times when the son of the deposed king had returned to lay claim to the crown. The young king had been smashed by Cromwell's far superior New Modelled Army, a battle that had effectively put an end to the wars that had stolen a decade from the people of the British Isles. Cromwell had called Worcester a *crowning mercy*, but all Lyle remembered was bloodshed and panic, and a populace worn to wraiths by plague, starvation and fear. "Lucky to get out of it with my hide in one piece."

"A king's man?" said Grumm.

"None more so."

Grumm raised his pot. "May he rot, then." He took a long draught, belching when he was done, and wiped his glistening beard with a grubby sleeve. His eyes narrowed as they searched Lyle's face. "And yet?"

"And yet it would seem he now languishes in Goffe's clink," Lyle replied. "If he's to be moved down to Portsmouth, then perhaps transportation awaits."

"Why would you care? An old enemy imprisoned by a new one."

Lyle shrugged. "Because the enemy of my enemy is my friend, Eustace. Wren was an honourable fellow, for all his malignant allegiance, and I would see him free if it hurt the Protectorate."

Grumm still stared hard at his friend, his blue eyes alive with suspicion. "I do not like that look."

"You mentioned a masquerade?" Lyle said, snapping his head round to address Bella. "Hippisley's place at Hinton Ampner?"

"Aye," Bella nodded. She clutched her pot in both hands, cradling the warm vessel against her chest as though it were full of precious gems.

Lyle drank slowly, luxuriating in the spices that fought away the autumn eve. "Not far from here. Out to the west above the Winchester road. When was this event to take place?"

"On the morrow," replied the girl. She gathered up a handful of the long, mousy hair that fell to her shoulders, running it through her fingers, her face wistful. "Wish I could be a great lady at a dance."

Lyle grinned. "You are already a great lady. But perhaps your wish is not so far-fetched. I believe we have our solution, praise God."

"Our solution?" Grumm spluttered as Bella beamed. "You cannot possibly..."

"Worry not, old fellow," Lyle cut in. "You need not embroil yourself in this."

Grumm lifted his pot. "Suits me well, and no mistake." When he had swallowed, he fixed the highwayman with a drilling stare. "You're a damnable fool, Samson Lyle, I do not mind telling you."

Lyle raised a single eyebrow. "Evidently."

"Anyone who is anyone will be there, for Christ's sake. God-rotten magistrates. Bureaucrats. Soldiers. Any number of Major-General Goffe's lackeys." He shook his head in bewilderment. "Zounds, the Mad Ox too, I shouldn't wonder." He leaned in suddenly. "He knows what you bloody look like, you fool!"

"But not what *you* look like," Lyle replied. "Or Bella. Besides, it is a masquerade. Every man and woman will wear a disguise." He rubbed thick fingers over the emerging bristles of his chin, the scraping sounds seeming unnaturally loud in the empty taproom. "I have to go, Eustace. I have to go. If Sir Frederick Mason is in attendance then we may discover when they plan to move Wren. It is a chance to strike at our enemies."

"Well do not count on my assistance, you bee-headed bloody frantic," Grumm retorted hotly. He folded his arms, setting his jaw and staring at the blackened beams above. "I shan't have any part in it, as God is my witness."

PART TWO: THE DANCE

Hinton Ampner, Hampshire, November 1655

Hinton Ampner was a tiny village straddling the road between Petersfield and Winchester. The land was thick with forests that stretched in all directions into the chalky South Downs, only occasionally broken up by patches of open farmland that sustained the smattering of timber-framed hovels clustered like toadstools about the hamlet's core. And that core was the Manor House, the huge edifice of red brick and grey stone that had been built in Tudor times as a hunting lodge and grown into the most imposing structure for miles.

It was evening as Samson Lyle and Eustace Grumm stepped over the threshold. The surrounding trees darkened an already grey dusk, but the great house glowed bright, basking in the tremulous light of a thousand candles. No stinking tallow, Lyle noted, for Sir John Hippisley had done well out of the revolution, seen his star rise with the other hard men of the new order, and the old Roundhead's home was sweet with the scent of beeswax, a touch of wood smoke and a great deal of perfume.

A footman in a fine suit of shimmering red and blue strutted confidently out to greet Lyle like some over-sized kingfisher. At his flank was a soldier clutching a halberd. Lyle felt his pulse quicken. The footman held a mask attached to a thin rod, which he lowered to appraise the new arrivals. "Sirs?"

This was the first test of Lyle's nerve, and he held his breath behind his own ostentatious mask of gold and black. It was fastened by a string about the back of his head so that there was no danger of it slipping, and he bowed, the mask's goose feather fringe wafting at his scalp and tickling his ears. "Sir Ardell Early," he said, his voice sounding so peculiar in the muffled confines of the disguise. He glanced over his shoulder at the figure who had accompanied him to the door. "And Winfred Piersall."

The footman considered the names, and for a terrible moment Lyle thought they had been discovered, but the man offered a wide smile and a deep bow and swept his arm back grandly. "Your servant, gentlemen. I hope you enjoy your evening."

The men allowed themselves to be shown into the house's inner sanctum. There would be no further need to prove their credentials, for a masquerade ball was precisely that - a masquerade. Men and women were not themselves on an evening such as this. They were whoever they wished to be, hidden by their disguises and afforded complete anonymity for the night. It was a fashionable pastime on the continent, and would, Lyle suspected, have become quite the thing in England had the Stuart dynasty survived its time of judgement. But now such public displays of opulence, not to mention the private exchanges of carnality that inevitably went on in darkened corridors behind the bright ballrooms, were not condoned by Cromwell and the men, like William Goffe, who ruled in his name. And yet, though theatre had been banned, and many of the great pagan-spawned festivals that had been adopted and adapted by the High Church were doggedly repressed, the new regime understood when it was politic to cool their instinctive censoriousness. Their great supporters - those strongmen who had killed a monarch, purged a Parliament and made Cromwell king in all but name - were occasionally to be allowed down from the giddy moral heights to which they had been thrust. When it served a purpose.

"Your lad did well," Grumm, upholstered in a green suit and mask so that he looked to Lyle like a huge frog, muttered under his breath as they were ushered along a well-lit corridor.

"Pays to know a Little Mercury or three," Lyle replied in hushed tones. The highways and lanes of Hampshire were abuzz in daylight hours with boys and girls around the age of eleven or twelve, delivering letters and invitations from one great house to another. They were the life-blood of rural communities, and Samson Lyle had recognised their worth almost as soon as he had embarked on his criminal crusade. He had several in his pay, who provided him with gossip and occasionally intercepted useful correspondence. In this case, he had asked his contacts to keep their eyes sharp for letters bound for Sir John Hippisley's estate. One lad had brought him two such documents. Both declining invitations to this evening's masquerade. One from a wool merchant known as Sir Ardell Early, the other from Winfred Piersall, a moderately successful goldsmith.

"You think Sir Frederick's here?" Grumm asked.

"Aye," Lyle replied just as quietly. "Goffe wants something from Hippisley. Money or land. This dance is part of the payment. Mason will be here reminding Sir John of his obligations." He noticed the kingfisher-clad footman glance over his shoulder. "I was just saying," he added in a louder voice, "that this place is exquisite."

The footman nodded. "Quite so, sir. Sir John purchased the seat five years ago, yet still he improves upon it. We have a large hall, as you will presently see, two parlours, and twenty-one chambers. There is a brew-house on the estate, along with a malt-house, stables, barns, and our own hop garden." His ears quivered, and Lyle assumed he was smiling behind the mask. "Even a bowling green, would you believe?"

"I look forward to complimenting your master on such a fine home," Lyle said.

They reached the end of the corridor and the footman pushed a set of double doors that opened into a sizable room that might have been used to entertain dinner guests once they had removed themselves from the grand hall. There were tables lined against one wall, crammed with goblets full of various types of liquid, while a small choir of perhaps a dozen children were arranged opposite. They wore white robes and masks, which, to Lyle's eye, made them look like faceless cherubim. Something he found profoundly disturbing. They sang a high, lilting tune that was sweet enough, but did little to assuage his unease. More mirrored doors were on the far side of the room, flanked by a pair of retainers as luxuriously dressed as the rest of the staff, and Lyle guessed they would lead into the main hall. He gazed left and right. This was to be a grand affair; that much was clear. The panelled walls carried a near impossible shimmer, polished to within an inch of the servants' lives no doubt. Every mirror gleamed, every floor tile squeaked its cleanliness beneath every boot heel, and every tapestry had been dusted and straightened in preparation for the most discerning of guests. Lyle was glad he had dressed in his very best finery. Bella had gone to great lengths to scrub his long riding boots and bring his favourite shirt to the whiteness of virgin snow. She had chosen for him a black coat with slashed sleeves that revealed the yellow lining beneath, and, though he had complained of looking like a gigantic hornet, she had insisted that nothing less would do. The brilliance of the newly freshened shirt collar offset the coat nicely, she had said, and, even Lyle could admit, the delicate lace at his cuffs certainly provided a deal of beauty to the ensemble. It was all finished off, of course, by the gold mask, and now, as he and Grumm were shown into the great hall, he thanked God for it. For he stepped into a roiling cauldron of bodies, all immaculately attired, all disguised, and each one an enemy.

The choir song was overwhelmed by louder, jauntier music from the balcony, even as the rest of Lyle's senses were assailed. It was as if Sir John Hippisley had squandered his entire fortune on this one gathering, such was the display of wealth that greeted Lyle's gaze. A vast hall of polished floor and high ceiling, awash with colour, draped in bright tapestries, transformed for the night into a Venetian ballroom that thronged with figures dripping in gold and silver, lace and satin, feathers and fans and pearls. Music played above the incessant chatter, masked men and women danced in the room's centre, laughing and whooping and calling to one another like so many rainbow-fledged birds. The women wore swirling dresses, voluminous and shimmering, while the men were adorned in such gaudy attire that Lyle felt as though he had stepped into a room full of peacocks.

Lyle could not help but laugh at the sight, and he sensed Grumm at his shoulder.

"Strange," he said, comfortable that the din of the dance would obscure his words to all but his friend. "Always considered this kind of thing belonged to the past."

Grumm gave a low snort. "The lofty peaks we are ordered by the good book to scale, are not always attainable. It is man's nature to kick back at the chains of morality once in a while."

"You're in the right of it. I imagine we shan't find any ardent Puritans here." That was the irony of this brave new world, he thought. The Parliamentarian faction had never been unified in search of a republic. Indeed, the vast majority of the old Roundheads - himself included - had enlisted to oust the king's corrupt advisers, not bring down the entire monarchy. Where the Royalists had fought for their king and the status quo, the rebel cause had been one of disparate factions, all brought together through a common enemy. They were not all dour Puritans, but a violent concoction of Presbyterians and Independents, soldiers and merchants, aggrieved aristocrats, rebellious Members of Parliament, and radical commoners seeking to level the very foundations of society. Little wonder, then, that no sooner had the shared enemy been vanquished, the factions began to rupture. They turned upon one another, tearing the hard-won peace to shreds. It had taken two more wars to finish the quarrel, leaving the Independent party supreme and unassailable: Oliver Cromwell its figurehead, the New Modelled Army its muscle. But that meant a great many of the ordinary rebels had never been as sober and pious as their new masters. They had supported a cause that had overtaken them, overwhelmed them, and now many - most, perhaps - yearned for the old days that, though far from perfect, were not as stifling as life under the Major-Generals. They went to chapel, they prayed and fasted, but if ever an opportunity to while away an evening with dance and song presented itself, the people would flock to it like so many months to a flame.

"Not any proper ones," Grumm muttered, his mind evidently in tune with Lyle's. He inched closer. "What do we do now?"

"Find Mason."

"How?"

"He's a sober sort," Lyle replied, hoping he was right. "He'll be plainly dressed by comparison with the majority. And he's run to fat. Shouldn't be too hard to spot."

"Conspicuous by his banality. What if he knows Sir Ardell Early?"

"I'm in disguise. Besides, we took a nicely bulging purse from Early once, if you recall, and he was not too dissimilar to me in height and build."

"Then what?"

"Then I'll get him on his own."

Grumm jabbed him with a sharp elbow. "And *then* what?"

Lyle shrugged. "I'll think of something."

They moved into the crowd, buffeted by sweeping skirts as couples breathlessly whirled past. He noted the smells. Heady perfumes, lavender oil and rose water, all mingling strangely with the sweat and stale tobacco of the men and the smoke of the hearths. He extricated himself from the mad rush of the wide floor and eased through the bodies to the outer wall, where he turned to observe. It was surreal to see such flamboyance in these austere days, and he felt himself smile at the sight. The men at the apex of society, power-brokers like Goffe and Cromwell, would probably endorse this event for reason of political expediency, but the hearts of those that gave them their power - the radical Puritans at Whitehall - would give out on the spot if ever they knew what Cavalier pursuits went on in this far-flung part of their new Godly empire. He found the idea infectiously pleasant. But more than that, more than the idea of human nature pushing past the grey barriers of England's incumbent rulers, Lyle simply enjoyed the spectacle. The women threw back their heads and laughed, their forms elegant and their hair released from the coifs they would wear during the day. The men seemed freer somehow. No longer tethered to the stakes of probity driven into the nation by the Lord Protector and his formidable army. And there were jewels here too, glimmering, glinting garnets and rubies and sapphires. They winked at Lyle, dazzled him, and he beamed back. Because Alice would have loved an evening like this. She would have danced until dawn and burst with the sheer joy of it.

There were warnings too. Soldiers stood sentry at the four corners of the room, and he guessed there would be more patrolling the rest of the house. He steeled himself against the nonchalance such a lavish spectacle could engender. The waters in which he and Grumm paddled were infested with the most dangerous sharks imaginable.

"I'll take my leave," Grumm said after a short while.

Lyle looked across at him. "Aye." He reached for the green-swathed elbow as the old man went to move. "And Eustace? Take care."

"Gah!" Grumm hissed, shrugging him off. In a matter of seconds he had dissolved into the throng.

Samson Lyle remained in position for another hour, observing discreetly from behind his mask. Occasionally folk would nod to him, and he would return the gesture, but there was no challenge, and the grim sentries knew better than to accost Hippisley's guests without due cause. As the evening wore on, the energetic chaos of the early throws had given way to a more relaxed atmosphere. It was convivial, but more languid somehow, the men having drunk their fill of the best claret money could buy and the women resting their dance-worn feet beside the great tables that verily groaned with a feast fit for the old king. And yet of Sir Frederick Mason there was no sign. Lyle scrutinised every guest as they passed, searching for a man with the lawyer's portly frame, but, though a few came close, none matched the description well enough. He became increasingly frustrated, his plans apparently coming to nothing, and he moved away from the main crowd, slipping out through a small side door and into a quiet chamber that had evidently not been intended for use this night, judging by its lack of decoration. On its far side was a door that occasionally swung open to reveal a bustling servant, and he guessed the kitchens or cellars would be somewhere beyond. Another door was located in the wall to his right. It was made of thick oaken timbers, squat and studded, and he presumed it must lead outside. He went to lean against the cold wall, pleased to have found somewhere peaceful in which to gather his thoughts. He swore softly, infuriated by his own miscalculation. He had been certain that Sir Frederick would attend. He slapped his thigh hard in frustration.

"You seem a tad vexed, Sir Ardell."

Lyle spun on his heels, his heart suddenly frantic inside his chest. It was not the unexpected words that had startled him as much as the identity of the speaker. "Colonel Maddocks, I..."

Colonel Francis Maddocks was not in costume, but had nevertheless donned a fine suit for the occasion, one of all black that made him look like a raven caged amongst parrots. He wore a saffron-coloured scarf to denote his allegiance, pristine and bright as it crossed his torso, complete with his family crest at the shoulder. His hair, silver-flecked black like the head of a jackdaw, fell about his shoulders in matted strands, while his grey eyes were bright in the candlelight. His sword and pistol were the marks of a man on duty, charged, Lyle presumed, with the safety of the illustrious guests, but his face creased in a friendly smile as he stooped a touch to stare into Lyle's mask. "It is Sir Ardell Early in there, is it not?"

"Aye, Colonel, it is," Lyle said, forcing calm into his tone as best he could. "How did you...?"

"Oh, the footman pointed you out to me," Maddocks explained. The deep creases at the corners of his eyes became more pronounced. "I know he should not - and believe me when I say that he did not wish to unmask you, so to speak - but I fear I can be persuasive." His brow furrowed slightly. "But how, Sir Ardell, did you know who *I* was?"

"You wear no mask, sir," Lyle replied, confounded.

"But we have never met. Not in person, leastwise."

Sweat prickled at Lyle's neck. His cheeks felt suddenly clammy beneath the black and gold disguise. "Someone mentioned you were here to keep us all safe, Colonel. And you carry weapons at a masque. It is not so taxing to deduce your identity." He let his eyes flicker briefly across Maddocks' shoulder, where the lion roared in black thread. "Your strength brings you fame, sir."

Maddocks shrugged, playing the game of self-deprecation poorly. "Ah, well, it is good to know my services are appreciated." To hide his reddening cheeks, Maddocks turned slightly, showing Lyle to a bench at the far side of the small room. "I must say, I am surprised to find you here, Sir Ardell."

"I am not so dour as you might suppose," Lyle replied cautiously, thinking back to the letters they had found in Mason's possession.

Maddocks laughed as they sat down, white teeth glowing beneath the coarse bristles of his moustache, and raised his palms in supplication. "I meant nothing by it, sir, truly. But since your good lady wife..." he trailed off as awkwardness overtook him.

So Early's wife had died, Lyle thought. He dipped his head. "I have not found pleasure in many things, tis true," he said, for once needing no pretence. He swallowed the lump that had thickened at the back of his throat. "You were looking for me, Colonel?"

Maddocks nodded. "How fares business, sir?"

"Business?"

"It is my business to keep your business safe, Sir Ardell. Major-General Goffe has entrusted me with a mission of great importance. The safety of his supporters across the Downs is paramount to him. I would speak to those I must protect. This evening seemed a good time to introduce myself, though I confess it is difficult."

Lyle took the hint, but tapped a finger against the corner of his feathered mask. "My apologies, Colonel, but I like to maintain the charade at all times. What is the purpose of a masquerade if our faces are exposed? I would not insult our host by removing my guise." He noted Maddocks' disgruntled shrug, allowed himself a tiny smile, and continued. "But I will tell you that business is well, thank you. The trade thrives, I thrive. The hills hereabouts are ideal for pasture."

"And you've received no trouble?"

"Trouble?"

"Bandits, Sir Ardell," Maddocks replied earnestly. "Brigands. Footpads. Call them what you will."

"Vermin."

"Aye, vermin," Maddocks echoed, eyes gleaming as though they belonged to a fox. "To be exterminated."

"Please God."

"They've not harassed your work?"

Lyle paused for effect. "Oh, they have, to be sure. And it's affected my profits, I don't mind telling you." He gazed across the bench at the colonel, imagining what Grumm might say if he knew he were stringing the Mad Ox along in this manner. "One in particular."

Colonel Maddocks sat back, balling his fists. "The Ironside Highwayman."

Lyle nodded. "The same, sir. By God, I shall skin him alive when he is caught. String the knave up by his entrails."

"Not if I catch him first," Maddocks replied darkly.

"Do you think you will?"

The door swung inward suddenly and both men fell silent as a couple bowled in from the ballroom. They seemed to hang off one another like a pair of old soaks outside a tavern, before the woman, resplendent in billowing blue and yellow, took her young companion by the wrist and dragged him through another door and out into the labyrinthine passageways beyond.

"Be sure of it, sir," Maddocks said when the couple's laughter had faded. "It is purely a matter of time." He stood suddenly, issuing a tight bow. "Part of my task is to make myself known to those I am charged to protect, so I am pleased we are now acquainted. But now I must see to the men. One can never be too careful."

"You do not think Lyle will strike tonight, though, Colonel?" Lyle said, staring up at the soldier. "Not here."

"One can never be certain where that villain is concerned." Maddocks blew out his cheeks, wide nostrils flaring. "I am not fond of masquerades, Sir Ardell. In my view, the likes of that young pair," he indicated the far doorway through which the laughing couple had vanished, "are little more than preening popinjays and wanton harlots. The very epitome of that which we fought to eradicate." He offered a weary shrug. "But they are valued by my masters, and I must see that they are left in peace by this nation's less desirable elements. There are those who would steal the very shoes from their feet, let alone the jewels from their fingers and necks."

"It is a rich prize, I readily concede," Lyle replied, labouring his incredulity, "but there is as much cold steel here as warm gold. The Ironside Highwayman is a mongrel of the road. Such a dog would not bite so large a beast, Colonel."

Maddocks gave a rueful smile. "He is no common villain, Sir Ardell. He cares not for mere thievery. His targets are the new elite. The people of the rebellion. Those whose stars rose as the old regime's fell. Men such as Sir John. Men like us. If I were him, I would be sniffing out this place like a fox eyeing the largest hen-house in the land."

Lyle stood, extending a velvet-gloved hand for Maddocks to shake. "He'll not get past the likes of you, sir."

"You flatter me, Sir Ardell."

"You are not to be trifled with, Colonel, and he knows it. And there are others here. Hippisley himself marched with Cromwell, did he not? Hinton Ampner is this night filled with the men who made the rebellion. Won it." Grumm's disapproving face resolved in his mind's eye, and he inwardly smiled, adding, "Heroes all."

"Well it is kind in you to say," Maddocks said, making for the doorway that would take him back to the ballroom. To the surprise of both men, the door burst open before he reached it, through which blundered a tall man draped in voluminous robes the colour of salmon, his face obscured by a long, hooked beak that was studded with nuggets of pink and yellow glass.

"Colonel Maddocks!" the newcomer exclaimed in a loud voice that echoed about the small antechamber. "All is safe and well within our humble walls, I trust?"

Maddocks bowed, deeply this time, his face splitting in an obsequious grin. "Safe and well, Sir John, naturally." He waved a hand in Lyle's direction. "I was just saying as much to Sir Ardell."

Lyle took to his feet. "Sir John Hippisley?"

"Ha!" Hippisley barked, slapping his silken thigh in delight. "Do not indulge me so, Sir Ardell! You know me well enough, despite this infernal beak. Worn at my goodwife's suggestion, and rued every moment since."

Lyle felt his mouth contract around his tongue as the saliva dried to dust. He realised he was holding his breath and forced himself to release it lest it affect his speech. "It is an admirable disguise." He hurriedly dredged what he knew of the wool merchant from the back of his racing mind. "And we are not so well acquainted that I might instantly know your voice. Not yet, least wise. I fear I do not often have cause or need to leave my estates."

Hippisley nodded, the aquiline nose bobbing in a manner that reminded Lyle of a peculiar pink bird he had once seen in a Parisian circus. Though that animal had stood entirely on one of its thin legs, while the one before him seemed to hop excitedly from one to the other. "Quite so, quite so. But I trust our friendship - and our respective business interests - will flourish side by side, Sir Ardell. Tell me, do you enjoy yourself this night? My little soiree is to your liking?"

"I am enjoying myself greatly, Sir John," Lyle said, beginning to relax now that Hippisley seemed content with his identity. "The good colonel was just assuring me of his intent to rid our fine county of that base rogue, Samson Lyle."

Maddocks cleared his throat, bowing as he shuffled backwards. "I will take this moment to excuse myself, gentlemen, if it please you. Patrols to see to, you understand."

"Of course, Colonel Maddocks, of course," Hippisley said gravely, watching the soldier disappear into the great hall. He turned to Lyle when the door had clunked shut in his wake. "I fear he will lose his mind over that man."

"Lyle?"

"The same. Maddocks makes it his life's work to catch the so-called Ironside Highwayman, but I can tell you that bringing Major Lyle to ground will not be easy. He was a renowned fighter. And I hear he became a master swordsman during his time in exile."

Lyle was astounded at the man's familiarity, given the fact that they had never met. "You knew him?"

Hippisley shook his head. "No, but I am acquainted with many of his old friends." He was a big man, broad as well as tall, so that when he leaned forwards conspiratorially it seemed as though a the whole room dimmed. "The story goes that he fought with Henry Ireton - God preserve his eternal soul - in

Ireland. Smashing the papists as was his right and his duty before God."

"Amen to that," Lyle intoned.

"Quite so. But I heard that he lost his nerve. Saw one too many death."

Lyle felt instantly sick and he swallowed back the bile that always singed his throat when Ireland was mentioned. One too many death? Whole towns sacked, their people put to the sword. The smell of smoke and sulphur and roasting bodies came to him like a living nightmare. He breathed deeply, the pungent fumes of the masquerade suddenly as fresh as a meadow by comparison. "What happened?" he heard himself say.

"Argued with Ireton, stormed out of camp, made ship back to England," Hippisley said bluntly. "That was in the last weeks of '51. But Ireton's messengers reached the motherland first, and when he arrived he was arrested for desertion. He escaped, of course, and fled to France."

Christ, Lyle thought, but that was a frighteningly succinct description of the gauntlet he had been forced to run. The journey across the Irish Sea had been a vomit-washed hell, the ride from the northwest of England had been wet and cold, and then he had been run to ground and beaten bloody by the men who had been his subordinates until that moment. When finally he had extricated himself from the dank confines of his cell and found the terrified Bella, they had walked barefoot through marsh and over hill, crossed the snowy peaks that formed England's spine, and made it to the coast where they had stowed away in the hold of a cargo ship bound for the continent. They had been shadows of their former selves by then, half-starved, weather-ravaged and trawling the very depths of despair. He swallowed thickly and somehow conjured an amused grunt. "What exquisite irony. An arch rebel forced to cower in France with the last of the Cavaliers. Forced to swerve both sides of the divide."

"Quite so!" Hippisley bellowed happily. "Deserved nothing less."

"He deserved the noose."

The master of the grand estate seemed to appreciate that, for his pink plumage juddered as he laughed, deep brown eyes twinkling above the beak. "One day, please God."

"But why is the rogue back?" Lyle asked, unable to stifle his intrigue at the breadth to which his notoriety had evidently stretched. "Why risk returning? Especially now that Cromwell rules so completely through his major-generals. Is it true that he was done a grievous wrong?"

"Not a bit of it, sir! Soldiers were sent to his estate to the east of here, charged with confiscating the knave's assets. He was a traitor, after all. His goodwife was home." He dropped his voice to a clandestine murmur. "There was an altercation and, I'm sorry to say, she was killed. Trampled by the horses as she tried to keep them at bay. A terrible accident."

In that moment Samson Lyle could have wrung Hippisley's neck as though he were the very bird he portrayed. "Accident, sir?" he said, every ounce of strength poured into restraining his ire. "It sounds like murder."

No sooner had the words left Lyle's mouth than he knew he had overreached himself, for Hippisley's shoulders were suddenly squared like a defensive barricade, his eyes somehow darker. "Does it now?" he retorted coldly, the mirth all gone. "Then I commend you to keep your thoughts to yourself in company such as this. It was ruled an accident."

Lyle took a small rearward step. "My apologies, Sir John. It was wrong of me to suggest."

"Wrong of you to think, Sir Ardell. Suffice to say, however," Hippisley continued, apparently content with the retraction, "that Lyle believes you are right. He returned last year. Rides with two others, one a woman of all things! Both are masked, though he is not. They target members of the ruling class. Judges, soldiers, lawmakers, tax collectors, businessmen, merchants. The common sort love him, as the peasantry are wont to do. William Goffe, as you'd imagine, would rather like to see him dance the Tyburn jig."

"As would I," Lyle intoned gravely.

"Quite so, my good man, quite so." Hippisley clapped his hands together, the big palms slapping loudly despite their covering of kid skin, and he made for the door to the ballroom. "Now, I must not neglect my guests, though I know not who they are behind their guises, and you must come too."

Lyle tensed. "Very kind in you, Sir John, but I would not be such an encumbrance on my gracious host."

"Not a bit of it, sir! You said yourself that you do not often leave your estates. This is the opportunity to meet folk that might be of interest to you. Those of a like mind and mutual interests. This is why I have been permitted to hold such an event, after all."

Lyle could only nod. How could he refuse? And now he would be escorted about the crowd, directed from one foe to the next, each with their own tale of how the Ironside Highwayman had menaced them, how he should be gibbeted on the highest point of Butser Hill as a warning to others. Each man and woman would look into his eyes, and one, he knew, would eventually recognise him. With creeping trepidation he followed the big man into the main hall. People still mingled, chattered, ate, drank, danced and brayed to the high ceiling. A few heads turned to appraise them, eyes glinting with intrigue. He noticed one woman, resplendent in green and silver, took particular interest, her almost black eyes bright within a mask that had been styled to resemble the face of a cat. She held his gaze for a second, the eyes at once unreadable and intense, and it took all his willpower to tear himself away.

"Might I ask, Sir John," he said as he moved in the wake of Hippisley's imposing frame, "if Sir Frederick Mason is here? I have been meaning to speak with him for some time upon a certain matter."

Hippisley paused, turned, drew breath to speak.

"Sir John!" a man exclaimed with startling breathlessness, bursting from the crowd. He was a servant, wearing the ubiquitous kingfisher livery of the house, and his face, uncovered, was flushed and glistening with sweat.

Hippisley swung the long beak on him. "What is it? Well, spit it out, man!"

The servant stared at the floor. "We are running low on the good claret, sir."

For a moment it looked as though Hippisley might explode in rage, but his broad chest suddenly deflated as he sighed in exasperation. "Must I deal with everything myself?" He turned to Lyle. "Forgive me, Sir Ardell. I will return forthwith."

Lyle nodded rapidly, thanking God for His timely intervention. He might have been denied Hippisley's answer, but at least he would avoid the inquisitive gazes. He watched Hippisley stalk away, now alone in a sea of people, the thrum of the dance like waves lapping all around.

Lyle took the opportunity to flee, making for the antechamber from whence they had come. He needed to clear his head, walking straight to the ugly exterior door that he had guessed would open out into the gardens. It was not locked, the bolt sliding back with a deep rattle, and he stepped quickly into the night air.

The area immediately surrounding the house had been landscaped and planted with various kinds of shrubs and bushes. There were several rows of what he guessed to be fruit trees running through the lawns, their branches naked under the moonlight, and a maze of ivy and honeysuckle sprawled over a complex of trellised fences. Beyond that was the high, moss-clothed wall, keeping the garden separate from the rest of the large estate, and Lyle instinctively walked towards it, wanting to be as far from the heady masquerade as possible.

The sounds of the ball faded as he strode into the night. The air was crisp and fresh, chilling his nostrils and throat, making him feel as if he could finally breathe freely. He paced steadily through a miniature orchard of wizened apple trees, the ground slick beneath his boots, until he came to the ivy-woven trellis, moving to the far side so that he could not be observed from the house. There he paused, tilted back his head at the night sky, wondered how best to abort this evening's reckless task now that it had been shown to be borne purely of hubris. The stars winked, mocking him. He removed his mask, worked his jaw to free it of the stifling feeling the disguise had engendered, and blew a warm gust of air through his nostrils. He knew he needed to find Grumm before he could do anything, so, with another steadying breath, he turned.

"I'm surprised you found the time to attend this evening, sir, given your busy schedule," Felicity Mumford said. "Robbing honest folk, and such." She sniffed daintily. "Still, at least you appear to have bathed for this engagement."

"Madam, I..." Lyle spluttered, replacing the mask despite the terrible knowledge that it was all too late.

She grinned. "Fear not, Major Lyle. I had rather hoped I would meet you again. Though I confess I am surprised it is so soon".

"Thank you," Lyle said, lowering the pointless disguise. He stared at her. In her hand was her own mask. It was green and silver, like her dress, the eye holes turned up at the corners in a distinctly feline manner. "You saw me in the hall."

"I did. I knew it was you. Could tell by your eyes." She ran her free hand through hair that had been freed of the coif she had worn when first they met. The gesture mesmerised him. "Who are you supposed to be? I cannot imagine you were invited in person, sir, for where would they send the invitation?"

He laughed at that. "Sir Ardell Early."

She raised a single brow in amusement. "Not a great likeness, though perhaps similar in height. Besides, Sir Ardell is a bore, and not many here would know him."

"That was my hope." He stepped forward a fraction. "Why did you not raise the alarm before? Why not now?"

"My uncle is a vile man, Major. He despises me, I despise him. We must suffer one another, since he is my only living kinsman, but that does not compel me to like him." The corners of her mouth twitched almost imperceptibly. "And I like you. Lord knows why, but I do. I suppose you were kind to me, even as you threatened me with that ghastly pistol you carry." She shuddered, casting her gaze to the grass between them. "But will you tell me the truth?"

"Truth?"

Now she searched his face again, her dark visage illuminated by the warm glow from the house at her back. "They say you ride against the government for the memory of your late wife. Is that really why you turned outlaw?"

He nodded. "Aye. She was murdered in vengeance for my betrayal. Her and my unborn child."

Felicity's fingers went instinctively to her lips. "Oh, Lord. I am sorry, Major. Truly."

He looked away, unable to meet her eye. "No matter." He found himself walking amongst the dense barricades of ivy and honeysuckle. She was with him. "The passage of time serves to numb the pain, if not the fury," he said after a short while. "I have rebuilt my life. Made my money. I am, I suppose, content. But I'll wage my private war until there is no more breath in my lungs."

"And why did you betray them?" she asked tentatively.

"I joined the Parliamentarian struggle when I was a child, Miss Mumford. Served under Cromwell at the age of sixteen at Naseby. A boy before the drums began to beat: a man after they fell silent. Campaigned against all the bitter uprisings of the second war and rode with our newly made force in the third. I saw many terrible things. Too many horrors to number. And yet none of that mattered when we went to Ireland. Women and children. The infirm, the weak. They were as rodents to us, and we exterminated them as we would a nation of rats. It was no longer war. I decided to ride away. A decision that I have paid for every moment since."

They reached the end of one of the ivy corridors where it met with the sheer face of the high wall. The moonlight was shut out of this corner and it was utterly dark. "Why are you here, Major?" Felicity asked. "It is unimaginably dangerous for you."

He hesitated, wondering whether a confession would be sheer folly. But she had known it was him, and done nothing about it. "I would free a prisoner held by Goffe's men," he said. "Your uncle's strongbox..."

She smirked. "The one you ruined?"

"Aye. It contained a letter mentioning this man. One James Wren. He will be transferred from Newbury to Portsmouth."

"When?"

The sounds of giggling carried to them on the breeze and they both looked round. Nothing came from the darkness. Another couple escaping the crowds.

"That, Miss Mumford, is my difficulty," Lyle said. "It did not indicate when."

"Watch the road," she suggested bluntly.

He shook his head. "Wren was a prominent Cavalier. The guard will be heavy."

She arched an eyebrow. "Too heavy for the great highwayman? Could you not leap out in surprise?"

"Imagine a cat leaping out upon a flock of sparrows, only to discover that they're hawks."

She laughed at that. "So you require time to plan."

He dipped his head. "I need to know when he will be moved. And I had hoped Sir Frederick would attend this evening."

Her jaw dropped. "And you were simply going to ask him?"

"Yes."

She laughed again in the darkness. "You are a strange creature, Major Lyle, that is for certain." Before he realised she had moved, her hand was on his cheek. It was warm and he angled his face, pressing against it. She was so close, though he could only discern her outline in this sepulchral recess of the garden. But he could smell her, and feel her breath.

He inched away. Just a fraction, but enough to break the trance. She was perfect to his eyes, and that knowledge hurt him. Brought guilt crashing through his chest to invade his heart. He thought of Alice.

Then she moved, closing the divide just as he had opened it, climbing to the tips of her toes, and her lips were on his, parting a fraction so that he could feel the lambent tip of her tongue. And then she was gone, stepping away from him as his rushing pulse hammered in his ears.

"He is here," she said. "He does not condone such events, of course, but even dour men like Uncle Frederick concede such frivolity must be allowed on occasion. Hippisley is to be rewarded, for he served the revolution well, and his allegiance must continue to be nurtured. His charisma holds a deal of sway here in the Downs, so says my uncle."

"Where is he?" Lyle managed to say, his mind still clouded by her actions. "Where is Sir Frederick?"

She gave a sharp, bitter chuckle. "Uncle will not dance, or be seen to give it his blessing. But he is here. Put that mask back on, and follow me."

The drawing room was on the far side of the house, looking out onto the front courtyard via a pair of large, rectangular windows that were crammed full of diamond-shaped panes of glass. Samson Lyle waited in the corridor outside, watched with disinterest by a bored looking footman, but he caught a glimpse of the room's interior as Felicity Mumford half-opened the door and bustled in. Lyle watched as she walked, skirts hissing like a chorus of serpents behind, and, just as she disappeared inside, he spotted two familiar faces. One was that of Sir Frederick Mason. He wore no hat, but the rest of his attire had not changed since the robbery. Felicity had said that he disapproved of such events, but Lyle could see that such a claim was a stark understatement, for the sober black coat and plain white shirt were conspicuous in their absence of colour. Mason sat at a large table scattered with papers and scrolls. He studied one intently, not looking up as his niece entered, a quill poised in his right hand. The other man was standing at his shoulder. He wore the attire of a soldier, even donning a breastplate for the occasion, though it was no masquerade costume. Kit Walmsley, Mason's bodyguard, was grim-faced and alert. He looked up immediately upon seeing the door open, one hand reaching for the hilt of his sword, and frowned when he saw that it was her. For a heartbeat his little eyes flickered past her shoulder to stare at the doorway. They met Lyle's gaze, held firm. Walmsley cocked his head to the side like a confused hound as he stared at Lyle, and then the door slammed shut.

Lyle did not know whether to linger or make good his escape. If Walmsley had somehow recognised him, then trouble would be quick on his heels. But he could not afford to flee. He needed to know when the authorities planned to move James Wren, and the chief lawyer to the Major-General of Berkshire, Sussex and Hampshire was the only man who had that information. He had come too far to let the night's efforts go to waste.

A bell tinkled gently from somewhere further down the passageway, and the glum footman trudged away, leaving Lyle alone. He edged closer to the door. The murmur of voices carried to him, muffled and too quiet to discern, but no shouts came forth, no hue and cry was being raised. He held his breath, stepped back. The door handle clicked, light streamed out to illuminate the dull corridor, and there stood Felicity Mumford. She stared hard at him, gave the tiniest shake of her head, and called a friendly farewell over her shoulder. Lyle needed no further encouragement and made to leave. He strode quickly over the polished tiles, footsteps echoing in the confined space. He could sense Felicity walking behind, deliberately slower, and knew she was making out that she was not associated with him. Then he heard a man's voice, deep and authoritative. He recognised it immediately. It was Walmsley.

Lyle cursed viciously and picked up the pace, searching for somewhere in which he might hide. There was some kind of altercation behind, raised voices, a man and a woman, and he knew Walmsley had accosted Felicity. His instinct was to double back, knock the bodyguard onto his rump for speaking to her thus, but knew he could not. He did not even glance round at them, instead reaching the end of the corridor, pushing through a small doorway, and finding himself in a room full of liveried servants. They called to one another angrily, anxiety the common vein through each voice. The room contained a large table at its centre, men and women round the outside, each in position by various work-surfaces. One woman in heavily stained apron stood like a sentinel before an imposing hearth, overseeing a pair of young lads tending the fire. Above the flames, spitting and hissing as teardrops of fat plummeted into the white-hot embers, a pig turned on a spit, its skin darkening from the heat. Lyle realised he was in the kitchens, the very heart of the house, and he recalled that the little antechamber where he had encountered Maddocks and Hippisley was on the far side. He ran now, dispensing with any show of decorum, baffled members of the house staff left slack-jawed in his path.

He passed through to the chamber beyond, pleased to discover it empty and silent. He considered going for the little studded door that would take him into fresh air, but he knew he had to find Grumm. With a pounding heart and twisting guts, Lyle entered the main hall.

The ball went on unhindered, ignorant to his private fear. Lyle plunged into the throng, forced to use more force than he had wanted as he cleared a path, much to the consternation of the revellers. Hands grasped at him, wanting to know why he shoved so rudely, and then he heard the word he dreaded. His name. His real name.

The hall fell silent as one. The musicians up in the gallery ceased as though some mystical conflagration had devoured their instruments in the blink of an eye. He kept going, kept pushing his way through the bodies.

"Lyle!" Kit Walmsley's stentorian voice ripped through the pungent air again. "Samson Lyle! You will halt, damn your eyes!"

And then he knew it was over, for more and more masked faces were looking at him. Those strangely blank expressions examining him as though utterly dispassionate, yet behind the disguises he knew they would be far from disinterested. A few brave souls placed themselves in his path, slowing his flight, then others grasped his shoulders and arms, clawing, dragging. He felt as if he waded through molasses. A huge paw landed hard on his shoulder, wrenched him round, its match grasping at his face until the mask slid free. Silence again. Samson Lyle had been captured, the wolf run to ground. Kit Walmsley's wide, ruddy face grinned back at him as the former Roundhead tossed Lyle's mask away in disgust as though it were a lump of rancid meat. His nose was still swollen, the nostrils scarlet tinged, and his eyes were slung with heavy blue bags.

Lyle's brain raced. The colours and scents and sounds of the evening swirling like storm-harried leaves. Christ, he thought, but it was all over. They had failed. A year of evading - taunting - the authorities had come only to this. A pathetic flash in the pan, his audacious shot at greatness fizzling to nothing, the powder dampened by arrogance.

"I see your snout has yet to recover," Lyle said defiantly.

Walmsley's hand fell to his sword, thick fingers snaking round the grip. The stunned revellers gasped, letting their quarry go so that they might move clear.

Samson Lyle punched the stout old soldier in the face. It was not as hard as it might have been, for he had only time and space for a straight, sharp blow, but Walmsley's recent wounds were fresh and vulnerable, and his nose caved in like a sodden honeycomb. He wailed, the anguished bellow reverberating around the high ceiling as he staggered backwards. He did not fall, but blood spouted freely down his chin and between the fingers that pressed over the damage in a futile attempt to stem the flow and numb the pain. Lyle saw his chance, rushed into Walmsley, shoving him back further with one hand and gripping his sword hilt with the other. The blade rasped free as its owner fell away, and Lyle spun on his heels. The crowd screamed, sheered away from the glittering steel like a flock of sheep in the face of a rabid dog, and a path soon opened up.

"That's two blades you've given me now, Kit!" Lyle called over his shoulder. "You really are a tremendous benefactor!"

Walmsley brayed into his cupped hands. Lyle laughed. The crowd screamed. More shouts erupted as Lyle moved, though this time he recognised them as the soldiers who had been set to guard the room. There would be at least four, he knew, perhaps half a dozen, and each would have a musket. But they would not dare discharge the lethal weapons amongst the packed gathering, and he gauged there might be a few moments to carve a path through to the entrance hall that he remembered from when first he and Grumm had entered.

"Lyle!" another challenge snarled above the panicked din.

Lyle turned to see a familiar face. "Ah, the Mad Ox. Have you enjoyed your evening?" He backed away, the gaudily clad revellers parting like the Red Sea to let him through. "What was it you said? Sir John's guests are little more than preening popinjays and wanton harlots, was it not?"

Colonel Maddocks advanced passed the reeling Walmsley, his face dark with barely restrained fury. He had been duped and he knew it. He did not draw his pistol, for the crowd was too deep and fluid to guarantee their safety if a shot were discharged, but his brutish broadsword was in his hand in the blink of an eye. "You're trapped, Lyle," he said, voice a seething rasp. "Fodder for my hounds."

"We shall see, Ox," Lyle replied as calmly as he possibly could. He had reached the doorway now, and backed into the entrance hall where the choir had earlier sung so sweetly. They were still there, bunched like penned lambs, but now their mouths were shut, eyes wide, faces pale.

The entrance hall was different than Lyle remembered, if only by way of atmosphere. When he and Grumm - Ardell Early and Winfred Piersall - had crossed its polished tiles, the place had been a picture of serenity. The choir chirping like baby birds, the candlelight flickering, the mirrors and tapestries bringing brightness and warmth to the grand stone structure. But now the room was one of bleak horror. The mirrors reflected only stunned faces and sharpened blades. Men, women and children pressed back in a terrified crush against the walls, desperate to be away from those who would brandish cold steel on so merry an occasion.

Lyle ignored the cries and gasps. He was an animal cornered, senses suddenly keen. His enemy stalked into the chamber too. Behind him the revellers were pressing into the doorway from the ballroom, desperate to witness the confrontation unfold, as long as they stayed safely out of range. Maddocks was sneering, swishing his heavy blade out in front, beckoning Lyle onto its tip. He had plenty of courage, Lyle knew well, but no doubt revenge gave the colonel an extra impetus this night. After all, their last meeting had ended in abject humiliation for Maddocks, despite the fact that Lyle had hardly behaved with any chivalry.

Maddocks lunged. He did not have the finesse of Walmsley, but nor did he require it. His tutelage had been gained on the field of battle, and he knew how to fight without the airs and graces of the fencing masters. His arm was extremely strong, the blade a single-edged cavalry sword that was intended for cleaving rather than duelling, and though Lyle parried easily enough, he was forced to give ground simply to avoid being overwhelmed by the sheer power of his old comrade. Lyle jabbed with the blade he had taken from Walmsley, striking out at Maddocks' sword arm, but the colonel was alive to the threat and patted it away.

"I will fight you!" Samson Lyle bellowed, but he did not mean Maddocks. "All of you! Every soul here!" The crowd murmured uneasily.

"You will not fight after this day!" Maddocks spat back. "You have nowhere to go, Lyle! Nowhere to hide!" He glanced about at the assembled faces. "This is Major Samson Lyle. Look upon him. See the fear in his eyes. This is the Ironside Highwayman. Maker of the republic, breaker of oaths. Deserter! Traitor! Outlaw! He has no home but the road. No cause but the memory of a dead wife!"

This time Lyle attacked, thrusting the long rapier at Maddocks' face. The colonel swept away the threat with contemptuous ease, whipping the point of his own sword at Lyle's lower ribs. Lyle parried, flicked his thinner, lighter weapon up in a darting riposte. He felt the point scrape at something, jumped back to assess, and saw that a thin crimson line had been drawn vertically down the centre of Maddocks' wide chin. Maddocks looked stunned. He lifted a hand to the graze, winced as he stared down at bloody fingertips, and a low, guttural growl seeped from his throat.

The colonel lurched forward, fat droplets of blood flinging from his chin to spatter the floor. He slashed the air between them in a series of lightning arcs that threatened to smash through Lyle's defences and eviscerate his chest. Lyle barely had time to react, recoiling and parrying, the shuffle of skirts and feet ever-present as the ring of onlookers surged out of the way. He blocked a low strike, then one from on high, twisted out of range of the next, and felt his back collide with the cold wall. Women screamed on either side as Maddocks advanced, bringing across his blade in a savage horizontal swipe designed to cleave Lyle in half. The highwayman managed to get his own steel in its path, but Walmsley's rapier was no match for the solid weight of the broadsword, and Lyle felt his stomach turn as the thinner blade snapped in two. It was enough to send Maddocks' blow skittering off to the left, beyond Lyle's elbow, and a spray of hot wax showered the side of his face as a fat candle was cut in two. He dropped the useless hilt, hooked an arm around Maddocks' elbow so that the colonel's sword was locked against the wall.

They were inches apart now. "You'll be strung up on the Downs, Lyle," Maddocks rasped as he struggled to wrench his sword arm free, his fetid breath invading Lyle's nostrils. "It is over."

Lyle kicked the soldier hard in the crotch, twirling away as Maddocks cried out. He stared about the open space, searching for a weapon, anything he could use. Out the corner of his eye he caught sight of a man dressed all in green. From behind the green mask, eyes of pale blue glistened. Lyle thanked God, because it was time to leave. "Bella!" he shouted.

Maddocks had straightened. His face was deep red, breathing laboured, his eyes like bright orbs. He still clutched his heavy blade, and he levelled it, the point in line with Lyle's throat.

And someone stepped out from the choir.

Maddocks and Lyle both turned to look at the masked child who had walked into the blood-streaked ring.

"Enough play, Samson," the girl's voice announced. It was a surreal and incongruous sight. A girl clothed all in white, her appearance and tone angelic, yet when she drew her hands from behind her back, they bore objects synonymous with death. She raised both pistols, ugly and black in her grasp. One was pointed at Maddocks, the other swept perpetually back and forth, threatening every soul in the room. "'Bout time we went home, I reckon."

Lyle went to her, feeling Maddocks' gaze like a dagger in his spine. He took one of the pistols, checked that it was cocked, and stretched out his arm. "It has been a wonderful evening," he announced, "and I have thoroughly enjoyed myself. But now it is sadly time to take our leave." A murmur of impotent discontent rustled through the room, like a stinging breeze heralding a storm. He noticed the crowd at the doorway, faces still clamouring for a view of the incident, bodies pushing through to the small chamber from the great hall beyond. Foremost in that pack was the stocky form of Kit Walmsley, his

nose a ragged mess. Lyle winked at him, causing the older man
to step into the temporary circle as he took the bait like a crazed
animal, but a shake of Lyle's pistol halted him just as quickly.

Silence followed. Tension. People were still moving at the
entrance to the hall, and Lyle knew that the armed guards must
surely be moving through the throng. He glanced over his
shoulder. "Ready?"

Eustace Grumm, still masked in green, was standing beneath
the lintel of the rear door. "As I'll ever be, you mad fool."

Lyle laughed. He and Bella edged backwards, pistols still
poised. The circle of onlookers seemed to contract as they
moved, terror at witnessing the fight turning rapidly to rage. A
pair of soldiers broke through the crowd, as Lyle had predicted.
They each brandished muskets, the wheel-locks wound and
ready to fire. Still, though, the risk seemed to deter them. The
range was nothing, a matter of yards, but a misfire would kill
innocents and they were too timid to take the chance.

"Shoot!" a voice barked suddenly, making the soldiers - and
consequently everyone else in the room - flinch violently. "I
said shoot the villains, you spineless women!"

Sir Frederick Mason's rotund form waddled into view. He was
ruddy faced and furious, spluttering indignantly as he spoke, the
veins in his nose raised and livid like a blood-spun cobweb.

At his shoulder another, taller man appeared. He had
discarded the salmon-hued beak to reveal a handsome face that
was lantern-jawed, with a wide mouth and deep-set eyes.
"Hold!" he ordered.

"Why thank you, Sir John," Lyle addressed Hippisley.

The master of the house ignored him, turning instead to
Mason. "I'll not have muskets fired in my damned house, Sir
Frederick. No, sir, I will not. The safety of my guests is
paramount."

"Now, Sir John," Lyle said, "I would ask these men to leave."
He nodded at the guards. "Both of you. Back into the hall. Have
a dance, perhaps."

The soldiers looked bewildered, uncertain, but Hippisley
raised a staying palm. "You will remain." He swung his gaze
upon Lyle. "You are trapped, Major Lyle. You cannot possibly

hope to make it out of Hinton alive. There are guards everywhere, you fool. Not only these, but at the door. Out in the grounds. You think me a dullard?"

"No, Sir John, not a bit of it. Indeed, that very fact is what has made this night so utterly thrilling."

"Then admit when the game is up. Hand yourself in. No one else need be harmed."

Grumm and Bella were with him, which meant he had no further need to linger, and Lyle took a step rearward, ready to make for the door. The musketeers might shoot when they were out in the open, but he wagered they would not discharge their weapons inside the house. He drew breath to call to his companions. It was worth the gamble. But at the corner of his eye he caught movement. A woman with long, dark hair, dressed in green and silver. She had discarded the mask, and he saw the corners of her mouth twitch upwards as, he had come to learn, they often did when she regarded Samson Lyle. He knew he should just flee while he had the chance, but something in her eyes made him act. He lunged for her. She resisted, screamed. He kissed her hard on the lips, their teeth clinking. She struggled, screamed again.

Sir Frederick Mason stepped forward, his face taut. "Touch her again, you evil filth, and I shall have the skin flayed from your bones!"

"Unhand me, sir!" Felicity Mumford shrieked. The crowd echoed her anguish.

"I'm afraid you're a tad late for that, Sir Freddy," Lyle grinned, and he kissed her again, more softly this time, before spinning her about, pinning her against him with one arm, and lifting the gun to her throat with the other. She twisted as if to resist, but it was not a concerted effort. "Now, if you'd be so gracious, please remove those ghastly muzzles from such a well-appointed room."

"Sir John," Mason bleated at the renewed threat, his bluster punctured.

"You'll die a criminal's death!" Sir John Hippisley bellowed, but he waved the musketeers away. They melted back into the crowd.

Lyle put his lips to his captive's ear. "Well? What is it?"

"A traitor's death!" Colonel Maddocks, sword still in hand, snarled over the thrum of the guests who were in equal parts appalled and enthralled.

Lyle dragged Felicity away from her uncle, and from Hippisley and Walmsley and Maddocks. Her heels scraped as she lost her footing on the tiles, but he took her weight easily. The crowd shifted to let them through, Grumm holding the doorway, Bella swinging her pistol in warning against any who might think themselves courageous.

Felicity tilted back her head as they moved. Her breath was warm as she whispered. "Three days, Major. At dawn."

"I would kiss you again," Lyle hissed.

"Please do not. I fear it would rather compromise my position."

"Thank you. I will come for you, Miss Mumford. I swear it."

"Do not bother, sir. The life of a brigand is hardly something to which I aspire."

"In time, they will know you've told me," Lyle said as they reached the doorway. "What will happen to…?"

"Me?" she cut in. "I can deal with Uncle Frederick, do not worry."

Lyle stared at their pursuers. "Have the dowdy wench, Sir Freddy!" He released her, slapping her rump hard as she bolted back into the room. She yelped in exaggerated outrage. He laughed. "I grow tired of her already!"

Lyle, Bella and Grumm raced along the passageway through which they had earlier been conveyed, the small flames of candles guttering madly as they rushed past. There were a couple of footmen in their way, shimmering in their red and blue suits, but they did nothing in the face of the armed fugitives, instead pressing themselves tight against the timber clad walls to allow the trio through. Bella was laughing, high-pitched and giddy with excitement. Grumm was cursing their collective stupidity, though Lyle wagered he would be grinning behind his mask. They knew a pursuit would already be underway, Maddocks and his men charging out of the mirrored chamber like a herd of stampeding heifers, but they were already at the large porch, the door open, stars pricking the black sky beyond.

"Took your time," Lyle called as they burst out into the fresh night.

Grumm ripped off his mask, tossing it into one of the shrubs that lined the path along which they ran. "There were eight, Major. Eight o' the buggers to gather. Not easy, I can tell you."

"But you succeeded?"

"I'd have told you by now if I hadn't, you beef-witted lump."

Lyle eased his pistol's pan cover closed, thrust it into his belt, and clapped Grumm between the shoulders. "You're a grand fellow, Eustace!"

Shouts rang out behind. Lyle glanced back to see a score of men pour out from the manor house. "How far?"

"See for yourself," Grumm rasped.

Sure enough, as they passed a stand of ancient elms, the three came to a small clearing. The main high road lay just beyond, but before that, tethered loosely beneath the branches of a soaring ash, were Star, Tyrannous and Newt. The horses looked up from their grazing, whickering gently as they recognised their respective keepers.

Star snorted irritably when Lyle untied the reins and leapt into the saddle. The big grey evidently sensed the urgency in his master's actions, and Lyle stroked the beast's thick neck, praying there would be no panic this time.

Shots split the night. The trio flinched, ducked down, though the musketeers would be too far away for the range to be effective. "Calm, boy, calm," Lyle murmured softly into Star's sharp ear. He straightened, looked across at Grumm. "What did you do with them?"

Grumm grinned, his face a rictus of wolfish pride and sharp, crooked teeth, as he pointed away to his left. "There. Took an age to get 'em comfy enough to share my wine."

Eustace Grumm had been chief of a complex ring of smugglers in his native Cornwall. He had used intimidation, poison, steel and guile to outwit his rivals and the Customs men alike. But after a rival had tipped them off as to his whereabouts one balmy night a year after the First Civil War had reached its bloody conclusion, he had barely escaped England with his life. He spent the following years living as a vagrant on the Continent, frightened and destitute. Surviving off scraps discarded by the kitchens of the great town houses of Calais, stealing when he could, and spending much of his time existing in the shadows, evading the thief-takers who lurked in his wake. And then, on the road south to Paris, the lawmen had caught up with him. They found him in a busy coaching inn, beat him and dragged him outside, the noose already slung over the bough of a stooped tree.

But a man named Samson Lyle had been in that same tavern. He had watched quietly from the within the fug of tobacco smoke as questions had become quarrel, and quarrel had become arrest. And as the five thief-takers had laughed their way out to the place of summary execution, that silent, watchful man had appeared in the night air, double-barrelled pistol in one hand, blade in the other, and he had prized Eustace Grumm from their clutches. The old man had latched onto him like a limpet after that. Riding with him through northern France, providing the former cavalry officer and his young ward with companionship and laughter, while his expertise in the ways of the outlaw had often proved invaluable. Indeed, thought Lyle as he squinted into the inky darkness to discern the row of eight prone bodies that had been left at the foot of one of Sir John Hippisley's trees, the irascible old criminal possessed knowledge that extended far beyond contraband. He looked up from the row of saffron-scarfed soldiers as more guns spat their fury from the direction of the house. "Just wine?"

Grumm's face twisted in its ugly tick. "And a sprinkle o' certain mushrooms."

"You are a marvel, Mister Grumm."

"Thank you, Major Lyle," Grumm replied as they kicked hard at the mounts.

"They ain't dead, are they?" Bella asked.

"No, lass," Grumm replied, loudly now above the crash of hooves and crackle of musketry. "But they'll have sore skulls in the mornin', I promise you that!"

PART THREE: THE BRIDGE

Near Liphook, Hampshire, December 1655

The driver's name was Tomkin Dome. He was not yet fifty, but he knew his days were numbered. He could feel it, feel the burn in his chest with every breath, the innate brittleness in his bones. He could taste the acrid mucus he hawked clear of his throat each morning, certain it had become tainted. And his skin. God, but it itched. Gnawed at him during the night like an army of rats, pus-filled boils forming on his forcarms and face, livid and moist. The jangling of the cart did not help matters. Every judder and jerk made a patch of corrupt skin sear with pain, or burst, soaking his clothes with stinking moisture. Christ, but he hated his life.

He took a flask of wine from a small bag beside him on the seat and pulled out the stopper with his teeth. When the liquid burned his throat, he closed his eyes, finding happiness only in its richness. He had tasted better, of course. Back before the rebellion, in the good times, when his trade in Lymington and Hayling sea salt had thrived and he could afford the very best that life had to offer. But then the wars had come, and Tomkin Dome had pinned his colours to the wrong mast. Now he had nothing but a waggon to his name, bitterness in his heart, and relentless, grinding agony.

Dome thrust the flask home and squinted into the murky dawn. It was close upon eight o'clock. A thin mist crept up off the River Wey to extend white fingers between ancient boughs and over the wide road. Grey clouds, pregnant and vast, loomed ominously overhead. The air smelled of rain. There was no breeze so the trees were still, darkening the land either side of the highway, their branches, mostly stripped of leaves, straining for the sky like so many talons. A boil smarted on his rump and Dome shifted his skinny frame irritably, spewing a savage oath as he did so. One of the riders out in front turned back to admonish him in clipped tones. Dome's seething retort was lost, he hoped, amongst the sound of hooves, and he turned his attention back to the job at hand.

The cart was small in size. Not the massive, gilt coaches of the rich and powerful, but an unprepossessing vehicle, plain and functional. It was drawn by a pair of strong horses, a chestnut and a grey, the traces jangling behind as wheels creaked and bounced noisily. The cart had been agrarian in nature at one time, flat and open for grain or hay, but now it was a perfect box, for a metal frame had been placed upon its rear platform, like a giant aviary, with a small door against which a heavy lock clanged. Within the cage, slumped against the bars and swaying with the motion of the vehicle, was a figure. His hair was long, unkempt, framing a face that was bowed from view, as though dipped in prayer. Occasionally the horsemen would call to him. There were ten of them; five out front, five at the rear, and they would make sport of taunting the captive, sneering when he ignored them, laughing when the gaunt, stubble-shaded face deigned to look up.

"Steady!" Tomkin Dome snarled as the horses rounded a kink in the road and approached a small stone bridge. "I said steady, you flea-bit buggers!" He received a host of withering glances from the pious troopers for his trouble.

The cart slowed to walking speed. The vanguard of horsemen - heavily armed harquebusiers - trotted forth first, clattering onto the stone slabs that spanned the Wey. Below them the water meandered lazily. The river was deep here, clear as crystal so that the grey silhouettes of fish could be seen darting in the shadows cast by the grassy banks and amongst the gauntlet of smooth rocks and straggly weeds.

Dome scratched at an ulcer beneath his armpit as he waited for the troopers to wave him on. He was a frail man, given to feeling the cold more than most, but his brow prickled with sweat nevertheless. He drew a cloth from his sleeve, mopping his face. "Well?"

The troopers had gathered at the centre of the bridge. One of them was speaking, but not to the driver. Dome looked past him to see a lone man on the far bank. He looked, to Dome's poor eyes at least, like a scarecrow. A thin, gaunt, crook-backed bag of bones, white-bearded and deeply wrinkled, a filthy bandage wrapped round his skull to cover what was left of an eye lost long ago. The scarecrow seemed to whisper to himself, admonish himself. He would suddenly bellow a scrap of scripture, arguing with some unseen spectre. Occasionally he would twitch, his neck convulsing, one cheek jerking hard as though tugged by an invisible rope.

Tomkin Dome stood. "Long way to go yet, Lieutenant Chickering!"

The most advanced rider twisted in his saddle, his face taut behind the trio if vertical bars that hung from the hinged visor of his helmet. "I am aware of that, Master Dome," he replied testily. "I shall move this doltish beggar off the bridge and we'll be on our way."

The scarecrow shuffled forward a couple of paces. "Doltish, sirrah? No, sirrah! Not I! Not ever!"

Lieutenant Chickering drew his sword, leaned to the side so that his saddle creaked. "No further, old man, I'm warning you. Move off the bridge or I'll move you myself."

Tomkin Dome sniffed hard, feeling mucus bubble into his throat. He hawked it up and spat onto the grass at the road's verge. "Enough o' this, Lieutenant. Run the bastard through, or trample him or boot him into the river. I care not, sir, but we must be off." He lashed his horses with the reins and they lurched forth, clattering up onto the bridge. Behind him he could hear the five troopers follow. But Chickering could not move for the scarecrow remained steadfast, gibbering at the dark clouds and dancing a mad little jig, and the young lieutenant seemed unwilling to follow Dome's ruthless advice.

Tomkin Dome laughed heartily, despite his various pains, because he knew Chickering was a kind man at heart, too pious for his own good, and that meant he was stuck for at least the time it would take to dismount and forcibly remove the old vagrant from their path. He did so just as Dome steered his cart up to the apex of the bridge, the rear-guard trotting blithely in his wake, so that the vehicle and all ten of its escort were crammed on the smooth stones above the gargling water.

A pistol appeared in each of the scarecrow's hands.

Chickering seemed to be half dozing, for he did not react for several moments. Eventually he stepped back a pace, jaw lolling, as he absorbed the implication. "Wh... what the devil?"

The scarecrow straightened, losing the curvature in his hunched spine as though a miracle had been performed. He brandished a crooked grin. "Don't do anythin' silly now, me old cuffin. Ground your arms, get your men off their nags, and point to those angry-looking clouds, if you please."

Chickering was a young man, and rolled his shoulders to affect a bluff courage, but the delicate whiskers of his upper lip quivered ever so slightly. "We are ten men, sir."

The scarecrow's blue gaze flickered between the officer and the men mounted at his back. "Ten finely appointed fellows, sir. Shiny armour and pretty weapons. Which of you thinks he might prime his pistol before I stick a bullet twixt his eyes?" No one moved. The scarecrow spat bubbling saliva through the gap in his front teeth. He trained one of the pistols on the lieutenant's crotch. "No plate there, I'd imagine. Now ground arms, you ballock-brained maggot, less'n I turn your cock to a cunny."

"Why you treacherous cur!" Chickering hissed, but he dropped his sword nonetheless. His pistols were holstered in his saddle, too far away to be of use, but he still turned to order the troopers to discard their own.

The scarecrow broke into his little jig once more. "Poor old crump-back! Crazed as a headless cockerel! You might be more respectful o' your elders in future, son."

Up on the cart, Tomkin Dome felt his heart race and he wondered if he would expire there and then. He heard hooves and murmurs behind, and turned, expecting to see Chickering's rear-guard following the order, but they had yet to relinquish their arms.

"Oh God," he whispered, understanding that resistance would catch him firmly in the cross-fire. Then out of the mist came a grey stallion. Its head resolved first, eyes bulging and wild above a diamond-shaped patch of pristine white, steam pulsing in roiling jets from nostrils flared black. It seemed to Dome like a ghoul rising from the very bowels of hell, a snorting demon come to claim souls for torment. He shuddered at the thought, but knew it was no spectre, for a man emerged from the wisps, perched atop the beast. He was dressed in dark clothes with a cloak of mossy green, reins in one hand, a curious double-barrelled pistol in the other. The man's face was sharp and lean, the deep lines at cheeks and brow making a once handsome appearance craggy like a sea-smashed cliff. But there was brightness too. In the green eyes, almost glimmering below the brim of his black hat, twinkling from the miasma like lonely stars on a cloudy night.

Dome stood on his rickety timber platform and pointed at the newcomer. "Might wish to check your backs."

The five troopers behind the cart twisted as one. All at once the horses were still. They were trapped on the bridge between two shooters. Yet still they had the superior numbers, and a mad rush at the brigands would certainly sweep them away. Dome swallowed hard, wondering if the soldiers were weighing up their chances.

As if reading their minds, the newcomer let his ghostly grey lope up to the bridge. "This pistol has two shots," he called. "My friend has two also. Fight if you must, but be certain some of you will perish." He lifted a gloved hand to push a tendril of matted sandy-coloured hair from his eye. "Drop your weapons. I will not ask again."

The troopers did as they were told, dismounting and filing up the side of the cart to join their comrades. The cloaked man remained in his saddle, watching from on high, while the scarecrow corralled them like armoured sheep, impotent in the face of the elderly footpad's wolfish delight.

"You," the man in black said, green eyes darting to the waggon.

Tomkin Dome touched a hand to his breast. "Me?"

"Get down and collect the weapons. Toss them in the river."

Dome dropped his reins and scrambled down to the smooth stones. "Aye, sir."

"Then be rid of their mounts, save two."

Dome nodded, already cradling three swords, a pair of pistols and a carbine. "Right away, sir."

As he scurried about his work, he saw that the scarecrow was jabbing his twin pistols in the faces of the soldiers. "Over there, and be quick about it," he ordered, forcing them back against the side of the bridge. "Any one o' you makes a move, you'll get a ball in the throat." He looked between them at the crystal water. "Or maybe I'll save the lead and shove you straight into the drink. Pretty deep, ain't it? Wonder how well you'll swim with all that plate weighin' you down."

"Cover yourself, Eustace," the man perched on the big grey called.

The scarecrow screwed up his face. "They've seen me."

"They've seen a haggard old man. Give them no more to recall than that."

Reluctantly, and with a spiteful sneer, the scarecrow tore away his eye bandage and pulled a black cloth over the lower portion of his face. Chickering bristled, his own features crimson with rage. "You won't get away with this." He glanced across at the mounted assailant. "You'll swing. Both of you."

"Both?" a new voice startled the lieutenant. It was high pitched, the tone of one very young, though it came from the river.

Chickering's eyes widened, as if the speaker were some kind of mythical creature, a nymph dwelling amongst the reeds. The scarecrow grinned and nodded, encouraging the troopers to look down at the water. When the lieutenant turned back, his face was a picture of bewilderment. "A girl? What kind o' highwayman brings his slattern on the road?"

Tomkin Dome had an armful of weaponry, and he staggered to the side of the bridge and dropped them into the glistening depths. He saw her, then. Her face was covered in a silken scarf, but her long hair cascaded over her shoulders to the base of her spine. She too held a pistol, but it was what her other hand clutched that interested him. The girl held a pair of ropes, each taut as they stretched out into the centre of the Wey. Bobbing at their far ends were two small skiffs. She looked up at the bridge. "Get down here, piss-a-breech. And I ain't no slattern. Not any more, least wise."

The scarecrow cackled. "You heard her," he said to Chickering. "Off for a nice trip down the river."

The mounted man walked his horse up to stand beside the cart. He gazed down at the cage, then at Dome. "Do you have the key?"

Tomkin Dome shook his head. "Alas, no, Major. The key is at Portsmouth. None here may open it."

Lieutenant Chickering had been trudging at the head of his men towards the far bank and waiting boats, but now he froze. He turned slowly back, eyes settling on the carter in a look of blazing malice. "You? You have betrayed us?"

Tomkin Dome's entire body hurt. His lungs felt weak and sore, his skin crawled. But he managed a deep bow in spite of it all. "I am a loyal subject of King Charles. And his murdered father before that."

"You will die too, you pathetic little worm," Chickering said darkly.

"I embrace it, young man, for I have taken this small revenge and will die happy." He turned to look up at the horseman. "Thank you."

Major Samson Lyle nodded and slid from his horse. Star grumbled, but kept calm enough. He thanked God for His providence, for the plan had worked. The party had left Newbury on time, and Bella had tracked them so that he knew when they were likely to cross the River Wey. He felt so alive, his blood zinged through his limbs in a way that it had not done since before Ireland. He thought of Felicity Mumford, and, for the first time, felt no guilt.

Lyle reached for one of the saddle's leather loops, through which hung a long war hammer. They were designed for piercing or crushing plate armour, though he had used it against many an infantryman, and the effects on an unprotected skull had been more horrific than he could ever have imagined. Now, though, the target was not skin and bone. It was the heavy lock that hung from the doorway to the cage. Lyle lifted the hammer, poised to strike. "See to our friends, Eustace!"

"Pleasure, Major!" Grumm called back. The old man jerked his pistols and the prisoners resumed their slippery progress down to the grassy bank. "Couple o' nice, cosy boats for you to try, chums," he chirped at the backs of the crestfallen troopers. "Perfectly river worthy I assure you."

Lyle swept the war hammer into the waiting lock. It clanged, the sound echoing about the trees with unnatural loudness, the gurgling of the river its only competition. He repeated the blow twice more with deep grunts, the flapping of startled birds shaking the canopy above, and then there was an almighty crack as the lock twisted and broke. Lyle slid the bolt back, tugged open the door. "Sir James Wren?"

The man in the cage had barely reacted to the frenetic action swirling around him, but now he crawled stiffly to the little doorway. "Aye."

"Then come. The coast awaits. You must take a ship."

Wren took Lyle's proffered hand, bracing himself against it as he stepped out. His hair was lank and filthy, falling over his face in greasy clumps. His eyes stared out from behind the dark veil. He seemed exhausted, broken, though a new light came into his face, as though waking from a terrible dream. "I know you."

"Lyle."

Wren seemed puzzled. "A Roundhead, were you not?"

"I was."

"Allied now to the king?"

"Allied to none but myself."

It was Wren's turn to extend his hand. "I shall tell the king of your service nevertheless."

"As you wish."

Tomkin Dome had chased off eight of the troopers' mounts. Now he came to stand before the man who had hitherto been a captive of the Protectorate. "Sir."

Wren stared at him for a few heartbeats, before his eyes widened. "Sergeant? Sergeant Dome?"

Dome beamed. "You have it, sir, and good it is to see you again."

They shook hands. Wren swept the hair from his face, the life pouring into him with every moment. "What risk you have taken in this enterprise."

Dome's face became sad, and Lyle thought of their first meeting, when the brittle carter had told him of his illness. It had been a Godsend for the mission, but that did not make him happy. Dome cleared his throat awkwardly. "I am not long for this world, Sir James. I would fight for my king one last time." He glanced at Lyle. "Thanks to this man."

Lyle could not stifle a smile. "A small matter, gentlemen. Now if you wouldn't mind, I must be away from here. And you have a ship to catch."

"How?" Wren said.

"The major has arranged our passage to France," replied Dome. "We must ride hard for the coast."

Lyle nodded. "Ride like devils, for they will hunt you."

Wren was already walking gingerly towards the two mounts Dome had selected for their journey, but he looked back at his rescuer. "Why are you doing this, Major? You were a rebel."

"It will hurt Goffe and Cromwell, Sir James," Lyle said as he watched the two men hoist themselves into the saddles and quickly kick the beasts into a canter. The hooves clattered south over the bridge. "That is enough!"

Lyle went to the side of the bridge. He leaned over the stonework to peer down at the two skiffs. They each carried five passengers, fury etched into every face. He waved. "Give my regards to Major-General Goffe!"

Lieutenant Chickering tried to stand, causing the boat to list violently, throwing him back onto his rump. "He will track you down," he snarled as Lyle, Grumm and Bella brayed to the scudding clouds at his floundering.

"I count on it! Be sure to tell General Goffe who it was that outwitted him."

Chickering stared up at him as the boats slipped swiftly downstream. "Then who are you?"

"Major Samson Lyle, sir. The Ironside Highwayman!"

Historical Note

The Rule of the Major-Generals was a 15 month period of direct military government during Oliver Cromwell's Protectorate.

The new system was commissioned in October 1655 and the country divided into 12 regions, each governed by a Major-General who was answerable only to the Lord Protector. The first duty of the Major-Generals was to maintain security by suppressing unlawful assemblies, disarming Royalists and apprehending thieves, robbers and highwaymen. To assist them in this work, they were authorised to raise their own militias.

Colonel Maddocks and his men are figments of my imagination, but William Goffe was indeed Major-General for Berkshire, Sussex and Hampshire, and it would have been his responsibility to hunt down Samson Lyle and men like him.

Sadly, Lyle himself is a fictional character, but he is indicative of many outlaws of the period.

Contrary to the classic tradition of the 18th Century dandy highwayman, mounted bandits have infested England's major roads for hundreds of years.

Indeed, in 1572 Thomas Wilson wrote a dialogue in which one character commented that in England, highway robbers were likely to be admired for their courage, while another suggested that a penchant for robbery was one of the Englishman's besetting sins.

During the years immediately following the Civil Wars, highway banditry became more widespread simply due to the sheer number of dispossessed, heavily armed and vengeful former Royalists on the roads. This idea was the inspiration behind *Highwayman: Ironside*, though I felt it might be more interesting if my protagonist had been a Roundhead rather than a Cavalier.

The locations in the story are all real. The London to Portsmouth road became a major coaching route in the eighteenth century, but it had already been an established highway for centuries. Many inns punctuated the route, and the Red Lion at Rake (now a private house) was certainly present in 1655.

The Manor House at Hinton Ampner was indeed purchased by the Parliamentarian, Sir John Hippisley after the wars. The current house was built in 1790, and is now owned by the National Trust.

The Ironside Highwayman will ride again.

Michael Arnold

HIGHWAYMAN: WINTER SWARM

Michael Arnold

1

Priors Dean, Hampshire, December 1655

The White Horse was not a large establishment. Indeed, the tavern's low ceiling, supported by tobacco-stained beams and mellow walls of wind-smoothed stone, reflected a former life as a modest farmhouse, the kind of place a small family might congregate after a day of toil in the seemingly endless hills. But this night, up high on the Froxfield plateau where the downland chalk was made sticky by clay and the frozen fields were smothered in a glittering blanket of snow, the White Horse seemed like the very centre of the world.

The noise emanating from its windows was raucous, pulsating over the gently undulating terrain and through the dense blocks of white-capped woodland that marked the plateau's fringe. And the light — warm and tremulous — blazed between shutters flung wide, bathing the snow and the outbuildings and the distant hedgerows so that the deep night glowed orange for fifty yards in all directions.

Towards the light walked an old man, a young girl and a large dog. They trudged carefully, steps crunching but gently placed, along the track that bisected the field from the main road. Their breaths plumed thick and white, a rasping chorus, unnaturally loud in a land muffled by the long-dwindled blizzard. The clouds scudded above them, by turns masking and revealing a bold moon, though they hardly needed its guidance when the boisterous hails of the isolated inn beckoned them so readily. The smash of a dropped — or thrown — pot rang out suddenly, followed by a fresh guffaw, and the dog froze, jerking its leash taut. The girl swore, for the rope was coiled about her thin wrist. She twisted back, tugged hard, forcing the frightened animal to proceed. It was a huge thing, brindle-coated and wide-pawed, but it was clearly disquieted by the light and the noise. She coaxed the loping creature to her hip, its half-raised hackles climbing higher than her waist, and patted its head as she walked.

The man spat into the snow. "Craven mongrel."

The girl laughed beneath the brim of a wide hat worn at an extreme slant. "He's a timid thing, is all."

"He's a bleedin' ban-dog," the man snapped in the rounded drawl of his native West Country. "A throat ripper. And he hides 'twixt your legs like a blue-eyed pup. How old are you now?"

She shrugged. "Twelve?"

"Pathetic," the man said. "He's mad."

"The dog?"

"The major."

The girl rolled her eyes. "He ain't mad, Eustace. It's a plan."

The old man had a long nose that was bright red at the hooked tip. He wiped it with the sleeve of a buff coat that hung incongruously loose on his brittle frame, like a sack draped on the end of a broomstick. "A mad plan. An ill-considered, pottage-brained, slop-pale of a bliddy plan."

"It'll work."

"Better plans have been conjured in the cells of Bedlam."

The girl snorted. "Leave off, Eustace, you miserable old stoat."

The man flashed her a deeply creased grimace. "Don't you address me thus, *Dorothy*," he warned, emphasising the name with a malicious sneer, "lest you wish a taste o' this stoat's backhand."

They were at the extent of the White Horse's projected light now, almost visible from within the alehouse. The girl stopped abruptly, leash straining again. "I do not like Dorothy."

Eustace sniffed. "Bella, then."

She grinned, a gesture as bright as the moon, the smattering of freckles vanishing in the wrinkles of her snub nose. She bent to stroke the dog. "He's a nice boy, ain't he?"

"A flea-bit mongrel." He unslung the old army-issue snapsack that had dangled across one shoulder, upending the contents. A ball of twine and two brush-like objects dropped free, and he quickly scooped them out of the snow. They were made of many sheafs of bracken, left to dry out and bound tightly at one end. He moved for the dog, but it growled deeply, making him jerk back. "Bastard beast. You do it."

Bella smirked and took the bracken bunches. The dog made no sound as she bound them about its big ears, a pair of rustling antlers. She fanned the foliage out, making them as large as possible. "There, you handsome thing."

"Have you the tail?" Eustace asked.

She shook her head. "You picked it up."

"I did not." He scratched his unkempt beard, as white as the snow, with nails that were jagged and yellow. "I took the horns only. You were to bring the tail."

Bella made to argue, but something caught her eye. She handed the rope to an uneasy-looking Eustace and darted a few paces into the gloom. When she returned she was clutching the half-rotten remains of a discarded willow broom. It was wet, mould-darkened and heavy, but the dog seemed to acquiesce to Bella's soothing tones as she tied it about its thick tail with twine. "There." She stood back, fists planted on hips, admiring her work as though the panting hound were carved in alabaster. "This'll work."

Eustace blew a gust of air through his thin nostrils and screwed up his leathery face. "None of this will work."

She fixed her brown eyes on the twinkling blue of his. "Do you wish to back out?"

He handed her the leash. "'Course I bleedin' don't."

*

Inside, the White Horse looked to be bursting at the seams. Three of its rooms were dedicated lodgings for weary travellers, and more than half of the ground floor had been given over for use as a smithy, so the taproom itself was disproportionately small, and consequently heaving. It was clogged with rough-hewn tables and crooked chairs, a large, roaring hearth and a counter lined with tapped hogsheads. The chamber would have been cluttered with no patrons at all, but, as it was, the place was alive with chatter and acrid with the aroma of so many unwashed bodies. A dozen locals — grizzled shepherds and foresters in the main — had been drawn to the hearty haven by the noise and the song and the sporadic fits of laughter, a cosy remedy for the affliction of a wintry night, but they had been joined by at least a score more. These extras were not local. Hampshire men, by their accents, but up from the coastal cities rather than the hill-hidden hamlets of the Downs. They were passing through, stabling their tired mounts, rejuvenating aching bones in the comfortable surroundings, sheltering from the forbidding darkness and from those who might think to menace their progress. They wore tall boots and coats made of oiled buff hide. A couple still donned gleaming breastplates, though most had long since discarded the encumbrances, while one man, hunched peaceably over one of the tables to stare down into his ale pot, had a wide scarf the colour of saffron fastened about his waist.

"To Midhurst," the man in the scarf said. It was tied in a large knot at the small of his back and he reached behind to adjust it as he spoke. "We ought to be there now, by rights, but I could not risk the ride."

The fellow seated opposite, dressed in a simple farmer's smock, bobbed his head and gulped down a lingering draught of ale, belching softly when the pot was empty. "From the Alresford garrison?"

"You have it. No great distance, I grant you, but we tarried too long."

"And the weather must have hindered, L'tenant."

"A great hindrance, for certain. I feared the very heavens had opened."

The farmer leaned back, stretching like a cat. He was lean, with strong, calloused hands, and a face that was deeply lined and burnished by years of exposure to the elements. "All done with now, thank God. Clouds are spent."

The lieutenant pulled a sour expression, tugging at the strands of a dark beard that belied his youth. "But hardly conducive to our ride, nonetheless."

"No? Your horses looked strong, sir."

"Strong, aye," the young officer agreed. "And expensive. Not the kind of beast you wish wrong-footed by a snow-hid branch or burrow."

The farmer spread rough palms. "I would not know such things, sir. A simple ploughman am I, unused to soldierly ways. You are dragooners, as they calls 'em?"

"Lord no, friend. The dragoon is your mounted musketeer. We are harquebusiers. Cavalry of the proper sort." The lieutenant rubbed his face with delicate fingers. "Charged with duties of singular import."

The farmer smiled, eyes of emerald narrowing to craggy slits below a fringe of straw-coloured hair. "The chest."

The lieutenant seemed to spring from his weary reverie at that, sitting bolt upright as though suddenly branded. "What do you...?"

The farmer's hands were up immediately, flattened, placating. "I could hardly miss it, sir, is all. I meant no mischief."

"You see I am on edge, somewhat," the lieutenant muttered, slumping back again. He fell silent while a girl came to refill their pots from a large, craggy blackjack. They both watched the swing of her hips as she retreated into the mass of revellers. "The colonel would hang me from the rafters by m' ballocks should I make a sow's vittels of this task," he said eventually, glancing over his shoulder to where the small, iron-bound box rested on the rushes amongst the troop's piled effects. "It is a pay chest. The Midhurst garrison's money is overdue." He let his voice drop to a hushed rasp. "By more than two months, 'tween you and I."

A great burst of laughter rumbled out from a party of soldiers gathered about one of the hogsheads. The farmer flinched nervously, looking back at them as though they were a pack of wolves. "Jesu."

The lieutenant shook his head. "Worry not, sir, they merely take their ease. No harm will befall you."

The farmer nodded gingerly, his throat convulsing with a thick swallow. Evidently content that he was in no immediate danger, his eyes returned to the box. "Lord, I'll wager they're smarting. The Midhurst men, I means."

The chuckled reply was rueful. "That word does it no justice, friend, believe me. They're angry as hornets. Talk of mutiny, though it won't come to that. No man wants his neck stretched."

"Thanks to you, L'tenant, their gripes will vanish soon enough."

The lieutenant nodded happily, eyes markedly glazing as the drink settled in his stomach. "On the morrow, God-willing."

The farmer grinned, offering a conspiratorial wink. "To Lieutenant Puttock and his brave lads," he toasted, raising his pot. "May they rest easy by night and gallop hard by day."

Puttock gave a languid nod. "I'll drink to that."

They both drank deeply, the farmer finishing first. "You do not concern yourself with," he leaned closer, dropping his voice, "*him*?"

"Him?"

A wince. A furtive glance left and right. "I daren't speak the devil's name."

Lieutenant Puttock covered his mouth with a fist as air rumbled from his guts. "The Ironside Highwayman?" He forced an uncomfortable cackle. "Samson Lyle is a disgrace. A common brigand."

"They say he was General Ireton's friend. His right hand no less."

"No longer. If I were to lay eyes upon that vile traitor, I should spit in his face and stick my blade in his belly."

"They say the Ironsides murdered his goodwife." The farmer's voice was a whisper. "That he will wage war upon his former comrades until the day he dies."

"Then may God ensure that blessed day comes swiftly."

The farmer raised his pot again. "Well said, Master Puttock. Well said indeed."

*

The demon came in through the window. It was a hideous thing, dark and howling, teeth bared, saliva frothing at its mouth. It smashed through the legs of the first two people as soon as its paws slammed and slid amongst the trampled rushes, then collided with a knot of shocked revellers with a guttural snarl that knocked them asunder like so many skittles. It slewed to a halt against one of the table legs, splitting it with a crack, and the wooden slab toppled over him, followed by a shower of ale, blackjacks and pots. The men at the table scrambled clear as the beast reared against its entrapment, the splintered shards eschewed with a great shrug of its muscular frame, and it howled again. The blaze in the hearth was reflected in its eyes, and they were as cold as the flames were hot, tiny and black as the night. It had fearsome spines thrusting from the wide expanse of its skull, and they shivered at the creature's every move. Its tail was a long, sharp spike that looked like something from the hellish murals that had once adorned so many churches, drowned now by ubiquitous whitewash for the sake of spiritual austerity. Its violent, snapping arc had soldier and local alike scrambling for the door, jostling and screaming and desperate not to be the one who would be sucked down to Satan's realm.

It was chaos. The demon turned circles, its din as deafening as it was fearsome, and the folk finding themselves in its way bellowed for divine intervention. Jars shattered, chairs tumbled, barrels toppled and rolled, ale and wine dashed the floor and hissed in the hearth.

Lieutenant Puttock had been sipping his drink, and he rocked back, spitting the liquid in a spray down his coat and scarf as he leapt to his feet. His heart felt as though it would give out there and then, his guts turning to water and the very skin feeling as though it would melt with sudden heat. He heard himself curse as he twisted, groping for his scabbard. It lay with the troopers' pile of effects, and he crashed through three or four breastplates before he managed to snag his baldric in the crook of a finger, yanking the belt and its weapon into the air. He grasped the hilt with his free hand, and the sword was naked, the manic firelight snaking along its length.

"Hold!" he bellowed at his men. "Hold, damn your meek minds!" But most were streaming out through the swinging door as though their very lives depended on it. And perhaps they did, thought Puttock as he edged forth, pushing past the table and the frightened farmer with whom he had been drinking. The creature was in a corner, a half-hidden puckrel, eyes agleam, body immersed in shadow. Was the horned beast waiting to pounce, sent by Lucifer to rip souls to hell? The inn had mostly emptied now, its patrons high-tailing out into the snow, and

Puttock had only to pick his way through the debris. He heard the shifting of paws in the darkness. Claws scraped on the floor. Or were they talons? He knew he should have paid more attention to the regimental preacher's ranting. What good was cold steel against a harbinger from the very bowels of the earth?

The demon moved out from its hiding place. Puttock raised the sword in one trembling hand and the scabbard like a shield in the other. He had the vague idea to slide one over the other, making a rudimentary crucifix of them, but knew such a thing would be too sinful to risk. And then he swore, because the demon had cocked a hind leg, tossed its head to shake loose the bracken that had been tied to its ears, and pissed on the floor.

Puttock sheathed his sword and went to the dog, which immediately rolled onto its back. He shouted at the doorway, and, after a moment's hesitation, his men began to make their sheepish return. "A trick," he said, anger at his cowardly charges somewhat assuaged by the absurdity of the situation. "A child's game and nothing more. Your demon is nought but a poor mongrel, transformed by twigs and a broom handle."

One of the more senior soldiers pushed to the front of the shame-faced crowd. "Forgive us, Lieutenant, sir. These hills are ripe for witchin', is all."

Puttock shook his head and cast his gaze about the ruined taproom. The tapster, a stoat-thin man in his fifties, was ringing blue-knuckled hands and muttering in evident distress. Two of the locals were already putting things right, lifting tables back into place and collecting up fallen pots. Puttock shook his head. "What fools we are, eh?"

He went back to his own table and picked up his stool. It was only then that he noticed the pay chest. Or rather, the gap in the heaped belongings where once the chest had been. "By Christ, no." He took a step towards the pile, eyes transfixed on the void. "No!"

"Sir?" one of the troopers said at his back.

"The strongbox," Puttock managed to murmur, the rush of blood louder in his ears than his own words. He forced himself to turn. "It is gone."

The trooper frowned, then set his jaw determinedly as he turned to the men. "Search every man here. Now, God rot your slovenly carcasses!"

"Wait."

The trooper paused at the command. "Lieutenant, sir?"

Puttock felt as though he might vomit. "Where is he?

"He, sir?" the trooper echoed, nonplussed.

"The man I was speaking with," Puttock said. His head swam, his stomach churned. He stared about the tavern's dim interior, pointing to the stool where the emerald-eyed farmer had perched. "There. He was sitting there."

2

Stoner Hill, Hampshire, December 1655

The crack of the pistol echoed back and forth across the soaring hangers, flung like duelling cannon-fire through the snow-capped woodland of the steep escarpment fringing the north and east of Petersfield. A host of rooks alighted from the thick canopy, squawking angrily at the slate dawn and somewhere, far off, a dog replied with a high-pitched yap. Then all was silent.

The shooter blew the last wisps of smoke from the warm muzzle. He was standing in the centre of a raised platform that was hidden deep within the dense forest. It was a square within a square, a ditch edging it, and too precise to be anything but man-made. It was the work of ancients, he had long since decided. A fort or camp, a place to defend, once imbued with views across the whole, cavernous valley. Now, though, it was home to the tools of the countryside. Scythes and shovels, old clay pots, two double-ended saws, a long-hafted axe, a rickety dog cart loaded with empty cloth sacks, and a couple of tatty barrels. There was a harrow lying in the bracken, its wooden frame wide and its spiked teeth rusty, while a tangle of netting hung limp from a tree. The place was overgrown, mouldering and invisible to the outside world. Perfect for one such as he.

His green eyes sparkled as he regarded the box, heavy enough that it had not rolled back with the bullet's impact, then winked at the scrawny girl, who immediately scampered out from the square's edge. She kicked snow in tiny flurries as she went to the prize, kneeling beside it to heave open the iron-bound lid. She looked back at him, eyes as bright as the metal within the chest, and then she plunged her hands into the drift of coins, letting them envelope her forearms as her laughter rolled out over the snow.

"The Midhurst garrison wages," Samson Lyle said, returning the pistol to his belt. "A menace of a thing to get out of the tap room. Heavy as a ... well, as a box full of treasure."

"I cannot fathom it," the cracking voice of an elderly man came from below the torn sinews of a wind-felled oak. He stood in the bowl shaped crater left by the roots, absently inspecting one of several domed baskets that had been positioned within, upended and propped on a stout timber to keep them from touching the earth.

Lyle turned. "The pay, Master Grumm. The soldiers undertake soldierly duties, and they are given metal disks in return, by which they might make purchase of such things as they desire."

Eustace Grumm's antique face twisted with a sudden, violent tick. "A pox on your wit, Major, for I've a stomach full of it." He fingered one of the baskets, picking at the strands of woven straw that pushed through its daub skin. "I cannot fathom the events of last night. How came General Goffe by such cowardly troops? They ran like goddamned conies."

Lyle stamped his feet against the cold, disturbing bits of grey rubble and ochre tile from beneath the snow. "Folk fear the night. They fear the shadows. The war hardened some of us till there was no fear left. But the rest? They fear God, they fear Satan, they fear witches, warlocks, demons, Papists, Fifth Monarchists, Frenchmen, Dutchmen and Spaniards. They fear the forests and the lakes and the hills." He winked. "And it appears they fear dogs dressed as puckrels."

"But soldiers?" Grumm went on. "Gaggle o' craven piss-a-breeches."

"Soldiers are more superstitious than most," Lyle said. "And you'll be running too if the bees feel you picking at their skep."

Grumm removed his hand from the woven basket, stepping back sharply. "What fool keeps bees up here?"

"The flowers on these slopes are particularly fragrant," Lyle said. "Produces a wondrous honey." He closed his eyes, dragging a scrap of schooling from the recesses of his memory. "Leonardo da Vinci once said that the humble bee was a marvel of nature. It gathers its materials from the flowers of the garden and of the field, but transforms and digests it by a power of its own."

"Who's Daventry?" Grumm asked in evident distaste at the unfamiliar name. "A monk?"

"A painter, and many more things besides. Long dead, more's the pity."

"Bees are all at winter slumber," Grumm scoffed, giving the hive's hard shell a gentle rap with his bony knuckles.

"Honey bees do not hibernate, Eustace," Lyle warned, chuckling as Grumm jumped back in alarm. "They cluster to keep warm, but they are not asleep."

"Samson?" It was the girl who spoke. Bella was still crouching over the box, but she held up a couple of thick coins, rubbing them between thumb and forefinger. "This do?"

Lyle nodded. He turned to another corner of the square, where a fourth person loitered. "For the damage, John."

The man hovering at the edge of the snow-filled fosse had a balding pate and reedy frame. He flinched as Bella tossed him the money, but caught the coins deftly enough, and nodded his thanks to Lyle. "Pleasure, Major."

"Lieutenant Puttock suspects nothing?"

"Nowt, sir," John said. "They searched the roads most of the night."

Lyle had known they would, which was why he had decided to take the fox tracks through the thick forests and meet at the remains of this old look-out of which only a handful of souls were aware. "And they dwell at your tavern no longer?"

John shook his head and pocketed the money that would more than compensate him for the destruction wrought by the demon dog. "Buggered off to Midhurst."

"Shame-faced and empty-handed," Eustace Grumm cackled. "He'll be in the dung by noon."

"A shame for Mister Puttock," Lyle said, for he had liked the young lieutenant, "but he is Goffe's creature, and I am at war with Goffe."

"You are at war with everyone, Major," Grumm replied.

Lyle thought about that. Ever since turning his back on Ireton's mission in Ireland, he had been a hunted man. But then Alice had died. His childhood sweetheart, his goodwife and best friend; beautiful, elegant, wise. She had been trampled under the hooves of the Protectorate's Ironsides, the same cavalrymen who had once been his comrades, and it was then that prey had become predator. Now it was Lyle, the most feared highwayman in all England, who hunted quarry on the nation's roads. Lawyers, bureaucrats, tax collectors, politicians and soldiers. Any who performed the duties of a cog in Cromwell's grand machine. He supposed Grumm was right. It was a war that would never end — but that did not mean he would give up the fight.

"We have weakened Goffe's arm," he said, unwilling to be drawn into Grumm's game. "It is enough for now."

"William Goffe is Major-General of Hampshire, Berkshire and Sussex," Grumm said. "The iron fist of the Lord Protector. He'll feel our sting as a bullock feels a tick on its arse."

"He hates me, Eustace. Now he'll hate me even more. A success, to my mind. And how fares the hero of our play?"

"Just fine," said Grumm. "The smelly beast has a thick hide."

"But you stuck it with something, Eustace," said Lyle, "or it would hardly have yelped so."

Grumm's thin lips parted to reveal his empty gums. "Holly branch. He barely noticed when I whipped his rump with it, so I raked his undercarriage."

Bella laughed. "Did the trick, right enough."

"I can imagine it did. Was he well remunerated?"

The girl wiped her runny nose with a sleeve. "He had a bucket-worth of offal for his trouble, aye."

"Then all our cast find their efforts rewarded," Lyle said, glancing at the innkeeper. "Just as it should be. And my thanks again."

"Where to now, Major?" John asked.

"You know I cannot tell you that."

John pulled a hurt expression. "I'd not let slip."

"Nor would you, till they yanked the teeth from your jaw."

Grumm smacked his gums wetly. "You'd spill by the third."

"The second," Bella added.

John blanched, swallowed thickly, and offered a shallow bow. "Good health to you all."

"You're a grand fellow!" Lyle called after the innkeeper as his skinny frame vanished into the trees. When the man was gone, he turned to his companions. "Let us remove this loot to a place of safety."

"Well?" Bella pressed as she shut the strongbox. She stood, hands on hips. "Where we going?"

"To market, Bella," Lyle said. He patted his coat. "The Royal Wardrobe is in dire need of refurbishment."

3

Petersfield, Hampshire, December 1655

"They house orphans there now," Eustace Grumm called from the front of the cart.

They were rumbling into town at a slow lick, careful to watch for lingering gazes. The snow down here, in the valley between the southern chalk hills and northern clay ridge, had all but gone, turning the roads to slush-swamped morass, and a thick spray flung up from the wheels to leave a brown haze in their wake.

"Orphans?" Samson Lyle replied from his seat at the rear. He alone wore a cowl to disguise his face, for he alone bore the risk of recognition. The others covered their features during a robbery so that they could live in peace when the sun was up.

"At the Royal Wardrobe," Grumm answered, lifting himself a fraction to scratch his rump. "Since the king lost his bonce."

"Best use for it."

"Did you ever see it, Samson?" Bella asked, sitting opposite Lyle in the main body of the jolting vehicle, legs drawn up to her chest against the cold.

Lyle tugged back his hood a touch, peering into the bright green eyes that peeked above the sharp rise of the girl's bony knees. "The king's head? Aye. A gruesome thing."

Bella's freckled nose creased deeply. "Samson," she protested. "The Royal Wardrobe, I meant."

"Aye," Lyle said. "Near Blackfriars, as I recall. My troop was billeted nearby for a time."

Bella tilted back her head to stare at the bilious grey clouds, then swept her gaze across the line of shops and homes that flanked the High Street. "Imagine it," she said wistfully as the cart slowed to negotiate the way through a gaggle of angry geese being driven by a small boy toting a large stick. "Packed to the rafters with finery. Silks and satins, feathers and frills."

"Not no longer," Grumm called from the front. "Now tis packed with London's urchins!" He spat over the side. "The world turned on its head, an' no mistake!"

"For the good, Eustace," Lyle chided.

Grumm cackled nastily. "Only a bleedin' Roundhead would drool such nonsense."

"And only a Cornish Cavalier could be so blinkered."

"I was never no Cavalier, Major, and you knows it. But that don't make me no Roundhead neither." They went deeper into the town and the traffic became dense as folk thronged towards the market. "Roundheads," Grumm muttered. "Brutes, the lot."

"Saith the smuggler."

"To feed my family, Major!" Grumm argued as he steered the cart through a dozen heavily laden pack horses.

"To feed yourself, you old liar."

Grumm twisted round, face tight. "Cut me to the quick, you do," he hissed. A pair of horsemen cantered past on mud-spattered mounts, and he eyed them furtively. They doffed hats and went on their way, leaving Grumm to fix Lyle with a caustic stare. "Christ, Major, but keep your bliddy hood on!"

Lyle swept out an arm to indicate the thronging streets. "The town is to a vagabond what the greenwood once was. A maze of anonymity."

"A snake pit of danger," was Grumm's retort.

"A warren of refuge and opportunity," Lyle countered coolly, though he could not deny the quickening pace of his heart.

"Delirious," the Cornishman muttered in exasperation. He worries at the tangled strands of his beard. "Every man to lay eyes on you is trouble, you damned fool. Bella and I may be seen, for we cover our faces when we... *work*... but you let your victims bear witness to their persecutor. Christ, man, but your face is known and there is a price on it."

"It adds to the legend."

"It allows the more fragrant among them to swoon before the dashing high lawyer, once friend to the Protector, now his nemesis."

"Nonsense."

"Arrogance."

"We arrive," Bella cut in, craning her head over the side of the wagon to feast wide eyes upon the bustling market that juddered into view.

Grumm blew a blast of air through his nose. "Just keep your hood on and your head down, Major, that is all I ask."

The market place itself was set in the open space in front of a large church. It was the fulcrum of the town, its beating heart, crammed with traders and fringed with steam-wreathed livestock pens. Lyle tightened his cloak, ensuring his hood covered his features, and alighted from the vehicle. He helped Bella down, went to join Grumm, and the trio moved quickly into the crowd, crossing through the ring of enclosures. Beyond the cattle, sheep and pigs were the tradesmen, standing sentry beside stalls piled high with wares of every kind. They stamped feet against the cold as white vapour spilled from mouths that bellowed competing slogans to the bustling crowd. Around them, weaving through the throng, were the sellers with barrow and basket. Warreners with skinned conies and cordwainers with fine shoes, hawkers pushing strips of ribbon, scraps of lace, sugar plums, and tallow candles. There were baker boys jostling for custom with itinerant apothecaries, fishermen touting the latest catch, and pie sellers hoping the waft of hot mutton and pastry would prove enticement enough.

"What'll you buy, Bella?" Lyle asked. "It is deserved. The pooch was demonic indeed."

She grinned. "Viper broth."

Lyle looked down at her. "Boiled adder guts?"

"Amongst other things," she sniffed. "It preserves a woman's beauty."

Eustace Grumm interrupted with a hacking cackle. "You ain't yet a woman."

Bella rounded on him. "And you ain't no man, you old weasel."

"Peace, peace," Lyle interceded, trying not to laugh. A grubby-faced lad of five or six snaked between them, and he slapped the boy's probing hand sharply, sending the would-be pickpocket scurrying into the multitude. He turned back to Bella. "You are not yet grown, child, whether you welcome the

100

fact or no. When I took you into my household you were no older than that brazen cut-purse."

Bella eyed the gap in the crowd that had swallowed the urchin. "That was five year gone," she protested indignantly.

"And drinking so noxious a brew," he persisted, "will see that you never reach majority." He knew his right to admonish her was forfeit the moment he had embroiled her in his criminal career. She was wise beyond her years, of course. Before Lyle had interrupted the life of the girl then named Dorothy Forks, she had been used and abused by any man with coin and a taste for childlike flesh. After joining his motley band, she had become the landlady of an alehouse by day and the accomplice of a notorious highwayman by night. Such an existence would corrupt even the most lily-white innocence. And yet Lyle could barely stave off the paternal urge that so irked his hot-tempered ward. "Viper wine is pure poison."

Bella looked as though she might argue, but made do with a theatrical sigh instead. "A dress then."

"Fine and well."

"You?"

Lyle glanced down at his clothes. "A new shirt." He winked at the girl and addressed Grumm, holding up his forearm. "Some handsome fringe at the cuffs, yes?"

Grumm pulled a sour face. "Christ, Major, but you're as dandy as Prince Rupert."

"Never compare me to that scoundrel," Lyle answered. "The Duke of Plunderland is long vanquished, and good riddance to him."

Bella cooed like a dove. "He is the most handsome man in all the world, so they say."

"And a good Cavalier," Grumm, a Royalist sympathiser like most of his fellow Cornishmen, whispered in deliberate needling.

"And do they say," Lyle said to Bella, "how many men went to their deaths at his hand? Do they speak of the hangings? Of the sackings? Of the destruction of Bolton and its people?" He felt heat pulse at his cheeks, saw the girl visibly balk, and was instantly ashamed. He extended a hand, which she shied from.

"I apologise. I am a Roundhead of old. I shed blood to rid this land of that German poltroon and his cronies."

Bella nodded, smiled tentative acceptance, and they pushed on. Lyle bought three pies, handing one each to Bella and Grumm, and went deeper into the throng. Stray dogs slunk between the makeshift alleys, sniffing the ground and hunting for edible scraps. A group of children ran past a stack of cages, clattering the wicker bars with sticks to the incensed chorus of squawking hens within. Loosed feathers billowed madly as the irate chicken farmer spewed threats at the backs of the giggling gang who were already well clear of his vengeful grasp.

Voices beckoned from all quarters, silky suggestions writhing in the cold air with abrasive bellows. "Here, good fellows!" one shouted. "The best price anywhere in the county!"

"Eels!" another brayed. "Fresh eels, caught this very dawn!"

But Lyle had eyes only for one place. Petersfield prospered on the back of the wool trade and, as such, the lion's share of coin changed hands at the centre of the trading space, where there was a dense cluster of stalls owned by cloth merchants. There were raw fleeces too, and haphazard sconces constructed of wool packs, but the cloth, produced by expert weavers in the surrounding villages, was the driving force of the town's economy. As Lyle moved closer he was compelled to squeeze between men of the finer sort, wealthy merchants, stylishly upholstered, servants buzzing at their backs like so many flies. Many were foreigners, come from the Low Countries to do business now that the fetters of the Dutch wars had been cast off. Some would have bodyguards close at hand, so he kept his eyes sharp and darting within their veiling shadow, always alive to danger. He eased his way to one of the tables, stacked high with bolts in various shades.

"I will buy if you will sew," he said to Bella, handing Grumm his heavy purse. "Agreed?"

"Agreed."

"Ah, Master Brown!" a man exclaimed in a voice that swept across them like a sudden gale. He came from the nearest stall, a hugely fat trader, sweating in spite of the cold, scattering bodies like a bullock amongst reeds, and made his way directly to the old man at Lyle's side. "Fare you well?"

"Well enough, Master Tincey, aye," Grumm managed to reply as the man clasped his shoulders in an embrace that reminded Lyle of a bear savaging a whippet.

The fat man turned red jowls and bright eyes upon Bella. "And young Mistress Lucy. You assist your uncle as best you can?" He winked. "The tavern will not thrive without you, I am certain."

Bella winked back. "My great uncle would forget where the Red Lion was without me, sir, so addled is his ancient mind."

Grumm wriggled loose. "Why, you cheeky..."

Tincey brayed, slapping Grumm's shoulder with a meaty paw. He glanced sideways at Lyle. "And is this lummox still of use?"

"He may have the wit of a mosquito," Grumm answered with unconcealed relish, "but he can shovel dung like a titan. Works hard for his scraps. Knows he'll receive a few more for Christmas, though the authorities would stifle celebration."

Tincey frowned. "Vulgar holy days have no warrants in the Word of God, Master Brown."

"He is right, Uncle John," Bella chided.

Grumm's leathery face creased sourly. "I will let you fast, Master Tincey, if you would only let me feast."

Tincey laughed again, unwilling to let the argument impinge upon business. Instead he performed an ostentatious half-turn, sweeping a brawny arm towards his wares. "Shall we?"

Bella was already at the table, rummaging through the bolts, placing one against the next as she assessed colour and texture. "This one, this one and..." she squinted at three examples of intricate lacework, jabbing one with a finger, "this one."

Tincey's small team of adherents rushed forwards to help, but the merchant dismissed them with a wave. He gathered the cloths himself, holding the first out for Lyle to take. "Goffe's men are in town, Major."

They were close, Tincey and Lyle, for the former had not released the item, tugging instead to draw Lyle nearer. "Where?" Lyle hissed.

"The big house behind me," Tincey said, not looking round.

Lyle let his hooded gaze drift beyond his old friend's ear to take in the impressive edifice of a two-storied home built in rich red brick. It dominated the south-west angle of the market place, wide mullioned windows frozen in melancholy stare below bushy ivy brows, as if the house itself spied on proceedings. "Then we must be swift. What else?"

Tincey shrugged. "What do you imagine General Goffe considers in so dreary a season?"

"Warmth," Lyle answered. "And provisions, of course." A caught a flicker of something cross the merchant's expression. "He must keep his soldiers alive and happy."

Tincey nodded. "Quite."

"The burden of being lord of Hampshire, Sussex and Surrey," Lyle said wryly. "Poor creature."

"And to ensure his soldiers will last the winter, what must he master?"

Lyle shrugged, nonplussed. "Tell."

The broad canvas of Tincey's face wrinkled in a conspiratorial smirk. "Preservation."

"Salt?"

"Salt indeed. And from whence will this salt come?"

It only took a moment for Lyle's mind to catch up. "Hayling."

Tincey nodded. "The island's salterns produce the very best quality."

"White gold, they say."

"Not far short, I'd wager. The likes of Goffe would pay a pretty penny. His garrisons can use the stuff for curing hides too, and it has power in a poultice." Tincey glanced at the iron clouds. "But in the depths of the freezing months, food is scarce and meat must have salt."

Lyle edged closer. "You are telling me because?"

Tincey brandished a triumphal grin and let go of the cloth so that they might part. He reached for the next, twisting back and speaking softly as the bundle crossed into Lyle's waiting grasp. "There is a convoy bound for Winchester. A man would find it in Havant this very day, should he take the time to look."

The soldiers appeared before Lyle could open his mouth to reply. They came from the house, just as Tincey had forewarned, a stream of leather and steel, spilling across the threshold so swiftly that a dozen had invaded the market before Lyle could consider his options. He dipped his head by instinct, praying the hood would do its job, while Tincey kept talking. The big man twisted back to his piled bolts, grabbing three at once and presenting them for Lyle to take. Lyle followed his lead, staggering with the increasing weight.

"There's a good fellow!" Tincey bellowed happily. He glanced at Grumm. "Good for something, I do declare!"

The soldiers moved with purpose. They were not wandering, but searching. Lyle could sense them behind and in front, to the sides of the cloth stalls and out towards the road. They were isolating this section of the market, hands resting on the hilts of sheathed swords, passive but prepared. They were harquebusiers, to judge by their buff coats and lobster-tailed helms. Cavalrymen in the normal run of things, but dismounted now for this ominous duty, mounts tethered elsewhere while they stalked.

"There!" an iron voice called. They closed in, shifting closer to Tincey's stall.

Lyle shut his eyes behind the textile shield, his pulse a torrent in his ears. He could smell the men. The stink of horse flesh wafted from them, unmistakable in the nostrils of one who had counted so many years in the saddle.

"There, I say," the speaker barked again. "Take him."

Lyle tensed. Not only by instinct, but because he recognised the voice. His guts churned in response. Men moved a little way to his right. His eyes were still clamped shut, but he could sense them, their shadows dimming the watery light. They could not recognise him, for he had barely looked up since arriving in the market place, but here they were, swarming like moths on a summer's eve. The smell grew stronger, but no hands gripped him. No steel tickled his belly. He held his breath.

There was a short scuffle, all grunts and shifting feet, and then the light came back, the musk diluted in the crisp air. He risked a sideways peek. The soldiers had taken a man, bound his wrists at his back, and dragged him free of the crowd. They compelled him to stand before one of their own; the one in command — the one whose words had clamoured like marriage peals in Lyle's mind. The man, another soldier, was as tall as Lyle, but with a bearing set thicker by an extra decade of life. His hair flowed to his shoulders in silver and black tresses from below a felt hat that looked new and expensive, while his grey eyes shimmered as they regarded his captive.

Eustace Grumm appeared at Lyle's flank. "Shit on a short stick," he muttered under his breath.

"Calm," Lyle spoke into the cloth.

"Calm?" Grumm hissed. "What is the Mad Ox doing here? Christ's wounds, but we're for it now."

"Whatever his purpose, it is not we three."

The leader of the soldiers fiddled with gloved fingers at the scarf that formed a diagonal band across his torso. The golden-yellow material was fastened in a large knot at his hip, while the wide jaws of a roaring lion were embroidered at his shoulder in blackest thread. His poise was casual, a wolf in a flock of frightened sheep. He revelled in it.

"What is the meaning of this?" the apple-eyed captive bleated. He was skinny and slightly stooped, hollow cheeks pitted by spent disease, but his garb bore the well-appointed style of the town's mercantile elite. "By what right do you treat me thus?"

"By the right of Major General William Goffe. You are Matthew Mallory?"

The rapidly blanching face betrayed the prisoner's disquiet. "And who the devil are you, sir?"

The soldier tugged gently on the saffron silk so that any wrinkles jerked taut. "Colonel Francis Maddocks. The man whose duty it is to uphold General Goffe's law." He jabbed a finger at Mallory. "And you, sir, are accused of flouting said law. You are a coiner."

Mallory puffed out his chest as far as his skinny frame allowed. "Not so, Colonel. Not so. A goldsmith, am I. Reputable, honest, and..."

"The very finest coin clippers are those whose fingers work metal by instinct."

"How dare you, sir!" Mallory blustered. He looked into the faces of the growing crowd. "Which of you is my enemy? Which brazen viper makes such a claim?"

"Your own apprentice, Master Mallory," the colonel said bluntly.

Mallory gulped air in preparation for a new tirade, but his lips simply smacked dryly. Terror had finally got the better of him, and quickly his vigour ebbed away. His face was drained, tinged a slight shade of green, and he stooped suddenly, as though he would vomit at any moment. When he looked up, there was nothing but pathetic resignation in his eyes. "But it harms no one, Colonel."

Maddocks waved a hand, summoning dour-faced soldiers who immediately compelled Mallory into a stumbling walk.

"It harms none!" Mallory bawled in sudden, querulous explosion. "Coining is not mentioned in scripture, sir! Ergo, it is not a true crime!"

Maddocks snorted his derision and executed a crisp about-turn. "Put him in irons."

The crowd disbursed as quickly as it had gathered, folk returning to the business of profit as though the martial sideshow had never transpired. The procession of soldiers clomped out of the cobbled space with their plaintive prize, grimly satisfied with the day's work. Colonel Maddocks swaggered in their wake, a hand propped casually on the ornate hilt of his sheathed sword, his free hand clipping the brim of his hat as he acknowledged the grandees of the town.

"Lord have mercy upon us," Eustace Grumm's words tumbled on a lingering out-breath.

Lyle stifled his own relief, handing the makeshift palisade of cloth back to the merchant and gathering up the rolls Bella had selected. "Let us be gone," he muttered, dry-mouthed, when the business was complete.

The trio slipped through the market place, stunned mute by the close call, oldest and youngest in the lead with Lyle, playing overburdened servant, traipsing in their wake. They were quickly aboard the vehicle, turning back towards the highroad that would take them north and east.

It was only when they were well clear of the town that any of them spoke. "To the Red Lion and safety," Grumm called above the trundling cartwheels. "Some fine tobacco, some rich cheese, and a goblet o' claret. That'll settle my nerves, an' no mistake." His satisfied expression soured as one of his cheeks twisted in sudden spasm. He eyed Lyle through narrowed eyes. "Wait."

"Wait?"

"I knows that look."

Lyle, sitting amongst the bundles of cloth, could not prevent the half-smile that tickled the corners of his mouth. "Whatever do you mean?"

"You cooking somethin' up, Samson?" Bella asked, the hint of mischief inflecting her tone.

Grumm glowered at them both. "Major?"

"It's what Teensy said," Bella guessed.

"Tincey," Lyle said. "Teensey he ain't."

"What he said," she persisted. "Talk o' salt."

Lyle nodded. "General Goffe is on the move, my friends. The Ironside Highwayman must ride again."

4

Rake, Sussex, December 1655

"They depart on the morrow." Lyle yawned away the final word as he closed the door and walked into the Red Lion. It was light in the taproom, pale morning rays streaming through unshuttered windows on a cold, crisp breeze, but his legs felt leaden as he sidled across the rushes to the table Grumm had just wiped clean. He pulled up a chair, slumped heavily into it and yawned again. "Rendezvous with escort today, in Havant. Leave at dawn."

"So says Celia," Bella muttered. She was already squeezed up against the table edge, working her way through a chunk of bread that smelled like heaven to Lyle.

He chose to ignore the sneer in his young ward's voice. "So she says." He had passed the night elsewhere, a fact that increasingly brought simmering hostility from one particular quarter. But he would bear Bella's jealousy, for Celia Hart's bed contained more than lithe limbs and warm breasts. She was the widow of one of Havant's more prominent parchment makers, and maintained an interest in the trade that made the town wealthy. That interest kept her involved in the comings and goings of the place, and few rumours passed through without reaching her delicate ears. Lyle reached for the loaf-laden trencher. "The commander at Havant has few men to spare."

"Then the escort will be weak?" Grumm called from the hearth, where he was busily dusting the large pewter plates that shone like silver moons atop its mantel.

"Indeed. They bring the salt in bags. A single wagon."

"What if it rains?" Bella asked.

Grumm paused in his duty to reply, "They'll have it under oiled sheets. That's how we used to move the stuff."

Lyle eyed the Cornishman's work, appreciating his attention to detail. The Red Lion was the Ironside Highwayman's bolthole, his hideaway, just off the Portsmouth to London Road at a little hamlet called Rake. It was ideally situated, a bridgehead on the highway from which he could attack the machinery of Goffe's administration, but it was also Lyle's second livelihood, his second line of defence from hunger when illegal pickings were slim, and he was glad the others, whose aliases officially owned the modest plot, took as much pride in it as he. The inn had ample stabling, a well-appointed and homely taproom, and lodgings for a dozen. He sat back, threading his fingers behind his head, and revelled in the contentment he had once considered unattainable. "One cartload, escorted by a small party of musketeers commanded by a fellow of meagre repute."

Grumm had stopped now, tossing his rag over a stool. He planted bony fists on his hips. "All this risk for sacks o' salt, Major."

"You would have us take aim at the more lucrative prizes?" Lyle said. He winked at Bella. "There are no ships hereabouts to lure onto rocks."

Grumm's ashen face coloured dramatically. "I was never a wrecker, God rot you!" he snarled, stabbing the air with a bluish finger. "A smuggler only."

Lyle laughed. "That was all I meant." He pushed some of the bread into the side of his mouth. "You have a smuggler's heart, Eustace. You would catch the pike and let the stickleback swim free."

"I simply would not advise takin' on a company of bleedin' muskets for such mean reward."

Lyle finished chewing and waited for his friend's bluster to ebb. He leaned in on his elbows, propping his chin on his hands. "For what do we fight, Eustace?"

Grumm shrugged, as though the question was foolish. "When my... *past*... went awry, I was destined for the noose." His rheumy eyes drifted into the middle-distance, and Lyle knew he was dragging the scene from the depths of memory. Grumm had been driven out of his homeland by underworld rivals, only to find himself snared by lawmen on an anonymous French road. It was only the intervention of a gaunt-faced Englishman that had saved his neck from a fatal stretch. The man — a wanderer with grief in his gaze — had appeared like a twilight wraith, armed with a long sword, an unusual, double-barrelled pistol and a vicious looking war-hammer, and he had seen off Grumm's persecutors as though they were nothing but a gaggle of belligerent geese. "You saved me, Major."

Lyle smiled. "You fight for me, Eustace. And I value that. But *I* fight for vengeance. Only vengeance. At night I dream of what was lost, and by day I look to hurt those who took it from me. Ireton is dead, but Oliver Cromwell is not. Francis Maddocks is not. William Goffe is not."

"But salt?"

"If I could hurt the Lord Protector I would, but I cannot. I am no more irritating than the warts on his face. So I am reduced to small victories. I cannot bring down the government, so I must make a nuisance of myself to those who adhere to it, profit from it. Spike a cannon, though I can never destroy the battery. Salt is life for a garrison of hungry men, Eustace, which makes it important to Major General Goffe." His palms suddenly hurt, and he realised he had been holding his fists tightly bunched. He uncurled the fingers, lacing them beneath his chin. "And if it is important to him, then it is vital to me."

Bella nodded firmly. "And us." She twisted to look back at the old man. "Right?"

Grumm sighed. "Foolish."

Lyle pursed his lips as he drew a map in his mind's eye. "They will not travel far in one day."

Grumm snorted scorn as he glanced out of the window at the snow-dusted courtyard. "Not a road worthy o' the name. Especially with so heavy a bounty."

"Once they are across the hills," Lyle went on, imagining the route north from Havant, "they will rest at Buriton, like as not. The village boasts more than one tavern to accommodate them."

"Then a short dash to the Mad Ox at Petersfield," Grumm warned. "And he'll see them safe to Winchester from there."

"Then we cut them off beforehand," said Lyle. "Before Buriton."

"How will we know which road they take?" Bella asked, her keen eyes darting between the two men. "There are many choices northward."

Lyle nodded, closing his eyes as he studied his private map. There was a network of routes criss-crossing the land between the coast and Petersfield like a sprawling cobweb, and, in summer at least, a traveller could select whichever took his fancy. But in deep winter? Lyle placed himself at the head of the convoy, imagining the young officer's possibilities. "Most are impassable with a heavy cart. I'd wager they will travel either by Finchdean or through the hills at Butser and Wardown."

Grumm's face convulsed as his tick held momentary sway. "The Finchdean road is better," he finally managed to say.

"Aye," Lyle agreed, "but it is perilously close to the Forest of Bere. The greenwood is infested with footpads."

"Like us," Bella grinned.

Lyle flashed her a crooked smile. "Not exactly like us."

"The convoy has protection," Grumm went on sombrely.

"Enough to risk the forest?" Lyle enquired of the smoke-black eves.

Grumm screwed up his leathery features. "You tell me."

What had Celia Hart purred in his ear? Lyle turned her words over in his mind. Eventually he looked at Grumm and shook his head. "They will avoid Bere."

Grumm lifted a hand to his beard and tugged at the wiry strands, twisting them into white bands about his fingers. "The hills it is, then. God help us."

5

Gravel Bottom, Hampshire, December 1655

Of all God's many phenomena, it was mist Samson Lyle loved the most. He had learnt to embrace it during the wars, when a lingering skein could hide a pike and a thick pall might even smother the glow of a match tip. Mist was the seasoned campaigner's friend and the raw recruit's waking nightmare. And Lyle's quarry, he had discovered on his reconnaissance between Mistress Hart's thighs, were as raw as he might have hoped. He licked his lips slowly, moist skin tingling in the cold air, and squinted through the murk towards the unseen curve of the road. He forced his breathing into a slow, shallow, quiet rhythm, listening for the tell-tale clank of traces and chains. "Ireton was one for a good mist," he said to no-one in particular.

Beside him, Eustace Grumm tugged his scarf up to hide his features, and spoke through the muffling cloth. "Ireton fought with the New Model. He'd have won whatever the weather."

An image of town walls — tattered and crumbling — skittered across Lyle's mind, and he gritted his teeth. "It was misty at Limerick."

Grumm cleared his throat awkwardly. "*Star* and *Tyrannous* are tethered back in the trees, just as you asked."

Lyle nodded absently, still dreaming of Ireland. His lungs involuntarily convulsed, as though the deep, painful breath might ward off the memory. It did not. The heady, metallic odour of blood filled his nostrils as it always did. The stench of bloated corpses and burning thatch. He had turned his back on the all-conquering English army when the massacres had begun. But his abandonment of the cause — of his friend, General Ireton — had lit a powder train that had burned its way through his life, through everything he loved. Ireton's swift, brutal revenge had spared nothing, leaving Lyle with wealth measured only in regret and guilt and fury. Ireland would remain a wound on his mind, festering and painful, never to heal.

Noises climbed out from the misty afternoon, searing away Lyle's melancholy like flame-bathed brands. He glanced down at the pistol in his hand, already loaded and primed. Its maker, a renowned Rotterdam gunsmith, had been a marvel, a genius of the craft. Lyle squeezed the stock, reassured by its familiar contours. It was hefty, longer by a hand's length than its English cousin and bulkier in its unique design, but perfectly balanced for all that. The weapon had two barrels —- a rarity in itself — but this one was particularly unusual for its single lock, cock and flint. One barrel was set above the other, with a release lever that would shift them on an axis when one charge was fired, revolving the twin muzzles so that the second might be immediately presented and discharged. It was an object of formidable beauty, and had become the mark of the Ironside Highwayman.

"The time is upon us," Lyle muttered. "Bella had better be ready."

*

The convoy consisted of one large wagon hauled by a quartet of mud-caked, steaming ponies that slipped and slid alarmingly in the slush. It had snowed during the night, just enough to deposit a shallow white crust, which, in itself, was no cause for anguish, except that the dawn had been mild, and the snow had thawed, and now the road was a cloying quagmire. The driver did his best, snarling and whipping like an angry Bedlamite, but the weary beasts could do little to improve their sluggish pace, and the seven surly firelocks who escorted the vehicle were left to grumble in the roiling miasma that tumbled from the roadside woods. The lone officer was on foot too, though he clung to the shaft of a glinting partisan, employing the butt-end as a walking stick.

Lieutenant Gilbert Amberley silently cursed as he drove the staff hard into the filth with hands numb despite their kidskin sheaths. He cursed the feeble sun, cursed the hills for their evil depths, and cursed Temperance Rathbone, the brewer's daughter, whose pouting scorn had put him here. A vixen shrieked somewhere distant, making him start. He patted the pistol jutting from his belt, then hauled on the partisan to pep lethargic strides. *Be a man, Gilby*, she had whispered. *Ask for my hand then, and it'll be freely given*. Well God damn her, Amberley thought, as his eyes strained against the never-ending whiteness. No pair of tits was worth this.

It was a haunting place. Forbidding. The chalk hills were smothered in yew, beech and conifer, and the dark bowels of the wood seemed to whisper to him, calling him to his doom. The gully through which they now slogged was known as Gravel Bottom, the low road between the twin humps of Butser and Wardown. Was it a road? Barely, to Amberley's mind. Admittedly, in many sections of this northward route, the going was not entirely ruined, for quarried chalk, smashed and compacted, made for a robust surface when treated with a layer of flint. However, such stretches of hardy thoroughfare were to be found only in the towns and villages such as the salt road on Hayling Island, the passage through Havant, and patches around Horndean and Buriton. In between, in those great swathes of crop and forest linking village to village, it was nothing more than soil, pounded by heel and hoof, sunken over centuries to carve a discernible scar against the open countryside. This was one such place, a backwater, not far short of twenty miles from the brine pans and harbours of the coast. This was farming country, peasant country, and, Amberley suspected with a new chill; pagan country. England's deep, unenlightened underbelly, where illiterate folk prayed to demons and sought wisdom from witches and warlocks. He shuddered. By Christ it was a terrifying place. The mist made it infinitely worse.

The forest crackled. Amberley twisted back, peering along the narrow road that snaked into the distance, its breadth a mess of hazardous ruts, gnarled roots and water-filled boot prints. Further back they had noted a small, decrepit cottage. It had appeared to be empty, and he was sorely tempted to scurry back to its dank rooms to wait till the misty blanket had lifted. Yet he knew a detachment of dragoons awaited his unit at Buriton church, and he was so close now that it hardly seemed right to delay.

Above and to the sides, bare, silvered branches protruded through the miasma like huge talons, preparing to drag unwary pilgrims into the murky abyss. Black crows flared suddenly from shrouded perches. Men flinched at the maddened caws. Amberley felt a powerful urge to sketch a cross over his chest, but knew his Puritan-minded charges would lose what little respect they held for him. He prayed silently instead.

And then the music started.

*

There was no breeze, so the chimes needed a helping hand. They were on a bough close to Eustace Grumm, and he snaked his fingers through the hollow shafts of wood, tickling them with a tender caress, letting each swing back and brush the next by sheer momentum. The song was at once gentle and haunting, and exactly what Samson Lyle had asked for. He crouched low and moved through the rotten brown bracken fronds to the edge of the road. He could not yet see the wagon or its guards, but he could hear them clearly now, the voices of the men shredded in their disquiet. The chimes played on and he flashed a smile at Grumm. He stepped onto the road. "Shall we?"

*

Lieutenant Amberley felt a patch of moisture bloom in his breeches. He stepped back, levelling the partisan at the empty road and drawing the pistol with his free hand. He pointed the firearm into the mist, but became aware of his trembling hand and lowered it quickly. The musketeers trudged past the wagon to come up behind him, following his gaze to scrutinise the obscured near-distance.

The imp appeared at that moment. It came from the mist, bolting across the road, from right to left, not twenty paces in front of Amberley. He could have sworn his heart ceased beating in that instant. He backed away by instinct, mouth painfully dry. He knew of witchcraft, had been warned of it from a thousand pulpits, and was acutely aware of its insidious but very real threat. He had once even seen an ancient harridan hanged for souring a neighbour's milk by way of dark power. But this was the first time he had encountered evil in its rawest form, wickedness in its own realm. The terror was palpable.

It was only when he wandered into the first of his musketeers that Amberley managed to take hold of his fear. The firelocks muttered and whimpered behind, like so many pups scolded by a snarling bitch, and they began to shuffle away, too frightened to proceed, too tense to hightail it into the woods. He was ashamed of the very sight of them.

"Hold!" Amberley ordered. "Keep still! Make ready your weapons!"

One of the firelocks, thick brows furrowed tight beneath the peak of his Montero cap, shook his head rapidly. "What use'll they be, sir? Leaden bullets against witchery?"

"Enough, man!" Amberley hissed. He put the pistol away and took the partisan in both hands, jabbing it towards the shoaling group. "Do as you are told or find yourselves on a charge!"

"Christ," the musketeers' spokesman whimpered, eyes drifting beyond the lieutenant's shoulder. "Jesus protect us."

Amberley wrenched himself round. There, in the road, was the imp. It was small, hooded and dark, a living silhouette risen from the forest murk. It stood stock still, tiny claws clasped out in front, and laughed in a tone that was pitched querulously high. Then the white talons parted and objects fell to earth, scattering in the mud. The visage sunk away as quickly as it had appeared, vanishing into the mist from whence it was born. One of the firelocks was praying at Amberley's back as he summoned the courage to advance a pace, squinting to inspect the macabre seeds that had been sown by the creature.

He saw dolls; tiny figurines, carved from some kind of dried root and clothed in paint. There were four of them, laying pell-mell in the mud, staring sightlessly back at him with beady black specks. He stooped to pick one up, turning to show it to his men.

"King Jesus!" the heavy-browed musketeer began to babble. "King Jesus help us!"

The soldiers were all praying now, and some even crossed themselves. They stumbled backwards, colliding with one another, and with the horses harnessed to the vehicle. One of the horses tried to rear, flailing legs only missing skulls by fractions. Amberley looked down at the doll as the realisation dawned. It was a poppet, a thing of magic, the tool of the witch. He dropped it as though it burnt a hole in his glove, and reeled away, staggering back to his men, some of whom were edging beyond the wagon in thought of desertion.

Fear was giving way to flight. Better the noose of a mutineer than the unknown fate of a man taken by the devil himself. Gilbert Amberley knew he should berate them, for his duty was paramount, and yet he could see the horror in their eyes, hear it from their lips, and shared it in his own tightening breast. He was only snatched from the mind-swirling reverie by the click of the pistol pressed above his ear.

*

"Ground your arms!" Samson Lyle bellowed. He was among the musketeers, so that a small voice might otherwise have sufficed, but cacophony naturally exacerbated terror. "Ground them, I say, or this man shall die!"

"Who the...?" one of the soldiers managed to blurt.

"My name is Major Lyle."

"The Ironside Highwayman!" another of the stunned guards exclaimed. They exchanged flickering glances, seemed collectively stricken with guilt, and already the weapons began to shift.

"Put 'em down, gentlemen," Lyle warned. He kept the double muzzles firmly poised against his captive's skull, pressing hard enough to extract a wince, while with the other hand he took the man by a slender elbow, guiding him backwards and out of the soldiers' reach. "Advise your fellows to ground their arms, sirrah, lest you would ruin this nice coat with a smattering of brains."

The man was clothed in a suit of grey. The feathers in his hat were the colour of saffron, worn to compliment the scarf that crossed his torso from shoulder to hip. It was Goffe's scarf, the major-general's device, and Lyle knew that Celia Hart had proven as veracious as she was voracious.

"The ghoul?" the officer managed to hiss, his body tense but not struggling.

"An associate of mine, of course."

The officer's shoulders seemed to sag. "You have fooled me."

"So it would seem." Lyle shook the officer gently. "Well?"

There was a moment's hesitation, during which Lyle prayed his bluff would not be called, and then the man drew a sharp breath. "Lower your muskets, men," he ordered. "Ground them."

Lyle watched as the soldiers, albeit grudgingly, did as they were told. He glanced at the razor-tipped partisan. "And drop the twig, there's a good fellow."

The man did so through muttered derision. "*Major* Lyle," he said scornfully. "You hold no commission."

"And you are?"

"Lieutenant Amberley. Langstone garrison." The man's neck wrenched about so that he could glimpse his enemy. "You are a vile traitor, sirrah."

"And you, sirrah, are a terrible bore. I have heard the cry of treason more times than I care count."

"Are you not ashamed, sir? A man of your birth?"

"If shame is what a man must feel for choosing peace over war, then I embrace the sensation gladly."

"You are an outlaw."

"In the eyes of General Goffe and Colonel Maddocks," Lyle said.

"They *are* the law," Amberley retorted caustically.

"But ask the common man," Lyle went on, ignoring the assertion. "See what he has to say on the matter."

Now Amberley struggled, bucking against Lyle's grip with startling ferocity, but Lyle held him firm, jabbing again with the pistol's cold muzzle. All the while he kept the younger man's body between his own and the disarmed but twitchy musketeers. Eventually Amberley's fury ebbed, like a broken colt, and he became still, resigned to his fate. Lyle nodded, then, without looking round, roared, "Bella! Eustace! I'd welcome your company, if you please!"

Bella appeared first, coming out of the mist to the south. Her face was masked with a wide kerchief below the eyes, and she led a large, roan mare by its head collar. Harnessed in its wake was a shallow cart set on a high chassis and huge wheels. It was packed to the full with hogsheads. Water slopped from each of the open casks. Lyle had known that the salt wagon would not be easy to turn or pass, so he had stationed Bella at the tumbledown shack that haunted the road further back, a position from which she could access the convoy's rear, and now she coaxed the doughty beast and its trundling burden all the way up to the lower-slung vehicle.

From the north came Eustace Grumm, grey cloth smothering his white beard. He coaxed two larger horses by reins looped tight about his sharp knuckles. One was a black gelding; his own mount, *Tyrannous*. The other was an imposing grey stallion, its face marked out by a brilliant white diamond that seemed to glow despite the murk. It was a handsome creature, imperious in its height and musculature, and yet Lyle's eyes could not help but dwell upon the large patch of mottled pink skin that ruined one of its long flanks. *Star* had been wounded by an exploding cannon during the wars. The stallion was his oldest companion, and he still felt a pang of culpability for the injury.

Lyle nodded to the old man and stole a glance back at Bella. "At your leisure, Mistress."

The mask shifted above the girl's wrinkled nose as she evidently grinned, freckles dancing along the line of cloth, and she went to work, first cutting the ponies loose from their harnesses, and then leaping up onto her high cart like a squirrel dancing a lofty bough. The water had been an easy thing to source, for they had simply shovelled snow into the barrels and let it melt. Now they had a cartload of the deadliest weapon imaginable to a convoy out of Hayling Island's famous pans, and it took the girl a matter of seconds to unhitch the side of the vehicle adjacent to the piled sacks. She took a few seconds to haul away the oiled coverings. Then she kicked. The first hogshead crashed over the side, toppling into the salt wagon. Its upper surface had been cut away, so that its contents gushed manically over raggedly splintered wood and onto the budging bags, darkening the cloth and saturating everything within.

The driver of the cart, a sickly looking fellow with meaty jowls and rivet-head eyes, remained frozen to his seat. He gave a disconsolate whimper, and shrank down, head and arms thrust between his knees as if he were attempting to burrow his way to safety.

Bella laughed through the kerchief. She placed her boot heel against the next cask, shoving hard, and it toppled too. Again and again she kicked, and even the vessels packed deeper within the cart emptied their bowels as they fell, the torrent coursing over the nailed slats and pouring over the side, a waterfall that drenched and dissolved General Goffe's precious salt.

It was over in a matter of seconds; the sacks a sagging mound, the salt utterly ruined.

Samson Lyle released Amberley and stepped away. As he moved, he drew his sword with his free hand, using the point to prod gently at the lieutenant, ushering the crestfallen officer back towards his men. Amberley turned, glanced at the blade, and temptation flared in his brown eyes.

Lyle knew the look well enough. He shook his head. "You have heard of Charles Besnard?"

Amberley eyed him warily. "The fencing master?"

"My tutor, Lieutenant."

Amberley stared again at the sword, though this time it was as if the weapon had become a hissing viper in the highwayman's grip. His neck convulsed as he swallowed thickly. "I do not fear your bragging, sirrah. I can fight."

"Then you have my respect," Lyle said, flashing a grin. "Perhaps one day we shall sing the song of swords. But not today. My work here is complete, and I've little wish to see virgin snow tainted red."

*

It was the driver who changed things. Grumm had brought up the horses for their escape, Lyle had returned Amberley, but still held his pistol level with the cluster of soldiers so that they remained appropriately meek. The driver — a cowering, quivering wreck — had been duly ignored.

His terrified mewing might have been real or fake, it was impossible to tell, but now that he stood tall on the back of the salt wagon, a long, thin dirk poised in one hand and a thrashing, cursing girl dangling from the other, it all seemed academic.

Grumm pulled his pistol, the soldiers gasped, Amberley brandished a tight grin of triumph, and Samson Lyle swore.

"Cut her, m'lord?" the driver called, his voice tremulous, as though the magnitude of his action was only this moment dawning. "Cut her?"

The lieutenant balked. "What? Good God man, no." Then, stifling the natural slant to chivalry, he skewered Lyle with a narrow stare. "That is to say, not unless Major Lyle prefers stupidity above sense."

Time was as frozen as the forest. The musketeers gathered up their firearms, checking locks to ensure the flints had not worked loose. Grumm and Lyle were still armed, but now they were hopelessly outgunned. The driver waited, his dirk partly concealed beneath the scarf that hung across Bella's chin.

Lyle eyed Amberley warily, gauging the younger man's temper and courage. "The salt is gone, Lieutenant. What have you to gain?"

"Everything."

"Oh?"

"An exchange. The girl," Amberley said, jabbing a finger towards Lyle, "for the Ironside Highwayman." He stooped briefly to retrieve the partisan. "My reputation dies with the salt. It is rekindled with you."

"Me for the girl?"

Amberley nodded. "Aye."

Eustace Grumm inched forward. "Nay."

"Aye," Lyle said.

Grumm's pale eyes widened above the edge of his mask. "Major!"

Amberley nodded, his face taut with triumph. He glanced back to the driver. "You, sirrah. Bring the whelp."

"Very good, m'lord." The driver removed the blade just enough to avoid stabbing Bella as he coerced her from the wagon. She knew better than to resist, but the terrified look she threw Lyle was enough to twist his guts.

Snowflakes — like huge white feathers — began to tumble from a sky that was uniform grey. They settled on hats and coats, in the road ruts and on ancient branches. Lieutenant Amberley waved them from his face as he paced carefully backwards, distancing himself from Lyle but never breaking the gaze. He returned to his men, who grumbled for vengeance, and muttered soothing words as though they were a pack of unruly hounds. The driver, hauling the girl by the collar as though she were a stray cat, joined them too, and the group began to move southward along the road.

The outlaws pursued at a distance. "What are you about, Lieutenant?" Lyle called. "You wish an exchange; well let us exchange!"

Amberley turned. "You have three pistol balls aimed at our backs, and your very name cries treachery!" He shook his head. "No, sir! I am duped once, but never twice!" He stretched out the partisan, so that its glittering blade pointed to the bend in the road. "To the cottage, Master Lyle!" he shouted. "I will treat with you there, in good faith!"

*

Gravel Bottom Cottage — though it barely deserved the name — had once, Lyle supposed, been a most welcome sight on the tree-choked and lonely saddle between the rising crests of Butser Hill and Wardown. A marker on the passage through the dangerous belt of high chalk downland that spanned the waists of Hampshire and Sussex. It was still a marker, of course. A place to be expected, to be noted in one's mind as the miles meandered, but no longer was it a haven. It had been habitable once, at least a generation ago, but now it was a mouldering hovel of crumbling daub and rotten, fractured beams. Its windows were black holes, shutters long since plundered by man or torn by gale, and its thatch blown to the depths of the forest. Through its roof grew the boughs of an adjacent oak, its bare limbs threading the rafters to form a gnarled latticework, as though God Himself could not abide the cottage's nakedness. The building — erected by man and absorbed by nature — sat back from the road, a silent sentinel, glowering at travellers foolhardy enough to brave the elements and tempt the criminals.

Two such criminals pushed their wagon through the snow, inching it into the roadside some seventy paces to the north of the building. They had released the roan mare, *Newt*, so that they might use the vehicle as a shield against attack, and now, as the daylight began its slow ebb, they were distant enough to be out of realistic range of Amberley's muskets. Lyle would take no chances, and thus, to the tune of the Cornishman's incessant grumbling, had set their own animals back in the protective embrace of a gargantuan elm and pushed the vehicle by manpower alone for the final yards.

"When we complete our trade," Lyle said, crouching behind one of the wagon's big wheels, "you must take yourselves far away from here."

"She is lost to us," Grumm, beside him, hissed bitterly. "We must put her from our minds."

Lyle chuckled softly. "You do not mean that."

Grumm sighed. "No, I do not." He thumped his own thigh. "God damn her recklessness. A girl should not partake in such work."

"You would hardly have been able to scamper across those barrels, Eustace," Lyle chided gently.

"I'd have managed," Grumm retorted hotly. The snow was falling in thick sheets, muffling his voice as it had their footsteps. "And without prancing about that cart like a bliddy June chough. She has put herself in the dung, an' no mistake. Brazen, snot-nosed little dell."

"Brazen she is," Lyle agreed. An image of the girl when first he had encountered her fluttered through his mind. She had been six or seven years old. Embarking on a whore's life to survive, beaten onto that path by an avaricious man with a black heart and a gnarled cane. Lyle had cracked that infamous cane across its owner's skull and plucked little Dorothy Forks from the only life she knew, and she had not left his side since. He had gained the most loyal friend, and she had bestowed upon herself a new name and a new career. He could not help but smile. "And brave."

"What good is bravery when they have seen her face?" Grumm replied. "We are lost."

"Not so," Lyle said, keeping his eyes on the cottage.

"Not so? This..." Grumm waved an emaciated hand as he tried to conjure the right word, "this... myth we have created. The Ironside Highwayman, wronged by his former masters, hell-bent on revenge for a lost life, attacking the machinery of State from his brigand's paradise. It thrives purely on our guises; mine and Bella's. You only exist because you may hide in the Red Lion, secure in the knowledge that we who play characters of taverner and serving wench are never seen at our shadow work." He flicked at the dirty folds of the scarf about his throat. "Our faces remain concealed so that we may continue our pretence of uncle and niece, landlord and ward. Now it is gone. The veil quite literally torn away."

"The convoy guards have seen her," Lyle conceded. "But Amberley and his party are not local men."

"They are Goffe's men."

"Goffe controls three counties in Cromwell's name. He has many men. Our pretence is not lost, and nor is the Red Lion."

Grumm looked poised to argue further, but evidently thought better of it, for instead he leaned closer to the wheel, pressing his bearded face up against the spokes. "Why hide?" he asked. All around them the snow was filling the undulations of a thaw-churned earth and settling in glistening beauty upon every naked branch. "The two of us against the eight of them? Nine, if you count that bastard carter. They would shred us like rags on a harrow."

"At what cost?" replied Lyle. He could see movement within the cottage, wraiths sliding within the sepulchral heart, but nothing discernible. And no sign of the girl. "If Amberley gets himself shot then how will he collect his prize? Besides, he fears the snow."

"He can discard his wagon now," Grumm scoffed.

"Aye, thanks to Bella. But the snow lies deep. The journey to Buriton would take time on foot, tempting an ambush."

"Then what will he do? Sit there all winter?"

"Will you come to me, Major Lyle?" a voice called suddenly, cutting across Lyle's intended reply. "The girl will not be harmed!"

Lyle exchanged a glance with Grumm, then squinted through the spokes to ascertain the speaker's position. "And then what, Lieutenant? You have rope enough to hang me?"

"No, sir!" was Amberley's bellowed response. "To Petersfield with you, for just and fair trial!"

"You cower in your crumbling castle from just two men, yet you would bravely drag me all the way to Petersfield? You will still feel lead in your back, sirrah, I guarantee you that!" At his flank, Eustace Grumm muttered grisly agreement.

"You dissemble, sir!" Amberley called. "Let us get this business done with! Come hither and we will exchange one brigand for another!"

Grumm placed a hand on Lyle's elbow. "He plans to take you captive but not string you up? He will not risk the journey to Petersfield, you said so yourself. He lies, Major. He can hardly sit there, in that dank shack, and await spring! No, he plans to lure you in, then stretch your neck."

Lyle considered the assertion, but somehow it did not ring true. He shook his head. "To claim my quiet death will not be nearly so rewarding as to haul me before a magistrate in chains. Amberley would see his star rise, and for that he needs pomp, he needs circumstance, and he needs a warm body; *my* body, to dangle where all might see. The good folk of Petersfield must witness the piss drip from my boots and all will know who to laud."

"Then?"

"Then he knows something we do not." Lyle stared at the old cottage. Nothing appeared to stir therein. The snow kept coming, blurring the view. "They expect him at Buriton," he said eventually. "He knows Maddocks will come searching."

"Or p'raps he is already there?" Grumm ventured. "We've gambled the convoy would be reinforced at Petersfield. What if we got it wrong? What if the Mad Ox is closer than we thought?"

Lyle looked at the Cornishman, a dread pang settling in his guts as he met the blue eyes. "You are right. He does not await the thaw, Eustace. He awaits rescue."

6

Bella watched the lieutenant closely. He was nervous, for his left eye trembled gently at one corner. "How old are you?"

Amberley looked back at her from his position to the side of the window. "Nineteen," he replied brusquely. "What matter is it?"

"None," she shrugged. "The Major is just seven years your senior."

"And?"

"He has seen a great many battles."

The muscles of Amberley's lean face tightened, but he chose to stifle whatever retort had come to mind. Instead he turned away, staring out into the afternoon murk. "The coward lost his nerve. He scuttled into the trees like a frightened fawn."

Bella was seated on the floor at the rear of the room, legs drawn up to her chest. She propped her chin between her kneecaps. "He will come for me."

Amberley nodded. "You had better pray that he does." He was clutching his partisan, which he levelled at Bella. "And you will go in his stead."

"You are mistaken. There will be none left behind but you and your men."

The musketeers — poised with weapons at the edges of the ancient home — did not bother to stifle their amusement. Amberley smiled too. "The mistake is yours, little mistress."

Bella looked around the room. "Why do you hide from him? You have so many weapons."

"I am not a monster, girl. The exchange must take place, be it bloodless or no, but I would rather the latter. No one ought die in this godforsaken wood."

"But one must die in Petersfield marketplace, the life choked out of him as the townsmen gape and giggle?"

"Lyle is a criminal."

"He is a good man. His only crime was to refuse Ireton's bidding."

"You know nothing," Amberley said bitterly.

"The Major was a hero," she persisted. She took the scarf, still knotted at the nape of her neck, and lifted the folds to wipe snowflakes away from her face. "A true Roundhead. An Ironside. He fought at Naseby, at Preston and Dunbar and Worcester."

Amberley looked as though he would argue, but instead he twisted his thin mouth, a thought apparently sparking in his mind. Eventually he asked, "Is it true what they say of his horse? That it will no longer suffer a fight?"

"You disgust me, sir," Bella retorted angrily. "Fascinated by the very legend you strive to destroy."

Amberley looked genuinely affronted; hurt, even. He lowered the pole-arm and stepped closer, boots smearing black tracks through the thin dusting of snow that had come through the jagged roof. "I was merely..."

"The poor beast," Bella interrupted softly, "was grievous wounded at Worcester Fight, where the tyrant king's son finally tasted defeat. The animal cannot abide gunfire."

Amberley was clearly startled by his captive's sudden softening, but chose not to press the issue. "Then why does Lyle abide the horse?"

"As I said, he is a good man," Bella replied. In truth, she had seen a boy. In Amberley's crestfallen expression, in his hurt at her rebuff. In that moment she knew he was no match for Lyle. "A kind man." She felt her expression tighten a touch as she considered those who would dance a jig upon Lyle's grave, given half a chance. "What do they say about him? Out there, in the world."

Amberley shrugged. "That Ireland turned him into a craven rogue. That he shrank from blood. That he deserted his post."

"They did slaughter in Ireland, sir," she said. "He was a soldier, not a butcher. He refused the orders and was hounded out of the New Modelled Army for his conscience. Do the poisoned tongues wag of his goodwife? How she was killed by Ireton's riders?"

"There was no proof of malice in that."

"Is that what they say?"

Amberley's shoulders tensed and he spun away, growling, "He is outside the law, girl, and that is all that matters." He reached the window and glanced back, eyes dark in the shadow of his hat. "He will give himself up and I will free you. And if he tarries any longer, we will simply take him without an exchange."

Bella laughed, shaking her head with a deliberate look of sympathy. "You will struggle from in here."

Now it was Amberley's turn to seem amused. "It is not I who will capture him, little mistress. I will simply wait." His thin mouth spread in a slow smile as he let the implication settle. "Oh, I would see the barter done, by my word. If the brigand will give himself up, then you will be released, and I will assuage the shame of losing the salt. But there is a company of dragooners awaiting us at Buriton."

"Buriton?" she echoed softly, her stomach twisting with the word.

"You supposed we would be alone until Petersfield?" He tutted, like a schoolmaster admonishing an errant student. "Sadly not. They will soon be here, searching for us. Lyle should ride away while he still can. But, of course, we both know he will not."

7

Buriton, Hampshire, December 1655

Dusk turned the village slate-grey. On its main road, a horseman in polished plate and oiled leather drew his steed to a stop twenty yards ahead of the rest of his mounted company. He patted the animal's vapour-wreathed neck with a gauntleted hand and removed his helm. Long hair — sweat-matted and black — tumbled like a silver-flecked fountain about his shoulders, and his grey eyes speared the nervous man who had scuttled to his bridle. "Where is my salt?"

The villager flinched at the stentorian tone. "M'lord?"

Colonel Francis Maddocks sucked impatiently at his front teeth. "Salt. There is a convoy out of Hayling Island. A large consignment bound for the garrison at Winchester."

"Ain't seen it, m'lord."

"It was due to arrive here some hours ago."

The man eyed the huge horse anxiously, as if the beast would twist back to bite him at any second. "Roads are spoilt, m'lord."

Maddocks wrenched the horse away abruptly, sending the villager skittering back to the road's edge. He fished in his saddlebag as an officer wearing the same saffron-coloured scarf cantered out from the troop. "Cardamom."

The officer frowned. "Sir?"

Maddocks held out a flattened palm, in which nestled a pale green pod. "From the East Indies. Praise God for peace with the Dutch, eh?"

"Praise God, sir, aye," the officer answered dubiously. "You... cook them?"

"Break the pods, thusly," Maddocks said, splitting open the thin, papery outer shell with thumb and forefinger, and tipping the contents onto his tongue, "and chew the seeds."

"To what end, sir?"

"A man's breath is revived, Captain," Maddocks said as he chewed, the intense flavour filling his mouth and cascading to the back of his throat so that water pricked at his eyes. "And other things. You are a widower, correct?"

"My wife fell to an ague last spring."

"Then you must partake. They say many a bonny maiden has found herself drawn to its aroma."

"I'd rather trust in the Lord, sir," the captain balked piously, glancing by instinct up at the jagged outline of the church that dominated the village centre, dark behind the tumbling snowfall. "He will provide."

"Perhaps it is the lord's work that cardamom finds its way to Petersfield," Maddocks countered archly. "But the fact remains that such commodities are the life's blood of a nation. Trade and commerce are how this great Commonwealth will thrive. Now let us consider another commodity due to grace our fair town."

"The salt should be here, Colonel. That was the agreed schedule." The captain pursed his lips as he considered the conspicuous absence. "But what with the snow..."

"Snow?" Maddocks cut in. "Or enemies of the state?"

The captain frowned behind the bars of his helmet. "We took substantial precaution, sir."

"And what, pray, constitutes substantial?"

"A squad of firelocks, sir. Eight, including the officer. He would not..."

"No?" Maddocks paused to pick a speck of cardamom seed from between his front teeth. "Need I remind you of the tavern up at Priors Dean? How many men did the fiend deceive? Thirty? More? That is why we freeze to the marrow in this wretched little backwater. Why I am compelled to deal *personally* with this business. General Goffe is none too pleased with the loss of the Midhurst garrison pay. I cannot risk another failure."

"He would not hit the salt convoy. It is small beer by comparison."

"It is just this unpredictability that makes him dangerous, Captain." Maddocks thrust his own helmet atop his head, tucking back the hair and fastening the strap tightly. "He would rob a coach as soon as loot a castle."

The captain blew out his cheeks. "Major Lyle is an enigma, that is for certain."

"Never afford him the courtesy of rank in my presence," Maddocks snarled, the sudden ferocity making his subordinate's horse skitter sideways across the filthy road. "I knew him before his fall from grace. He is never to be underestimated. Not ever."

"I apologise, sir," the captain blurted as he desperately tried to bring his animal under control.

Maddocks waved the man away, taking up his own reins and signalling to the waiting dragoons with a barked order. "Perhaps the snow has delayed Lieutenant Amberley," he muttered to himself, "and perhaps not." He looked at the captain. "Let us ride south and discover the truth of it."

8

Gravel Bottom, Hampshire, December 1655

Night was drawing in quickly, making the fat flakes glow as they wafted from the pregnant clouds. The trees at either side of the road had all but vanished, swallowed by the encroaching realm of darkness.

Samson Lyle could barely discern Gravel Bottom Cottage as he made his approach. He had elected to remain armed in the circumstances, jamming plenty of wadding into both of his belted pistol's barrels so that the bullets would not fall out. He rested his left hand on the hilt of his sword, the other on his heavy war-hammer. His pulse raced, rushing in his ears.

"Are you ready, Amberley?" he called as he halted sixty paces from the shack. No lights flickered within, reminding him that the soldiers bore flintlock muskets. They were unlikely, he hoped, to be concealed within the depths of the forest, for he had watched the old shack intently during the fading light, but still he found himself wishing Amberley's men possessed the old-style muskets where permanently lit match-cords would mark each man out at nightfall.

"Approach!" Amberley's disembodied voice came in reply.

Lyle's throat burned with a jet of bile. At this range the musketeers would do well to pinpoint him, especially in the dark, but he had seen plenty of lucky shots in his time. He swallowed hard, bit down on the urge to turn tail, and stepped forth. "I am here, do you see?"

"You took your time, sir!"

"A doomed man has matters to put in order! I am here now! Send her out, and I will come freely!"

"You think me a fool?" Amberley shouted. "First come to the cottage, Lyle, and I will release her!"

Lyle went closer by ten crunching strides. He could smell smoke now. "I was at Basing House, you know."

Amberley finally showed his face as he moved to stand beneath the lintel of the open doorway. He held his partisan, leaning casually against its shaft, and spat at the ground. "That bastion of popery is long crumbled, Praise God."

"I was there when the flames took hold," Lyle said, just managing to discern the black muzzles of half a dozen muskets emerge from the windows. If Amberley wanted it, he would be eviscerated in moments. "An accident, though the malignants do not believe it. We eventually took the place by storm."

"Common knowledge."

"But before that, Colonel Dalbier made an ingenious attempt to draw them out."

"Blather, sir. This is not a coffee club."

Lyle ignored him. "He had bales of wet straw lit, so that the smoke slewed across the battlements. And the straw was laced with arsenic and brimstone, so that the nature of the fog was most noxious."

Amberley hissed an exasperated oath. He opened his mouth to speak, but held the breath, and Lyle knew that the scent of smoke had reached him too. The young officer hesitated, utterly thrown. He peered out from the cottage, craning his neck to search the abyss for the tell-tale flicker of flame. What he saw was thick smog, swirling at head height from the forest's wild heart. It was yellow against the snow, cloaking against the night, and it rolled with the slight breeze from infernos unseen to swirl about the tumbledown building with curling, probing fingers.

Lyle thanked God for the breeze and Eustace Grumm for the fire. He breathed in the aroma, revelling in the rich smoke that he knew carried no poison. But Amberley did not know, and Lyle was laughing as panicked voices rattled in the night. "Arsenic and brimstone, Lieutenant!" he shouted, retreating a short distance, lest fear made them eager on the trigger. "A bitter brew indeed!"

Amberley was at the gaping doorway again. "You cannot mean it, Lyle! You will poison your little punk as you poison us! No, sir, it is bluff and bluster!"

"Is that so?"

"You'll not scare me so easily, blackguard!"

"Your choice!" Lyle called, the smoke beginning to screen him. "Either way, Lieutenant, you and your men cannot huddle in your nest like so many ants!" He was on the move now, keeping low, running close to the haloed shack and cupping his hands to his mouth to bellow, "The men of experiment are like the ant, are they not? They only collect and use! Bella! Do you hear me? They only collect and use?"

*

Bella Sparks, still crouching at gunpoint in the rearmost recess of the building, drew her heavy hood up and over her scalp. "Gathers its materials from the flowers of the garden," she said, "and of the field, but transforms and digests it by a power of its own."

Lieutenant Amberley was pacing like a caged animal, unsure of what to do. He paused, glowering. "Have you a fever, girl?"

She gathered up the folds of her scarf and lifted it across her face. "It is da Vinci."

"Vinci?"

"Leonardo da Vinci," she said calmly, voice muffled by the cloth. "Said the men of experiment were like ants. But bees? Well, it seems he liked 'em a lot, did old Leo. So does the Major."

Amberley stalked across the room, skewering her with his eyes. "Speak plainly, girl, or so help me God, I will..."

"The smoke, Lieutenant." She rose to her feet. The poised muskets twitched, their owners looking to Amberley for instruction. She pulled her sleeves down over her hands, so that the only patch of skin now exposed was the narrow slash surrounding her eyes. "It is not so much bluff, as distraction."

"Distraction?" Amberley hissed.

"Buzz buzz, Lieutenant." For the first time she looked up at the open roof, its splintered maw filled with oak branches. "Now, Eustace! Now!"

9

Eustace Grumm was not a brawny man, but he had spent decades smuggling contraband goods from Clovelly into the Cornish mainland, and that had lent him something of a knack for handling unwieldy loads. Lyle's suggestion had brought his dissent, naturally, on the grounds that the objects he had once hauled into caves and up cliff faces had been sacks and bushels, rather than domed sculptures covered in dried dung and filled with bees, but the plan, in the execution, had not proven as difficult as he had imagined. Now, as he lay flat like some gigantic lizard across one of the oak branches that formed the snow-dusted ceiling of Gravel Bottom Cottage, he used a large knife to cut through the ropes which harnessed a hogshead against his spine.

Grumm had taken Bella's cart, emptying it of all but a single barrel and hitched his black gelding, *Tyrannous*, out front. He had gathered up the robust sheet that had once protected the army salt shipment, and plunged through the snow and the tangled undergrowth, climbing the hangers until he had located the regular lines of mossy stone that marked out the ancient fort which had been their rendezvous some days before. He found the skeps in situ, resting on their timber perch beneath the shelter of the exposed root ball, and, after selecting the largest, he had torched wet hay to smoke the bees to docility. Then he had blocked their entrance hole with rags and carefully lifted the dome of woven straw from its wooden base. It was heavier than he had imagined, though he supposed much of the weight was due to the cowcloome caked on its outer surface. The concoction of manure and clay protected the straw hive against the elements, and had dried hard as rock, and it took a great deal of effort to lift the thing while keeping his movements smooth so as not to rouse and enrage the creatures within. Then he lowered the skep into the waiting hogshead, jammed the thick oiled sheet over it so as to smother any escape, and loaded the vessel onto the cart. As dusk had arrived at Gravel Bottom, so had Eustace Grumm.

The barrel hitch, expertly fastened by a master in the dark arts of smuggling, was quickly released, and, with a shrug of his shoulders, the hogshead toppled. It plummeted into the very centre of the room, staves smashing apart, leaping out of the iron hoops as the barrel splintered. The soldiers reeled instinctively away, but swung their weapons round to fire upon this unexpected intruder, their shots ringing like mortars in the confined space. The sulphurous stink of powder-smoke filled the cottage, rising in a thick pall, and for a moment Grumm could not see a thing. With pounding chest he called Bella's name, and was relieved to hear her muffled reply.

He waited, braced himself. There was nothing but eerie silence. He swore viciously, knowing all had gone awry. Voices began to break the calm, orders given and received in the gloom below, men making sense of what had happened as their collective vision began to return. Smoke still roiled manically, and Grumm prayed the acrid smog had not dampened the bees' ire. But then he heard it. Faint at first, but persistent for all that. A hum, low and constant, like waves on a shore. Then he realised that it was not like a tide at all. It was like a thousand bees emerging into a confined chamber.

The voices were growing louder now, but they were also becoming shrill with rising panic. The skep had broken. The bees, finally, had come.

Grumm disentangled himself from the rope and slung it over the broad bough, fastening a fool-proof knot as he shouted for Bella to make her move. The soldiers were beginning to shriek as the noise of the bees overwhelmed all. They were evidently as angry as Lyle had predicted, and woe betide the enemy they would first encounter.

The rope jerked taut, creaked loudly, and there, out of the thinning mist, was Bella Sparks, only her eyes exposed to the risk of stings. Below her was a world of chaos, of men flapping wildly at swirling black smudges that cascaded about their heads. They pushed and shoved their way out of the building, braying like whipped cattle and shedding garments every few paces.

Grumm held out his hand. Bella gripped him hard, let him take some of her weight, and together they dragged her up onto the sturdy branch. They let the rope fall away, and slithered back towards the trunk without a word.

*

Samson Lyle waited for Lieutenant Amberley at the front of the cottage. He did not wait long.

The soldiers came first, scrambling out into the snow to flap wildly at the angry bees swarming about their heads. They cared nothing for him. Barely even noticed his presence in their desperation to flee.

But Amberley froze. He had tumbled out over the cracked threshold, flailing like a madman, hat and partisan long discarded in the melee, and then he had looked up into Lyle's green gaze, and the bees had suddenly meant nothing. "You," the lieutenant managed to say, his throat constricted by simple fury, "have caused me such woe, villain." In a flash his sword was free of its scabbard.

"You insult me yet again, sirrah," Lyle said. "Do you never learn?" He glanced pointedly over both shoulders. "Seems as though you are abandoned."

Amberley swallowed thickly, raising the blade. "I will run you through."

A distant rumble rolled from somewhere to the north. Lyle did not risk a look behind, keeping his eyes firmly on Amberley's, but he knew the provenance by instinct. "Be brief, sirrah, for I must depart."

"Major!" the voice of Eustace Grumm, shrill with alarm, rent the snow-stifled air. "Horses!"

The approach of heavy horses bearing heavily armed men was a sound ingrained upon Lyle's heart and mind. He dragged his own blade free, lifted it to acknowledge Grumm, who would be waiting with Bella, and then levelled the weapon, beckoning the younger man to test him.

Amberley lurched forwards, raising his blade high, slashing down in a crushing arc that would have cleaved Lyle's skull in half had he not parried. Lyle slid away, aiming low with a jab designed to test his opponent's reflexes. Amberley met it well,

138

turned it away from his thigh, but his breathing was already laboured, and Lyle lunged thrice at his face with vicious slashes that sent the officer staggering rearward out of range.

The noise of hoof-beats was growing louder. Lyle could hear Grumm and Bella calling to him, urging him to leave. Amberley was panting, still holding his sword high in challenge, malevolent stare blazing beyond the curling hilt, framed by brown hair that was now dishevelled and darkly matted with sweat.

Lyle twitched his own sword. "This is a Pappenheimer, named for the German count who made popular its style."

"What of it?" Amberley rasped.

"You are not worthy to face it, Lieutenant," Lyle said levelly, keeping his knees slightly bent, his elbow gently flexed. He turned the hilt so that the watery moonlight glittered over the symmetrical shell guards. "See here? Decorated by a master craftsman. The shapes are hearts and stars."

Amberley reacted as Lyle had hoped, launching himself forth like a crazed bullock. Teeth bared in a snarl, he lashed his sword in ever wilder arcs, murderous in their intent but loose in form. Lyle ducked under one sweep, stepped round another, and parried the last so forcefully that Amberley was knocked clean off his stride. As his boots slid, Lyle stepped close, slicing clean through Amberley's saffron scarf with his rapier's razor point. Amberley tried to retreat further, but could not avoid the solid pommel that crunched into his nose, shattering the slender bone in a gush of steaming blood.

"That is for threatening Bella," Lyle said, letting his enemy recoil, and using the respite to clean the hilt on his coat. "You see the pommel is sculpted into the shape of a mushroom? Beautiful, is it not?" He threw Amberley a half-smile. "Heavy, though."

Amberley spat a thick gobbet of gelatinous blood. "Traitor!" He rolled and squared his shoulders, ignoring the pain that must surely have been lancing through his head, and went forward again.

Lyle parried the oncoming blade easily, laughing with deliberate scorn, and flickered the tip of his rapier at the sides of Amberley's head like a gigantic silvery tongue. Amberley stumbled backwards, his chest heaving, eyes like twin moons, and raised a hand instinctively to check if he still had ears. "Traitor," he said again, though his voice was barely more than a whisper now. "Your bitch died for your perfidy."

"Come," Lyle beckoned, forcefully biting back a sudden flare of anger. "See what Besnard taught me."

"Enough, Major!" Eustace Grumm yelled away to Lyle's right.

This time he glanced at his friends, both mounted, and was gratified to see that Bella had indeed been liberated. Perhaps now was time to make haste.

Amberley almost killed him. In that second of slipped focus, soldier caught highwayman with a despairing lunge. Lyle turned it away, but could not gather himself to riposte before Amberley had closed the distance between them, trying to overwhelm Lyle's defences with blows of unfettered ferocity, his bloodied grimace like a cathedral gargoyle in the encroaching darkness. Lyle danced away, blocking and writhing, but now his own pulse raced and sweat began to prick his forehead. Beyond his opponent the canopy was shifting, and he realised that the horses were almost upon them. He took a strike high, double-handed, letting the blades push against one another, and stepped in, the steel singing as edge slid against edge. Then the hilts clanged like church bells, but Lyle's fingers were entirely protected by his Pappenheimer's broad shell guards. They pushed like wrestlers, braced hilt to hilt, forearms quivering with the strain. Lyle eased off, letting Amberley believe he had the better of the bout, then wrenched his wrists over in a single, savage twisting motion. Amberley's sword was gone in a trice, clattering into the space between them. Horror ghosted across his lean face.

"And this," Lyle said as he kicked out, sinking his boot heel into Amberley's midriff, "is for insulting my goodwife."

The soldier doubled over with a guttural groan and emptied the contents of his stomach onto the snow.

Lyle stood over him, sheathing his sword, just as a column of mounted soldiers in golden yellow scarfs thundered round the bend in the road. "Godspeed, Lieutenant." He glanced at the riders, giving particular attention to the leader. Even in the gloom he could see that there was a black smudge at his shoulder, where the head of a lion was embroidered upon the silk. "I've a feeling you shall need it."

10

Colonel Francis Maddocks knew the Ironside Highwayman the moment he saw him. Lyle's lean, spare physique, his dark cloak, his wide hat with fair hair sprouting beneath the rim, were the stuff of Maddocks' nightmares. He kicked hard, raking his horse's flanks brutally, and jerking one of his twin pistols from its holster. "We have him now, men!" he brayed, standing in the stirrups, and shooting into the darkness. "We have him now!"

He galloped through the plume of smoke, squinting hard, but evidently the pistol ball had flown wide. He yearned for the others to shoot, but knew they could not. As mounted infantry, dragoons carried muskets, and could not discharge them effectively from the saddle. With a roared oath he thrust his weapon home and did not bother with the second, the range too great. Instead he drew his long backsword, straightened his arm and peered along the steel's sleek length, the point hovering over Lyle's chest.

And Samson Lyle ran.

The outlaw spun on his heels, bolting back towards the cottage, and for a moment Maddocks thought he might entrap himself within, the dandy fox finally brought to ground. But then he veered right, away from the road, and Maddocks kicked again, determined the undergrowth would be no hindrance to pursuit. Only then did he see where the fugitive was headed. Three horses waited in the tree line. Two — a black and a roan — bore figures on their backs, both masked. The third carried only an empty saddle. The beast was a big grey, and he knew it instantly. Had ridden at its side in more fights than he could remember. He hated the mere sight of it.

"Cut him off!" Maddocks screamed above the cacophony of his own stallion's hooves. "Cut him off, damn your eyes!"

Already the trio of waiting horses were turning. The mounted pair spurred forwards, passing between two wizened trees to vanish onto an ancient track, leaving the grey in their wake. Lyle reached it, hooking the toe-end of his boot into the stirrup. Maddocks howled in rage, released the reins to steer with his thighs, and freed his second pistol. His dragoons were charging in his wake, but their slung muskets rendered them impotent. Only when they halted could the weapons be brought to bear.

Lyle swung himself up into the saddle with the agility of an acrobat. He was lashing the grey with hands and feet, willing the creature into a gallop.

Maddocks was thirty paces short now. "Shoot!" he screamed left and right. "The mount will take fright!" He knew his was the only firearm worthy of the name in a chase, but perhaps the sounds of the muskets might take a toll upon the cowardly stallion.

Some of his dragoons were firing now, having slewed to a standstill and dismounted. They would be unsighted and next to useless, but the noise was as terrific as he had hoped. He emptied his own pistol at Lyle's back, blinding himself by the flashing pan and gout of smoke. Then he was through it, and immediately he saw that Lyle was crouching low, nuzzling his horse's thick neck as bullets flung past to shred leaves and splinter bark.

The huge grey reared violently. Maddocks crowed up at the snow-swollen clouds. He tossed the pistol away in his urgency, took up the reins again, and ripped the night apart with a war-cry he had not uttered since Ireland. The grey was running again. Somehow Lyle had regained control of the fainthearted creature, but at huge cost. The remaining dragoons had swallowed up the ground between them, so that now there were only a dozen yards left before they could skewer his spine with their butcher blades. Moreover, Lyle seemed lopsided somehow, for he was carrying his head cocked on one side, as though a kink had formed in his collar. "He's hit!" Maddocks shouted. "We have him! On! On! On!"

As the words left his mouth, he knew that victory was secure, for the grey was slowing, lifting its legs in an awkwardly high step, suddenly tentative.

Such was the elation coursing through the colonel's veins, he almost galloped headlong into the barricade.

*

The harrow rose like a drawbridge as Bella and Grumm hauled on the ropes.

It had not been part of the plan, but the shrewd Cornishman had noticed it when collecting the skep, and the notion now implemented had dawned upon him. He had tied ropes to either side, set the spiked frame flat across the track, and left it in situ.

Lyle had worried that *Star* would not make it across. The frame's wooden limbs were treacherous enough for any horse to negotiate, least of all one frightened half to death by gunfire. Yet the redoubtable beast had made it across in the nick of time, and the ropes had twanged taut, the rusty teeth rising to block Maddocks' path.

He had taken a pistol ball in his right shoulder. Flames of agony lapped up and down his neck and spine, but he clung on with grim bloody-mindedness. *Star* wickered softly as if to reassure him, even as liquid snaked, sticky and lambent, down the inside of his shirt sleeve. He twisted back as best he could. It was anarchy on the far side of the harrow, the appearance of which had so terrified the government horses that they were reluctant to even attempt the hazardous undergrowth that choked the flanks of the old bridleway. Thus they were reduced to curses and insults as they threw themselves down from their saddles to prime muskets for an improvised volley.

But it was only moments before the drawbridge ropes were tied off on low branches. Bella and Grumm spurred away, plunging into darkness, but Lyle alone paused. Despite the pain, he bade *Star* perform a tight half-turn, and dipped his head to Maddocks, who was furiously ordering his men to risk the forest's tangled grasp. The dragoons, though, were mounted infantry, and did not have the skill or reckless abandon of full-blooded cavalry troopers.

"A pleasure as always!" Lyle called with an impish grin. "Oh, and Francis? Do be kind to Lieutenant Amberley! Poor fellow has a sore nose, and, I'd wager, a good few stings!"

Colonel Maddocks glowered, his eyes glittering orbs, incandescent with impotent rage. "I will kill you yet, Lyle! You will dangle by your neck, sirrah, and I will drink to your demise! That is my solemn pledge!"

"I expect nothing less, old friend!" Lyle called, kicking gently at *Star*. His shoulder seared white hot, and his eyes watered, but he no longer cared, because a winter swarm had saved Bella. That was all that mattered.

And then the Ironside Highwayman was gone, swallowed by the night.

HIGHWAYMAN: WAR'S END

Michael Arnold

© Michael Arnold 2020

Michael Arnold has asserted his rights under the Copyright, Design and Patents Act, 1988, to be identified as the author of this work.

First published 2020 by Sharpe Books.

MICHAEL ARNOLD

For my niece, Isla

JANUARY 1656

Grange Farm, Petersfield, Hampshire

A vixen's cry shredded the night.

Startled, the thief crouched low against the crumbling cob wall, the rasp of his heaving chest overlaid by the rushing blood at his ears. The surviving three fingers of his right hand were braced against his thigh and he dug the nails hard through the wool of his breeches, relaxing his grip only when the pain had chased away the panic. He swore softly at his own temerity, reminding himself of the growl in his belly and edged eyes and nose above the makeshift parapet.

The pirates were directly to the south, forty paces away or thereabouts. He counted them in silence. Eleven, all present and correct, seated on logs and discarded barrels, knees drawn up before the remnants of a glowing fire. The men were at the centre of an unpaved yard, its craggy terrain of wheel-ruts and boot-prints frozen solid by the bitter winter. Beyond them, looming over the farm's half-dozen outbuildings, was the great barn, its stone walls pale in the moonlight, soaring rooftop gilded by a gossamer of frost. Distant storm clouds swelled and rolled far beyond, surging in from the coast.

Outside the barn, its shafts roped to iron rings set into the building's masonry, was the high-sided wagon the pirates had brought with them. The thief had watched as their weapons and personal effects were stowed within. Absently, he wondered why they did not seek shelter inside the barn.

The pirates laughed and chatted. One of them took a long drag from an earthenware flask and spat into the orange embers, causing a tell-tale hiss and a flare of new flame. A man struck up a slow tune on a flageolet, another of his comrades accompanying him with a mournful voice. The thief waited and watched. He checked over his shoulder, squinting through the darkness to perceive the outline of the town, chimney stacks silhouetted by the moon, thin smoke-trails smearing the stars.

Locating the line of the Portsmouth road, he let his eyes trace its route towards the farm, dipping low before rising again as it passed him, becoming the long, straight causeway that elevated travellers above the treacherous, marshy terrain on their way into the chalky hills. All was empty, all was silent. He pulled on his trusty Montero cap, tugging the sides down to cup his face and slung his snapsack over a shoulder.

To the thief's right, at the west of the yard, a flurry of sound came from a low timber block as the pirates' pair of bulky brown draught horses bickered with their new stablemates in the stalls. One of the men around the fire snarled a command. No-one bothered to investigate but their attention had been collectively engaged and they all squinted towards the stable in the gloom. The thief thanked God for His providence, pressed closer to the wall and prayed hard.

The prayer was answered more swiftly than he could have hoped. Soft whickering grew to a chorus of angry whinnies as the cramped horses jostled for space and fodder, all of it played out above the beat of iron-shod hooves against the stable walls. This time the thief did not wait to see if the men reacted. He was already on the move. He vaulted the wall, ignoring the scrape of loose stones and scuttled, hunched and crablike, into the open. His breath was white in the biting air, haloing his wool-wrapped skull, a beacon for his every movement. He clamped shut his mouth, allowed himself only to pant through his nostrils in sharp, shallow bursts and prayed that he might be spared the watchman's cry.

Gradually the horses became calm but still the pirate sang his melancholy refrain. And the thief went to work.

TUESDAY

Idsworth, Hampshire

St Peter's Church stood alone on a high sweep of chalk downland as the storm vented its fury. Stinging rain beat at the valley in diagonal sheets, dashing the isolated building's flint walls and forming rivulets between the roof tiles that bubbled and gushed as they poured onto the gravel path below. The surrounding hills seemed to quiver as their deeply forested slopes leaned before winds that screamed like a host of banshees, the last vestiges of snow purged ruthlessly from the highest boughs. Above the straining canopy, boisterous rooks banked and twirled beneath bruise-coloured skies. Through it all, a single bell began to peel, its mournful call echoing stubbornly from crest to crest.

On the chalk ridge, the doors of the little church groaned open. Figures swathed in heavy winter coats and cassocks, streamed in pairs from the west porch, some linking arms against the howling gale, all tilting forwards as if wading through treacle. The procession fought its way along a track that cut through a wide field, sloping down towards the main road some two hundred paces below. There they would find the waiting carriages, drawn up in a long line before the gated entrance to a substantial, if a touch dogeared, manor house. Coachmen squinted back up the rise, shielding rain-slick faces with wide hats and waxed sleeves, attempting to locate their masters as swiftly as possible so that they might flee the hostile afternoon. Irritable horses whinnied and snorted. The road's edge, still patched with thawing slush, steamed and turned yellow beneath their raised tails.

From the porch, the elderly man placed a woollen cap upon his snow-white pate and watched the last of the storm-harried congregation fight their way to the roadside, hands clamped tight to their own hats, wasting no time on pleasantries as they clambered into their vehicles. He saw the carriages lurch, heard the whips crack above the whining wind. Drivers barked, their voices deep and resonant below the shrill caws of the obdurate rooks. The old man could not stifle a rueful smile. The great and the good of the parish would walk into the very eye of a hurricane if there were enough witnesses to report it. As dusk crept ever closer, he felt sure word of their attendance on this most inclement day would spread like the sickness that had placed his beloved wife in the very casket around which they had all brandished their piety. Some, he knew, had come here out of genuine grief. Most had come to be seen.

The old man made to turn. It was then that he glimpsed the rider.

The horse was huge and grey, a pale smudge emerging from a stand of bare trees at the northern fringe of the ridge. In the saddle, hunched against the rain, was a figure draped in a cloak of dark green. A man, to judge by a frame that looked tall and lean but broad at the shoulders. Water dripped from the hem of his deep hood and from his long scabbard's pointed chape. They loped, man and beast, across the downland swell, buffeted on both sides by the malicious wind, the horse's fetlocks caked in mud. They were heading for the church.

The old man went inside. The nave echoed with the sound of his own footsteps. He searched the plain benches, the whitewashed walls, the little pulpit. He was alone. The bell continued to toll. He turned in the direction of the bell turret. There was, at least, one person left. A creak at his back. It was too late. He fished for the chinking purse at his belt, fumbling with the string so that it might be hidden.

"Master Spendlove."

The old man looked up at the speaker, the purse still clutched tight in his trembling hand. "I have, this afternoon, put my wife in the ground, sirrah. Have you no respect?"

The newcomer, standing in a gathering pool of rainwater, drew back his hood and glanced around the church. "She loved it here."

Spendlove gaped. "You." His mouth dried. He made a show of looking over his shoulder. "The rector is within."

The man in the green cloak gave a sardonic smile. "Busy at his chimes." He spread gloved hands wide. "I mean you no ill,

Master. How long has it been since last we spoke? A decade? I am sorry for that, yet still I grieve with you. Does that offend?"

Spendlove groped for words that were suddenly elusive, managing only a murmured, "No." He let his gaze roam over the tall man's features. Over eyes that were green like the cloak but paler, cooler and unsettlingly keen. They sat above a prominent nose that bore the kink of a long-healed break and a cleanly-shaven chin that was strong in an otherwise spare, thin-lipped face. The man's hair was a tousled mop, the colour of straw and his complexion was lined and weathered, though Spendlove knew the cragginess to be premature; owing to matters beyond the mere passage of time. He swallowed thickly, finding his voice. "You knew her. To mourn her is your right, just as it is mine."

The tall man winced as he bowed. "I loved her." He shifted his stance, suddenly awkward, the tall riding boots – bucket-tops pulled high over his thighs – clacking on the flagstones.

"You called her aunt."

"She was a second mother. When I heard of her passing, I knew it was to this old place that I should come."

A memory crept unbidden into Spendlove's mind and he could not help but smile. "You ever chided us, Ursula and I, for coming here."

The tall man grinned. "Chalton is your village, Master. Furnished with its own place of worship." The pale eyes surveyed the modest church again. There was the hint of a shudder. "Idsworth is a haunt of ghosts."

Spendlove pushed a lock of hair back under the edge of his cap. "But this ancient place lingers, in spite of it all. A symbol of the life that once thrived on these hills."

"A place now only of sorrow."

"Of stillness and contemplation." As he spoke, Spendlove noticed the hilt of the rider's sword, protruding through the cloak at his waist. It had an elaborate shell guard, the metal decorated with holes cut into the shapes of stars and hearts. It was a famous sword. No, an *infamous* sword. The sight of it jogged his mind, permitting the return of gnawing disquiet. "You should not be here."

The lean face tightened. "I will leave if that pleases."

Spendlove almost laughed at that. "Nothing of what has become of you pleases me, boy." The alternating waves of astonishment and anxiety gave way now to anger. He pressed a hand to his chest as he spoke in a cracking voice. "It is a dagger to my heart, Samson, as it was to hers."

"I did not wish to dismay you, Master," the rider blurted, the confidence fading from his tone. He reached out a hand, failing to conceal another wince. "That was not my intention."

"Dismay me?" Spendlove shrugged him off, twisting to one of the wooden benches, at the end of which was a short stack of pamphlets. He snatched one up, wielding it before the rider like a weapon. "You dismayed me, Samson Lyle, when you became the Ironside Highwayman."

Samson Lyle had been advised not to come. Had been subjected to a spittle-flecked rant during which the risks of coming out into the open had been colourfully extolled. He had ignored every word. Laughed the worries away. But now, as he paced at Spendlove's side, the bell's continuing toll reverberating about the high roof beams, he began to wonder at his own hubris. He glanced down at the man who had taught him to read and write, who had breathed life into Classical Greece and the emperors of Rome, who had introduced the joy of Shakespeare, Marlow and Johnson. A man to whom Lyle owed so much, yet whose disappointment hurt more than any sword thrust. He said meekly, "I had no choice."

They were walking down the nave, towards the porch. Spendlove did not look up. "There is always a choice, Samson."

Skirting a magnificent octagonal font decorated with quatrefoiled panels, Lyle noticed its broad base bore the marks of recent repair. He recalled hearing how the ancient object had been smashed by Parliament men during the war. Nothing but nothing, had been left unsullied by those bitter years, he thought. "You know what they did to her?" he asked tightly, feeling bile rise at the mere thought.

The porch, as they stepped inside, was still shut but the wind howled like a pack of wolves beyond the studded door.

Spendlove turned to him now. His face was lined like an ancient map but his blue eyes were as bright as Lyle remembered. "Of course. And I grieve with you, Samson, as you grieve with me but that does not give you the right to..."

Lyle had reached for the door's large iron ring. He let it go. "But do you know what happened?"

Spendlove's white eyebrows knitted together. "Kicked by a horse. A tragedy, Samson. God called your goodwife home, just as He has mine." He raised an admonishing finger, the school master resurrected. "That is no justification for what you have become."

"God did not call," Lyle said scornfully, his mind making the inexorable leap to another time and place, delving deep to mine seams of perfect sorrow. "Alice was dispatched." He had hissed the final word and regretted the rancour in his voice but was powerless to dilute it. "Thrust through the veil beneath the hooves of my enemies. Murdered out of spite that was meant for me."

The old man recoiled as though taking a dagger to the chest. "Murdered?"

"Trampled," Lyle said, voice clotting. He had not been present on that fateful day. En route, instead, to France and four years of exile. But still he relived Alice's killing every time he closed his eyes. Replayed every shout, every command, every scream. "They killed her because I was not there to kill. I am outside the law, Master and I know how it must unsettle you but the Army is *above* the law. Lambert and Cromwell and the rest." He heard himself laugh, though it was a dark, mirthless sound. "Major-General Goffe is ruler of Berkshire, Sussex and Hampshire. He *makes* the law. Bends it to his will. Who will resist, if not I?"

"Is that what Alice would have wanted? For you to forfeit your own life in her absence?"

"Alice is no longer in a position to want anything. And my life saw ruination the day I lost her. Thus, I shall haunt these roads. I shall hunt the Major-General's men. I will harry their convoys and I will make their lives unbearable, as they have made mine unbearable."

The silence that filled the porch was like a noxious fog, stifling them both. Lyle drew up his hood and went back to the door.

Spendlove reached for his elbow. "You mourn Ursula with me. I mourn Alice with you. Let us leave it at that. I harbour no ill-will, Samson. God knows there are plenty who do but I do not."

Lyle felt a torrent of relief. It was unexpected and for a moment he was dumbstruck. What had he hoped for, coming here? He had told himself it was an errand simply to pay his respects. Told his criminal associates, Eustace and Bella, that such gauntlets were there to be run. Yet now that he had received some measure of acceptance from his old tutor, he realised that was all he had wanted. He stooped, gathering Spendlove in his arms and hugging him tight. "Thank you, Master."

"Still, you should not be here," Spendlove whispered. "You run a great risk."

Lyle straightened. "Soldiers? Here?"

Spendlove shook his head. "But there is not a lane or bridleway they do not patrol."

Lyle shot him a crooked smile. "Even down in these forgotten places?"

Spendlove tutted, rebuking him as he had once done so often. "You mock, Samson but I will ever cherish poor Idsworth. The black death killed the people, right enough and left it empty. Nothing to show out there but a few crumbling walls and pastureland left for the forest to devour. Now it is mere memory."

"A memory with a church."

Spendlove turned back to examine the interior, his gaze wistful. "This place has seen much. Lost much." He pointed to the whitewashed chancel arch and the walls beyond. "There are wondrous murals here, Samson. Tales of scripture rendered in vibrant colour. Concealed after the fissure with Rome. My grandfather told me of those days. Of the men who came with grim faces and full buckets and sang Psalms as they purged every sublime brushstroke from every inch of every wall. But they linger, those marvellous creations. Hidden. Waiting for their time to come again."

Lyle arched an eyebrow. "And I suppose that *I* am St Peter's church, yes?" he said wryly. "A monument to memories stifled and concealed."

Spendlove pursed his lips in an expression of innocence. "Your words, Samson. Not mine." He winked. "But the murals here will one day bask in daylight. I pray what is buried in your soul will find its own way out."

"One day."

"And until then?"

"I have made my bed and I shall lie in it." Lyle opened the door. The wind threw it wide, almost wrenching off his arm to press the point. He hissed as white-hot pain lanced his left shoulder blade.

"Samson?"

"It is nothing," Lyle said. "I was wounded, before Christmas. Pistol ball. It heals nicely."

"Jesus love you, boy," Spendlove replied, shaking his head in astonishment.

"Come." Lyle staggered out into the rain-lashed open. The gloom was gathering apace. "It grows late, Master. These roads are not safe."

"Should I fear highwaymen?"

Lyle grinned. "Footpads, I was going to say." He had to shout to be heard, gripping a fistful of his hood just to keep it up. "Plenty shelter in the high hills. I would escort you back to Chalton."

The old man indicated a lone, open-topped carriage down on the road, its single palfrey sheltering beneath a tree. "I have my trap."

"And I my horse," Lyle said. "Poor devil's tethered 'neath a tree. Charred black by lightning by now, I shouldn't wonder."

"Let us travel together, then," Spendlove demurred, resigning himself to company. "There is a small gathering at the inn. Well-wishers, you understand. You remember the Red Lion?"

Lyle laughed. "I have become an outlaw, Master Spendlove, not a half-wit."

A cinder path took them to a beech tree, alone on the grassy hillock, its crooked branches making defiant gestures at the darkening skies. Lyle led the way, dipping his head against the rain while the bell sang on.

"Chalton will be busy," Spendlove muttered at his back, rapid strides crunching in the dusk. "You'll be seen."

"I am seen a great deal," Lyle said, squinting into the tangle of low boughs under which his pale horse shifted uneasily. "Context is all. If they do not expect to see a notorious highwayman, they will not see one. Besides, those who knew my face before the wars are few and far between. And I, of course, am hardly the fresh young stripling that once they knew."

"You have not changed as much as you might think," Spendlove replied. "You're as cocksure as ever and that's a fact."

Lyle smirked into the driving rain. "I feel I have changed a great deal but perhaps I delude myself. And what of little Botolph and Amelia?"

"They will be there," Spendlove said, presumably meaning the alehouse in Chalton.

"How do they do?"

"Grown now, almost. Amelia turned eighteen, July last. A man could not wish for a better daughter, though, Jesu forgive her, in possession of a loud mouth and a hot head," he chuckled, "not so dissimilar to your own."

"Her mother was the bold one, as I recall."

"Aye," Spendlove agreed with an aching sigh, "bold and courageous was dear Ursula."

"Botolph was the younger of the two," Lyle remembered.

Spendlove nodded. "By three years. A gentle lad but a good one. I thank the Lord for them both daily."

"I can trust them?"

"You can."

"Then I look forward to paying my respects."

They were ten yards out from the tree but Spendlove halted. "You intend to step foot in the tavern? This is folly, Samson and no mistake."

"If I am recognised, I will depart," Lyle reassured him, "after a positively Shakespearean display of blackguardly roguishness, of course. One mustn't have you implicated, after all. Perhaps I shall relieve you of a groat or two and you can play the stoic victim."

Spendlove fiddled with his hat, worry etched on the deep fissures of his face. "It is no laughing matter, Samson and..."

A raised palm cut him off. Movement had caught Lyle's eye. He stared through the blurring rain. His horse, Star, was there, the big stallion's grey coat a pastel smear amongst the gnarled tangle of branches but something was out of kilter. Something in the beast's movement, an odd crabbing, as though Star were shying from some danger at his flank.

Lyle ran. The wind snatched back his hood. The rain streaked his face. He ducked under the first bough, skirted another and he was into the patch of bare earth around the beech, a clearing rendered flat and barren by the tree's canopy. Star was there, attached to the truck by his reins but he was not alone.

"Put your sticky paws where I might see them, friend," Lyle ordered, lifting his voice above the rush of raindrops on leaves. He came to stand some half-dozen paces from the man who had been rifling through his saddlebags.

The man was short and wiry, clothed in rough apparel little superior than those of a beggar. His head was covered in a woollen cap, the sides unfurled to shield ears and frame a face that was pinched and rat-like. He was clearly startled but he managed to produce a short, curved knife from the snapsack slung at his shoulder. He jutted out his narrow chin and sneered. "Or what, *friend*?"

Lyle thrust a hand into the folds of his cloak and pulled the pistol from his belt. "Or you shall witness my weekly shooting practise at uncomfortably close quarters."

The man – who, to Lyle's reckoning, looked to have seen a handful more years than his own twenty-seven – let his mouth loll open, exposing the remains of blackened teeth and diseased gums. He spoke with a broad northern accent that was marked by a high-pitched whistle on the letter 's'. "What is that thing?"

The thing in question was one of Lyle's most cherished possessions. Created for a wealthy Frenchman by a Rotterdam gunsmith, it had found its way to him after a brawl in a Rennes alehouse during his time in exile. Longer than a typical English flintlock, the weapon was no less wieldy, its balance and workmanship exquisite. But what made it truly special was its ability to fire two shots in quick succession. "Double barrelled pistol," Lyle said, turning his hand a touch so that the reedy man might see it with more clarity. "Two strikers, two muzzles but the same lock, cock and flint." He trained the gun on the man's face. "One bullet for each of your eyes."

The stranger edged away from the horse but did not relinquish his blade. Around the hilt, his knuckles were white where he gripped and Lyle noticed that he was missing his two middle fingers. His eyes, gleaming brown beads beneath the edge of the brown cap, flickered restlessly between Lyle's face and the twin muzzles. "You'd kill a man in a church yard?"

"You'd rob a man in one? Besides, where better, sirrah?" Lyle jerked back his head in the general direction of St Peter's. "I believe the gravediggers are still here, as luck would have it. The ground's nice and malleable and I'd be delighted to lend them a hand."

The fidgety eyes narrowed a fraction, the thin upper lip curling. "Trust your powder to burn, do you?"

Lyle shrugged. "Do you trust that it won't?" A tightening of the northern fellow's expression spoke for his indecision and Lyle twitched the pistol. "Put the blade down, man, for Christ's sake."

Down it went, landing on its side in the leaf mulch. Down, too, fell its owner's façade. "I meant no harm, sirs," the three-fingered man blurted, his bluster leaking rapidly away while his gaze darted beyond Lyle's shoulder.

Lyle looked round to see that Spendlove had managed to pick his way beneath the beech's knotted limbs. "A would-be thief," he announced, throwing his gaze quickly over the horse to ensure nothing was missing. One holster was necessarily empty, its occupant currently in his grip but the butt of the second pistol, a regular flintlock, was present. Lower down, fastened in a leather loop, there glinted the fearsome war-hammer he had carried since the late rebellion, while his saddlebags did not appear to sag with tell-tale emptiness. He returned to his captive. "And what is the thief's name?"

"Thief, sir?" the man carped. "No no, not I."

"I suggest you return whatever trinkets you may have stolen," Lyle went on, ignoring the mealy-mouthed protest, "and tell me what business, other than the obvious, you have hereabouts." The villain, he decided, obviously required a timely reminder, so he moved the folds of his cloak aside to expose the hilt of his sword. "I am on familiar terms with Colonel Maddocks, if that serves to jolt your memory."

The words worked as surely as any dagger thrust. Foreboding etched itself into the northerner's sharp features. "The commander hereabouts?"

"You have heard of him, then?"

"Aye, sir. Who has not?"

"An old acquaintance of mine," Lyle said, which, in the most basic of terms, was true enough. It rankled to invoke the name of his nemesis and he heard Spendlove shift his feet. He turned to shoot him a wry glance. "Needs must when the devil drives, Master."

Spendlove held his peace. The increasingly nervous looking captive began to babble. "Jesu. I... I am sorry, sirs, forgive me. Forgive me, do. Maddocks is a terror, they say."

"Out with it, man," Lyle snapped. "It is getting dark and I am growing bored. What is your name?"

"Whistler, sir."

"Whistler."

The frightened fellow nodded rapidly. "On account of..."

Lyle interrupted him, "I have no doubt as to the provenance of the name. What do you do with yourself, Whistler, when you are not creeping about these hills?"

"I labour, sir." Whistler dug one of the remaining fingers of his right hand under the edge of his hat and scratched his temple. "Have dug ditches, knapped flint and worked the salt pans down at Hayling. Anything will serve, long as it puts food in my belly."

"Including thievery." Lyle looked directly at the mutilated appendage. "Not your first offence, either."

"Only when I have no other recourse," Whistler opined, unable to keep his eyes from straying between Lyle's sword and firearm. "I am hungry. What is a man to do?"

What indeed, thought Lyle, as he smothered the pang of hypocrisy that rose like damp through his bones. He told himself that his own crimes were of an altogether different substance. One of vengeance rather than simple larceny. Somehow innately more righteous. But, looking at the pathetic creature before him – drenched, hungry and frightened – he could not help but think that no man's circumstances were ever truly simple. "Where are you headed?" he asked eventually, filing the sharper edges from his tone.

"Portsmouth," Whistler said, exploring his armpit with his complete hand in search of an unseen louse. "There to seek work."

Except that possession of all five digits did not necessarily make Whistler's left hand any more useful. Lyle saw the scarring on the palm and ordered the man to hold it up. "What happened there?"

"A burn," Whistler mumbled, keeping the raised fist balled.

"A brand," Lyle replied.

Behind him, Spendlove enquired, "As punishment? Theft again?"

Lyle shook his head. He had caught a better glimpse before Whistler had grown wise to the scrutiny. Now, as he considered the doleful fellow without the focus upon his attempted robbery, he saw the man behind the misdeed. "That cap," he pointed at Whistler's head, "is a Montero. An infantryman's staple. See the flaps folded down against the ears? Useful as a blazing hearth on a long winter's march. Open your hand fully, Whistler."

The fingers slowly peeled back, staying curved like talons. It was clear the palm could never again become entirely flat. Spendlove stepped closer. "What is that mark?"

"Desertion," Lyle answered grimly, for he had seen such marks before. Whistler's hand had been placed on a tray of red-hot iron that was shaped like a glove and had been branded for all the world to see. A symbol of punishment but also of ownership. The fingers were covered with small blemishes, like smallpox scars, where searing metal studs had pressed against the flesh. The palm, however, bore far more elaborate markings. "Note the letters 'C' and 'R'," Lyle said, "either side of the crown emblem?"

Spendlove looked up at him open-mouthed. "Carolus Rex?"

Lyle nodded. "King Charles." He asked Whistler, "A Cavalier, then?"

Whistler inspected his blighted palm for a second, before confirming, "Sir Allen Apsley's."

"Foot?"

"Pike."

"What happened?"

Whistler's bottom lip trembled in the hoary gloom. "I were a'feared." His eyes glazed as they peered into the past. "You cannot know what it was like."

"I know well enough," Lyle replied. "When did you run?"

"After Hinton Ampner," Whistler said, his voice a monotone, still immersed in a flood of memory.

"Hinton Ampner?" Lyle echoed incredulously, for it was a place he knew well. A tiny hamlet on the Winchester road and seat of one Sir John Hippesley, a Roundhead during the civil wars, whose rebellion against the crown had paid dividends under the Protectorate. Only last year Lyle had visited Hippesley's grand house, there to infiltrate a masquerade in order to steal an important document. But it was not a country manor that had made Whistler abandon his post and Lyle recalled the name of the next village situated on that busy highway. "Cheriton," he said. "There was a battle at Cheriton. Parliament took the field."

Spendlove nodded sagely. "I remember it well. The rebel news-sheets made much of it."

Lyle frowned at Whistler. "You must have been very young."

"Too damned young," Whistler replied with the ghost of a shudder.

"It is often thus." And Lyle could not prevent his own mind tumbling back through the years to a little place in the

163

Northamptonshire wilderness. A place called Naseby. He had been sixteen, green as cabbage and frightened as a spring leveret. The blinding smoke, the stinking sulphur, the screams of grown men, the hoof-shaken ground and the heart-stopping drums. He had held his nerve. Kept the line. Followed orders and ignored the stench of his own piss as it warmed his breeches. Naseby had been hell on Earth. How close had he come to raking spurs into his mount's flesh and bolting for the hills?

Whistler swallowed thickly, his Adam's apple bobbing in that reedy neck. "My chin needed no blade. My voice high as a woman's. The guns. Jesu but they were loud. So loud."

"You retreated in good order," Lyle said, dredging up what detail he could from the back of his mind.

"The king's men, for certain," Whistler's reply was rueful. "But not I. I dived right under a hawthorn hedge, curled up like a new-born pup. No one noticed me. Not even the Roundheads as they swept through. Night fell, I was alone. Freezing my stones off but breathing yet."

"Never to return to Sir Allen's colour."

"Or so I thought." Whistler gave a wry smile. "Only to be snared like a coney outside Winchester."

"You were recognised?"

Whistler nodded. "One of the prison guards claimed he knew my face. I swore blind they had the wrong fellow. How could he prove it? In the end it did not matter. The example was all."

"Fortunate you were not hanged."

"Fortunate? Maybe."

Lyle sighed. He felt suddenly tired. With a jerk of his chin he indicated the way down to the road. "Begone, Whistler, before I change my mind."

"Gone, sir?" Whistler echoed as though he were a halfwit. "Truly?" He pressed his mutilated hands together like a penitent. "By God, sir, you are the Samaritan from the Book of Luke, leapt from the very pages. Nay, sir. An angel."

"Begone, sirrah," Lyle snapped, thrusting the pistol in its saddle holster, "before I deprive you of that yapping tongue too."

"I will." Whistler backed off, shuffling and bowing at the same time. He stooped to snatch up a threadbare snapsack from amongst the beech's roots. "That I will. I beg your forgiveness again."

Then he was gone, leaving Lyle and Spendlove standing beside the grey stallion, the only sound the hiss of rain on the canopy. The light was failing quickly now, darkness dimming the church to little more than an outline.

"You think me a hypocrite," Lyle said, impulsively wishing to deflect his old master's disapproval. "I take only from government men."

Spendlove shook his head. "I think you too soft, Samson."

Lyle gave a short grunt of laughter as he clambered into Star's saddle. "There but for the Grace of God, Master Spendlove. There but for the grace of God."

"It was God's grace that made you keep a loaded pistol."

Lyle grinned. "It wasn't loaded."

Spendlove's little pony, slopping bravely through roads that were now mere funnels of filth, made laborious work of hauling the trap and its rider up the hill to Chalton. The thatches of the village, nestled as it was amongst thick woodland, were all but invisible in the encroaching dusk but the square tower of St Michael and All Angels, one of the hamlet's two prominent structures, climbed over the swaying branches to guide them home.

The second noteworthy building could be heard before it was seen. The Red Lion, a tavern situated opposite the church on the far side of a triangular patch of lawn, was Chalton's beating heart. Like most of the surrounding homes it was a marriage of timber and thatch, though much larger than its neighbours, with rain-streaked windows all aglow and smoke tumbling thick from the chimneystack to mingle with the brooding sky and fragrance the air. The sounds of music and of laughter drifted down to them as they climbed, the weary traveller's siren song.

Lyle gave Star a final, gentle word of encouragement. The stallion, forced to drop pace to keep with the much smaller pony, snorted irritably, a spray of raindrops jetting from his muzzle. Lyle laughed. He breathed deep, letting the heady odour conjure warmth in his mind though there was none in his body. Water dripped from his hood as he rode, tapping rhythmically on the leather tops of the tall riding boots. Star shivered and he reassured his old companion with a soft voice and a patted neck.

"It is a dangerous game you play," Spendlove muttered as they drew up in the tavern's muddy yard. Two young lads, thin as whippets, dashed out from the shelter of a timber lean-to and took the horses' bridles.

Lyle slid from his saddle, boots immediately enveloped by the squelching mire. He pulled the double-barrelled pistol from its holster and delved in one of the saddlebags to fetch his wide-brimmed hat, then asked, "How often do you see soldiers in these parts?"

The boy holding Star peered up so that rain streaked his cheeks, eyes widening at the sight of the gun. "Not for weeks, m' lord."

Lyle looked at Spendlove. "You see?" He handed each boy a penny, then pulled back his hood and replaced it with the hat.

"I do not like it," Spendlove protested as they watched the lads unhitch the pony and coax both beasts to the stables.

"All shall be well," Lyle said, then caught Spendlove's pointed glance as he set about loading the pistol. He winked. "Just in case."

They entered the tavern as soon as Star and his new companion were safely ensconced in the stable block, a muggy, steaming collection of buildings that stank of horseflesh, hay and dung. The stallion had whickered at their backs in disgruntlement until the ostler, lurking out of the rain, had produced a sack of fodder, seemingly from thin air, clicking his tongue in some secret equine language that immediately compelled Star to settle. Lyle had shaken his head, produced more coins, sworn at the fussy beast and left.

The taproom was stifling, the blast of hot air assailing Lyle the moment he stepped onto the chalk floor's blanket of fresh rushes. Fragments of convivial chatter had drifted out on the heat, like leaves tumbling on an autumn gust but they faded as abruptly as the music, a dozen pairs of eyes searching the doorway anxiously.

"Major-General Goffe's responsibility," Spendlove said, "not only encompasses the suppression of Royalist sympathy but charges him with the reformation of public manners."

Lyle nodded but held his peace. It was safer not to explain that the protective guise he donned since returning from France was that of an innkeeper. In that role he saw at first hand the moral expectations to which the people of the fledgling Commonwealth were held. Ever since Cromwell had divided England and Wales into ten regions, each to be governed by one of his military grandees, the government's efforts to make the nation Godlier had become considerably more concerted, enforced now at sword-point as well as pulpit. Of course, the excessive imbibing of strong drink could not be stamped out altogether, any more than Goffe might end dancing or laughter but if drunkenness was detected, penalties could be harsh and swift. That was why every one of the Red Lion's patrons was nervous of strangers. Any new face could be that of a government informant.

"And that is why," Spendlove went on, nodding at a figure slumped on a low stool beside the window, "Rotten Jeremiah, there, takes picket duty."

Lyle cast his gaze over the wizened old man who had apparently been playing lookout. The fellow's face was so deeply lined that it looked like the shell of a walnut, while from his mouth dangled a long, cold pipe. His eyes were firmly shut. "If he were my lookout," he said sardonically, "I would have him shot."

Spendlove, apparently unaware of Rotten Jeremiah's less than attentive efforts, had already moved to the counter, where a couple of locals, relaxing now that they recognised one of their own, patted his back and shared murmured condolences. He caught the tapster's attention with a polite cough. "Wine, if you please, John."

Lyle went to join his friend, weaving through the tobacco fug, skirting tables, two sleeping dogs and a mangy looking cat. The brick hearth was away to his left, blackened spit-dogs flanking its flames, the chimney breast above adorned with an assortment of iron shears.

"Wardley Spendlove," the tapster was saying, "a warm welcome to you." He was a portly man in his mid-forties, with short, lank hair the colour of slate. "I was deep afflicted to hear the news of dear Ursula. Young Botolph ain't been the same these past days."

"Thank you, John," Spendlove said. He put a hand to Lyle's shoulder. "An old acquaintance, come for the funeral. He would share a cup with me in her memory."

John gave them both an earnest nod and jabbed a gnarled thumb in the direction of two nearby barrels. "Sack or Malmsey, sirs."

The older man deferred to Lyle, who indicated that Malmsey and John went to work. Spendlove turned his back to the counter, propping elbows on the sticky surface and pointedly cast his gaze upon the Red Lion's tosspot, who was snaking from table to table, gathering spent trenchers, blackjacks and pots. "Botolph. Not as you recall, I'd wager."

"No," Lyle agreed, watching the lad work. Botolph Spendlove, whom he had known as a flaxen-haired and knock-kneed stripling, was now a strapping youth of stocky frame and square jaw. A grown man, to all intents and purposes. Yet still his face retained the freshness of childhood, a patchy beard of auburn fluff, the same shade as the thatch on his head, doing nothing to add to his fifteen years. "He has become a fine fellow, Master."

Spendlove flashed a proud smile. "Has his mother's looks."

"And he works here?"

"To earn us a few pennies. He and his sister, both. Times are not easy. But we persist. I tutor the youngsters hereabouts, Botolph and Amelia clear the pots and tend the taps."

Lyle watched Botolph attempt to scoop up one too many cups, promptly dropping one that clattered noisily to the ground. "And his ailment?"

Spendlove shrugged. "Half as many hands makes life twice as hard. But he manages."

"Wardley Spendlove!" a large, sweaty patron at one of the tables suddenly exclaimed. He did not stand, the glazed look in his eyes providing explanation but he raised a dented pewter goblet in salute, slopping claret over the table. "My prayers are with you, sir! Goodwife Spendlove was one of a kind." He paused, quaffing the wine and belching prodigiously. "Now she rests with God for eternity. We were all of us the better for having known her."

"Thank you," Spendlove acknowledged.

"I see why this place requires a picket line," Lyle said dryly, making his former teacher laugh.

"Father," Botolph said, startling them. He had evidently been roused to their presence by the drunken toast and now came to address both men with a concerned frown. "Did you walk? I told you not to. The roads are dangerous and..."

"I escorted your father, young sir," Lyle said, "have no fear."

Botolph's brows knitted further together. He drew up his shoulders and, Lyle noticed, let his palsied hand slip behind his back. "And you are?"

"A friend of mine, Botolph," Spendlove said in a soothing tone. "An old friend."

"Thomas Smith," Lyle invoked the first name to form on his tongue. "When last I saw you," he whistled softly, "zounds, you were barely knee high to a palfrey."

Botolph seemed to relent, stepping back slightly. "Grown now, Goodman Smith."

"Indeed." Lyle extended his hand. "And well met."

Botolph grasped Lyle's palm, though he kept his ruined left hand concealed. "A friend of father's is a friend of mine, sir."

"Here," Lyle said, passing his Malmsey to Botolph and ordering a replacement for himself. "Join us." They went to the nearest empty table and sat down. Out the corner of his eye, Lyle noticed a small service door at the furthest reach of the room. It opened and closed like a yawning mouth, the gathering night visible beyond. A young woman, wearing an apron over a corn coloured dress, came and went, rolling hogsheads through from what was, presumably, a storehouse in the yard. "It seems the tapster is not short on supplies."

Botolph smiled. "Delivery came in last evening, before the rain, thank the Lord." Beginning to relax, he sipped from the cup, then said, "Might I ask how you are acquainted?"

"Your father was my schoolmaster," Lyle explained, "when I was but a snipe."

"Yours and many others."

"Right enough," Lyle agreed. "A grand man. His wife a grand woman. Showed me kindness that I shall never forget. That is why I have come." The new wine appeared and Lyle raised his cup and his voice. "To Ursula Spendlove, may she rest in Paradise."

Father and son joined the toast, as did half a dozen more across the room, their voices echoing amongst the blackened beams.

And then the strangers burst in.

Cold, damp air howled through the tavern, heralding the silhouettes that filled the doorway. Rotten Jeremiah was awake now, roused by the violence of the door slamming back to torture its hinges and he staggered to his feet, pipe skittering off his shoe, swaying wildly and spluttering a warning as incoherent as it was worthless.

"There!" the foremost silhouette snarled. "There's the villain!" His voice was guttural and harsh, the English stilted, unnatural, an accent borne thousands of miles to the east. "Duncan, Louis; take hold of the wretch!"

The night descended into chaos. More dark shapes forced their way over the threshold, breaking either side of the first man like streams about a boulder, gargoyle grimaces given life by shadow and candle-flame. Before anyone could react, the most advanced pair had kicked up the rushes on their way to Lyle's table, taking young Botolph Spendlove in hand and wrenching him to his feet. At their backs, blocking the doorway, more men came in single file. All were powerfully built, scabbards conspicuous at their waists.

Lyle instinctively glanced at the little service door but knew he could not hope to make it before he was overrun. Instead he held his nerve and his peace, trying to identify the newcomers before he did anything rash. They might have been soldiers of some kind, he supposed. They wore no uniforms, no plate armour or field signs, which made him doubt whether they were members of the Protectorate's irresistible military wing, yet to encounter sell-swords in the tranquil Hampshire hills seemed just as unlikely. Duncan and Louis, the vanguard, loomed over his table, shoring up the helpless Botolph like twin buttresses. He could see daggers and pistols jammed into their belts. The larger, Duncan, had the youthful aspect of one just touching his twenties. He was pale-skinned and red-headed, a wide cross-belt bracing his torso, around which was coiled a knotted whip. His compatriot might have been a decade older, with a fastidiously-trimmed and oiled beard that could not entirely conceal skin blighted by scabies. Both men wore high boots but no spurs, setting him to wonder whether they travelled on foot. The ripe stench of leather, sweat, ale and tobacco wafted liberally from them.

While the highwayman mulled his distinctly sparse choices, Wardley Spendlove decided to act. "What is the meaning of this?" he cried as his stool shot out from under him, clattering to the chalk floor as he lunged for his son.

The surly men gripping Botolph by the arms swatted Spendlove contemptuously away, one of them putting a boot to his rump for good measure. The old man careened headlong, flailing almost comically, to sprawl amongst chair legs. His persecutors guffawed; loudly, cruelly.

But the laughter died as rapidly as it had begun. The girl came from nowhere. Not nowhere, thought Lyle; but from the shadows at the back, near the crates and the pots and the yard, where the candles had not been lit and the hearth's flames made few inroads. From the modest service door that led to the storehouse and its casks. It was the girl he had seen bringing in the barrels, dirty apron strung at waist, yellow sleeves pushed up to her elbows, mind bent only to her work. Except here she was, standing tall, having inveigled herself into the midst of the standoff entirely unobserved, to snatch the whip from Duncan's belt. She snarled like a trapped wolf, lashing at the whip's owner with the knotted leather so that he released Botolph and shrunk back, clutching his face with his hands. Blood seeped through his latticed fingers as he roared English obscenities mixed with a stream of Scots Gaelic that echoed in the rafters. She drew back the whip again, turning on the bearded man who still held the boy firm and her coif, scraped by her passing forearm, fell away, long tresses of dark brown hair tumbling in its wake. Blades appeared from behind the bearded man, brandished by his comrades to glint in the soft light. Some of them grinned, enjoying the spectacle but the threat was clear enough. Knowing she had failed, the girl stalled, breathing heavily as she let her arm drop, though she kept a tight grip on the whip. Duncan took hold of Botolph again, spitting another vicious oath at her. There was a thin, red gash across his chin.

That was when Lyle stood up. He pulled the pistol from his waistband and levelled it, not at Botolph's captors but at their leader, who was no longer a featureless silhouette but a broad, tall, ruddy-faced and thickly moustachioed menace, with a feathered hat in one hand, his other resting on the sword pommel at his hip. Lyle retreated by a half-dozen paces, putting distance between himself and the strangers. The girl immediately fell back too, seizing the opportunity to move into the space he had created.

The leader of the armed men looked coolly at them both. His bright blue eyes sharpened at the metallic clunk of Lyle's pistol, the hammer thumbed back into the cocked position but he did not flinch, save the shifting of one cheek as it was wrinkled by a mordant smirk. He eyed the firearm. "A pretty piece. What kind of man might brandish such a thing?"

Lyle kept the weapon steady. The foreigner's florid complexion was blemished further by the pale white lines of aged scars and he picked one, a deep divot below the left eye, on which to train the muzzle. "The man who will kill you." He spoke truthfully, for, unlike at Idsworth, the weapon really was primed and ready to fire. There was always a risk that the rain had spoiled the charge, for black powder attracted moisture like the driest sponge imaginable but he was willing to gamble that Botolph's captors would not be eager to put it to the test.

The man with the bushy whiskers licked his lips slowly,

gauging the scene. "Two bullets."

Lyle nodded, retiring a couple of paces further. "For two men." He twitched the muzzle so it roved over the figures gathered in the doorway, a barricade of steel and flesh that would be impossible to breach. "You may choose, if it please."

The ruddy fellow canted his head to the side, as if deciding whether Lyle were short of wits. A golden hoop glittered in his right earlobe. "There are eleven of us, *Skurwysyn*."

"Then you will leave as nine." It was all Lyle could do to keep the pounding of his heart from manifesting as a trembling hand. "Is the boy worthy of such a price?"

"Is he worth your life?"

"Aye," Lyle answered. For the first time, he noticed the expression on Botolph's face. One of bafflement as much as fear. He realised, too, that the girl with the whip was looking at him with curiosity and now he truly saw her. Or, rather, he saw her mother in the face looking up at him. This was Ursula Spendlove's daughter, Amelia. She had the same dark brown eyes, brightened by touches of ochre that caught the candlelight like flakes of gold. The same wide mouth that gave her a serious, solemn countenance and the same petite figure that belied undoubted boldness.

Forcing himself to turn back to the man with the moustache, he said, "Well? How is this night to end?"

Silence hung heavy as a sodden robe. Lyle held firm, despite the aching of the wound in his back, wondering which of them would make the first move. These were hard men, any fool could see, utterly accustomed to violence. All it would take was a word, perhaps a mere gesture, from their leader and the Red Lion would be awash with smoke and blood. And yet something had given the foreigner pause. He had not anticipated resistance in this bucolic idyll, let alone outright threat and, as Lyle had hoped, he clearly harboured no wish to weaken his party on account of a spotty-faced tosspot.

After what seemed like an eternity, the moustachioed man cleared his throat to speak. "We want what is ours, nothing more." The corner of his wide mouth fluttered, the chasm in his cheek deepening. "And nothing less."

"Yours?" Lyle said. He stepped back again. Close enough now, perhaps, to bolt for the rear door. But could he leave the Spendloves at the mercy of these men?

"A treasure." The glassy blue gaze slid to regard Botolph, who dangled between the armed men like a doe's carcass. "Stolen by this knave." His hard voice dropped lower as contempt crept in. "This dead man."

Botolph thrashed at that, the precariousness of his situation finally crystallising in his mind. He received Duncan's backhand, swift and savage, for his trouble and went immediately limp.

Amelia Spendlove looked as though she would lash out again with the whip but halted when Lyle shouted, "He is just a boy!"

"My boy!" Wardley Spendlove, still felled but sitting up now, was covered in the filth of the floor. He sobbed pitifully as he cradled an elbow, tears sketching pale lines through the grime of his cheeks.

"Father," Amelia whispered. She dropped the whip and, all bluster gone, went to crouch beside the prone old man, weeping as he wept.

The moustache flinched, climbing on one side of its owner's face to reveal brilliant white teeth.

Lyle caught the look. One he knew all too well. "Come here, girl."

Botolph's sister glanced up at him, a mix of bewilderment and anger passing like a storm cloud over her face. "I think not, sir."

"Damn it all, Amelia, do as you are goddamned told!"

She flinched at that, then her sombre, earnest expression hardened into something more defiant and Lyle privately berated himself for the outburst. But Wardley was muttering with soft urgency in her ear and, to his surprise, she was kissing her father on the forehead and clambering to her feet. Without a word she came to stand behind Lyle.

Wardley Spendlove had not taken his eyes off his son. "He is my good Christian boy. Never has he hurt a soul."

The scarred man's half smile transformed into a sneer that was brimming with scorn. "I was younger than this whelp when I took my first life."

"As was I," Lyle responded as the Naseby drums boomed in his mind. "Providence conspires against us at times but that does not grant licence to torment every youth you see fit." He risked another glance at Botolph, whose wretched face had taken on the milky hue of the condemned. Wine-dark blood welled from an artificially flared nostril. "You accuse this boy of theft?"

"I do."

"When was this crime committed?"

"Yesterday," the man with the moustache said, taking a step further into the room. He wore a long cassock, the brass buttons glimmering in time with the hoop in his ear. The acolytes at his back shifted their feet, growling in low threat, evidently eager to take whatever revenge had been promised and planned. "At the big farm to the south of Petersfield."

"Yesterday?" Wardley Spendlove echoed indignantly. "My son was here." His voice faltered and cracked with the strain of the moment. "His mother passed away this last week. He has barely left our home, let alone the village."

That seemed to jar with the hitherto unyielding foreigner. He licked his lips slowly, eyes shifting from one face to the next as if he tried to read each mind in turn. "We have tracked our hare over the hills," he said eventually. "Followed his every footstep. We had a witness."

"Had?" Lyle asked pointedly.

Duncan, huge and malevolent at Lyle's left flank, flashed a dark, toothless grin of unholy relish. "The piglet did squeal," he said in a querulous tone that was incongruous set against an accent made in the Scots lowlands. "Oh yes he did." He gave the semi-conscious Botolph a jolt, like a hound shaking a rabbit. It elicited a soft, forlorn groan. "The piggy did identify this rogue as our quarry and that he did."

Lyle shook his head. "It cannot be. You are mistaken."

The man with the moustache caressed his sword pommel with the palm of his left hand. "I think it is you who are gravely mistook, *Skurwysyn*." He cocked his head like a curious dog. "Who are you, that you would court death in this manner? Soldier?"

"A soldier in an army of one," Lyle answered.

"Brigand, then?"

Closer to the mark than you realise, thought Lyle. "Will you release the boy?"

The foreigner lifted his feathered hat and placed it atop his head. A benign enough gesture, except that it freed up his right hand, with which he carefully drew back the cassock to reveal a large-handled pistol and the fat haft of a small axe. The sword, more fully visible now, appeared to be curved, broadening as it swept away from the hilt. "My name is Marek."

"Prussian?" Lyle said, stalling and planning in the same instant, bracing himself for a fight even as he prepared to leap for the door.

"Polish," Marek answered and he seemed to take a pause, as if anticipating recognition. When none came, he said, "But you can call me death, *Skurwysyn*."

Lyle chose not to enquire as to the meaning of the final term; the intended insult was clear enough. "Death, then," he replied, deliberately blasé to hide the chill that played at his neck. "Why are you here?"

"All you need to know, *Skurwysyn*, is that I *am* here and I will have my property, or the boy will die."

"You are footpads," Lyle said. "Outlaws. If you spill blood the Army will hunt you down."

Marek grinned. "And who will raise the hue and cry? You? A man who sups beneath a hat slanted to hide his face? You are unlikely to scuttle to the authorities, I suspect."

"You will get nothing from him," Lyle protested, desperate now, for he could see a night of frustration for Marek that could only culminate in the agonies of others. Botolph's innocence would achieve nothing but condemn him to a slower death.

Marek's smile widened. "Do not concern yourself, *Skurwysyn*. We have done this before. Why don't you take a seat and watch?"

*

Havant, Hampshire

Night was Whistler's friend. His ally. It was the time he came alive. Time for him to go to work. It was deep into the smallest hours and Havant slept. He had hoped for darker skies but the storm-clouds had inched inland at the harrying of the Solent's biting winds and the moon had revealed itself to give road, tree and rooftop a wan outline. Whistler, though, had learned to count his blessings. At least it was no longer raining.

Tugging down the flaps of his Montero cap to bring warmth to his ears and cheeks, he rubbed the ruined palm of his left hand with the mutilated nubs of his right, then edged out onto the road. A dog barked and he hesitated, shrinking back into the mouth of the alley from whence he had emerged but nothing came of the brief commotion. He checked the street again, before cautiously venturing forth.

It had taken almost three hours to reach the town, by way of rain-sluiced tracks that had cloyed at his every step in a concerted attempt to swallow his shoes. If his belly had been full then he would never have attempted the hazardous journey. If the confounded horseman at Idsworth chapel had not returned to his mount when he did, Whistler would have had an array of useful goods to sell. A trip to one of the taverns at Chalton, Finchdean or Rowlands Castle would undoubtedly have revealed some ostler or farmhand far enough into his cups to be parted with a few coins. A groat or two for a tinderbox, perhaps more for a powder flask or, better still, a nice saddle cloth. The transaction would have yielded enough for a meal and board. A place beside the fire. If he had managed to snatch the pistol or the exquisite war hammer, he would be set for the rest of winter. But it was not to be. The horseman, whoever he was, had been implacable. Frightening, even. Those cold green eyes had chilled Whistler to the marrow and he had known that it was enough simply to escape with his life.

So it was south that he had headed. He had told the green-gazed villain that Portsmouth was his goal and he supposed that was true, in a roundabout way, though he had little intention to seek honest employment within its fortress walls. But the harbour town was too far for one night's trudge and so he would make do with Havant, a couple of miles to the east of Portsmouth, at least until sun-up. And Havant was a plump goose to pluck, if ever there was one. A settlement that had sprung up around a road built by the Romans but that had truly flourished by dint of its natural springs. Water mills had been constructed here, with tanneries and breweries and all manner of manufacturing, so that the place, given its relatively modest size, was as rich as any outside of London. Whistler was cold, he was sodden and his stomach was so empty that it convulsed excruciatingly. But he knew that his stars were about to change. He was a fox in the proverbial hen house.

From the shadows at the road's fringe, he scanned the premises on the far side. Immediately opposite was a large tavern. The lure of the heady woodsmoke meandering from its trio of chimneys had been nothing short of a taunt for one without a single coin to his name. He could hardly loiter before the warming flames without purchasing a single drink, for the result would be a thick ear and a charge of vagrancy that would see him land a spell in the stocks or lashed to the whipping post. Thus, he had skulked in his alley during the late evening, jealously observing the rowdy establishment as the candles flickered in the windows, silhouettes of drinkers passing to and fro beyond. He had listened to the desolate moans of the dancing bear tethered to a stake in its yard, heard the laughter of men tossing coins at the pathetic animal as it sauntered for their pleasure and breathed the aroma of sot weed smoke, freshly baked bread and meat pies. All as the rain had come down, cruel and unrelenting.

Whistler had still been in his alleyway as the candles had finally guttered and the tavern's patrons filtered out onto the street, bound for home. Shutters had clacked into place all along the street, doors locked and barred. The sorrowful bear had ceased his call, presumably led away to see out the night in a cage. Whistler had waited patiently as the watchmen completed their rounds, calling the hour as they strode Havant's main crossroads by the light of swaying lanterns. They hummed tunes and spat tobacco as they paced, in pairs and threes, nodding to the last of the folk they encountered, reminding the citizenry of whatever new laws Major-General Goffe had deigned important.

He had still been there when silence had fallen and the clouds had lifted. Now the town was his alone.

*

Chalton, Hampshire

"What did your witness say?" Lyle's pistol was still trained on the men crowding the end of the taproom nearest the tavern's door. "Will you not reveal the charge, sirrah, so that this poor wretch might offer some defence?"

The Pole's smile coloured all but his eyes. "I am no magistrate, *Skurwysyn* and this is no court of law."

"Nor are you an executioner."

Marek inclined his head. "Very well. The answer lies in the hand." He turned his brutal face on the younger Spendlove. Duncan, the Scot, lifted Botolph's arm like a trophy. At the end of that limb, dangling like a limp flag, was the palsied hand, palm enclosed by fingers unnaturally curled inwards like the petals of a desiccated flower.

Lyle remembered the anguish of Wardley and Ursula Spendlove when first the afflicted babe had come screaming into the world. At the fear that their beloved son would suffer more than just deformed flesh when the fullness of time revealed the person he would become. He remembered, too, the whispers of the gossips, the greybeards' censorious glances and the open mockery of other children.

Marek was pointing at the hand. "The man I seek bears Satan's mark."

"His hand?" Lyle scoffed. "That is all? It contracts of its own accord. Has done since birth. A common enough disorder." To a man, Marek's company sketched crosses before their chests. The act was so brazen that it took Lyle aback and he heard himself say, "Papists?" The men did not answer but his mind was already putting the gesture together with the curved swords and the lack of military insignia. "You're sailors."

"Perceptive as well as suicidal," Marek said.

The attack came from the right flank. A short, strongly built man with a shaven scalp, an amber-toothed grimace and pock-pitted skin lunged out of the shadows. In his white-knuckled fist flashed a long, slender dagger, driving up and out from the hip, bound for the soft space immediately beneath Lyle's ribcage. At Amelia's warning shout, Lyle took one, two, three rearward paces, offering only air for the blade to slice. As his assailant flailed and overstepped, he drew his rapier with his free hand in one swift motion, the hiss loud beneath the low ceiling as it slid from the scabbard. With a staccato forward step, as if dancing a Galliard, he flicked his wrist and the sword's delicate tip darted upwards, just brushing the side of the shorter man's hand. The fellow recoiled, yelping as he let the knife drop to the floor. All the while, the pistol's twin muzzles kept level with Marek and his bunched comrades, so that no one else moved.

The tapster, cowering back against his hogsheads, gasped. "God save us, it is…" he began, then swallowed back whatever exclamation had begun to form.

All was still. Lyle steadied his frenzied heart and gritted his teeth against the pain in his shoulder blade, the scab encrusted wound leaving him in no doubt as to whether it had fully healed.

But Marek was looking at the tapster now. "What were you going to say?"

The grey-haired man opened and shut his mouth like a dying fish, stuffing his hands into the pockets of his apron. "Nowt, m'lord, honest."

Marek unsheathed his own sword now. Slowly, purposefully. He was close to the tapster, so Lyle could do nothing to intervene and he raised the blade above the height of the counter, letting the tip hover in line with the frightened man's belly like a poised serpent. "Use your tongue or lose it."

The tapster raised a trembling hand to point at Lyle. "I… I seen him afore, m'lord. Tis the Ironside Highwayman hi'self."

Only then did Lyle realise that, in the brief scuffle, his hat had shunted back and up, tilting away to shade his neck instead of his face. His heart sank just as Marek's brow rose.

"Ironside?" the Pole quizzed the room.

"Cavalry, m'lord," the tapster mumbled fearfully.

Marek's eyes did not move from Lyle. "Now your twinkling swordplay is explained."

Lyle shook his head. "I took instruction from Charles Besnard." He had been hiding in the Paris fencing school, of course. Grieving and recovering and learning by turns. But no one in this place needed to know that.

Marek whistled softly. "A master," he said in what appeared to be genuine admiration. "My compliments."

"The ironsides," one of his company interjected from the back of the armed group, the accent's hard vowels unmistakably the product of Ulster, "were Cromwell's goddamned horsemen. Murdering villains, all." He pushed his way to the front so that he could see Lyle. "Tell me. Were you in Ireland?"

"Hush," Marek ordered. "He may dress like a cavalry officer but that does not make him one." The corner of his mouth upturned in a sneer, animating his whiskers, as he appraised Lyle with new interest. "Highwayman? You are nothing but a thief. A ditch hider and a mask wearer and a coward."

"You know nothing," Lyle replied, all too aware that his tone lacked conviction. He was thinking of the thief at Idsworth and smarting at the irony of it all.

Marek's line of thought was straightening now, like a loosed arrow and he was not to be deterred. He laughed, loudly and mirthlessly, like a sudden thunderclap, then waved the sword at Botolph Spendlove. "He is in your employ."

"No," Lyle replied.

The exchange stirred Botolph, who brought up his head. "I've never seen him before tonight, I swear it."

A backhand from Louis clubbed him to silence. Wardley Spendlove, still prone, mewed like a wounded animal as fresh blood trickled from his son's mouth. Amelia started forwards but, to Lyle's relief, evidently thought better of it.

"This cursed creature," Marek was saying, pointing the steel at Botolph but keeping his glittering eyes on Lyle, "is your man. You are a renegade of these woods, *Skurwysyn* and he does your bidding. Why else would you be here? Why else would you intervene? You spoke of his Devil's hand, that you saw it when he was a baby."

"He stole nothing," Lyle protested, "and he knows me not."

"Why would you risk your life for his?" Marek made a tutting sound with his tongue. "Give me the treasure. End this foolishness."

"What is this treasure you have lost?"

"A book. A blessed book. But you know that already."

Lyle scanned the room for the dozenth time in search for a way to break the deadlock. He would not back down but nor could he give the man his treasure. The front entrance was well and truly blocked, while he would be hunted down by the sailors before he reached the rear door. He needed to stall for time while the wheels of his mind frantically spun. "The sailor's road passes near here," he blurted. "You're travelling from London, bound for ship at Portsmouth. Or the other way around."

Marek nodded. "The *Diamond*."

"Fourth-rater," Lyle said, dredging scraps of information from the back of his mind. "Forty guns. Part of Blake's fleet."

"Lately at Cadiz," Marek confirmed. "Returned home for refit and refreshment. My lads and I have been at Bankside," he shook his hip so that an unseen purse jangled with money, "at the prize play. Now we travel home. We will join the ship at Spithead on Friday."

Lyle risked a backward half-step. Marek's men flinched. The clicks of cocking hammers rang out in the gloom. He was stuck fast. Trapped like a fox in a snare. "Friday," he repeated the word. Time enough to act, he thought and a flash of memory cracked across his mind like Duncan's whip. "I do not have the book but I can get it for you."

Marek's eyes narrowed. He glanced at his bristling, glowering cohort, then at Botolph and finally let his gaze find its way back to Lyle. He pursed his lips in apparent contemplation. "You would strike a deal with me, *Skurwysyn*? You are brave, I give you that."

Lyle shrugged. "Do you want the book back or not? Kill us now and it is lost forever."

Nothing showed on the Pole's implacable face but his arm moved and the broad cutlass hissed its way into its scabbard.

"Very well. You will return my property by the time we cast off, or this pathetic specimen will bathe in the Solent."

"He is a good swimmer."

"Even when hogtied? Truly, the boy must be kinsman to Poseidon himself." Marek spat at Botolph's feet, inching closer to Lyle. "Please understand me, Ironside Highwayman. You and your associate have stolen something very dear to me. To us. We have run our quarry to ground, praise the Holy Mother and the devil-touched whoreson will come south with us at sun-up. Either our property is returned by the time we depart for Spithead, or he dies. You have my word on it."

*

Havant, Hampshire

Whistler scampered across the street, leaping glassy puddles and piles of horse-dung as he went. Hunger made him weak but it also made him resolute. The buildings on this side of the road were principally involved with animal skins. A tannery, a fellmonger and purveyors of vellum and ink all had their place. But the jewel in Havant's crown was the large parchmenter's premises that devoured the lion's share of the row and it was beneath its deeply jettied first floor that Whistler came to a halt. He pressed his back against one of the massive double doors, high and broad like those of a tithe barn, as he paused to catch his breath. The site was one of bustling industry during the day but now all was still, the gates firmly shut and barred and the challenge would be a matter of finding a way into the imposing building. When he had composed himself, he slid along the door, always searching the road for the return of the watchmen or prying eyes in overlooking windows. Nothing gave him undue alarm, so he continued until his shoulder blade felt the scrape of the building's corner. He rounded it, always facing outward, finding himself in a new passageway as he stumbled over a discarded hogshead, rotten beyond repair and slid along the gable wall. In and out he breathed, footsteps silent, craning his neck so that he could check for suitable features in the wall.

Like magic, it resolved from the gloom about a yard above his head. A rectangular ventilation grate, cut into the wall between two of the timber stanchions and sealed by a grid of metal bars. It was tiny, barely a square foot in dimension. A child would have struggled to fit through it. Except that it had rained all day.

Whistler returned to the broken hogshead and dragged it through the mud until it was positioned beneath the grate. He climbed, gingerly at first and bobbed his knees a couple of times to test its durability. Despite an alarming chorus of creaks and cracks, it held firm and he pulled a rusty and much-used chisel from his snapsack. Glancing over both shoulders, he jammed the sharpened point into the wall. The building's timber frame might have been stout but the spaces between the great oaken joists were made of wattle and caked in daub. The daub – a mixture of clay, straw, mud and chalk dust – had been whitewashed, to improve both the aesthetic and its resistance to rain. But it had rained a great deal and, while the wall was not about to melt into the gutter, it was soft enough to offer only meagre resistance to a chisel wielded by a tenacious hand. It took Whistler less than a minute to excavate the outer layer of daub into which the grate had been sunk and it came away with a concerted tug.

He placed the metal fixing carefully on the ground and peered through the hole. All was dark, too dark to take an effective inventory but that hardly mattered. He knew well enough that the open-plan space would hold the accoutrements of an industry delivering prodigious wealth to the town. Stone vats, containing a solution of lime and water, in which the valuable pristine-white skins of South Downs sheep would be soaked for days at a time. Wooden structures upon which the slippery hides, fresh from soaking, would be draped, ready for the remnants of hair to be scraped clean to reveal the pink skin beneath. There would be containers holding bare, tidy skins that were scheduled to be rinsed in the fresh waters of the local springs, purged of lime residue so that they might next be stretched taut on frames for drying. There would be a trove of tools, too. Good quality items that might fit discreetly about a man's person. Easy to steal, easier to sell. But there was something extra special about this place. It teased a particular kind of treasure. One that had Whistler grinning in the desultory moon-glow and redoubling his efforts. His ruined hands screamed with the strain, though he swallowed back the pain, proximity to his prize acting as a salve.

With each movement of the chisel more clumps came away, spattering his sodden shoes, exposing the latticed wattle beneath like the bones of a flayed carcass. When there was enough of the woven hurdle on show, he simply pulled. Returning the chisel to the snapsack and gripping the ends of the coppiced hazel strips where they had been cut to form the setting for the grate, he hauled with all his might, letting his feet dangle to the sides of the hogshead so that his entire weight might contribute to the struggle.

One by one, the sticks broke. The noise was excruciating in the still of the night but intermittent moments of frozen, ear-pricked terror gave way to frenetic action as he gradually enlarged the hole, each splintering spar a word of encouragement. It was not long before the modest vent had become a man-sized window into which Whistler hauled himself, hooking elbows over the edge of the jagged gap, scrabbling with his toes for purchase against the wall, cursing the height and the sharp spears of hazel and the day's foul weather and the green-eyed horseman whose earlier intervention had driven him to this. In moments his top half had slithered into the dry air on the far side of the wall, balanced by his waist on the fractured wattle like a seal about to launch from its rock into the surf. For a heart-stopping second, he feared he would be stranded there, snagged by his breeches on the split fronds but then the momentum shifted and down he went, plummeting into the shadowy abyss, arms outstretched, bracing against the unseen.

He hit the floor hard, rolled, clattered into something wooden that immediately toppled about him. But he laughed inwardly all the same. Because he was unhurt and he was inside.

He disentangled himself from the wooden structure that, with quickly adjusting eyes, he saw was a hoop-shaped frame, across which a pale skin was stretched, held firm by strings and pegs that could be altered to accommodate the inevitable shrinkage. He pulled the apparatus upright. The skin was rubbery and damp. It had been scraped to the blemish-free sheen of the latter stages of the process, left to dry before the final steps that would transform it into viable parchment.

More edges and lines resolved from the shadows as Whistler gauged his new surroundings. The vats were present as expected, flanked by tool benches, buckets and brooms. There were piles of finished skins, ready for cutting to shape and various crates and trunks that might have warranted investigation had time allowed. Shelves heaved with all manner of objects and hooks protruded from the high beams, from which dangled bunches of dried herbs that did valiant battle against the perpetual stench.

Whistler moved through the gloom, picking a silent path to the rear of the workshop, where three smaller doors implied rooms beyond. None was locked. He opened each in turn. The first was an office, perhaps that of the clerk. A Spartan environment inhabited by a huge table that was empty, save a jar of quills and two ink pots. There were a couple of chairs and a wide bookcase crammed and sagging with papers. He entered but only to quickly riffle through a drawer set into the table. Therein, he discovered a solid hunk of bread wrapped in an oily cloth and a scrap of some unidentifiable meat, dried and seasoned for longevity. He could have wept but staved off the pricking tears. He did not resist a breathless prayer of thanks. Then he crammed the lot into his mouth and closed his eyes as he savoured every morsel.

The second room was little more than a cupboard. A copse of tall brooms, boxes of bunched and balled cloths, some short-handled brushes and a collection of pails of various capacities. The third room, however, was the reason he was here. The reason he had especially chosen this factory in a town full of wealthy businesses. It was a storeroom. Lined all the way around its edge by solid chests, stacked three high, so that the top layer reached Whistler's chin. There were dozens and he could not hope to check the contents of them all, which was why it was a relief to know that what lay within each one was identical to the next. He simply went to the nearest and lifted the heavy lid, standing on tiptoes to peer inside.

Parchment. Pristine white gold, with the merest hint of yellow, made from Hampshire's coveted downland flocks and Havant's famous and mystical springs. This was the finished product; dried, cut, inspected, rolled and tied with ribbon, all ready to be transported to the four corners of the Commonwealth and beyond. Parchment was expensive and this stuff was the very best money could buy. Whistler unslung his snapsack and opened it wide, muttering thanks to the parchmenter for preparing his wares in such tidy and easily hidden scrolls. He allowed himself a smug smile, for this loot, when converted into coin down in Portsmouth by the hands of ship's captains and dockyard clerks, would see him through the winter.

When the bag was full, he closed the lid and turned. Which was when he was punched in the face.

WEDNESDAY

Near Rogate, Sussex

"I warned you not to go," the man muttered from high in the saddle as his black gelding negotiated sticky mire that had, until yesterday, been a firm trackway between dense gorse thickets. The horse snorted gently as if for answer, earning a patted neck, while its rider, as craggy and weather-beaten as his oversized buff-coat, continued unabashed. He craned his reedy neck sideways to address one of his two companions. "Did I not, girl? Don't go to Idsworth, says I, for some kestrel-eyed bastard'll know your face and trouble will surely follow. Is that not what I said?"

The girl in question, diminutive upon a bulky roan mare, seemed pained to agree but nodded nevertheless. "That's about the size of it."

The first man cackled triumphantly, revealing rotting gums that sprouted crooked, amber teeth. He was extremely thin, his coat hanging off his bony frame as though it had been draped over a broomstick and his shoulders were severely hunched, giving him the look of an ancient tree, bowing against the passage of time. His face was lined deep by years, furred in wintry white bristles and given a hawkish aspect by a long nose that was hooked and red at the tip. "But do he listen to old Eustace? Do he Hell. Now look." He cackled again, ruefully. "Shite on a short stick."

Behind the old man and young girl, Samson Lyle said, "My decision to pay my respects to Ursula Spendlove has no bearing upon our current predicament."

Eustace Grumm twisted all the way round to face him. "If you weren't at that God-forsaken ghost village, you would not have supped at Chalton."

The sun had not yet fully risen but a grey light showed the way as the narrow track joined an established bridleway, sunk deep over time, so that it was thickly fringed by brown bracken and bare lime trees.

"If he had not gone," a fourth voice spoke in the gloom, "my brother would have no hope at all." Amelia Spendlove, peering over Lyle's shoulder, fixed Grumm with a furious glare that made him turn quickly back to the bridleway. She rode pillion on Star's broad back, clutching tight at the highwayman's midriff. She had dispensed with the apron, replacing it with Lyle's spare coat against the cold, the hem of her skirts now brown with mud.

The trio of horses drew together as they eased watchfully out onto the cloying bridleway, collectively nervous of the peril posed by the wider road's high banks.

At the front, Grumm muttered, "And I'd be snug in my bed, none the wiser." He looked up as he spoke, scanning the darkly tangled boughs for signs of movement or the telltale glow of a slow match. Louder now, he said, "Not traipsing out through this bliddy muck and this bliddy cold."

"It is not that cold," Lyle said, running a gloved hand over Star's pricked ears as the animal took up position between the other mounts so that they travelled three-abreast. He studied the looming banks too. The thick blanket of rotting leaves, the gaping entrances to badger setts and the craters left by uprooted trees. It was a wolf-grey morning, the kind that could conceal all manner of danger. Crows cawed as they swirled high above, an unseen brook gurgled somewhere nearby but otherwise nothing stirred. He let a hand drop to the butt of his pistol all the same, reassured by its presence in the saddle holster. His arm pressed against Amelia's and he felt her tense. Withdrawing it quickly, he said, "And at least the rain has finally relented."

Before Grumm could muster what would doubtless have proved a less than sanguine response, Amelia cut in, "I would have no hope either."

Lyle's instinct was to play down her statement as hyperbole but they both knew he had saved her, despite her initial resistance, from the close attentions of Marek and his swash-and-buckler men. "You are safe now," he said.

"And you are certain that boy will find my father?"

Lyle nodded. "Young Hector is most reliable." When he and the girl had bolted for the little rear door and the yard beyond, leaving Wardley Spendlove on the tavern floor had been a wrench for them both. Yet Lyle had wanted someone trustworthy to remain and the old man had been the obvious – the only – choice. The first thing he had done, after riding Star into the rain-lashed night, was locate Hector, a shepherd's boy with the body of a seven year-old and the mind of the shrewdest card-sharp. "He'll find Master Spendlove and deliver the message."

"Tell it again, Samson," Bella said, with unapologetic relish. "These men were sailors?"

"With Blake's fleet, 'pon the *Diamond*."

"Thought the venerable General at Sea," Grumm sneered, "was down haranguing the Diegos."

"Blockading Cadiz," Lyle confirmed. "Part of the fleet has returned for a refit. This Marek and his lads have been enjoying the pleasures of Bankside during shore leave. He mentioned he had competed at the prize play and he certainly has the physique for it. Now they're returning to port." He cast his mind back to the previous night, replaying Marek's words. Seeing again the nonchalant brutality in that slab-like face, the predatory strength in his bearing. A chill formed on the surface of his skin. "They were hard sorts. Not common ruffians. Dangerous."

"And you have 'em riled," Grumm said bitterly. "Shite on a short stick."

Bella glanced across at Lyle, her long, mousy hair falling over a face full of freckles. "Best you ran away, then."

Lyle winced at her choice of words. "Not a decision from which I derive a deal of pride, I assure you. But I struck a deal with Marek, which has bought us time."

"You should have stayed clear of the whole bloody show, if you ask me," Grumm commented.

The arms wrapped at Lyle's waist tightened a fraction. "You would have had him sit back and quaff his wine," Amelia retorted acerbically, "while those vile creatures tortured my little brother for a book he does not possess?"

Grumm harrumphed theatrically into Tyrannus's thick neck, declining to pick a fight. Lyle stifled a grin.

Bella said, "Your old school master got the stones to keep up with these sailors?"

"To protect his son?" Lyle replied. "Aye, I'd stake my life on it." And that had been the plan, such as it was. Hector had told Spendlove that he was to stay with Marek's men. Take his pony and trap and shadow them all the way south, so that Lyle would be free to fathom an answer to Botolph's sorry predicament. Once they reached the coast, Spendlove was charged with noting the location of the sailors' lodgings and then finding an old associate of Lyle's who could provide a safe house where he could sit tight. Lyle and Amelia, meanwhile, had galloped Star hard all the way back to the Ironside Highwayman's bolt-hole, a tavern on the edge of the village of Rake, there to rouse Bella and Grumm, his companions in life and accomplices on the road, just before the sun took a foothold on the eastern hills. Now they travelled south as the sodden fields crackled and the birds began their song.

Bella, who was around twelve, they reckoned – though the matter was oft debated – clicked her tongue in gentle encouragement as her horse negotiated a felled log. "What now?"

"We shan't attack them," Lyle said. "I confess I had considered it."

"I bet you had," replied Grumm with dark amusement.

"Why not?" Bella asked, a lack of years never equating to a lack of courage. "The three of us can take them, can't we, Samson?" She glanced at Amelia, perhaps reflecting upon the tale she had heard regarding Duncan's stolen whip and added, "Four of us."

"I believe you could best anyone, truly," Lyle said.

"Ambush them on the road," she scoffed. "We know where they're headed."

"Marek's men are not common bandits," Lyle chided, though he could not stifle a laugh. In truth, while her bravado might one day be the end of her, he was proud of the indomitable young woman she had become. Dorothy Forks had been her name when first he had made her acquaintance. That meeting, on a thickly forested road not vastly dissimilar to the one on which they now travelled, had occurred by way of a proposition. Little

Dorothy, a raggedy, snot-nosed snipe with a well-practised curtsy that was as coquettish as it was repellent, had stepped into Star's path and offered all manner of favours in return for a few coins. Her pimp had lurked nearby, propped against a knotted blackthorn as he monitored the exchange with hungry eyes. Lyle had promptly snapped the stick over its owner's pate, scooped the girl into the saddle and offered her a different life. She had thrown herself headlong into Lyle's strange existence, taking on the daylight guise of respectable alehouse mistress, while at night she played accomplice to the region's most notorious highwayman, all on the condition that Dorothy Forks would cease to exist.

Bella pulled a sour face. "Well I think we ought to fight."

Grumm snorted. "We'd get ourselves killed, you daft mare."

"Tempting as it is," said Lyle, "we would not stand a chance. These are seasoned fighters, not green recruits."

"So are the Mad Ox's troopers," Bella countered, "and we best them all the time."

"This is different," Lyle answered levelly, conjuring this new adversary's image in his mind. The blue eyes twinkling from within that broad, florid face. The sardonic smile of neat, white teeth beneath that bristling upper lip. The cavernous scar blighting the man's cheek. He said, "The threat is real. I sense Marek and his company are capable."

"I'm glad it's not all wool in that skull o' yours," Grumm interrupted him brightly, evidently feeling an argument had been won.

"Yet I cannot leave him to the mercy of those men."

Now the old man wrenched himself about, glaring at Lyle with blazing eyes. "And I wonder if your wits have finally turned to suet, Major. You'd risk all our lives for a lad you barely knows?" He shifted his gaze to Amelia. "I am sorry, miss, it is a crying shame but-"

"You're in the right of it, Eustace," Lyle interrupted, "but his father and mother mean a great deal to me." And that fact was the axis about which his every thought revolved. Master and Mistress Spendlove had not raised Samson Lyle. Yet the task had been owned by parents who were as distant from each other as they were to their young son. They had money, the Lyles, a modest acorn of inheritance nurtured into a formidable oak by guile in the mercantile world, which ensured comfort at home that precious few could rival, especially when the first of the wars began. But his parents' match had been one made by others. A marriage of convenience that would forge alliances and oversee transactions but utterly inconvenient for those whose lives it would affect. Young Samson knew from almost the moment he could walk. A coldness between his mother and father. An estrangement in mind if not in body that was the hallmark of their union, a wedge driven between them, first by bitterness, then later by wine.

Thus, his modest, erudite and kind schoolmaster had stepped, unknowingly at first, into the breach. He had taught Lyle in a scholarly fashion, of course but also in life's intangibles. How to conduct oneself in polite company. How to treat others with respect and kindness. How to stand tall and defend a principle. Ursula Spendlove had made her own mark in Lyle's life, showing a young, impetuous man patience and empathy. She and her husband had demonstrated, in their quiet, unassuming manner, how successful a marriage could be and Lyle, when the time came, had modelled his own upon theirs. In so many ways the Spendloves had had a formative influence on Samson Lyle. Ultimately, he had to save Botolph, because he could not let them down. Could not disappoint Ursula's memory.

"Botolph is like a brother to me," Lyle said, dragging his thoughts from the hapless lad's parents, "though he knows it not."

"Well he ain't no brother to me," Grumm muttered.

"And that is why you are free to turn Tyrannus around if it please you."

"Good," Grumm grunted, patting his horse's neck appreciatively. "Then I shall."

They rode on in silence. The bridleway climbed a steep slope for a hundred yards, its leaf-littered banks diminishing. As it reached ground level, distant hilltops visible like dark etchings through the trees, it opened onto a broad fair-meadow of long grass that shifted with the vagaries of the wind. A nye of pheasants exploded from cover at the appearance of the riders, feathers flying as a half-dozen screeching birds scattered pell-mell in panic, while a small roe deer meandered further off, apparently untroubled as it tore up wads of grass and absently skirted patches of vicious-looking gorse. Thick stands of thistles marked a track across the field, flanking the hoof-worn route like a malevolent avenue. With their dark leaves and razor spikes, they were miniature pike-blocks to Lyle's eye and his mind wandered like the fawn, transporting him to other, distant fields, gore-spattered and smoke-wreathed. He had been blooded, the teenaged Lyle, at the decisive Battle of Naseby but the conflict had not ended there. Parliament's remodelled and formidable new army, with Lyle in its ranks, had barely paused for breath when they had been dispatched to deal with Royalists in Wales. Then it had been riots back in England, more Cavalier resistance in Kent and a new threat from the north as the Scots Engagers had crossed the border having made an alliance with the imprisoned monarch. There followed Preston and Winwick Pass, clashes of arms that had simultaneously annihilated the Engagers, ended the Second Civil War and made a man out of Samson Lyle. He could still smell those battles. Still hear them. Yet nothing could have prepared him for Ireland. The beginning of the end of his old life.

He had been a war hero by then. A dashing, deadly major in the formidable cavalry of the all-conquering Army of Parliament, sent to quell resistance across the sea. Except that war in Ireland was different. It was more brutal. Crueller. A conflict fuelled by hatred rather than principle. Finally came Limerick, where Lyle had seen and done things that had brought him such horror, such remorse, that he had thought he might drown in his own shame. He had turned his back. Ridden Star hard to the sea and then on to England. Ireton, his friend and master, had dispatched troops to intercept him and, somehow, they had reached Lyle's home first. He had arrived to discover that she was already dead. Alice; how he missed her. She was long gone. She was bones. A memory. Yet not a single hour slipped by without her haunting him.

"What's the bliddy plan, then, you mad bastard?" Eustace

Grumm's coarse voice grated across his bow.

Lyle blinked hard, forcing pin-pricks from his eyes and images from his head. He smiled at the Cornishman. "We find Marek's missing book and give it back."

Grumm sniffed. "He's probably offed the boy regardless."

"No, he wants his property. Botolph is surety. It makes no sense to kill him." In the distance a thick pall of smoke belched from what was probably a charcoal-maker's ferocious fire. He watched it gather above the trees. "Not yet, leastwise."

"Well then," Grumm replied with mock primness, "that's all tied up in a nice neat bow. We search the countryside for a special little book and just hand it back to Marek. No trouble."

Lyle laughed. "Ye of little faith, Eustace."

"Well forgive my sceptical heart, Samson Lyle but how in bastard blazes are we going to find the damnable thing?"

"We'll find it, old friend," Lyle answered, "because I know who really took it."

*

East Meon, Hampshire

The loud rap at the door echoed the length of the huge hall, forcing Colonel Francis Maddocks to look up from the thick stack of papers that had found their way to his table seemingly moments after sunup. With an irritable grunt he sat back in the chair, its polished stanchions creaking under his muscular frame and pushed the piled communiques away. "Come!"

His hair, raven black but shot through with silver flecks, fell loose about his shoulders. He quickly swept the strands away from his face as the young, mud-spattered soldier strode into the grand chamber on loping legs that were stick-thin and disproportionately long. Maddocks raised a single brow. "To what do I owe this dubious pleasure, Lieutenant Grimes?" He stood, moving away from the enormous hunk of oak and crossing the line of intricately patterned turkey carpets that had been laid out on his arrival. He reached the nearest window, a large rectangle of diamond panes and stared out at brooding skies that had dumped so much rain upon the outbuildings, orchards, forests and hills. The road that ran adjacent to the hall was empty still. In an hour or two it would be a morass. He turned to look quizzically at Grimes. "It is no easy ride from Petersfield in this weather. You must have departed before the sun."

Grimes, lobster-tailed helm wedged in the crook of his arm, bowed low, a particular effort for his willowy frame and, noticing watery filth forming a puddle about his tall boots, danced a brisk sidestep to put himself clear of the plush rug. The movement, all legs and arms, put Maddocks in mind of a giant crab scuttling across a rock. Grimes was a sallow specimen, with lower eyelids that exposed red-raw flesh where they drooped but his hazel eyes glistened with awe as they roamed the hall. "I was woken by word of a fracas, sir."

"Splendid, is it not?" Maddocks said, noting the lieutenant's interest. "When touring Major-General Goffe's territory, I am ever thankful to reach this place." He laughed as an image of his townhouse overlooking Petersfield marketplace pushed itself to the fore. "Tis more befitting of a man of my dignity than a view over cattle pens."

"It is like a fortress, sir," Grimes answered, still marvelling, "with walls so stout."

"Malmstone and flint," said Maddocks, "four feet thick." He could understand the younger man's wonder, for in a village of timber and thatch, the ancient complex of Court Hall was as unusual as it was intimidating.

Grimes's mouth twisted in evident distaste. "An old bishop's lair, so they say."

Maddocks nodded. "The Bishops of Winchester, no less. Maintained as a home and as a court house too. Praise God, such trappings were stripped from those ne'er-do-wells when their posts were abolished." He spread his own gaze appreciatively about the room. The hall itself, a throwback to times long faded, was almost fifty feet long, he reckoned and near thirty wide. The high, cavernous ceiling of black beams held up a magnificent louvred roof of many thousands of tiles and the glowing hearth could have accommodated an entire boar for the spit. Major-General William Goffe governed the region on behalf of the Lord Protector but it was his hand-picked commissioners and their military facilitators that did the real work. To the likes of Maddocks fell the enforcement of law and the reformation of public morality. Gambling dens, playhouses and baiting pits were to be suppressed. Public gatherings were to be broken up, old Royalists kept at bay, seditious activity crushed. Drunkenness, sexual licentiousness, foul-language and blasphemy were all to be severely punished, while alehouses known for clientele of an unruly nature could expect to be closed. And all that fell upon Maddocks's shoulders in the eastern and southern parts of the County of Southampton. To that end, he was compelled to travel, almost like a monarch of old, embarked upon perpetual progress. He had a dozen regular rest stops and of those, this was by far his favourite. If only it were his permanent residence, he thought ruefully but that privilege had been bestowed upon one of the Army grandees who had come out of the late war with gold-lined pockets and the ear of the Protector. The only condition to snapping up the manor at auction for a veritable steal was that the old bishop's court would be made available whenever it was requested by the new regime. "Now then," he said, clapping his hands. "This fracas."

Lieutenant Grimes scratched a chin crammed with white-headed pimples. He sniffed wetly. "Up in the hills, at Chalton. The Red Lion."

Maddocks knew the place and waved a dismissive hand. "Drunks comparing pizzles, no doubt."

The lieutenant licked thin lips nervously. "I fear it was a deal more serious than that, sir."

"Anyone die?"

"No, sir but there was some trouble with a parcel of foreign sell-swords, led by a fellow named Marek."

That gave Maddocks pause. He felt his features tighten, though he fought to remain impassive. "Mercenaries?" he said incredulously. "In Southamptonshire? What were they about; doing battle with sheep?"

"A lad was beaten," Grimes answered.

MICHAEL ARNOLD

"Not badly, Mister Grimes, or he would not have dragged himself all the way to your door."

Grimes shook his head, though the brown hair plastered to his forehead by sweat and mud did not shift. "It was not reported by the victim, sir. They drank the inn quite dry, these sell-swords. The tapster was forced to travel to town in order to replenish his ale."

"And he took the opportunity to lodge his complaint with you." Maddocks stared out of the window. The muffled sound of a watermill cranked and thudded outside. "Foreign mercenaries," he muttered, considering the assertion. "Man by the name of Marek. I wonder."

"He is known to you, sir?"

"Perhaps. Not mercenaries, Grimes," Maddocks said, for it just did not ring true. The old sovereign's three kingdoms had been infested with rough, godless killers during the civil wars. Men who had crossed from the conflict in the Low Countries when coins and enemies had begun to run dry. But those days had long faded. The creation of Parliament's New Modelled Army had initially stifled the need for such men. "Our final victory," he said aloud, "has ensured a peace that shall, God willing, last until Jesus' return." He snapped his fingers. "Not soldiers, Grimes but sailors. Pirates in all but name. Blake's squadron are in. The lawless knaves in his employ are worse than Barbary corsairs. General Goffe has petitioned the Protector on the matter, on account of the propensity of those same villains to roam his jurisdiction betwixt London and Portsmouth. Heathens in the main. Irish and French, Musselmen, pagan and Papist." He strode back to the desk, plucking a small, pale-green pod from a pouch that lay beside the papers. He offered it up. "Cardamom?" When Grimes politely demurred, Maddocks took a second to split open the thin outer shell with a well-practised thumb, tilted back his head and upended it into his mouth. A cascade of tiny seeds scattered his tongue and he chewed vigorously. "Restores the breath," he explained when Grimes stared in evident bewilderment. "In short, we have a pure Army and a rotten Navy. That's your answer. But what concern is it of mine? I would not readily

198

interfere with Blake's crews on account of a mere brabble in a tippling house."

"He was abducted, sir."

"The Chalton lad? The one they beat?" Maddocks grunted. "Condemned with shapely legs, was he? Months at sea and all that." He smothered his own mirth when he read only unease on his subordinate's face. After all, the lad had not ridden from Petersfield to share a jest. "Presumably you have dealt with this matter yourself, man?" He paused as a troop of horsemen, clad head-to-toe in leather and metal, thundered past the window to draw up outside Court Hall. When the thrum of their hoof-beats had ebbed, Maddocks continued, "Did you not make direct for Chalton?"

"I did, sir. The miscreants had already departed."

"They will be travelling down to Portsmouth," Maddocks said. "Hardly a pebble in a dung heap. Ride the lanes. Track them down, bring them in and free the bloody boy." Again, Grimes's expression struck a note of disquiet and Maddocks began to lose patience. "Lieutenant," he snapped, "speak plain. What the devil is this about?"

"The Ironside Highwayman," Grimes said pointedly, "was present at the Red Lion. Almost came to blows with the foreign ruffians."

Maddocks could not keep his features impassive this time, his brow screwing unbidden into a dark frown. "Indeed? You're certain?"

"Tavern-keeper told me so, sir. By his account, the sailors accused the Chalton boy of stealing something from them. Something precious. The Ironside Highwayman was supping therein and took it upon himself to intervene."

"He would not easily pick such men as enemies. The thief must have been a member of his sordid little gang." Maddocks knitted his fingers across his stomach. "Tell me they ran the blackguard through. Lord above but it would save me a deal of trouble."

"Alas, no," Grimes replied.

"Then?"

"There was something of a standoff, sir. Concluding only

when the bandit pledged to recover the missing item."

They were interrupted by a thump at the massive, iron-clasped doors. "Come!" Maddocks barked. The door opened and a servant ushered another soldier inside. He was a middle-aged man with close-cropped auburn hair, a broken nose and neat, white teeth. Maddocks acknowledged the man who had ridden at the head of the newly arrived group of cavalrymen with a curt nod. "Major Smith. Welcome. My man will bring refreshment forthwith." The major, as muddy and travel-worn as the lieutenant but devoid of the junior officer's temerity, gave his thanks and walked directly to the far end of the hall and the hearth's warming embrace. Already he was plucking off his leather gloves and shrugging his way out of the saffron coloured scarf – the mark of Colonel Maddocks' Regiment of Horse – that swathed his torso.

Maddocks turned back to Grimes. "This precious item. The Highwayman has it?"

Grimes shook his head. "He claimed not, sir but this Marek declined to believe him."

"Of course he declined," Maddocks gave a snort of amusement. "A weasel like Samson Lyle would not risk his skin for a stranger. You are aware of his treachery, yes?"

"Was a major," Grimes said, "in the Parliament's remodelled army. Fought to great acclaim, so I heard. A friend to General Ireton and," his voice took on a note of dread as he spoke the names, "even, they say, to the Lord Protector himself."

Maddocks nodded, unable to keep the sourness from his face or tone. "And to me, more's the pity. But he lost his nerve. When King Jesus called for warriors in Ireland, Lyle's ears were deaf. His pride and his cowardice condemned him to turn his coat and then his tail."

"They say his goodwife was killed," Grimes ventured tentatively.

"A mishap." Maddocks shrugged. "A tragedy, without doubt but not intentional. Troopers were dispatched to his home. Goodwife Lyle behaved rather rashly and was injured by one of the horses. If blame is to be apportioned, let it befall Lyle himself, whose treason brought about all. Now the Almighty sees fit for the knave to wander the roads with a price around his neck. Eventually, God willing, the price will be replaced by a noose." He hooked a thumb into his breeches. "Chalton, then. What was taken?"

"Treasure, sir and a book of some kind. The tapster knew only that."

Maddocks sighed heavily, not wishing to leave the comforts of East Meon prematurely. "I suppose I should investigate this business myself. Thank you, Lieutenant Grimes. You were right to inform me." He pressed the balls of his hands into stinging eyes. "Outlaws, pirates and treasure in our sleepy hills, eh? Whatever next?"

From the fireplace, a deep voice intoned, "You've heard the madman's rant too, Colonel? A good tale spreads on the wind, I do declare!"

Both Maddocks and Grimes looked to the medieval hall's far end. "Major Smith?" the colonel prompted.

"The madman," Smith said in jovial fashion, his palms held flat towards the heat. "Deserter, taken by my lads at Havant. Red-handed, no less, in the act of stealing parchment."

"What of it?"

"We found a deal of booty in his possession. Treasure, of sorts, that he claims he stole from pirates!" Smith brayed with laughter. "He's a talented storyteller, I'll give him that. A shame he'll soon swing for his crimes."

Maddocks turned back to the lieutenant. "Mister Grimes, rouse the men, if you please." He left the table and went to a low chest, upon which his sword and scabbard lay. Collecting them up, he added, "And fetch my horse."

*

Finchdean, Hampshire

Lyle had only Amelia for company when Star loped towards the hamlet nestled deep in the wooded hills. Misty fingers lingered stubbornly on the highest slopes, writhing over the treetops as the half-hearted breeze worked to push them clear.

"What happened to him?" Amelia asked as they came off the last hill and followed the line of a hawthorn hedge towards the clustered thatches.

Lyle felt her weight shift to the side and realised she was inspecting Star's coat. "Exploding gun at Worcester Fight."

She traced the patch of pink, mutilated skin that blighted the beast's flank. "Must have been a big gun."

Lyle nodded. "A scrap of iron near cut him in twain."

She straightened again. "I do not remember the war."

"Then you are fortunate."

"Bella told me about what happened." She hesitated, then ventured in a small voice, "To your wife, I mean."

"Bella has a big mouth."

"I… cannot imagine…"

"No," Lyle said curtly, "you cannot." He immediately regretted his tone, adding, "It is why my war continues." The addendum had been designed to offer some explanation, as if the information would go some way to softening his brusqueness but all it did was invite the memory of Marek's scornful words and they crowded in, like birds descending upon a new-sown field. *He may dress like a cavalry officer but that does not make him one.* Did the jibe ring true? Had he become, in truth, no different than a common footpad? No different than Whistler? He glanced down at the accoutrements of a warrior. The sword and the pistol. The dagger and the hammer. Baubles now. Used occasionally and then mostly for threat above substance.

"You fight to honour her," Amelia said. "To punish them for taking her from you."

"Aye," Lyle replied, his voice thickening with a sudden pang of loss.

"And to remind yourself of who you were," she added. "And are still."

Her understanding took him by surprise and all he could do was offer a dumb nod. He fought for Alice, certainly but also in a desperate attempt to piece together the fractured shards of his old self. The identity to which he still clung like a drowning man upon a disintegrating spar. Without the Ironside

Highwayman, there was nothing left of Samson Lyle. Just a ghost in a long cloak.

"Your reasons matter not to me," Amelia was saying, perhaps sensing his sudden unease. "You risk your life for Botolph and I am indebted."

"He is yet in danger," Lyle said as they moved beyond the hedgerow and onto the gravel track that led into the village proper. The surrounding fields were busy already with labourers and livestock but here, in the valley, Finchdean was almost silent. Smoke trails meandered from the rooftops, a pair of buzzards circled lazily far above but there was little beyond the lowing of distant cattle to greet them.

"And not only my brother," she said sorrowfully. "My father is an old man."

"Your father was the logical choice."

"What if they catch sight of him?"

"They will not *lose* sight of him, Miss Spendlove," he answered, amused that she would imagine her elderly father and his lumbering pony and trap could hope to follow a band of seasoned fighting men through the countryside undetected. "But they'll pay him no heed."

"I pray you are right."

They reached the triangular patch of turf at the village's heart. A tavern's painted sign creaked as it swayed gently on rusted hinges and the occasional clang and murmur came from behind the brick walls of a smithy.

"Ho, Ned!" Lyle called as Star crossed the green, slowing so that he could tear up wads of grass. At the farthest side was a hunched figure dressed in tattered breeches and a poor man's coat that would offer scant comfort against the cold. He was seated on a low bench, legs outstretched. He gradually stirred at the words, lifting his face to squint blearily at the newcomers. Lyle spoke again, "And how fare you this bright morning?"

"Major?" the man murmured softly. He was in his early thirties, with a dense thicket of brown hair, broad shoulders and a pulpy complexion. He shifted his rump, face creasing in an agonised wince. His legs only moved a fraction, accompanied by the clank of iron.

Lyle slid down from the horse, offering a hand to Amelia. As she moved, his nostrils were full of the scent of her hair and it was all he could do not to lean in. Clearing his throat awkwardly, he plucked an earthenware bottle from a saddlebag and inspected the stocks in which Ned's ankles had been fastened. His feet were naked and caked in grime. "How long have you been here?"

"A day and two nights, thus far." Ned hawked up a gobbet of frothy spittle and deposited it on the grass.

Amelia's face was a mask of pity. "What was your crime, sir?"

"Imbibed a cup or two." Ned gave a rueful grunt. "Or ten."

Lyle looked up and around. At Finchdean's doors and windows, into the mouth of every lane and up at the sheep-dotted fields. "Commissioner's men?"

Ned spat again. "Locked me up and sauntered off, God afflict them with plague. I'm to be released at noon, so they say but I shall not hold my breath for it."

Lyle nodded sympathetically. The intimation was that the local lawmen could do what they damned-well pleased and Ned was probably right. After the Instrument of Government had made Cromwell Lord Protector, he had divided the nation into regions that would be governed by his trusted major-generals. Assisted by their specially appointed commissioners and bolstered by an all-powerful army, the generals and their aides were effectively untouchable. "I will fetch my war-hammer."

"No, Major, do not," Ned warned. "I cannot be seen to gain freedom by such means. I'll find myself back here in a trice, with my sentence doubled."

Lyle sucked his teeth with irritation but eventually acquiesced. "I would speak with you, all the same."

"Jesu, man, do not be foolish," Ned said, palming his eyes. When he met Lyle's gaze again, his own was sharper than before. "Nowhere is safe. Get away before you are seen." He glanced across at the blacksmith's forge. "They'll open up soon. And Goody Pring will throw back the tavern's shutters in short order. They're honest folk, hereabouts but they'll sell you down the river for that plump reward."

Lyle crouched beside Ned. "I will not tarry long."

Ned's expression tightened. "Jesu, Major, pay heed. The Mad Ox has agents everywhere."

"The Mad Ox has chased me for many months without success."

Ned glanced up at the tavern's shuttered first floor. "He pays them well for information. They will see-"

"They will see a kindly Samaritan," Lyle cut him off, lifting the bottle, "offering water to slake a man's thirst. Let them report such a tale to their superiors. The constable has gone, you say. Well, are there soldiers hereabouts? Mounted men?"

"No," Ned conceded.

"Then let his spies watch." He handed Ned the drink. "Here."

When the fettered man had quaffed the water as though it were the very elixir of youth, sleeving his mouth and passing back the bottle, he said, "God bless you, Major, truly. But how did you know to find me here?"

"Here or the taphouse, old friend."

"The village drunk, you mean to say," Ned said, with a sideways glance of sheer embarrassment at Amelia. When Lyle did not respond, Ned sighed deeply, sadly, then asked, "What, then, of your friends? How fares that sharp-tongued stripling?"

"Bella is well."

"And your smuggler? Old goat dead yet?"

Lyle laughed. "Not when last I checked." And he prayed that was still true. He had dispatched them both to the south. Grumm to the next village on the road, Rowlands Castle and Bella all the way to Havant. There to ask questions.

"I am glad. And this young lady?" Ned looked pointedly at Amelia.

"The less said, the better for all," Lyle replied. "In truth, my presence at your beleaguered side is not entirely selfless."

Ned grimaced. "I cannot help, Major. I served you in the wars and I'm proud of that. But it is too fraught." He gave a bleak chuckle. "Look at me. This is what befalls a man who indulges in strong drink. What awaits he who treats with outlaws?"

Lyle could hardly blame his old comrade. That was why he had come prepared. He leaned forwards, placing the bottle on the grass beneath the bench. "Do not discard this, Ned. Drink the rest, take it home," he winked, "and throw it at a wall."

Ned glanced down at the bottle, then back to Lyle. After a moment's hesitation, "What do you need?"

"A thief may have come through here. A man I encountered first at Idsworth chapel. I have need of him." Lyle cast his mind back to the rain-soaked encounter beneath the solitary beech. "Said he was Portsmouth bound. If he spoke true, that places him on the Finchdean road, south, then on through Rowlands castle and Havant."

Ned's brow furrowed in consideration. "Name?"

"Whistler, he called himself. An old soldier, in fact. A malignant. Though this one deserted at Cheriton Fight. Earned a branded hand for his trouble."

"What's he done, this malignant?"

"Better that you steer a wide berth, Ned. But have you seen him? If anyone witnessed him pass through the village," he shrugged, apologetic for the statement, "it is surely the man who cannot leave."

It was a cruel thing to say, he supposed but truthful nevertheless. How far this man, this ragged sot, had fallen since riding to war on a noble destrier. It made him think of his words to Wardley Spendlove. There but for the Grace of God. How close had Lyle come to following Ned to the bottom of a wine cask after Alice had died? In the end, it had been the sword and the challenge of the duel that had brought him back from the brink. The time he had spent in French exile, the hours he had wiled in the school of Charles Besnard, absorbing the great master's knowledge. The more he had learned, the less his grief had hurt but it could all have been so different. Privately he shuddered.

To Lyle's relief, Ned laughed, this time with real mirth. "I seen many folk, sir. Pilgrims and traders. Children mostly. The little rats love to whip off my shoes and taunt my toes with feathers. I seen mariners too. A dozen or thereabouts. Fiendish looking buggers. Paid little heed to me and for that I was thankful. Haven't spied a motley company like that since before Worcester."

Lyle shared a look with Amelia. "Where are they now?"

Ned jutted his chin in a southerly direction. "Goody Pring wouldn't serve their like, so full are they of lice and pox. They've gone to find a steading with its own brewhouse. Plenty about."

"Did they have a prisoner with them? A young lad?"

"Not that I noticed. Mind you, they had a cart and nag. What I took to be a wounded comrade lying in back."

"Wounded, certainly," Lyle replied, "but no comrade." So Marek had been good to his word. They were travelling to the docks as planned. How close had they passed to the true object of their ire, he wondered, though they would not have known it? He pressed, "But not a lone stranger?"

Ned shook his head. "Regrettably, Major."

"Are you certain, old friend? A scrawny man, twitching and nervous, fingers missing on one hand and a deserter's brand upon the other. You saw no such fellow?"

Ned screwed up his face in apology. "Not a hide nor hair."

*

Rowlands Castle, Hampshire

By the time Lyle and Amelia had completed the two mile stretch down to Rowlands Castle, the day had begun in earnest. All trace of mist had gone, eradicated by a low-slung, dazzling sun and replaced in patches by vapour trails wafting from the mouths of folk about their business. The skies were no longer so brooding, which seemed to animate the carters and their whinnying palfreys, thundering back and forth along the ancient high road about which two-score homes, a chapel, a stinking tannery, cavernous warehouses and many more had grown. It was a small enough place, named for a Norman fort that had long since crumbled but, like Petersfield to the north and Havant to the south, the streets were well-maintained and the newer buildings mostly brick and tile, a sign of the prosperity brought by local fleeces that were unsurpassed for quality.

Lyle angled his hat to obscure his face as Star loped casually into the midst of the village. He had hidden his distinctive war-hammer and double-barrelled pistol in his saddlebags, though eyes were naturally drawn to the long sword at his hip and the woman with immodestly unbound hair riding pillion. He checked and rechecked the road behind, routes to the flanks and any other means of rapid departure, should such recourse become necessary. A gang of small children crossed the street ahead, scuttling like a gaggle of noisy geese towards a handsome, two-storied house of thick chimney stacks and mullioned windows. A petty school, he supposed and he wondered how education might have changed since Cromwell's rise. No more the endless recitals of kings and queens that he had been subjected to. No more High Church prayer book or the ingrained sense of fealty to prince or bishop. The brave new world left no part of society untouched.

He spotted Eustace Grumm, on foot and holding Tyrannus's bridle in a gloved fist, at the front of a bakery. He steered Star over to where the Cornishman waited. "What news?"

"Nowt," Grumm replied with a wet sniff. "And no sign of your pirates. What did you discover?"

"Hood," Lyle prompted.

Grumm's white eyebrows pressed together. "I am not known here, Major."

"When abroad, you conceal your identity," Lyle said. "That was the agreement."

Grumm blew a jet of air through his red nose but raised the hood all the same. Though Lyle was a well-known figure in the area, flirting with discovery always, his associates carried no such burden. When not assisting the Ironside Highwayman, Eustace Grumm played the part of John Brown, tapster at the Red Lion in Rake. Bella assumed the role of Lucy, his niece and together they were afforded a degree of normality. As long as they were never spied in the company of the notorious Samson Lyle. "Very well," Grumm muttered. "May I learn what you have learned, or must I guess?"

"We did not locate Whistler. He has vanished, it seems."

"Slippery little bastard," Grumm spat.

Lyle raised an eyebrow at that. "My, how you've changed."

Eustace Grumm had been chief of a smuggling ring in his native Cornwall. All manner of dark deeds had been the hallmarks of his illicit trade in the perpetual struggle with rival gangs and Customs Men alike. But after the latter enemy had been tipped-off as to his whereabouts one summer's evening in the uneasy and short-lived truce following the First Civil War, he had barely escaped England with his skin intact. The following years of exile and destitution had not been kind, culminating in a fateful run-in with thief-takers in a Parisian tavern and an impromptu meeting with a high branch and a makeshift noose. As fate or providence would have it, Samson Lyle, himself a landless, lawless traveller, had been supping in that same tavern. He had stepped into the argument like an avenging angel, with his soldierly manner and assortment of strange weapons and Grumm had been plucked from death's clutches. They had ridden together ever since, though that did not prevent Lyle from chiding his comrade when the mood took hold.

Grumm screwed up his face. "What I did," he answered sourly, "I did to survive. And you're hardly at liberty to deride, infamous outlaw that you be."

Lyle laughed. "Touché."

"Now tell me. Did you see the sailors?"

"They're near Finchdean," Lyle said.

"And the boy?" The Cornishman's wrinkled face tightened a fraction as he glanced at Amelia. "Young Botolph."

Lyle felt her move in the saddle and hoped she was acknowledging Grumm's inferred apology. He shrugged. "We must presume so."

Grumm made a clacking sound with his tongue. "Not in any haste, are they?"

"Their ship is not yet due for departure. And they're hardly concerned with alluding us. If anything, it serves Marek's purpose to remain visible, lest I produce the book."

"Must think you a miracle worker," Grumm said sourly. "What of the authorities? Surely Maddocks or his underlings have received word of these braggartly bastards? Traipsing cross country like blood-thirsty Landsknechts, kidnapping locals where they may. The Army cannot sit back and ignore such doings."

"*If* he has received word," replied Lyle, "then he'll be reluctant to intervene. These are Robert Blake's men and Blake is Cromwell's personal ban-dog against the Spanish. He has the Protector's favour."

"They're Papists!"

"They're experienced hands to a man."

"Ergo, they are above the law?"

Lyle nodded. "And they know it."

"What of Botolph?" Grumm asked. "They cannot simply swagger into Portsmouth with a youngster trussed up like a Christ-tide goose!"

"We are at war with the Spanish, Eustace. Any man-o'-war's crew may use impressment to bolster their complement."

Grumm pursed his cracked lips as understanding dawned. "And that's what the buggers'll claim they're about."

"The navy needs hands and the Protector needs victories. Maddocks would not lift a finger, even if he had a mind to. Marek will take his time, sample the local ales and wander down to his ship with Botolph Spendlove at his mercy. When the missing treasure does not find its way into his hands, the *Diamond* will set sail and Botolph will be doomed."

Grumm blasphemed softly, tugging the matted strands of his beard in frustration. "So it is down to us."

"And we cannot free Botolph without possessing either a small army or Marek's book."

"Which we do not have. And we cannot get it because we do not know where the real thief's bliddy-well at."

"Oh yes we do!" the words of a girl severed their discussion. Lyle turned, startled, in his saddle and Grumm looked up sharply, because the voice was coarser, brasher and pitched higher than Amelia's. The rider, grinning widely, brought her mare, Newt, to a fidgety standstill and offered a bow from the waist.

"Bella?" Lyle said.

"That whistling fellow," she answered. "I've found him!"

*

Warblington Castle, Hampshire

The prisoner was bound so tightly at the wrists that his skin bled. He could hear the guard's approach long before he saw him, for the jangle of keys at the man's belt was like a herald's trumpet in the silence.

He braced himself, screwing shut his good eye against the flood of light. He hissed aloud, jolted by the pain of the other eye that had been reduced to a blackened, puffy mess by a soldier's gauntleted knuckles.

He had been sitting against the damp brickwork of the cell wall when the iron-bound door juddered open but rose almost miraculously to his feet, his weight hauled without effort by rough hands at the scruff of his neck. He could not see the man who had dragged him upright, for the searing light cast the fellow in shadow but the familiar odour of onions and salted fish did the job of identification well enough.

"Where do you take me, Hobb?" Whistler blurted as his feet scrabbled in the soiled rushes, failing to keep pace with his body.

The prison guard, a squat, strongly built Kentishman, limped awkwardly as he spoke. "Colonel's here."

"Colonel?" Whistler echoed as they went through the doorway and out into the crisp noon air. He stole a look behind, finally getting to see in daylight the place where he had been incarcerated under the cover of night. It was a plain, single-storied barn, built in stone, with a tiled roof and only a single, high owl-hole for light and ventilation. Christ, he thought but how welcome a cold winter's day could be when one had been deprived of it. He breathed deeply, lungs smarting, as they crossed what he now saw was an expansive yard, the ground a muddy lattice of water-filled wheel-ruts. Outbuildings of various size and purpose fringed the open space, interspersed by great drifts of masonry, as if the rain clouds had contained bricks as well as water.

Hobb, leading the way with his strange waddle and a pungent onion trail, nodded a jowly head towards the far corner of the yard. "In there."

Whistler looked up. High above everything, an octagonal tower loomed, built in fine brick and dressed in grey stone. He knew it had been part of a larger structure once, the adjoining portions of abruptly ending curtain wall told him that much but those high ramparts had long been torn down, the once-formidable home undermined and slighted by a victorious, vengeful army. The tower was a lone feature now, incongruous and isolated above this modest wasteland. "What is that place?"

"Gatehouse turret," Hobb said, adjusting further his awkward gait to account for hidden pitfalls and slimy dung. "Only bit left of the old castle." He glanced back with a lopsided grin. "Garrisoned by your lot. Smashed up by ours."

Whistler watched a large kite do wheeling battle with a pair of noisy magpies above the crenellations. "My lot," he said bitterly.

The stocky guard grunted in amusement. "Yours forever, now that you bear the king's mark on your flesh."

Whistler stole a rueful glance at his bound hands, one of which would not open fully, for the seared and puckered palm had healed as tight as a drum skin. They had talked briefly, he and Hobb, after his arrival at the tumbledown castle. Hobb had been a Roundhead pikeman, seeing action in the early throes of the war, before the bullet from a harquebusier's carbine had shattered his thigh. It was strange for Whistler to consider the Royalist cause his own, since he had fled those terrifying ranks as soon as the chance had come but he supposed Hobb was right. He still stared at the remnant of what once must have been a magnificent gatehouse. Lower down, he noticed, part of the original arch remained. "Why leave that one turret?"

"Tis a landmark," Hobb answered. "Helps ships navigate Langstone channel." They were nearing the foot of the turret, where a set of time-smoothed steps led the way up to an open doorway. He grinned. "Also makes for a convenient home for miscreants such as yourself."

"Whistler, is it?"

The speaker had to be the colonel that Hobb had mentioned.

Of the trio of soldiers lurking in the gloomy, musty-smelling chamber to which Whistler had been conveyed, the colonel was the only man seated. He appeared to be in his early forties, with long, dark hair that was streaked with silver. His broad shoulders filled a fine green coat that was slashed at the sleeves to show a silken lining of rich yellow, while across his chest, right shoulder to left hip, there was wrapped a broad scarf, the colour of saffron, bearing the black insignia of a lion's head.

Whistler made the mistake of meeting the colonel's eye. He wrenched his own eyes away quickly, cowed by the nonchalant disdain in the cool grey gaze. "Aye," he managed to say, though it was an effort to force the words out of a throat suffering sudden drought. The colonel yawned expansively and licked his lips. He was lord of this place, a deadly beast in his lair and Whistler's eyes were drawn inexorably back to the lion. "That... that is to say, Whistler be my name."

The colonel glanced left and right at the other men, flanking the table on either side like a pair of grim sentinels, their faces devilish in the shadows thrown by tremulous candle flame. One was tall and stick thin, the other so portly that his scarf, fastened about his waist with a large knot, looked fit for tearing. The tall man, blighted by a facial tick that never seemed to settle, rubbed his hands together against the cold, putting Whistler in mind of a fly alighting upon meat. He glowered. "Sir."

Whistler nodded frantically. "Sir."

"Do you have a real name?" the fly asked. "A Christian name? What did your mother call you?"

"Never knew her, sir," Whistler replied, achingly aware of the final syllable's absurd trilling. "Was always Whistler, long as I can remember."

"A veritable songbird," the colonel said, then, "My name is Maddocks." On the desk before him was a small chest, a plate bearing a selection of marchpanes that had been cut into wedges and a large silver goblet, which he now lifted to his lips.

Maddocks. The name made Whistler's guts clench. It was all he could do not to fall to his knees and sob into the man's boots. He swallowed hard, forcing back a stinging surge of bile.

Unaware or unconcerned, Colonel Maddocks continued, "I

apologise for the crumble-down nature of this place but it will have to serve."

Instinctively, Whistler's eyes roamed. The place in question, he was beginning to realise, had once been a hub of work and governance. The ancient castle's chancery, perhaps, where documents were scribed, sanded and sealed. Besides the table, some of the accoutrements of administration remained, like fragments of memory. A couple of larger chests in the far corners. Shelves still clinging to the wainscoted walls between iron sconces adorned with elaborate oak-sprig motifs. But now the chests were empty, the wainscoting flaky and the sconces rusted. Like the rest of the castle, it was a place of ghosts and former glories, a chamber left to moulder.

As if reading his mind, Maddocks said, "The tower, here, makes for a convenient perch as I fly about the county."

Whistler managed a mute nod. While never claiming to be au fait with the logistical machinations of the Protectorate and its grandees, he knew well enough that Cromwell had devolved regional governance. The affable and talkative Hobb had told him that Colonel Maddocks, on behalf of Major-General Goffe, engaged in an almost perpetual tour of his jurisdiction, like the progress of a medieval king, centring himself on certain appropriate locations from which he might oversee the mechanisms of justice.

Maddocks reached for the tabletop chest, pushing back the polished lid and taking the topmost leaf of what looked like a deep ream of paper. "Now then, sirrah. Let us discuss your predicament."

Feeling all eyes on him, Whistler felt a sudden pang of terror. The fat soldier, ruddy face glimmering with sweat, sidled away from the wall to stand close. Whistler twisted back, hoping to see a recognisable face but Hobb had long since departed. Returning to Maddocks, he blurted, "I told the other men. The officers what took me. I-"

The fat man punched him. Hard, in the guts, so that Whistler folded in half. A thin trail of vomit erupted into his mouth, leaking from the corners of his lips to speckle his breeches and shoes. A strong hand snagged the scruff of his neck and wrenched him upright.

Maddocks, who had not flinched, scanned the paper in his hand, "You were taken at the parchmenter's, yes?"

"Aye, sir," Whistler uttered hoarsely.

"Theft is a very serious felony in the eyes of the Lord." Maddocks glanced up. "Thou shalt not steal. Tis the seventh commandment."

"What choice," Whistler croaked between heaving gasps, "do a man have?"

Maddocks cocked his head to the side, evidently amused. "Do not steal," he said slowly, as if to a dullard. "As choices present themselves, this one is simple enough, no?"

"When the alternative is starvation?"

"When the reward is eternity in paradise." He looked again at the sheet, then placed it back into the chest. Then he selected one of the marchpanes from the plate and crammed half of it into his mouth. "Now. You are a rotten apple, sirrah. A scourge. One lacking the moral fibre to be of any use to a community. In your time you have thieved," the grey eyes flickered to Whistler's hands, "you have deserted and you have trespassed. Lord only knows what other foul deeds will come to light on the day of judgement. You'll know, from your time as a soldier, that when a limb is rotten, the only remedy is the saw." He paused, letting the image hang in the dank air between them. "It must be cut clean away."

Whistler shook his head, frantically, dizzyingly. "No, sir, no, I beg of you-"

"Unless," Maddocks halted him, raising his hand as well as his voice. When all was silent, he took a long moment to eat the rest of the marchpane, licking his lips with a slowness that made Whistler want to scream, then leaned back, bending to take something from a low drawer by his knees. He raised it up for all to see and placed it gently on the desk. "This somewhat curious item was found in your possession. Enlighten me, sirrah."

Whistler gazed at the book. He had expected to be quizzed on the matter, for it had been in his snapsack when the watchmen and soldiers had seized him but, seeing it now, he was again struck by its beauty. It was a small thing, really. Not a great deal bigger than a man's flattened palm, its typeface so minuscule that it did not have the bulk of other bibles. But it had been crafted by artists. From the elaborate and vibrant illuminations within its fragile, yellowing pages, to the golden casing that had protected it for generations. "I took it off a party of pirates."

Maddocks had been staring at the bible too but now his eyes darted up to meet those of his prisoner. "Pirates?"

"Looked like the foreign killers we used to have during the late rebellion," Whistler said. "Paid to come to these shores for king or Parliament."

"Mercenaries."

Whistler nodded. "Excepting, this company wore curved cutlasses at their hips, so I took them for sailors of some kind."

"Where did you encounter these ruffians?"

"Up at Guildford. Followed them south."

"Because?"

Whistler glanced to the bible and back. "Because I saw that they did not lack for means."

"And you waited for your chance."

"God forgive me, sir but I did. Followed, watched, waited. Finally the moment came. The big farm above the marsh at Petersfield."

"The Grange. I know it."

"They rested." Whistler shrugged. "I snuck in."

"And you took this," Maddocks said and his hand slid across the golden book. "The Vulgate. The Papist bible." He looked at Whistler, though his fingers remained, tracing patterns over the metalwork. "Hardly a safe item with which to be caught, notwithstanding the precious material in which it is encased. A man could find himself mistaken for a Jesuit priest and disembowelled." Now he let go of the book and propped both elbows on the table, steepling his hands beneath his chin. His glare was hard and unrelenting. "Are you, in fact, an agent of Rome, posted to these Protestant shores by Satan's own Society of Jesus? Did not you hear word of the Lord Protector's recent proclamation? That popish priests be hounded and prosecuted with the full force of the law? That those who say masses and seduce people to the Church of Rome will be speedily and unmercifully convicted?"

"N... N... no, sir," Whistler stuttered, so taken aback was he by the accusation. He felt icy tentacles wrap themselves about his torso as his bowels turned to water and his heart threatened to pound his ribs to dust. "I... I did not know. I cannot even read!"

Maddocks pressed a forefinger against his lips. "Hush, Master Whistler. Hush now, there's a good fellow." He exchanged a smirk with the fat man and the fly. "Even the Jesuits have standards." As the others chuckled and Whistler came near to fainting, Maddocks picked up the bible, turning it in his hands. "So you stole this shiny bauble, not knowing what was within the pages. Blinkered by avarice, you saw only the gold."

"Aye, sir. I had planned to sell it at Portsmouth. Or have the gold stripped."

"But you never reached Portsmouth, on account of your greed."

"On account of my hunger, sir." Whistler felt his gaze slip, unbidden, to the plate of marchpanes.

Maddocks snorted derisively. "You are a villain and you will be dealt with as such. Next market day at Petersfield will suffice. They have room for one more at Gallows Field."

The fly moved in, rubbing his hands together gleefully, while his portly compatriot took hold of Whistler again. Into Whistler's ear, one of them snarled, "The noose awaits you, lad!" and he bucked and writhed in their implacable grasp but to no avail. They dragged him towards the door, his heels scraping and bouncing along the floor's shattered tiles and he began to weep.

Colonel Francis Maddocks waited for the rumpus to die down before returning his attention to the book.

"Exquisite, Captain Beck, is it not?"

The barrel-like physique of his subordinate filled the doorway. The man, sweating even more profusely than before, wiped chubby hands on his scarf as if to purge them of the prisoner's residue. He frowned at the bible in apparent distaste.

"A Romish trinket, sir."

Maddocks sighed. "One can despise the derivation of an object, John, without despising the object itself."

"If you say so, sir," Beck answered primly as he scratched his back against the wall, like a pig at a post.

"I do." Maddocks handled the book gently, reverently, knowing that his reformist officers would disapprove and not caring one jot. "Yes, I do."

Beck, as disparaging of Papist ornamentation as he was, appraised the object with a glint in his eye. "Golden filigree?"

Maddocks nodded. "Dominated by an image of the living Christ," he said, quietly now, unable to hide his awe, "triumphant before the cross." He ran a finger along the delicate patterns, some of which were inlaid with material the colour of oyster pearls. With his nail he followed each golden thread, caressing them as they swirled. "Around the edges, here, the goldsmith has set red garnets. And here," he indicated the space immediately beneath the cross, "you see these figures? Mourners, on Calvary. The Virgin among them. Such work, John." He breathed out slowly, savouring the moment. "To touch such work." He looked up sharply. "You've heard of Marek Nowak?"

The question clearly wrong-footed Beck, for the captain's mouth flapped silently for a moment or two. Then he shook his head. "I do not believe so, sir."

Lieutenant Grimes, stooping under the lintel, re-entered the room. "Nor I, sir."

Maddocks held up the golden bible. "Its previous owner."

"You know him, sir?" Beck asked, taken aback.

"*Of* him. He has something of a reputation."

"How so?"

Maddocks had studied the bible extensively since arriving in Warblington. The commanding officer of the Havant patrol, a pompous prig by the name of Delaney, had handled the gold-bound object at arm's length, as if the very stench of Beelzebub wafted in its wake. But if Delaney had been only too pleased to be rid of the Papist scriptures, Maddocks had been equally happy to receive them. He knew a valuable trinket when he saw one, even if it did contain the Latin poison that Protestant England spent so much time and energy attempting to eradicate. This wondrous thing had struck him like a heavenly epiphany the moment he had clapped eyes on its ornate cover and he had found himself scrutinising every pattern, every jewel and every page for allegories, maker's marks and any feature of note. "The letters 'MN'," he said, "written just inside." He laid the book on the table, beckoning the others to advance and opened the gold cover to reveal the first page. The initials, inked by hand, were set above the rough sketch of a bird of prey, wings splayed, talons bared. "See the crown atop its head? This is a Polish eagle, gentlemen."

"The pirate?" Grimes asked, reflecting on the prisoner's words.

"The same," Maddocks said. "Except that there are no pirates strolling through Hampshire. There are often, however, plenty of other kinds of mariner. Those who fight the Commonwealth's wars at sea. Shipwrights, caulkers, sailmakers. They walk the lanes between London and Portsmouth." He stabbed the handwritten initials with a forefinger. "There are not many foreign crews in the Commonwealth Navy. Fewer still boasting notorious Polish gun captains. The ship *Diamond* is one such vessel. Marek Nowak is one such gun captain." He sat back. "A fearsome rogue, if ever there was one. As lethal in the prize-fight as he is in battle. You've never heard of him?"

Beck and Grimes shared a nonplussed glance. The former shook his fleshy head. "Should we have, sir?"

"Something of a character amongst Generals at Sea Blake's forces," Maddocks said. "A monster of a pugilist when on land. A divisive figure for his Catholic faith and a fearsome creature for everything else. Fought for his homeland against the Cossacks and Tartars." He paused for a drink, then, clearing his throat, went on, "Survived the Batih massacre, where the Cossacks slaughtered Polish prisoners by the thousand. You'll doubtless recall the horrifying accounts of that atrocity." Invisible feathers played at the skin of his neck as his own memory conjured images he would rather not see. "Days of killing, Captain Beck. To bear witness to such slaughter can only warp the mind." His mouth had dried and he took another sip from the goblet. "After that, enlisted with a Polish merchantman, then found himself sailing under Blake."

Beck wrinkled his flat nose as if he smelled something rotten. "But a papist, sir. We'd not allow such delinquents to infest the Army."

"The Lord Protector's qualms on that score are not shared by the General at Sea."

"Then why does he not compel Blake?"

"Because Robert Blake wins battles, Captain." Maddocks shrugged. "Winning is everything." He left Beck to splutter indignantly and let his eyes slide back to the treasure. It glowed in the candlelight. Soft and rich and enticing. He smiled. "This is a blessed day, gentlemen. Do you know what this book is?"

"Bible, sir," Grimes offered. "Gold bible, sir."

Maddocks leafed rapidly through the pages of Latin until he reached the back of the text. On the final page there was more handwritten script, though these lines, tiny and faded, had been left by an entirely different scribe. "This is Spanish, gentlemen, which I know neither of you have. But note the date."

Grimes's tall frame leaned over the desk like a willow in a breeze. "1531."

"1531," Maddocks echoed. "1531. The very beginning."

"Beginning, sir?" Grimes said.

"When the heathen Americas began to bleed their vast wealth." He ran his finger over the faint note, silently rereading the words to himself. He looked up at captain and lieutenant in turn. "This bible was owned by a Spaniard. A sailor. He took it across the ocean with Pizarro. I had a suspicion, when first I set eyes on it. But to know the provenance of such a piece is truly breathtaking." Closing and lifting the bible, he rapped his knuckles on the metal bindings. "This is Inca gold, gentlemen. Captured by the conquistadors as they destroyed an entire empire. Some would say it is damned. Cursed, for the blood spilt in its taking. The Spaniards claim it is holy, given them by God for their conquest of a pagan land. Who can tell, truly? But sailors, ever a superstitious breed, revere such baubles as you or

I revere scripture itself. In short, Marek Nowak wants his book back and he'd walk through hell itself to get it. Oh, this really is a blessed day." He laughed when the others simply stared, slack-jawed and lost. "Not only do I have in my possession a priceless treasure but the most ruthless man in the Commonwealth Navy believes the Ironside Highwayman has stolen it. Nowak is not the kind of man to be duped. He and his gun crew are unrepentant papists in a ship full of God-fearing Protestants. They are an aberration in a fleet commanded by reformers. Blake owes his victories at sea to the certain fact that the Almighty is on his side. Yet there Nowak stands, beside his gun, firing hot iron at England's enemies while he counts his rosary and crosses his chest. Nowak is not liked, he is not wanted but he is tolerated. Firstly, because he is good – very good – at the business of killing. Secondly, because he is a man that other men fear. He is not one to be crossed. He is not one to be contradicted. He is not one to be made a fool of. And he believes Samson Lyle has made a fool of him."

Maddocks set the bible down and took another drink as he waited for his words to percolate through his officers' skulls. Captain Beck said, "If we keep the book, sir, this Marek will murder the Chalton fellow."

"An unfortunate consequence, to be certain," Maddocks acknowledged, "but a small sacrifice for the greater good, wouldn't you say?" When he saw Beck was unconvinced, he continued, "Lyle is the worst kind of hypocrite, Captain. A brigand and a traitor, yet brim-full with his own sense of righteousness. He has pledged to retrieve this book. Well, he cannot, for it is here, praise God! But he will yet try to rescue the Chalton man. He won't be able to resist." He looked at Grimes. "And what shall we do, Lieutenant?"

"Nothing, sir?"

"Nothing," Maddocks repeated, satisfied that at least one of his protégés understood the way real life worked. "You and I and Captain Beck, here and all our men will go about our business. We shall return to Petersfield. To Rowlands Castle and to East Meon." He picked up the bible again and opened the little chest. "We shall ride the bridleways, inspect the villages and keep law, order and public morality on behalf of Major-General William Goffe, God bless him. And we shall let Marek Nowak kill the Ironside Highwayman." He placed the bible in the chest and closed the lid. "A fine thing indeed."

*

Portsmouth Point, Portsmouth

The men circled one another like bulldogs in a pit, the fiddler played a jaunty reel, the crowd bayed for blood. The air was thick, hot, infused with spittle and blood, fuggy with the acrid stench of bodies and breath and ale and unadulterated excitement.

Marek Nowak blinked stinging sweat from his eyes, the blurry drape swept quickly away. Across the stained sawdust, panting hard, the twisted features of the leering Turk resolved before him. Like Marek, he was naked from the waist up, broad chest gleaming, the tuft of black hair at his sternum smeared with blood that dripped from his severely buckled nose. There were dark patches at his collarbones and biceps where Marek's attacks had been blocked, leaving bruises that would, God willing, take their own toll as the contest wore on. The Turk's eyes were puffing too, each cut deeply, one at the corner, one right across the lid but within the folds of livid, distended skin the glittering jet stare persisted.

The Jolly Sailor was located to the south of Portsmouth Point, adjacent to the gate that separated the lawless crescent of land from the rest of the town. It was slanted and timber-framed, squeezed in on both sides by hovels and bawdy houses, the epicentre of a rampart of debauchery and vice that glowered over the Solent's crashing grey waves. It hummed with the sounds of humanity; and Marek Nowak embraced it like a lover.

It had all started with a game of Ruff wherein the Turk, boatswain of a Portuguese slaver up from Senegambia, had won a deal of money at Marek's expense. That, of course, had all been by the Polish gunner's design, culminating in an escalation of stakes and coin that had climaxed with a final, lucrative challenge. Fists in place of cards. *Give me the chance to win it back, my friend. Double or nothing!*

Now, the better part of twenty minutes later, as the grimacing Turk spat a crimson gobbet onto the clotted shavings, Marek decided that enough was enough. It was time to collect his winnings. He squinted through the pungent pall of sot weed smoke. The sky outside had been pale grey when he had stepped over the Jolly Sailor's foot-worn threshold but now he could see only the room's glowing reflection in the black windows. Somewhere in the background the fiddle played on. The attack was low when it came. A lunge for Marek's midriff, the intention to hoist him bodily into the air and slam him to earth but Marek sidestepped, giving his opponent a shove so that he staggered past. The pair spun together, joined once again. Marek evaded a hammering right, the air pulsing at his ear and planted one of his own on the end of the boatswain's chin, snapping back the sinewy neck. The Turk, the taller of the two, rocked rearward to keep his feet and shook his head like a rain-drenched dog, dark droplets scattering from the matted ends of his long hair. The crowd yowled their appreciation. He put a knuckle to his chin as if checking it had not shattered, grinned crookedly from behind black stubble and spat a globule of tainted spittle onto the sawdust between them.

Marek snuck a downward glance, catching the bright wink of a couple of teeth and slid his tongue around his mouth to confirm they were not his own. Satisfied, he twisted his torso to present the smallest target for the Turk's superior reach, thrust his left foot out in front and bounced gently on his toes, ignoring the exhausted pleas of his aching thighs. His heart raced, his limbs felt white-hot, his swollen fists numb.

The Turk came again, his muscular frame gliding like a ghoul in the hellish torchlight, the crowd roaring him on. Marek dodged a left jab but could not avoid the heavy straight right that followed. He juddered back, stamping his feet to make sure he still controlled them. He could feel a patch at the corner of his mouth already beginning to swell, spat thickly as the Turk had spat and then they came together again. The Turk swayed around Marek's punch, came inside the range of his fists and grasped Marek's head, grappling at his ears, holding, twisting, forcing him down as if trying to drown him in an invisible pool. Marek could smell the Turk, taste the bloody sweat that showered them both and the pain at the base of his neck told him he would soon crumple. He lashed twice at the taller man's wire-haired midriff to little effect and launched upwards, clubbing the back of his skull into the Turk's face. Bone crunched, skin split, new blood fountained. Only when Marek pushed away did he see that the blood was the Turk's, the man's nose and mouth smashed to a gnarled mess, his bulbous fists clawing ineffectually as he reeled away.

The mob shrieked. Marek gave chase, hands locking at the Turk's arm and waist as his opponent floundered unsighted, mewing like a wounded calf. Marek dipped, twisted at the hips, wrenching hard and the Turk lurched off his feet, barrelling over Marek's dropped shoulder. Marek went with him, letting the bigger man's momentum take him and he left the ground too, tumbling onto the hapless boatswain so that he landed with an elbow driven hard into the dazed fighter's windpipe. The mob bellowed their delight and chagrin and from the corner of his eye Marek could see the glint of metal as coins slipped between avaricious palms. He rolled away, gasping. The Turk was clutching his neck, a drainpipe gargle easing between split lips.

Marek hauled himself to his feet. A grossly corpulent man – the local butcher if Marek recalled correctly – waddled into the makeshift ring and began the count. His was the role of fight custodian, employed to keep decorum when all around lusted for blood and violence. Steadily and with the echo of every witness's voice, the numbers climbed.

The Turk did not.

Then came a torrent of noise as the half-minute mark was reached. The Turk's second crouched over the prone form, pleading with him to stand but to no avail.

Hands came then, grasping Marek's drenched arms and holding them aloft. The pain descended, as it always did, fast at the heels of a fight finished. Marek was vaguely aware of his opponent beginning to stir, rocking to the side to vomit. He felt himself sway a little and a trio of barely pubescent pot-boys gathered around to bolster his bulk like snot-nosed buttresses. He waved them away in irritation, totting up his teeth again, just to be sure and made his way over to one of the tables his men had commandeered. They cheered him as ever and Louis, his oldest comrade, pushed a slopping pot of ale into his distended hand.

After slaking his thirst, his gaze fell upon the one member of the group manifestly not enjoying himself. "What did you think?"

The stocky but sallow adolescent stared, eyes wide as plates, around the smoky room. "You won."

"Good money to be made at the prize play, boy." Marek grinned as he followed the dour youth's gaze. "An education, yes?"

"It is a vile place," Botolph Spendlove said with revulsion. He rubbed a hand over eyes as bruised as Marek's, as if he might wipe away the sinful scenes. "A lewd place."

"That it is, boy," Marek said. "One of my favourite places on God's earth."

"Why are we here?"

"Spice Island lies outside the town boundary. Law extends only as far as the wall and gate, yonder. To lodge in the town invites the tentacles of your Puritan Parliament to entwine us, constrict us. But here? Here we are kings."

"Spice Island? They store spice here?"

Marek guffawed. "It is so named for its..." he pursed his lips as he sought the apt word, "*flavoursome* ways."

Botolph screwed up his mouth as if he tasted something putrid. "Drink, cards and pugilism."

"More than that, boy," Marek answered with relish. "So much more."

Botolph looked up at the balcony, where a party of wide-skirted women loitered. One appeared to catch his eye, waving. He cast his gaze hurriedly to the table's ale-rings.

"Ha!" Marek exclaimed, raising his jar to the ladies, who chirped vulgar remarks in response, making him think of budgies at the bars of a cage. "You're going to die soon, boy. I do not wish it but I have made a pledge. Get up there and become a man before it is too late."

Botolph's frame stiffened, the vein at his neck pulsing visibly. "You'll not get away with this."

"Is that so?" Marek answered contemptuously. "Have you any inkling as to my value aboard ship? Laws of the land do not apply. All the while I can bring my gun to bear with accuracy and speed, I am General Blake's man and none may touch me." He leaned in, jabbing a finger into the youth's chest. "I want my property returned. *You* stole it, your *master* has it. If he elects to deprive me of what is mine, I will kill you dead. Make no mistake."

Botolph's eyes glistened with a wellspring of tears. "I have no knowledge of this property, sir. None at all. I'm a God fearing man, not a thief."

Marek almost hit the boy for that but he wished no more burning pain for knuckles that had already served him so well. He glanced at Botolph's crippled hand, resting at the table's edge. "Your affliction is my proof. Christ but I should let Duncan take his whip to you again." He was gratified to see the boy wince at the prospect, for his back was well-striped already. "You are in the employ of this renegade; this Ironside Highwayman."

"I'd never clapped eyes on him till moments before you stepped into the Lion," Botolph bleated.

Marek drank deeply, quaffing the ale and belching. He inspected his fists, opening and closing the damaged fingers tentatively. "It is the same tired protest you have bored me with a hundred times, boy. I am no longer listening. The highwayman will bring my property, or I will bring him a corpse. There can be no other way."

THURSDAY

Warblington Castle, Hampshire

It was still dark when Hobb took Whistler from his cell. He was cajoled across the potholed yard, as he had been the previous day but this time there was no rendezvous with great men in the slighted castle's lonesome tower. This time he was shown through one of the breaches in the crumbled walls, with only a single lamp, a scattering of stars and a sliver of moon to illuminate the way and everything obscured by the billowing fog of his own breath. His feet crunched on frost-hardened ground and his chest rasped with trepidation.

"You're for Petersfield," Hobb, as pungent as ever, explained as they walked. "God have mercy on you."

Before Whistler could reply, they were out in the clearing beyond the wall. Here, where the foot of the fortress's old boundary was banked by a deep drift of rubble, the land had been transformed into a place of construction; or, rather, demolition. Planks criss-crossed like miniature roads, so that barrow wheels might traverse the worst of the mud, while workbenches could be seen in the gloom alongside earth-filled gabions and half-a-dozen wagons. They were removing the stone and flint from the ancient fortification, he realised. Bringing down the curtain walls, breaking up the largest sections and carting it away for works elsewhere. The nearby village, presumably, though that was anyone's guess.

Horses whickered out in the darkness. Whistler squinted after the sounds. Hobb gestured with a chubby hand towards the treeline, some thirty paces distant. Before the trees there was a black shape, blotting out the trunks, its outline – a regular square with a domed roof – similar to a house but smaller than he would expect. As they drew closer, the sounds of the horses grew louder and the detail of the place gradually began to resolve. It was a dilapidated old pug mill house, once used in constructing the castle and now, he thought wryly, most likely a shelter for the men who tore the place down. It was also a shelter for the soldiers who would escort him to his death, for he could see the four big destriers now, tethered to stakes at the side of the pug mill. There was a thick coil of rope attached to one of their saddles and Whistler's guts lurched as he understood that that was surely intended for him.

"Over there, fellow," the voice of a man came suddenly from the murk, putting Whistler's heart in his mouth. He looked round, searching for the speaker. The man growled, "I said over there."

Whistler saw his outline, tall and lean but, before he could respond, he noticed it was Hobb that was hurrying to remove himself. All at once, he noticed the speaker's outstretched arm and the unmistakable shape of the pistol at its extent and he saw, too, that the weapon was indeed trained upon his erstwhile gaoler.

As Hobb moved, the glow of his lantern briefly snaked across the scene. Before it was extinguished, Whistler saw a face he had seen before. Green eyes, glinting like a prowling tomcat's behind that poised pistol. He glimpsed the interior of the pugmill beyond. The men crouching, huddled together in fear, wrists bound between knees.

He gaped at the man he had encountered outside the rain-lashed chapel at Idsworth. "You."

"Where is the bible? Come, Master Whistler, do not play the fool with me."

"A soldier has it," Whistler replied. "A black-haired bastard with a yellow scarf."

"Maddocks?"

Whistler shrugged. "Might have been."

The man with the pistol advanced a pace. "I have no particular desire to turn you loose. If you would have your freedom, you must earn it."

Whistler felt the bravado leak away. He nodded quickly. "Maddocks, aye. A colonel. He has it. The soldiers took it from my snapsack and that bastard had it when he questioned me. That's the last I saw of it, I swear."

"Used it to wipe their arses by now," another voice, crackling

228

with age and coloured by the vowels of the westernmost counties, came from within the pugmill house. "Like as bliddy not."

Whistler laughed scornfully at that, despite his fear. "You think he's tossed a solid gold book into his fire?"

There was a pause, pregnant with realisation. "Gold?" Yet another new speaker from inside the shelter. This time a girl. Whistler wondered how many had come to affect this strangest of rescues. If a rescue was even what it was.

"You did not know?" he asked. "It is a bible. A popish one. All in Latin. Means nothing to me. But the bindings are covered in gold. Tis a very fine thing."

"Little wonder you pinched it," the old man's disembodied voice echoed in the dark.

"Aye, well, Jesu knows I wish I hadn't now."

The man with the green eyes said, "Is he there? Maddocks, is he still in the castle?"

*

"Jeremy?" Colonel Francis Maddocks called in response to the knock at his door. He was still in bed, the watery rays of a new dawn casting his chamber in dim grey.

"Sally, sir," came the reply from outside.

Startled to hear a female voice, Maddocks heaved his body up, tiredness counterbalanced by the relief of removing himself from the rudimentary straw palliasse that had made him itch most of the night. For the sake of decorum, he went to the wardrobe in which Jeremy, his usual servant, had hung his breeches and coat and quickly dressed before giving the order to enter. When the girl, who was about twelve at a guess, pushed open the door, he curtly demanded an explanation.

"An ague, sir," she explained, "God help him." She stepped into the room, bearing a large bowl of what he hoped would be warm water, a length of clean-looking linen draped over her forearm. "Taken to his bed. I have been sent in his stead."

Maddocks clapped his hands. "Smartly, then, for I cannot tarry."

She scurried to the low table beneath the room's only window and set down the bowl, folding the cloth into a neat square and placing it beside the water. "There's to be a hanging, so they say."

The casual tone annoyed Maddocks and he almost said as much but even the girl's impertinence could not dampen his mood. He gave an affirmative grunt as he bent over the bowl. "A prolific thief, aye." He splashed his face, pleased to discover that the water had, mercifully, been heated. When he straightened, using the cloth to dab away the trembling droplets from his nose and chin, he noticed Sally gazing absently out of the window that looked onto the castle's debris-strewn ward. "Not here, girl. It'll be done at Petersfield."

"Why, sir?"

"Propriety. Justice must be *seen* to be done in the appropriate manner. Even I cannot string an offender up from the nearest tree." Which was not strictly true, he thought, for he doubted any magistrate from here to Newbury would question the actions of Goffe's right-hand man but that did not mean Maddocks was keen to test the theory. "He'll meet his end at the town gallows on market day."

"Poor fellow," Sally said.

"We all must make our decisions in life and we all must carry the consequences." Maddocks cleaned his teeth with the linen, each tooth squeaking like an unoiled hinge as he buffed vigorously. When he was done, he dropped the cloth into the water and strode towards the door, fetching up his belt and weapons as he went. "Deal with that, girl," he commanded with a cursory wave back at the bowl. He took a sumptuous cape, the same colour as his capacious scarf, from a hook in the dark wainscoting. "I ride for Petersfield."

"To see justice done, sir?"

He could not help but smile at that. "Just so, Sally. Just so."

*

Near Widley, Hampshire

Star's lungs roared as he ran west.

Lyle leaned in, calling encouragement, urging the grey stallion to dredge more speed from legs that must have been growing heavier by the moment. But he could not relent. It was almost seven miles to Portsea Island and he had chosen to take the high road, over the hills, where the going was more hazardous but the lanes less conspicuous, which meant that a full gallop was impossible. And all the while the sun climbed out of the horizon at their backs.

Amelia clung on tight, squeezing Lyle's midriff, her cheek pressed against his back. He looked to his right, checking that Grumm and Tyrannous were managing to keep pace. Behind the Cornishman was Whistler. The deserter-turned-thief looked frailer than ever, as if the wispiest of breezes might topple him from the saddle. He seemed so feeble, so inconsequential, clinging to the former smuggler like a limpet on a rock and yet what chaos the man had wrought. What forces he had unwittingly unleashed. And now there was Maddocks. Lyle saw the colonel's face as he thundered along the track that was taking them up the chalky escarpment fringing the expansive harbours of Langstone and Portsmouth. His old comrade when they had fought under Ireton – ironsides together, zealous and triumphant – only to become his nemesis in the aftermath of Lyle's desertion and Alice's cruel death. Maddocks had hunted Lyle ever since, had chased him through forests and faced him at sword point and here he was again, dragged into Whistler's mess just as Lyle had been. Maddocks. The thought of him made Lyle shudder in the gloom. He was a reminder. Of a lost past and a futile future. And now Lyle would be forced to confront him again. Because soon, inevitably, the hunt would resume and Lyle would have to fight for his life.

*

Warblington Castle, Hampshire

"An ambush?"

The young cornet of horse, whose usual role of carrying his

troop's colour had been superseded this dawn by an impromptu prisoner escort, blanched under the severe gaze of his colonel. "It was dark, sir," he bleated, putting Maddocks in mind of a frightened lamb. He pointed at the domed pugmill some twenty yards to his rear. "They came out of the mill shelter. Tied us up."

"And took the prisoner," Maddocks completed the sentence. He had already clambered into the saddle and fastened his freshly polished helm before hearing the chorus of alarmed voices coming from beyond the castle ward. Making for the sound at a swift canter, he had come upon a scene of confusion involving a routine foot patrol and the disarmed, bound and gagged wretches they had stumbled upon. Those humiliated creatures had turned out to be members of Maddocks's own unit, which was something of an embarrassment but when he had finally grasped the implication, he had a mind to run each and every one of them through. He twisted, finding his immediate subordinate in the gathering daylight. "Captain Beck? Who, in Christ's holy name, would do such a thing? Why?"

Beck, who had scurried out of his own lodgings behind a suspiciously half-clad stable boy, had only just managed to gather himself for the breathless inquest. Red at the jowls and sweating profusely, he panted, "Fellow thieves, sir?"

Maddocks awarded the suggestion the scorn-dripping sneer it deserved. "We have not encountered a modern-day Robin Hood, Captain." He went back to the shame-faced cornet. "What did the culprits look like?"

The cornet was busily rubbing his recently untied wrists. "They wore hoods, sir. It was dark."

"Try."

The cornet risked a look up. "Three of them."

Another of the prisoner detail, a youngster with a dark complexion and a pronounced squint, cleared his throat nervously. "Four."

The cornet nodded vigorously. "Aye, four, that's right. The leader was a man. About my height."

"Accent?" Maddocks asked.

The cornet shrugged. "Local, sir but-"

"But?" prompted Maddocks.

"His accomplices were unusual," the cornet ventured.

Maddocks shifted his weight impatiently. "How so? Come, boy, do not be timid."

"One was elderly," the cornet said. "That is to say, he had an old man's voice. And, I may be mistaken but I reckoned on two women."

That caught Maddocks's attention. He edged forwards, ignoring the cornet's flinch. "Women?"

The trooper with the squint said, "He ain't mistook, sir. Women, for certain. One was very young, at a guess."

And in that moment Maddocks knew. His heart seemed to plummet from his chest into his stomach and back again. "It is Lyle."

Beck, apparently composed now, said, "The Ironside Highwayman? But why would he bother with that raggedy pilferer?"

But Maddocks was not listening, because something else – something worse – had occurred to him. Not occurred. The realisation had stabbed him full in the guts. "My lodgings," he said absently, almost to himself as the connotations squawked and swirled like birds through his mind. Then, louder, "To my lodgings, Captain Beck, immediately!"

*

Portsmouth Point, Hampshire

Botolph Spendlove had always wanted to visit the coast. A product of the rolling hills, he had walked those high crests and squinted into a horizon dazzled by the sea more times than he could count but there had never been reason or occasion to brave the roads that would take a traveller to the nation's southern edge. The miles between Chalton and the Solent were lush and bucolic but they also negotiated challenging terrain and footpad-infested forests. His life, therefore, had been one of gentle downland and sleepy village, cosseted by parents who knew too much of the world to risk exposing their precious offspring to it and Botolph had been left to stew in his frustration and long for the chance to see soldiers and bustling streets and mighty warships.

Now Botolph had it all and wanted none. He was in the thick of it, the lively, dangerous and depraved horn of dry land that served England but was not truly part of her. Portsmouth Point. Spice Island. There were sailors and dockworkers here. Privateers and pirates, hawkers and pickpockets, smugglers and swindlers, fishermen and ferrymen, gamblers, drinkers, whores and their pimps. Out in the harbour there were the warships he had craved to see, billowing shrouds rigged to masts as tall as great oaks. The streets were a cacophony of shouts and laughter, of foreign tongues and strange faces from all corners of God's creation, while the pungent scents of a hundred exotic spices mingled to make even the sharpest breeze heady and intoxicating. It was everything he could ever have imagined. And all he wanted was to go home.

"Come, lad," Duncan said, cuffing Botolph hard enough to make him stumble.

Botolph barely managed to keep his feet. He could hear the mocking laughter of his captors at his back. He could feel the heat of humiliation rise through his face and his swollen eye sockets began to pulse. As he straightened, he risked a sideways glance at the huge Scotsman, noticing with a shudder how Duncan pointedly fingered the knotted coil of leather at his belt. The wounds that striped his spine began to burn at the sight of it, reminding him of the first hours after his capture, when these evil men had attempted to extract information that simply was not his to impart. He noted, too, that with his free hand Duncan picked at the scab on his chin. It gave him a glimmer of pleasure to know that it was Amelia who had inflicted the wound.

Perhaps catching a shadow of defiance in the hostage's look, Duncan advanced with his black gums bared, unhooking the whip in one deft motion. He unfurled it, working his wrist so that it rippled from handle to tip. Botolph shied away, shielding himself with his arms, though bitter experience told him it would prove futile.

"Duncan!" Marek's harsh voice brought the Scot up short. "I want him in one piece."

The Scot furnished Botolph with a sour look but he stayed his hand nonetheless, letting the others amble past as he coiled the leather once more. They were on the move, the gunners, bleary eyed and ill-tempered after a night of debauchery. They had vacated the Jolly Sailor at dawn and now made their way north, intending to take new lodgings at an inn situated flush against the dock, there to await the ship's boat that would soon berth for the agreed rendezvous. *Diamond* was to sail back to Cadiz in a matter of weeks, Botolph had learned and all hands were expected back on deck to begin preparations.

Marek came alongside him, nodding at the cobbles to invite him to walk. "He does not like you. The book is," he waved a meaty hand, knuckles distended like knots on a branch, "priceless to us. But I must keep you whole so that that *skurwysyn* keeps his side of the bargain."

"Why do you call him that name?"

"*Skurwysyn*? Bastard. Whoreson. Your master-"

"He is not my master, you must believe me, I-"

"Your master," Marek said firmly, "is the worst kind of devil. A thief, for certain but also a liar."

Botolph abandoned the plea that had been forming on his tongue, for he could see plainly enough that Marek would brook no argument. Instead he gazed about the busy thoroughfare. "I have never been here before."

"Spice Island?"

"Portsmouth." He thought back to their brief conversation the night before. "You said it was an education."

"I was right?"

"You were." He looked up at the big gun captain, a heavy stone forming in his stomach. "How will I die?"

"The water," Marek replied, the frankness of his tone making Botolph shudder. "It is painless, so they tell me. I could make it worse for you, boy." His voice darkened in warning. "Do not give me reason."

"I will not," Botolph said hurriedly.

"Will he come?"

"This highwayman?" Botolph shrugged helplessly. "How should I know?"

Marek laughed at that. "You have spirit, boy, I concede. You'd make a fine hand aboard *Diamond*." He shook his head when Botolph made to speak. "Alas, that can never be. Your master has my book. I must be seen to fulfil my promise."

"But if he does not come with this book," Botolph said, "he will not be here to witness my death. What can be gained?"

"Plenty will bear witness, boy. Word will reach him and he will know."

*

Portsdown Hill

"I wondered why those bastards kept to their fire," Whistler said as the horses drew up on the escarpment's crest. The sun was fully visible now, the day cold but bright. "In the yard at Petersfield. Why not lodge under a roof, I thought? If not the farmhouse, then surely one of the stables."

"Sailors are not readily welcome," Lyle said as he gazed down on the flat expanse of Portsea Island. The view snatched the air from his lungs. The coastal plain stretched off to sea, a patchwork of field and marsh, road and hedgerow, with the rooftops of Portsmouth dark in the distance, a charcoal outline against the horizon.

Behind him, Amelia spoke. "For their rough manners?"

Whistler laughed. "For their poxed pizzles, Mistress!"

"That's enough," Lyle ordered. He was still staring into the distance, where land met water, examining the forest of bare masts that sprouted like black shoots from the glittering Solent, marking the bustling harbour and dockyard and, further out, the anchorage at Spithead, black hulls of the biggest vessels smudging the sky. Blake's great warships were there, sheltered from all but south-easterly winds as they awaited the order to set shrouds and sail for Spain. *Diamond* would be among them. He tried to guess which.

"And a man has more than thirst to be slaked," Whistler was

saying with obvious relish, "after many a month at sea. Any home with daughters to protect does not open the door to such travellers, no matter how weary they may be."

Lyle tore himself away from the ships and turned Star so that the grey stallion faced Grumm's black gelding. "Down you get."

When Grumm did not move, the light of understanding showed in Whistler's small eyes. His mouth dropped. "You mean to strand me?" His head jerked left and right, like a rat surveying potential routes of escape. "On this bloody hill in the middle o' nowhere?"

"Hardly nowhere," Lyle said. He pointed north, to the breeze-rippled pastures beyond Whistler and Grumm. "You'll find the Southwick road yonder."

"I will apologise to the lady, sir, I-"

Lyle cut him off with a shake of his head. "I owe you nothing but a thrashing, sirrah, so I would consider yourself fortunate that I am willing to turn you loose."

"I shall starve," Whistler opined, his tone growing shriller with desperation.

"Here." Lyle produced a small pouch from his saddle and tossed it to Whistler, who caught it with his scarred hand. "Get some food in your belly when the moment is opportune. But get away from here without delay. There'll be soldiers on this road soon enough."

The thief weighed the money in his ruined palm and slid out of the saddle, leaving Grumm to make theatre of stretching his shoulders, as if the weight of the world had been lifted from them. Whistler asked, "Where shall I go?"

"I care only that I do not look upon your face again," Lyle said.

Whistler glanced at the purse. "I can arrange that."

Lyle nodded. "See that you do."

They took the bridleway that led them south towards the vast island. Steep and winding, it cut a swathe through the white and green face of Portsdown Hill, small chunks of chalk skittering before them, kicked up by the horses' hooves. The slope was carpeted in long grass and thick brier patches, broken up by stands of trees and through the branches they could make out the rooftops of the villages nestling like mushrooms at the hill's foot.

"Wymering," Lyle said, indicating the buildings. "With Cosham beyond."

He felt Amelia lift her head from his shoulder to take an interest. "That is where we leave the horses?"

"And meet Bella, God willing."

They rode on. Resisting the use of their spurs to save the horses but always urging the tired beasts to push, for the road at their backs would not remain empty forever. Folk were abroad, though it was still early. Small children played and shrieked in the trees and Lyle's party were forced to negotiate their way through increasing amounts of traffic. Heavily loaded wagons, making hard work of the cloying terrain, travelled in the opposite direction, interspersed by a small flock of sheep, a sack-laden donkey and a gaggle of stick-driven geese, all noisily vying for space as their owners looked to do business on the first dry day for some time.

When they reached the village, Lyle made directly for the imposing whitewashed façade of Wymering Manor, a place so ancient that folk often found the detritus of Roman habitation in its gardens and cellars. From that landmark he was able to resurrect the lie of the land from memory and quickly located an inn just around the corner. The Bull & Gate was a modest, single storey affair but he recalled that it had adequate stabling and a discreet owner. He was forced to pay over the odds to the ostlers and landlord for a guarantee of security and anonymity, "But the crossing will be guarded by soldiers," he explained to a disgruntled Grumm, "so we must travel inconspicuously."

Bella arrived soon afterwards, having taken the low coast road around Langstone Harbour. "Ain't seen the buggers," she replied, swinging out of the saddle, as Lyle took hold of Newt's head collar and enquired as to any sign of trouble. "But I'd wager they've noticed the book's vanished by now."

A high-sided dray, drawn by two meaty cart-horses and driven by a portly bald man, with a slab face and thick neck rolls, came to a halt about forty paces away. The vehicle was packed full of tightly bound hemp bales and Lyle watched as the driver leaned back on his bench and lit a pipe. "You found it, then?" he asked Bella with a wry smile.

"Simple enough. Kept it in a little travelling chest." Bella gave an impish cackle. "Men like that do not need to hide their things. They're untouchable, ain't they? Who'd dare burgle them?" She winked at Amelia, who was watching with apparent astonishment as the little girl produced a gold-bound bible from her saddlebag. "Don't occur there might be a cuckoo in the nest."

Lyle took the gleaming object and thrust it into the folds of his cloak. "How fares the lad?"

Bella pulled an exaggeratedly sad expression. "Poor Jeremy!" She tapped her knuckles at her temple. "A sore head, I shouldn't wonder but he'll live. Now then," she clapped her hands and looked expectantly at Lyle, "we cannot stroll onto Portsea Island, Samson, so I hope to God you've cooked up a decent plan."

*

Portsbridge Fort, above Ports Creek, Hampshire

Maddocks dug his spurs into his mount's heaving flanks as the fort came into view. He had led a hastily mustered troop of forty out of Warblington Castle in something akin to blind panic, sending half up and over the hills, the rest staying with him on the marshy coast road and now they came together again in a flurry of hoof-beats and bellows. No one, it seemed, had been captured, nor so much as spotted. With frustration turning to rage, he directed his vengeful harquebusiers towards the narrow crossing onto Portsea Island.

Maddocks had known they would not find the book as soon as he had learned of Lyle's involvement. Why would such a man embroil himself with the likes of Whistler, the ever-sceptical Captain Beck had asked? The answer had rung like a bell in Maddocks's head. The Vulgate bible. And even as he had wrenched his horse's head about and galloped back into the decrepit castle's inner ward, he had known the golden book would not be where he had left it. There was nothing for it, except to rouse the men and hunt the malefactors to ground.

The high earthwork loomed above the road, dominating the landscape as it had for at least two centuries. The passage of time had weathered the rampart, stealing a few feet from the summit and filling parts of the defensive ditch but all that was counterweighted easily enough by the rows of fresh stakes, pale at the newly sharpened tips, that protruded like the teeth of some monstrous maw. The fort was shaped like a star, its high bulwarks reminiscent of the sconces Maddocks had seen at London, Worcester and Newark, yet this formidable obstacle was not designed to conduct or obstruct a siege but rather to protect the single crossing onto Portsea Island, thus giving landward protection to the crucial naval installations beyond.

Maddocks hauled on the reins as he reached the broad timber bridge over the ditch, noting the ominous black muzzles of half-a-dozen heavy guns on the rampart immediately above. His horse whinnied as it wheeled, great clods of mud flinging in all directions and he barked at the pair of sentries standing before the huge open gates. Their eyes wandered over him, taking in the cut of his expensive clothes, the gleam of his polished plate and the lion's head embroidered onto the saffron scarf. His pennant was coming, lofted on a long pole by a young cornet but they did not need to see the device to know with whom they were dealing. They stepped aside smartly and the troopers thundered across the ditch and into the open expanse of the fort, which proved to be a flat plateau containing a gravel track and a single wooden building that served as the soldiers' quarters. Told to take their ease, the troopers found space to dismount and went to sit on the grass, fishing hard biscuit, dried meat or wads of fragrant sotweed from their bags.

On the far side of the fort, in a reflection of the landward gates, the doorway above the creek gaped open, the flanking guards taking a markedly languid approach to their duties. Maddocks, still mounted, approached them, Captain Beck a few yards in his wake. "Riders," he called down to a swarthy sergeant who leaned nonchalantly against a halberd that was decorated with brightly coloured tassels. "Three, perhaps four. Have you seen them?"

The sergeant sucked at his black whiskers for a moment, then gave a noncommittal twitch of the shoulders. "Seen plenty o' folk since sun-up, sir."

"This party," Maddocks replied brusquely, "is led by a criminal. Tall, green eyes, into his late twenties. He is accompanied by a haggardly old clapperdudgeon and two females."

The sergeant glanced in amusement at his trio of subordinates. "Circus troupe, by the sounds of it," he ventured in an accent native to the West Midlands, "though we haven't seen the like."

Maddocks sucked his teeth in frustration. "Brigands, all"

"Lady outlaws, sir?" The sergeant's surprise was evident and he looked round at his men. "We'd not let in that kind of miscreant, would we, boys? Goodness me, no."

Captain Beck asked, "What think you, Colonel? Back on the road?"

Maddocks adjusted his cloak, buying time for consideration. He let his horse walk between the sentries and under the arch, to look upon the mossy blocks of stone that formed the bridge onto the island. Either side, the waters of the creek ran fast and murky, foaming thick where it parted around the base of each pier. He twisted to look back at Beck, who had come up to occupy the arch. "If Lyle had merely freed that flea-bitten little weasel then maybe. But he stole the bible."

Beck's fleshy face screwed into an expression of incredulity. "He's gone elsewhere, sir. Up country to sell his ill-gotten loot."

"Marek Nowak has one of the highwayman's gang," Maddocks answered, his tone firming with rapidly increasing certainty. "Lyle will not stand for such a thing, I'd stake my life on it. He has stolen the bible in order to return it. Exchange it for his fellow criminal."

"Then where is the blackguard?" Beck said in exasperation.

They were interrupted by the sergeant's voice, orders spilling loud and fast as he hurried to direct newly arrived traffic towards the crossing. Maddocks went back to look upon the commotion. Several wagons, stacked high with wool bales, had come down off the hill, it seemed and, funnelling through the earthwork, they would now need the cavalrymen to move aside. Between them and with the sergeant's profuse apologies as accompaniment, Maddocks and Beck managed to corral their resting troopers onto their horses and into a double file. When they were ready to ride, the colonel let his cornet come up, raising the colour for all to see and led them in a clattering chorus across the creek and onto Portsea Island. The hunt would resume in earnest.

Because the wagons had given him an idea.

*

Portsmouth, Hampshire

It had been years since Lyle had ventured down to the coast, where the Solent lashed the shore and the gulls wheeled and cackled but Portsmouth was just as he remembered. As the afternoon leaked away, the light gradually washing out, the cart had squeezed its way into the town, waved through the ornate gateway that was set into a huge, flag-topped and crenelated bastion, the jaded-looking sentries offering the most cursory of glances as they processed a line of vehicles that ran into the dozens. The muddy road beyond the long defensive wall had instantly become paved, sporadic steadings giving way to tightly packed terraces, thatch-work replaced by tiles in an evident effort to negate the effects of fire. The streets were busy, the bellows of barrow boys and basket wielders vying with purveyors of ribbon and string, eggs and milk, apples and leather and shoes.

All this Lyle and his companions heard, rather than witnessed, for theirs was a journey glimpsed via the chinks of light between their covering of hemp bales. In other circumstances the commandeering of the vehicle would have been a source of deep regret, for he had genuinely sympathised with the unwitting driver. The poor fellow had been taking his ease, eyes firmly shut, as he drank the tobacco smoke and let his cares drift into the crisp air. What a rude awakening it had been to feel the cruel press of cold metal as Lyle had pushed his pistol's twin muzzles into the bulging folds of skin at the nape of the terrified man's neck.

"You're travelling to the docks," Lyle had whispered into the man's rapidly reddening ear. It had not been a question, for where else was a huge consignment of hemp destined?

"Aye," had been the murmured response, from one too frightened to nod, "to the new ropery."

And so, with the promise that the driver's brains would be splattered over his cargo if he gave them away, the Ironside Highwayman and his accomplices became stowaways.

"Baltic hemp, out of Königsberg," the driver, doing his utmost to convey a calmness that he cannot possibly have felt, had explained as the chief sentry at the Portsbridge Fort had questioned him. "Comes into Port of London and I takes it out to Chatham, then down here. Makes the finest cordage on God's earth."

"I'm sure it does," had been the bored-sounding reply and then, to Lyle's palpable relief, they were out and away, the dray's wheels bouncing alarmingly over the stone bridge and onto the low-lying island, immediately picking up the road that would snake its way through village and field, all the way to Portsmouth and the sea. The gaps between the bales allowed Lyle to see the high bulwarks of the fort sink into the distance, eventually replaced by the scarp of Portsdown Hill and an empty sky that was a uniform grey. Then it had been a matter of nervous patience. Of waiting and listening. But, despite the occasional pocket of heavy traffic and a couple of mud-stuck wheels, they had made it to the town without significant hindrance.

Portsmouth itself was a bastion of civilisation at the southwest corner of Portsea Island. As the dray bounced and juddered along High Street, the frontages of shops and taverns raced past Lyle's little peephole in a blur. Fishmongers were abundant, along with net makers and boatwrights. There were at least two coopers, a large smithy, a chandlery, a bakery and so many more. Storehouses for raw fleeces stood shoulder to shoulder with brewhouses and tanneries and everywhere folk walked and rode, clogging the street, while sailors stood in the doorways of drinking dens and young lads darted hither and thither bearing parcels, goods and messages. The stink of the place reminded Lyle of London, a pungent concoction of seaweed and sewage, while the noise of lowing livestock and haggling shop-keeps overlaid all.

They trundled on, Lyle silently noting The Greyhound tavern, in which the Duke of Buckingham had been murdered during the old king's reign. It was the first of his signposts. In quick succession came the second, the large edifice of the Guildhall, its painted timbers dark in the fading light. Immediately he thumped a fist against the side of the cart.

"Here," he whispered to the others, "is where Master Spendlove should be."

Without further discussion, they waited for the dray to rumble off the cobbles and into a muddy side road, where it immediately came to a halt. Cautiously they pushed the bales aside and emerged like larvae from a dung hill, wriggling free and shuffling on their backsides to the end of the cart. The driver, eager to be rid of his unwanted cargo, had already leapt down from his seat and unhooked the rear panel, so that the four stowaways could jump clear. With Lyle's contrite thanks ringing in his ears, the man closed the vehicle, gave a surly nod and clambered up.

In moments the huge dray had juddered into life, hemp bales tumbling and resettling like a disturbed leaf pile as it rounded the corner. In the street, all fell to silence. Rows of narrow, two-storey homes flanked the strip of mud on which Lyle and his companions found themselves.

"What now, Samson?" Bella asked.

Lyle opened his mouth to answer but someone else spoke first.

"Praise be," Wardley Spendlove said as he came out of one of the low doorways. His mouth twitched into a smile at Lyle, growing to a delighted beam when his gaze fell on one of the other faces. "Oh, Jesu, it is my Amelia. Praise be."

A tear welled at the corner of Amelia's eye, trembling there for a moment, before plunging down her cheek. "Papa," she whispered and ran to embrace him.

*

Night had well and truly fallen when Maddocks called off the search.

The colonel, as a matter of efficacy as well as dignity, had perched atop his skittish, snorting destrier and overseen a methodical afternoon's work while his troopers, on foot and cursing their ill-fortune, had waylaid as many wagons, traps and coaches as they could manage along the road from Wymering to Portsmouth. Maddocks had ridden up and down the wide thoroughfare, scanning every face, for only he would know his former friend on sight. But the stretch, however flat and unobstructed, was all of five miles, busy as any road outside the capital and the task's futility had quickly become apparent.

The troop filed through the gate at Portsmouth's main bastion as a bright half-moon, smudged by fingers of cloud, spread silvery film over houses and battlements. With Maddocks, Captain Beck and the cornet at the fore, they made their beleaguered way south, along St Thomas Street to the huge Romanesque church dedicated to the martyred Archbishop of Canterbury after whom the street was named.

"Took some iron during the wars," Beck said.

Maddocks glanced at his captain, realising the man was staring at St Thomas's large central tower. It was difficult to see in the gathering gloom but the high walls were jagged in places, as if giant jaws had taken great bites out of the stonework. He nodded. "True enough. From our side, God forgive us, when the king's men held the town. The malignants used the tower as a lookout post, for its vantage cannot be bettered." When they reached the church, he signalled for the column to veer left, cutting across the junction with High Street so that they headed south and east. "There was no alternative but for our gunners over at Gosport to subject the place to bombardment. The nave was dire harmed too, though I pray one day the Parliament will see to its improvement."

"The conflict spared no place," Beck muttered sombrely.

"Nor any person," Maddocks replied, unable to keep his mind from wandering to a former major in Henry Ireton's regiment. That man had been his ally once, trusted and valued but the events of the last decade had tainted him, corrupted him. It was a point of bitter regret for Maddocks but also of stinging betrayal. Even as he considered the souring of his relationship with Samson Lyle, his heart hardened, his resolve to capture the fugitive setting a new fire in his belly. "See there?"

Beck touched at heel to his horse and the animal quickened to keep pace with the colonel. "Domus Dei?"

"As was," Maddocks confirmed. They were approaching another impressive complex of buildings, some constructed in the pale dressed stone of Norman churches and castles, while others, like new buds sprouting from an ancient bough, were made up of timber and brick, painted brilliant white and adorned with huge windows, ornate chimney stacks and smartly tiled roofs. It was an incongruous hotch-potch of a site, set just within the easternmost line of the town wall, all enclosed by a well-tended green and several large, timber outbuildings. "Domus Dei," he repeated the name. "God's House. An almshouse and hospice before the Dissolution."

"The new parts are the Governor's residence?"

"A modern mansion," Maddocks said with distaste. "Slapped on the side. Government House, we are now to call it." He shrugged. "Whatever its name, it has roaring hearths and plenty of good stabling. We shall dwell therein and see to our cursed quarry on the morrow."

Beck, evidently content with the prospect of food and lodgings, sat straighter in the saddle. "How will we locate him?"

"Marek Nowak. It is too late, too damned dark to ransack every smuggler's haunt and drinking ken in Portsmouth but he and his men will be here somewhere and they'll prove a sight simpler to track down than Lyle and his little parcel of thieves." They turned into the grounds of the Governor's House, hooves suddenly loud on the cinder path that would take them to the gates. "Tomorrow, Captain," Maddocks said, mood beginning to lighten with renewed hope. "We shall prevail, have no doubt.

Find the sailor and we shall find the outlaw."

*

"They lodge at The Bridge tavern," Wardley Spendlove said as he took his place on a low bench, leaning over his knees to enjoy the warming flames. "I followed them all the way to its threshold." His nose and upper lip crumpled in disgust. "It is out on The Point, so called Spice Island by the locals. A den of iniquity, full of houses of ill-repute, overflowing with strong ale and more illegal stills than you could possibly sup from. It is a lewd, violent place of danger and temptation."

Eustace Grumm, at the other end of the bench, gave a salacious chuckle. "Sounds wondrous."

It was pitch dark outside, the clarity of the night sky letting a hard chill descend. The only light in the fisherman's home came from the hearth, dancing and crackling as logs blackened while hands and faces were held out for as long as could be tolerated. Bella and Amelia sat cross-legged on the rushes, either side of the chimney breast, while squeezed on the bench between the two old men, Lyle asked, "What is Botolph's condition?"

Spendlove's features tightened at whatever unhappy image the question conjured. "He lives," he said simply.

Lyle took his roasting palms away from the heat and rubbed them across his freshly shaved cheeks. "Then let us consider extricating the fellow."

"Thorny task, that," replied the owner of their new bolthole. In order to safeguard the man, who lived alone in what was a clean and well-appointed dwelling of just two rooms, Lyle had introduced him simply as Tom. Distant kin to Lyle's late wife, the fisherman – as white-bearded as Grumm, if not nearly as thin – had welcomed Spendlove when the old man had appeared at his door. Now that the group had come together under his roof, he provided a much-needed fire, fresh bread and a dish of turbot and mushrooms. They would sleep on the floor, for there were no beds to spare but that mattered not a jot now that they were warm and full-bellied.

Lyle glanced across at Tom, who sat in a cushioned chair

nearest the hearth, a clay pipe dangling from the corner of his mouth. "How so?"

The fisherman sucked the pale stem, a stream of smoke tumbling from his nose and peered back with milky blue eyes that were sagging and wet, reminding Lyle of half-open clams. "The Bridge is out on The Point."

Lyle sketched a map in his mind's eye. At the westernmost edge of the town, beyond the main defences, he remembered there was a small tidal bay that was almost entirely enclosed by a crescent-shaped spit of land. That spur, Portsmouth Point, being a landing place for many of the sailors coming ashore from the Spithead anchorage, had its own gate in order to protect the town from interlopers. "Do they man the wall there?"

The fisherman dragged on his pipe again, speaking through the roiling smoke screen. "They do."

Grumm looked across at Spendlove. "You got in."

"One man, infirm and unarmed," Spendlove replied, "may slip through Point Gate unhindered but you?" he said pointedly, shaking his head, "With your guns and your blades?"

Grumm sat back, pulling a sour face. Lyle stared into the flames for inspiration. "Is there another way in?"

Tom leaned forwards, the bench lurching alarmingly and knocked his pipe bowl against the brick of the hearth. "Aye, I'd say there is."

FRIDAY

Oyster Street formed the western extremity of Portsmouth, hugging the foreshore, the town on one side, the grey waters of the harbour on the other. It was a commercial hub, smartly paved and packed with taverns and shops, with a huge pipe manufactory in the centre that seemed to hum with life, workers coming and going like bees at a gigantic hive.

Lyle took it all in as they walked south in the fledgling dawn, painfully aware that it would only take one person to recognise him and the day would quickly tumble to chaos. They moved in single file, Lyle, Amelia, Spendlove and Bella, leaving plenty of space in between so as not to be perceived as a group. Tom, leading the way, slowed his pace. "That there's the Camber," he called over his shoulder.

Lyle looked to his right, along the alleyway between two pubs. He could see water on the far side but it was evidently not the harbour proper, for a low-lying strip of land, complete with its own quay and buildings seemed to cut it off. This, then, was the bay he remembered, known locally as the Camber and soon he found himself hooking a right, down another of the alleys to leave Oyster Street at his back. They passed several warehouses, full, no doubt, of goods to be brought into the wharves further along the shoreline. Then they emerged at the water's edge. Here there was a timber jetty set upon slime-clothed stone footings that might have been centuries old. It jutted into the mouth of the Camber, the dock and quay of The Point lying across the water, immediately opposite the two structures separating the bay from the rest of Portsmouth Haven. On the far side, set a short way back from the quay, Lyle saw a large tavern, its name daubed in thick letters above the door. "The Bridge," he said aloud.

Beside him, the fisherman grunted. "Not a place I'd choose to visit." He paced along the length of the jetty, indicating a small boat that was tied alongside. "Here. Your vessel awaits."

*

"You mean to tell me that Samson Lyle has not made contact?"

Francis Maddocks stood over the Polish sailor, keeping his clenched fists collected at his back so as not to show his bubbling annoyance. It had taken less than an hour of daylight to locate the gun crew, for he had dispatched a score of troopers to the various inns and brothels dotting the community and such men were neither subtle, nor in hiding. Early hope, however, had quickly turned sour upon discovering that Lyle had not come to make the exchange. The revelation was as confusing as it was bitter.

Marek perched on the edge of a low palliasse to pull on his boots. Behind him the bed sheets were heaped in a haphazard hillock, out of which a slender leg protruded. "What concern is it of yours, Colonel?"

"Word reached me that you had kidnapped a citizen of the Commonwealth."

Marek shook his head, still fiddling with a boot. "Untrue."

"And that the taking of said citizen was enacted as a matter of ransom, in lieu of the return of a certain book. The Roman scriptures, no less."

Now Marek looked up, his expression impassive. If the colonel and his heavily armed riders, milling about the downstairs taproom, were intimidating, he did not show it. "I would not know."

"Scriptures," Maddocks went on, "stolen by one Samson Lyle, former officer in the army of Parliament, latterly and commonly known as the Ironside Highwayman."

The woman in the bed rolled over, exposing a little more skin as she made a drowsy mewing sound. Marek ignored her, though he caught Maddocks' furtive glance and gave a wry smile. "She is available, Colonel. I'm done with her."

Maddocks felt himself colour and cleared his throat angrily. "I know Lyle will make contact with you, Master Nowak. I would simply see the criminal dead. I am not your enemy."

"I wish only to rest here," Marek said, pushing up from the

bed to loom over the cavalryman, his myriad scars a map of violence across his ruddy face, "until my transport arrives at the dock."

"And when will that be?"

"This afternoon. A boat will be dispatched from the ship *Diamond*."

"I will not interfere with your plans." He glanced again at the mound in the bed, lowering his voice. "I care not for the man you have allegedly abducted. I want only to see Samson Lyle dance the Tyburn jig."

Marek ran a hand through his hair, the gold hoop glinting in his ear and went to a side table where he perused an impressive array of weapons. "I intend to board my ship, Colonel. Nothing more. Nothing less."

Maddocks ground his teeth so hard he feared they might shatter. He nodded sharply. "Thank you, Master Nowak," he said tersely, "and good sailing."

Maddocks glowered as he strode back to the waiting mounts. He could not have expected any help from Nowak but still the man's pigheaded silence was infuriating. It had occurred to him that full disclosure of the recent whereabouts of the Vulgate bible might coax some semblance of cooperation from the slab-faced Pole but, equally, a confession that he had possessed the book at Warblington might have had the opposite effect.

"Petersfield, sir?" Captain Beck asked as Maddocks gave a slight shake of the head.

The colonel adjusted his long cape and took his horse's reins from one of his troopers. He looked up at the plump form of Beck, high in the saddle. "It is not over until that pirate and his motley gaggle of rakehells are aboard their warship. We wait and we watch."

Beck stared out at the weed-flecked surface of the Camber. "To the Governor's House, then?"

"To Point Gate," Maddocks replied once he had hauled himself up, pushing his toes through the stirrups. "We'll search every soul attempting to pass through. If we can intercept the sly fox before he so much as reaches that foreign pope's-turd, then we get Lyle *and* the golden book. Marek Nowak can do what he likes with the Chalton boy, as long as I have the honour of handing General Goffe Lyle's head on a plate."

Beck grunted in black amusement. "A golden book and a silver platter, eh?"

"And a dead highwayman," Maddocks said. "Pray Jesu."

*

The carter muttered irritably to himself as the two watchmen emerged from guard huts set at either side of the wide entranceway. There were large wooden gates behind them, strengthened with thick, black iron strips but they had been jammed open for the day's expected traffic. The watchmen were Army personnel, pristine in the red coats and polished plate of the Lord Protector and both carried polearms topped with vicious-looking steel that immediately crossed to block the way. One of them, a burly man with a thick red beard, asked what business would concern the carter within the Commonwealth Dockyard.

"Shite," the carter answered.

The guards exchanged a glowering glance. The red-bearded man shouldered his polearm and took a step closer. "Mind your manners, my wizened friend, or pass you shall not."

The carter gave a high-pitched cackle that made both sentries start. "Shite, lad! Dung! I am here for your dung! That is to say, the dung of your chooks."

The second soldier – tall and gangly, with a prominent nose that glistened at the tip – tapped his helmet with a gloved knuckle. "Scrambled wits, Corporal."

"I'll scramble your wits, boy," the carter hissed, leaning forward above his mud-spattered palfrey, "and that dripping beak besides!"

The tall soldier advanced, his expression murderous. "Why, you haggardly old clapperdudgeon, I'll-"

The corporal's pole-arm swept across his comrade's path, clanging off the breastplate. "Hold, Stephen. He's harmless enough." He looked up at the carter with a wry chuckle. "Age loosens the tongue as sure as any strong drink." His eyes, small and keen, roved over the cart. "Empty. You're a gong farmer?"

The carter leaned to the side to peer into the bustling dockyard beyond. He could see long boathouses flanking a central thoroughfare, interspersed with rows of dwellings that were presumably built to house shipwrights, labourers, victuallers, officers and the many other tradesmen that would populate such a place. There were administration buildings, constructed in rich red brick, alongside busy workshops, brew-houses, storehouses and a multitude of other such places. It was a gigantic place, a town within a town and, with defences continually strengthened due to perpetual conflict with the Spanish and Dutch, it put him in mind of a small fortress.

He sniffed, offended. "Not any old gong. I've no interest in cowpats and dog turds. I am here at the behest of the venerable Doctor Phineas Welch. You've heard of him?"

The corporal shook his head. "I have not."

"Then it is a sore loss for you." The old man squinted at the peaked morions that protected the soldiers' skulls. "I cannot tell if you yet require Doctor Welch's services but time will surely compel you to seek him out."

"The fool speaks in riddles, Corporal," the taller guard, Stephen, said angrily, still smarting from the previous exchange. "Send him on his way!"

The carter shook his head. "Phineas Welch has made his name and fortune by coaxing the most lustrous locks from the most hirsute of pates."

"He cures baldness?" the corporal asked.

"Cures?" The carter tilted back his deeply lined face to guffaw at the sky. "Purges, banishes, expels!" He tapped the side of his nose conspiratorially, dropping his tone as if spies lurked on all sides. "But his secret ingredient is the dung of chickens. To be mixed with ash, oak bark, walnut leaves and the fat of a brown bear."

The corporal frowned. "A bear?"

"The fiercer the better! Now, you have poultry here, yes?"

The corporal shared a glance with Stephen and the pair instinctively looked back through the gateway and into the

253

dockyard. "More than the sea breeze can contain."

Stephen cursed at a private memory. "If I had a penny for every time I'd fouled my boots in droppings, I'd be able to buy one of these ships."

"There you have it!" the carter exclaimed. "Divine providence at work! Praise be and hallelujah!" He winked, gathering up the reins with one gnarled hand and pointing into the dockyard with the other. "I have my wagon and my shovel. Sally forth, master soldier and let us relieve your besieged nostrils!"

*

Marek Novak could not wait to return to the high seas. He had rested well since arriving in England all those weeks ago. The blockade of Cadiz had hardly proved a great strain, for the Spanish treasure fleet Blake had intended to waylay had never arrived, the great galleons, pregnant with gold, sitting tight in the Americas, far beyond the Commonwealth's reach. Even so, that did not render shore leave unwelcome. After months of gales and rainfall, weevil infested victuals and grinding monotony, a spell upon terra firma had been just the tonic Marek's mind and body required. The exotic delights of the Southwark stews and the profits of pugilism only enhanced matters. Yet now, an hour before dusk, it was time to go home, to the creaking timbers and the roaring waves and a bed slung from rafters. A warship was the kind of place that a man like Marek could make his own. A little floating fiefdom, where the murky, dangerous world below decks offered opportunity for one willing to impress his captain and cut the throats of his rivals.

Yes, he thought, as he stepped out of The Bridge and buckled his sword belt, it was time to take to the sea once more. He imagined the ship *Diamond* waiting for them just over the horizon. "Come, my boys, let us make ourselves known to our brethren."

At his back came the rest of his company, most pressing calloused palms into eyes assailed by the fresh breeze and bright sunlight. A heavy night had come at the usual price and more than one man vomited on the cobbles. Marek was unconcerned with their collective stupor, so long as each man had legs enough to make it to the end of the dock and board the pinnace that had moored above the mouth of the Camber. He breathed deeply of the salt air, revelled in the caws of the gulls and resolved not to dwell on a former Parliamentarian cavalry officer who had stolen his most prized possession. The arrival of Maddocks had thrown him off kilter, admittedly, with claims that Lyle intended to bring the bible to its rightful owner but Marek's time had run out and so, therefore, had Botolph's. A pity but not something over which to lose sleep.

He looked round at the bleary gathering, finding one face in particular. "I salute your courage, young Botolph, for you walk to your death like a man."

The boy, wrists bound tightly at the small of his back, did not answer. On either side, Louis and Duncan, his perpetual gaolers, gave grim smiles. Their saturnine captive had grown a sparse layer of fluff upon his upper lip over the last few days, which made him look a fraction older, but it also provided stark contrast for his sickly sallow skin. He had suffered, it was true, so perhaps putting him out of his misery was, in some way, a kindness.

Marek sucked at his own whiskers, a veritable hedge in comparison to Botolph's. "There are worse ways to die than drowning, boy, believe me. Your wits would scatter if I described the things I have seen." He clapped his hands suddenly. "Let us be done and away, my friends. Bring him to the water's edge."

It was a matter of yards from the door of The Bridge to the end of Camber Dock, though they were forced to run a gauntlet of netting, discarded cordage and crab traps over the slick cobbles. Below them, bobbing in the teal waters of Portsmouth Haven, was a large pinnace, the boat dispatched from the *Diamond* to collect its hands. It dwarfed the only other moored vessel, a tiny skiff, with its rows of benches and banks of oars, the two boats putting Marek in mind of a whale and its calf. The majority of the pinnace's oarsmen were absent, having slipped over to The Point's central street, no doubt, to seek a pot of ale while the moment was opportune. One man had drawn the short straw, left behind to hail and board the passengers. He was laid out on one of the rowing benches, catching a surreptitious moment's sleep, watched only by a pair of beggars who were huddled beneath a painted mooring post at the edge of the quay. As he led the way to the pinnace, Marek barked in irritation at the slumbering sailor, expecting more pomp and circumstance for a man of his repute. Across the short stretch of water that formed the Camber's mouth, startled seagull chicks scattered en masse from the edges of the boats tied to the wooden jetty that served the main town. The birds screeched madly, their speckled brown bodies a blur against the grey sky.

"Alms, sir."

Marek slowed, looking down as he noticed a single arm, slender and bony, protrude from the filthy bundle of rags at the foot of the mooring post. Two pairs of eyes glinted up at him like jewels in a dung heap. The ripe stench of excrement drifted off the threadbare scraps in nauseating waves, making Marek put his sleeve across his mouth and nose. "Get away, you filthy crones."

The arm retracted but the beggar went on, "Alms for a poor, blind veteran."

Marek stopped just short of the reeking creatures. "Veteran of what?"

"Naseby Field," came a voice that was weak and cracking. "Worcester and many more."

"Very likely, I am sure," Marek scoffed.

"Veteran of a campaign in the Hampshire hills too," the beggar said, "at a place called Chalton. Perhaps you know it?"

Marek Nowak drew his sword. "You!"

But before he could lunge, the rags fell away like the scales over St Paul's eyes, to reveal a man and a young girl, both crouching, both holding pistols that were primed and cocked. The man's firearm consumed Marek's attention, for it was large and double-barrelled and it was trained directly on his stomach.

The Ironside Highwayman stood up. He gave a wry smile, even as Marek's men drew their own weapons. "Well, gentlemen. Here we all are once more."

Marek did not expect to see Lyle again and the surprise only now gave way to a smouldering rage. Through clenched teeth he said, "Let us hope *something* is different from our last meeting, *Skurwysyn*."

The beggar, Lyle, stooped briefly to pick up a cloth sack, hitherto obscured amongst the stinking rags at his feet. "You mean this?"

Marek watched the sack hang heavy in Lyle's grip, knowing immediately what lay within. "You have it," he said softly and the knowledge kindled new flames within his chest. "I knew it," he tried to say, though his voice had become a deep growl. He glanced over his shoulder to the men braced for violence. "Did I not say?" He was answered by a ripple of snarls and oaths and pledges of murder.

Lyle was standing straight now, gathered to his full height. "For what it's worth, it was stolen by a man named Whistler."

Marek spat derisively. "I care not for the web's threads, only for the spider."

Lyle shook his head. "Not one of my people. I merely found him for you." He gave a sardonic smile. "By rights, you owe me a bounty." He shook the sack. "You can have the pages and I'll take the cover."

Marek was positively alight with rage now. It took every ounce of strength to keep himself in check. After all, what good was his bible if it accompanied a bullet in the guts? "Return my property and I will return this streak of piss."

Lyle's green eyes drifted past Marek to take in the sight of Botolph, bruised but whole, pinioned between Frenchman and Scotsman, just as he had been at Chalton. "What is so special about this book? It has a goodly amount of gold, I grant you but I'd wager a man such as you has plenty more treasure stowed away."

Marek stared at the sack that still gently swung like a pendulum from his enemy's hand. "That is Inca gold. It has..." he paused, groping in his mind for a word to do it justice, "power."

"Inca?" the little girl at Lyle's side chirped, astonishingly brightly for a child caught in a standoff.

"One of the tribes of the Americas," Lyle explained.

"Tribe?" Marek said contemptuously. "It was an empire. That gold was taken from the Ransom Room itself." He could hear his own voice thicken but was powerless to stop it. The provenance of the bible was what made it so special. "The very room where Atahualpa surrendered his kingdom to the conquistadors. After the battle of Cajamarca, Emperor Atahualpa offered Pizarro to buy his liberty by filling the room where he was kept prisoner with gold. That blood payment was melted down into ingots, divided amongst the conquering Spaniards and shipped home." He pointed the tip of his cutlass at Lyle. "Tell me. Have you heard of Batih?"

"The massacre?" replied Lyle.

Marek nodded. "I was there. After the battle, the Tartars of Crimea sold us like cattle to Ukrainian Cossacks, Satan devour them all."

"They executed many of your countrymen, I know."

"Many?" Marek echoed disdainfully, the choice of word utterly offensive to his ears. "There were five thousand of us, *Skurwysyn*. Hogtied and helpless. They disembowelled and beheaded us." He felt tears prick his eyes, hot and unstoppable. "It took them two whole days."

"But you survived."

"I worked the ropes loose. Hid under the corpses. When the Cossacks were gone, I crawled free." He twitched his wrist so that the cutlass slid down to point at the sack. "That book was in the hill of corpses. Right there with me. I do not know where it came from or who dropped it. But it found me. Saved me then and kept me alive since. That book is a potent thing. God's word and a blood curse, combined. It has kept me safe these many years, when, by rights, I should have perished a hundred times." He risked a quick glance back at Botolph. "I will return this whelp to you, upon my honour, if you hand me that sack."

Lyle seemed to wait for an age as he weighed a decision that was cruelly limited. Marek heard noise, the muffled voices of men calling to one another in the distance and recognised them as those of the *Diamond*'s oarsmen, returning to the pinnace for the journey out to Spithead. He could have laughed aloud. The highwayman had placed himself between Marek's dozen killers and the Camber's inky depths. A fool, if ever there was one. Lyle moved then and Marek felt his entire body zing with relief, for the Englishman had handed his pistol to the girl so that he might step forwards in unarmed parley, breaking the spell of the standoff. After three tentative paces, as if he approached a crazed colt, he lowered his hand to put the cloth sack on the ground. He kicked it, once, sending it tumbling over the cobbles to rest between the two parties. Then he retreated, as slow and measured as his advance had been. The first move had been made. Marek bowed. When he straightened, he twisted to jerk a chin at Duncan and Louis, who immediately shoved their captive away from the gathered men.

"You're free, boy," Marek said as Botolph, hands still bound, stumbled and lurched his way to the far side of the quay. Lyle's accomplice, the little wench, took hold of the bewildered boy and guided him by an arm to the small skiff that rose and fell gently in the shadow of the pinnace. Marek caught Botolph's eye as the lad made an ungainly descent of the dock's sandy slope. He read confusion there and well he might, for the Pole had promised a death this day. But it was not Botolph's death Marek so desperately sought. He raised his cutlass and went to the slaughter.

Lyle knew that Marek would attack and he knew that the sailor would be fast but still he was unprepared. The cutlass lanced forth as its bearer skipped half a dozen staccato steps in what seemed like the blink of an eye. Lyle only just managed to slide his own blade from its scabbard in time to bring it up for the parry and his twisting, grunting retreat was met with a thunderous cheer from the watching crowd, a couple of whom made to lend their leader a hand.

"Hold!" Marek snarled, spittle flecking his whiskers. He stood poised for the next attack, sword high like a battle standard. His face was reddening rapidly and he breathed hard but bloodlust made him dangerous and Lyle stayed back. "Any man interferes, I'll run him through myself!"

The mariners stood firm. The duellists were ten yards apart

now. Lyle pushed forwards his left foot and turned his shoulders, presenting the narrowest target possible behind the ornate Pappenheimer rapier in his left hand. He edged in, getting the measure of his opponent and the blades touched at the tips, their metallic song ringing across the water.

Marek's eyes tightened and he sucked in a quick breath. Lyle read it and danced backwards as the Pole lunged, wildly and with a great roar that had the gulls scattering and the sailors bellowing their support. Lyle swept the cutlass aside; once, twice, thrice. Each blow sending spears of pain through his half-healed bullet wound. He bit down on the inside of his mouth as if he could distract himself and jabbed his own blade up at the bigger man's throat, feeling Marek bat it away with his iron guard. Then Lyle went low, for the groin and Marek managed to twirl aside, saving himself by a fraction.

They set themselves again. Lungs heaving in time. Marek growled, "You thought your actions-would go unavenged, *Skurwysyn*? You think me a man to be deceived? To be made a laughing-stock?"

"I did not steal the book," Lyle said, though he knew his protests were futile. "Botolph did not steal the book."

Marek spat. "I will cut you for every lie to roll off your forked tongue." He laughed maniacally, drunk on bloodlust and violence. "Then I will cut off your tongue too!"

They came together. Marek slashed in huge arcs that might have felled trees, trying to take Lyle's head clean from his shoulders. The highwayman, surprised by the brawny sailor's agility, scrambled backwards, swaying out of range, then spun like an acrobat, countering the assault with a flurry of his own blows that had Marek recoiling haphazardly.

The sailors brayed as though betting on a dog fight. Lyle grimaced at the burning pain in his shoulder-blade. Marek stooped slightly, bracing one hand on a thigh, chest heaving in and out.

"Enough?" Lyle said. "Take ship, sirrah. Let us leave here with the boy, with no more harm done."

Marek pounced. Baring his teeth like a crazed animal, he screamed a war cry in his native tongue and swung the curved cutlass in two hands, a Viking berserker at a shield wall. Lyle parried the first sweeping cut but lambent flares of agony licked at the tender flesh at his left shoulder and he could not mount a riposte, reeling away instead.

Visibly short of breath, Marek slowed, swashing the cutlass in front like a scythe as he kept his furious glare fixed on Lyle. "You'll die, *Skurwysyn,*" he sneered. "Your corpse will feed the fish."

If Colonel Francis Maddocks could have reached Portsmouth Point at a gallop, he would have but Point Gate was narrow and, at the zenith of a short winter's day, heavy with traffic. It was a bottleneck of the most infuriating kind and it took several minutes of berating by the colonel and his officers, all standing in stirrups and waving pistols, to get the carts, animals and pedestrians moving. The fact that the congestion had been exacerbated by his own meticulous searches was not lost on him.

The point, though, was moot. For a message direct from The Bridge tavern had reached him at his roadblock. The place was a bawdy house as well as a tavern, its patrons savouring a good deal more than local ale and, though Maddocks was technically obliged to close such an establishment down, he had taken the opportunity to place the lewd women in his pay, just in case Lyle managed the impossible. Now, according to one of the resident slatterns, the impossible had happened. Somehow the infernal highwayman and his gang had inveigled their way onto The Point. Well, thought Maddocks as his troopers clattered through the gates, the elusive and arrogant brigand had finally come unstuck. He kicked his mount so that it brought up the rear of the riders as they funnelled into single file behind their flapping colour. "They're rats in a barrel, my lads!" he called exultantly. "Rats in a barrel!"

They managed the hint of a canter as they moved north along Broad Street, the central artery along which The Point's life teemed. Maddocks urged his horse to extra speed as he gradually made his way to the front of the line, bellowing at folk too stupid or too lazy to move out of his way and nearly trampling a youngster who was not paying attention as he pushed a barrow of wizened apples across the road. It was only a matter of half a mile, taking a right onto East Street and then straight onto the quay but it was a maddeningly sluggish business nonetheless and he feared he would be too late, that his men would thunder onto Camber Dock only to discover Marek reunited with his precious bible and Lyle vanished back into the town.

It was with pleasure, then, that he caught sight of the duel that was playing out on the slick cobbles between the dock and The Bridge tavern. Samson Lyle and Marek Nowak, soldier against sailor, rapier against cutlass. Maddocks could only see the confrontation because of the saddle's high vantage, for the patch of land given over to the snarling contest was entircly shielded by thc bodies of bellowing, jeering men he recognised to be the members of Marek's gun crew. Which gave him pause. He had imagined joining the fray. Surrounding Lyle and lending the might of his beloved harquebusiers to the chase. But to do that he would have to first make a path through the sailors.

"Clear them, sir?" Captain Beck said, reading his thoughts as he reined in at his side.

Maddocks shook his head. "Why bother? Lyle is trapped. Nowak has apparently decided not to make the exchange in a gentlemanly manner." He took a drink from the flask in his saddlebag while he watched the fight unfold. "Send a squad back to Point Gate, Captain. A matter of precaution."

"By the looks of things," Beck said, "Lyle is taking a hiding. I had heard he was a master."

Maddocks nodded. "Was." He swigged again. As he did so his eyes slid across the tiny bay to the row of fishing boats moored beside the Oyster Street jetty. There were just two figures on the timber walkway, presumably attracted by the noise of clashing steel as it drifted across the water. "Pity there aren't more witnesses to this most joyous occasion, eh?" He arched his back, cracking it and yawned. "No, Captain. The playhouses may have been suppressed but entertainments can yet be found. Let Nowak make an end of the Ironside Highwayman and we shall cheer his every strike."

262

Lyle's left shoulder blade burned like the fires of damnation. He gave ground again and again, wheeling about when space was short, offering painful ripostes to buy time and push Marek briefly onto the back foot. But he was losing. He was the superior swordsman, they both knew it but Marek's unrelenting attacks, fuelled by his bullish size and terrible rage, simply battered his smaller opponent, the clash of steel deafening as he smashed his way into – and through – Lyle's defensive postures. Closing on him, devouring the open-air Lyle so carefully maintained between them.

Marek, his heavy, rasping breaths audible above the shouts of his comrades, girded himself for a wild lunge. Lyle bit down on his bottom lip to distract from the pain and leapt backwards to receive the frenzied onslaught. The blades collided high, slid down the length of the killing edge and hilts clanged so that the pair came together in a strange embrace of snarls and grimaces. Lyle did all he could, lent his whole strength to the wrestle but he felt himself wilt beneath Marek's irresistible power. He jumped away, jabbing the rapier at Marek's windpipe to force the Pole into a desperate parry that would temporarily staunch the tide of his attack.

"You have been tricked, *Skurwysyn*!" Marek snarled, grinning and he danced on tiptoes for a moment, demonstrating an evident reserve of stamina and belying a face of livid crimson. "I am a pugilist. A good one. I do not tire!"

Lyle braced again. Marek had his back to the dock and Lyle leaned to the side to look past him at the waiting pinnace. The boatman was standing on the rowing bench. To Lyle's unqualified relief, the man raised a hand and waved.

Colonel Francis Maddocks did not even bother to affect the dour dignity demanded by his rank. He grinned as he chewed cardamom seeds and witnessed the demolition of his nemesis. It would have been more satisfying – downright poetic, even – if it had been Maddocks' own sword that made the final cut but greed and pride were both sins. He would have to make do with the memories.

And the end was close. Jesus but it was achingly close. Lyle had crumpled, forced into desperate evasion that could not last when pursued with such venomous alacrity. He found himself recalling that moment before Christmas, when he had pulled his pistol's trigger in the woods below Butser Hill. It had not been a killing shot, the range too great but the ball had found its mark nonetheless. Had punched into Lyle's upper back to make him sway and lurch and cling onto his mount's neck for all he was worth.

"Not all blows are immediately fatal," Maddocks muttered.

"Sir?"

Maddocks glanced to his side. "No matter, Captain Beck." As his gaze returned to the crowd and the duel, he noticed once more the figures on the timber jetty. He might have paid them no heed, except that they had moved to the middle of the long platform that stretched into the Camber from the town wharves. Idly, he watched them. They were kneeling together, huddled beneath their hoods like a pair of incanting witches. Then he saw the glow. Dim and orange, even gentle. Not a flame, as such but an ember.

"Slow match," he said to himself.

Beck, enthralled by the fight, answered distractedly, "Match, sir?"

"Jesu. They have slow matches over there. Look. See it?" A low, whispering dread came over Maddocks then. A knot started to form, deep within his core. "Wait. Something isn't right."

Lyle gave up his fencer's stance and stood flat-footed, lowering the Pappenheimer as if to concede the day.

"Come, *Skurwysyn*!" Marek roared, his nostrils flaring, eyes wide like twin moons. He tilted back his head and laughed; a sound that was wild and visceral. "And I thought you were a master! Let us finish this!"

Marek had his back to the water, blocking Lyle's view of the boats but he glimpsed the man in the pinnace as he jumped nimbly from the warship's vessel over to Bella's boat. "I was shot in my left shoulder," he called, loud enough for the baying mob to hear. "The wound has not yet fully healed. Saps my strength something grievous." He shifted his hips and torso, resuming the fighter's stance but this time it was his right foot that slid forwards. "Fortunately," he went on, swapping the rapier into his other palm. "I am not left-handed."

Marek's jaw dropped open. He stood there, dumbstruck and confused, as his chest heaved, his face a scarlet mask. The other sailors, deafened by their own shouts and blinded by shared bloodlust, simply called him on, charging their leader with finishing the job.

Indignation lit up Marek's eyes then. Lyle could see that the revelation would not smother the fire in Marek's belly but add fuel to it and he inched back voluntarily, letting the bigger man come on.

And Marek charged.

He raised the cutlass high and bolted like a demented ox, oaths tumbling from his mouth as he roared. Lyle bent at the knees, placed his aching left arm safely at his back and gauged the distance. He transferred his weight onto the front foot as Marek loomed above him, flicked out his blade to receive the blow, then pirouetted like a dancer. Steel met steel, Marek's huge power absorbed by a rejuvenated Lyle and the highwayman deflected the cutlass, sending it wide as his body ghosted under Marek's right arm. He completed the turn as Marek blundered past and lashed out with the flat of his sword, striking the Pole across his rump.

Marek brayed like a mule. Overreaching himself and unable to reel in his lunge, he was thrown off balance and he stumbled forth like a toppling building to smash, face first, onto the cobbles in a tangle of limbs, his cutlass skittering and clattering away.

The crowd fell silent, every man stunned into dumb inertia.

Every man except one. Samson Lyle did not linger or gloat. He ran for the edge of the dock, not breaking his stride as he stooped to scoop up the cloth sack and bounded straight down onto the sandy slope. He leapt for all he was worth, sailing over the sloshing shallows and crashing, pell-mell, into the little boat that Bella had managed to extricate from its mooring rope. It lurched under his weight, water slapping the sides and spilling over to shower the hull.

"Could have stabbed us with that," Eustace Grumm said, still breathing hard from his exertions over on the pinnace.

"My apologies," Lyle answered, grinning at Bella as he sheathed the Pappenheimer. He dropped the sack in the bottom of the boat, gathering up the oars and hauling hard, pulling against the tangled weeds with their fat bubbles. His shoulder wound made it a struggle and Grumm gathered up the second pair, swearing viciously as he bent himself to the effort. Between them on the middle bench, Botolph shivered. Bella wrapped her beggar's rags about his shoulders. The thud and slap of the oars played a rhythm under the growing chorus of incensed shouts coming from the quay. But they were building momentum now, edging away from The Point and into the expanse of the harbour with every oar stroke. The dark water, flecked with bits of pale crab and green weed, sluiced about the hull in time with the boat's motion, shifting the bible in its cloth sack like flotsam on the tide.

Up on Camber Dock, the crowd surged. They were a matter of yards away and Lyle twisted to look into their grimacing faces. They spat curses and threats, jabbed the air with swords and several were kneeling to load firearms. Lyle caught sight of Marek. The huge gun captain, beside the mooring post, was unflinching, impassive, though his gaze contained a wrath that almost made Lyle quell. Almost.

He inclined his head, acknowledging their duel. Marek's eye twitched at the corner and he said something, though Lyle could not hear it and then the sailors were cascading down the slope to the pinnace.

"They're coming," Botolph said. His voice was weak, a mere husk but there was vigour in his trembling hands and raw intensity in his gaze. He was staring in abject terror at the pinnace. "They're c… c… coming."

Lyle leaned forwards and patted Botolph's shoulder. "No, young sir, they are not."

Behind him, just as the first of Marek's howling pack reached the water's edge, the pinnace exploded.

Maddocks' horse was turning circles as he bellowed, whirling his sword above his head to provide a focal point in the commotion. "On me! On me!"

The harquebusiers, many having dismounted during the duel, scurried like mice to their positions, leaping up into saddles without even bothering to cram helmets over their heads or fasten gauntlets to their arms. Many were utterly bemused by the sudden turmoil, for they were spread thinly across the lawless spur of land, manning checkpoints at major taverns and street junctions all the way back to Point Gate and had no idea of what had unfolded. But they all heard the explosion.

The horsemen gathered en mass, churning about their leader like an iron-clad eddy, eyes darting back and forth between colonel and quayside.

When enough of his troopers had coalesced, Maddocks gauged the situation. His first thought was to storm the dock but the sailors had recoiled from the slope amid a shower of water and splinters. They congregated now about the mooring post, impotent in their rage, still screaming obscenities into the harbour as a thick pall of white smoke roiled about them like acrid fog. If they were a hindrance before, they were downright impassable now and he knew the chance to ride Lyle down had gone. He wrenched savagely on the reins, levelling the long, single-edged blade in a south-easterly direction. "To the town, damn your eyes! The town! Make for the jetty!"

Lyle and Grumm rowed hard. Marek and his men were stranded on Portsmouth Point but that did not mean the fugitives were home and dry. They could not rest until they had cleared the harbour and its formidable gun batteries. Still, though, Lyle felt a tide of relief swell in his chest and dampen the pain in his shoulder.

"What was that?" Botolph Spendlove said. His eyes, red-rimmed and glazed, were fixed on the entrance to the Camber, where a warship's large boat had erupted in a column of flame and timber and froth and now, as shards rained down to dapple the surface of the water, the pinnace had already lost its stern to the chill depths, the bow sitting high, right out of the water, as if lifted by some invisible sea creature. "Cannon? Mortar?" Now he turned, becoming frantic as he looked to the blockhouse on the Gosport side of the harbour. "Do they bombard us from the fort?"

"A petard," Grumm answered, proffering the puzzled young man with a decayed grin. "One of God's most sublime creations."

"There's nought of God in it," Lyle admonished the Cornishman. "A rudimentary device," he said to Botolph. "Highly dangerous, which is why," he winked, "it is crucial to have it set by an eminently expendable personage."

Grumm snorted but chose not to take the bait. "You takes a bell, cast in iron or brass. Fill it with black powder and fix it to a wooden base. Or, in this case, simply prop it in the floor of a wooden boat. Light the fuse and," he briefly released the oars so that he could clap his hands together, "boom."

"Evil contraptions," said Lyle. "Had occasion to employ them during the wars." He slid his backside round to take sight of the dock. The sailors were still there but the pinnace had all but gone. His gaze drifted to the left, to the jetty that extended from the Oyster Street wharf and the small fleet of fishing boats moored on both sides, noses inwards, like so many piglets at a sow. From the town came a sudden, deep thrum of hoof-beats and out from one of the alleys streamed horsemen. Dozens of them. They galloped in pairs, wrapped in leather and metal, barred visors pulled over most of their faces, a saffron-coloured cornet fluttering in the van. The small flag bore the head of a black lion.

The cavalrymen began to shout threats, just as the sailors had done but they were quickly silenced by the barks of officers. Then they were dismounting, gathering about one man in particular and Lyle saw that it was Francis Maddocks himself.

All eyes in the skiff had gone to the jetty now. "He found us, then," Bella muttered, her attempt to keep her tone light undermined by an unmistakable tension.

"Now, your petard," Lyle went on as they watched the troopers file onto the timber walkway, evidently intent on commandeering the fishing fleet. "One might secure it to a gate using hooks, or prop it against a bridge with beams."

"They're going to catch us," Botolph whispered.

"The shape of the thing," Lyle went on, undeterred, "concentrates the explosive so it may be targeted. In this case," he jerked back his head to indicate the sunken pinnace, "it was discharged downwards. In that case, however," he said, levering up an oar to point it at the jetty, "you will note the blast goes up."

Botolph frowned, opening his mouth to speak but the words were drowned out by a deluge of concussive noise as the second petard ignited, ripping through the end of the jetty from one of the footings beneath. The soldiers recoiled as one, scrambling away as the water and the sky seethed and kindling tumbled through a new bank of sulphurous cloud to scatter Oyster Street, The Point and the modest bay in between.

Then all was silent. Marek and his crew stood, mutely now, on Camber Dock, while Maddocks and his harquebusiers milled before the jagged remains of the jetty, their senses scrambled by the huge explosion, their plans in disarray. Just below them, tantalisingly out of reach, the empty fishing boats gently drifted loose to bob into open water.

Lyle let go of his oars. He reached out to pat Botolph's shoulder. "You're safe now, lad. Let's get you home." Then he stood up, taking a fistful of the soaking cloth sack. The skiff pitched alarmingly as he turned but he managed to pull the golden bible free, the pages within utterly ruined. Mercifully, that mattered to Lyle not a bit. He held it aloft, for Marek and Maddocks to see and offered a deep, lingering bow.

*

Near Alverstoke, Hampshire

The skiff slid onto the pebble beach with a hiss. Lyle jumped, boots splashing and crunching at once and dragged the vessel a few more yards so that it was safely grounded. It was dark but the sky was clear and the moon iridescent. He scanned the ridge at the top of the beach. It was empty, save for a line of grass tufts that curved before the salty breeze.

"Come," he said. "We'll find the road beyond that low dune."

They abandoned the boat, pushing it back into the sea so that, wherever it finally washed up, it would not give a clue to their whereabouts. Then they trudged up the beach, the gushing surf at their backs, tired bodies stumbling over the ever-shifting shingle.

Botolph was first to speak. The miseries of his captivity and the shocking nature of his rescue had seemed to tip him over some imperceptible ledge, so that he had withdrawn into himself as they fought the Solent's pernicious currents. He had hunkered into his blankets as dusk had crept in, his eyes staring vacantly at the shore and battened down any words that might have come. It was a revelation for the others, then, when his pale face shone with sudden animation at the ridge's summit.

"Papa!" he exclaimed, shedding the makeshift shawl so that it was snatched by the wind to tumble back down the beach. "Papa, I am here!"

The north face of the ridge was a gentle slope that began as stony sand and finished as grass, joining a narrow trackway that plunged into rolling pasture. There was little sign of civilisation in any direction, save for the vertical lines of smudged stars, about a mile to the northeast, that spoke of a village's thin smoke trails. All around them the landscape was empty, except for the lone wagon, down on the trackway, that was hitched to a pair of strong looking horses. Seated above them on the wagon's bench were two figures. Their faces were too far off to identify but one had a head of silver hair and the other wore a simple white cap.

Botolph was already running when the people in the wagon clambered down. Arms aloft, he dashed over the sand, sliding and leaping by turns until he hit the firmer grass and all the while he called for the father he thought never again to see.

The Spendloves embraced. The three of them, down beside the waiting horses, locking arms and weeping as one, voices muffled as temples pressed. Lyle, Grumm and Bella grinned and laughed as they strode to meet a family reunited.

It was Amelia who broke away first, coming to stand before Lyle, the highwayman gingerly rolling his damaged shoulder. She reached out, touching his elbow. His eyes fell unbidden to her hand.

"How do you fare?" she asked, squeezing his arm gently.

"Hurts," he said, self-consciousness making him brusque. He forced himself to look up, softening his tone. "I shall be hearty enough before long. Bullet wounds are generally not hospitable to fighting duels or rowing the Solent."

She smiled at that. The ochre flecks in her brown eyes shimmering like quicksilver in the moonlight. "Everything you have done, Major Lyle," she shook her head in wonder, "we can scarcely fathom, let alone repay."

Lyle placed his hand across hers. Her skin was warm despite the chill in the night air. "Be glad you have your brother back. It is enough."

They parted as her father approached, Lyle grudgingly letting her fingers slip away. Before he could react, Spendlove thrust out his arms and enveloped him in a tight embrace, sobbing through his joy.

"You must thank your friend, Samson," Spendlove said when they parted. "Dear Tom risked so much."

Lyle produced the golden bible from within his coat. "He and the other fishermen will have this. Payment, in lieu of their jetty and fleet, most of which is now scattered about the harbour, I'd wager."

"Did you ever intend to return it to Marek?" Botolph said, coming to stand beside his father.

"Certainly," Lyle replied. "I changed my mind when he tried to run me through." He was gratified to see Botolph's mouth twitched at the corners. It was the first time he had seen the lad smile.

"Pious men are wont to do foolish things," Spendlove said sagely.

"Not piety," said Lyle. "It was not the scriptures he revered but the gold itself. Inca gold. He believed it offered him protection. A talisman." He glanced down at the book. "Now it can be another's talisman. Tom can melt it down and buy new nets."

Spendlove laughed. "A whole new fleet!"

"They lit the fuse," Botolph said to Lyle, his voice querulous with evident astonishment. "My father and sister. Did you know? Out on the jetty!"

Lyle slapped him on the back. "I am aware of that."

"It was the major's idea," Amelia chided her brother, punching his shoulder playfully.

"Secured," their father said, "in ominously professional fashion by Mister Grumm, here."

"Those petards," Botolph addressed Grumm now. "How did you come by them?"

"Made them with mine own fair hands, boy," Grumm said with a roguish cackle.

"He stole them," said Bella.

Grumm held up his hands as if surrendering to some unseen force. "Stole is a strong word."

She snorted. "It's the right word, you sly old stoat."

He screwed up his craggy face. "The bottles and the fuses I stole." He leaned in to Botolph's ear, whispering, "Inveigled my way into the navy dockyard, didn't I, lad?" He laughed when the young man's mouth flapped in amazement. "Dressed myself up as a gong collector, of all things!"

"You are a marvel, sir," Botolph said, his tone hushed with awe.

"That I am and you can be sure to remind the major, here, eh?"

"What of the other ingredients?" Wardley Spendlove asked.

"Half the black powder was purchased with the major's funds," Grumm said.

Spendlove shook his head at the audacity of it. "You bribed a dockyard worker?"

"Indeed. The other half came from a crate of grenadoes, which were gifted to me, on account of this blade," he patted his waist as he spoke, "and its proximity to the storeman's stones. Then I loaded up my cart, buried the lot under a pile o' chicken dung and off I went."

"I thank you, sir," Botolph said.

Spendlove gathered his son and daughter in his arms. "We all thank you."

Grumm waved them away, suddenly embarrassed. "Never a doubt nor hesitation."

Lyle smiled, deciding not to mention Grumm's early views on the matter. Instead he looked over at the wagon that would be their transport for the next couple of hours. They would travel together initially as they departed the Gosport peninsula, seeking tracks with the deepest hedgerows and always scrutinising the horizon for horsemen. But they had rowed west out of Portsmouth, agreeing to rendezvous here, thus placing the entire harbour between them and their pursuers. Maddocks would be forced to ride the full fifteen miles around the water, with no clue as to where his quarry would alight. When the sun finally made inroads, the two groups would have parted, the Spendloves taking the highroad to the west while Lyle's gang would plunge into the vast countryside to the east, keeping to the sunken, shadowy lanes that criss-crossed field and forest. He said to his old school master, "Wales for you?"

Spendlove nodded. "I have kin in Pembrokeshire. Seems a good moment to pay them a visit."

"You have money?"

"Enough to see us there safely." He gathered his children close, one in each arm. "And you?"

An intense feeling of longing smouldered like a brazier in Lyle's chest as he watched Spendlove's hand slide about Amelia's shoulders. He cleared his throat, suddenly ashamed. "Retrieve the horses," he said thickly, "and wend our way back."

"They'll hunt you," Amelia said.

"I wouldn't have it any other way." Lyle disguised the lie with a broad grin. He turned to Bella and Grumm. "Ready? Then let's go home."

Historical Note

The Rule of the Major-Generals was a 15-month period of direct military government during Oliver Cromwell's Protectorate. The new system was commissioned in October 1655 and the country divided into 12 regions, each governed by a Major-General who was answerable only to the Lord Protector.

The first duty of the Major-Generals was to maintain security by suppressing unlawful assemblies, disarming Royalists and apprehending thieves, robbers and highwaymen. To assist them in this work, they were authorised to raise their own militias.

Colonel Maddocks and his men are figments of my imagination, but William Goffe was indeed Major-General for Berkshire, Sussex and Hampshire, and it would have been his responsibility to hunt down Samson Lyle and men like him. Sadly, Lyle himself is a fictional character, but he is indicative of many outlaws of the period. Contrary to the classic tradition of the 18th Century dandy highwayman, mounted bandits have infested England's major roads for hundreds of years. Indeed, in 1572 Thomas Wilson wrote a dialogue in which one character commented that in England, highway robbers were likely to be admired for their courage, while another suggested that a penchant for robbery was one of the Englishman's besetting sins.

During the years immediately following the Civil Wars, highway banditry became more widespread simply due to the sheer number of dispossessed, heavily armed and vengeful former Royalists on the roads. This idea was the inspiration behind the Ironside Highwayman, though I felt it might be more interesting if my protagonist had been a Roundhead rather than a Cavalier.

The locations in the story are all real. The Red Lion at Chalton and The Court House at East Meon still stand today, while the gatehouse tower is all that's left of Warblington Castle. The site of Grange Farm in Petersfield has, in the intervening years, been home to a gas works, an abattoir and, latterly, a supermarket, but the impressive stone barn and coach house remains, and is now home to a GP surgery.

Portsmouth Point, or 'Spice Island' as it was (and is) often known, really was outside of the city boundary, separated by walls and a gate. It gained quite a reputation for lawlessness, vice and villain. The ideal place for a group of sailors to pass the time before joining ship! Incidentally, the Portsmouth Point name was commonly contracted to Po'm. P. when recorded in ships' logbooks to , giving rise to the nickname of "*Pompey*".

The Saxon church at Idsworth (Lyle would have known it as St Peter's, though it was later rededicated to St Hubert) is a gem, and highly evocative. Built by Earl Godwin (King Harold's father), it stood at the heart of a village that was ultimately abandoned during the Black Death. Now it stands alone and isolated, looking rather incongruous amongst the sweeping hills, but its interior bears the marks of the thriving community it once serviced. During Victorian renovation work, a range of beautiful 14th Century murals were discovered beneath layers of paint that had presumably been applied during the Reformation. Well worth a look if you're visiting the South Downs National Park.

Also by Michael Arnold

The Civil War Chronicles
Stryker and the Angels of Death (Novella)
Traitor's Blood
Devil's Charge
Hunter's Rage
Assassin's Reign
Warlord's Gold
The Prince's Gambit (Novella)
Marston Moor

The Highwayman Series
Highwayman: Ironside
Highwayman: Winter Swarm

The Joshua Hawke Thrillers
Corpse Thief

About the Author

Michael Arnold's interest in British history is lifelong, and childhood holidays were spent visiting castles and battlefields. He became a Sharpe junkie at the age of 13, and his particular fascination with the seventeenth century was piqued partly by the fact that his hometown, Petersfield, is steeped in the history of the period. Michael is the critically acclaimed author of The Civil War Chronicles, featuring the indomitable Captain Stryker, and is also the creator of the Corpse Thief series, in which he turns his attention to the dark underworld of Regency London's resurrectionists.

You can find out more about Michael by visiting the following places:
www.michael-arnold.net
Facebook: MichaelArnoldBooks
Twitter: @MikeArnold01
Instagram: michaelarnoldauthor

*

Printed in Great Britain
by Amazon

16070025R00164